C000258526

Praise for Mark Morris

'Mark Morris is one of the finest horror writers at work today.'
Clive Barker

'Mark Morris writes from the heart and strikes you to the depths of your soul. He is one of the best horror writers out there.'
Stephen Volk

'A strikingly imaginative mixture of horror and fantasy, with a real sense of supernatural terror and with scenes of horror so strange they border on surrealism.'
Ramsey Campbell on *Toady*

'Morris has assembled an especially strong group of stories with dazzling, diverse approaches to horror. Highly recommended.'
Cemetery Dance on *Close to Midnight* (ed. Mark Morris)

'*Close to Midnight* illustrates what great shape the genre of horror is in... If you're a reader who enjoys quality fiction of the dark kind, this is a series to be cherished. There isn't a bad story in the entire book.'
Stephen Bacon

'Heart-rending, powerful, and distinguished by Morris's dynamic and insightful writing.'
Tim Lebbon on *It Sustains*

'A skilfully constructed tale, topped off with
a mind-boggling twist.'
The Times on *The Immaculate*

'Eerie, assured and utterly compelling, this
is a novel you will not forget.'
Michael Marshall Smith on *Fiddleback*

'I'm impressed with the imagination and variety coming
from the writers. *Beyond the Veil* (ed. Mark Morris) is another
happy clump of ickiness...and I mean that in a good way.'
The Happy Horror Writer

'I'd happily recommend this series to anyone and
everyone, Mark Morris is writing up a hell of a storm.'
The Eloquent Page on the *Obsidian Heart* trilogy

'A sizzling banquet of the bizarre that simply
demands to be read.'
Julian Lloyd Webber, *Sunday Express*, on *Stitch*

'Beautifully written pieces that lean
into the intuitive and fantastic.'
Publishers Weekly on *After Sundown* (ed. Mark Morris)

'This rich and masterful collection of horror highlights
both up-and-coming and established authors in an
interesting twist on the standard anthology... Highly
recommended for longstanding horror fans and those
readers who may not think horror is for them. There is
something for everyone in this one.'
Booklist on *After Sundown* (ed. Mark Morris)

MARK MORRIS

THAT WHICH STANDS OUTSIDE

This is a **FLAME TREE PRESS** book

FLAME TREE PRESS
6 Melbray Mews, London, SW6 3NS, UK
flametreepress.com

US sales, distribution and warehouse:
Simon & Schuster
simonandschuster.biz

UK distribution and warehouse:
Hachette UK Distribution
hukdcustomerservice@hachette.co.uk

Thanks to the Flame Tree Press team.

The cover is created by Flame Tree Studio with
thanks to Shutterstock.com.
The font families used are Avenir and Bembo.

Flame Tree Press is an imprint of Flame Tree Publishing Ltd
flametreepublishing.com

A copy of the CIP data for this book is available from the British Library and the Library of Congress.

PB ISBN: 978-1-78758-933-9
HB ISBN: 978-1-78758-934-6
ebook ISBN: 978-1-78758-935-3

Printed and bound in Great Britain by Clays Ltd, Elcograf S.p.A.

MARK MORRIS

THAT WHICH STANDS OUTSIDE

FLAME TREE PRESS
London & New York

To my buddy Al, for all the years of telly,
tea, biscuits and fantastic friendship.

PROLOGUE

For several blissful seconds after waking up the girl forgot she was dying.

Staring ahead of her, she saw nothing but darkness. Listening, she heard nothing but silence. She felt neither hot nor cold, had no awareness of her skin, her bones, her flesh. Idly she wondered if she was in bed. Wondered what time it was, and whether today was a school day. Then, instinctively, a breath hitched in her chest; a muscle jumped in her thigh.

Her leg jerked, scuffing rock.

And with that, it all came rushing back. The pain. The memory. The fear.

A sob tore its way out of her, and it was like regurgitating splinters. She curled around it, trying and failing to stifle further sobs. She became aware of her gritty eyes, of her tongue and throat swollen with thirst, of her stomach cramping with hunger. Fatigue crawled hotly in her limbs like fever. One by one her injuries blazed into life like igniting bulbs. The bruises, the scrapes, the sprains, the gashes. All at once there was not a part of her, inside or out, that was not hurting.

After the initial crash of memory, her thoughts started to break up again, to recede like a wave into a vast and depthless sea. How long had she been here? Everything was being taken from her: time, light, comfort, hope. Even though she could no longer think straight, she knew her body was shutting down, little by little, layer by layer, and that soon there would be nothing left.

I'm dying, she thought, and deep down that frightened her. But also it felt like a dream, like something that was not connected to her at all, and maybe that was a good thing. Maybe she should just close her eyes and push the hurt away, give herself up to—

No.

Her eyes opened again. Who was that? She expected to see someone beside her, scowling down at her – her mother maybe – but there was no one.

Someone, though, didn't want her to give up. But it wasn't them that was hurting, was it? It wasn't them who was so tired they could barely move?

They're coming for you. They'll find you.

This time the voice was so close, so loud, she actually used her aching, feverish arms to push herself upright. If the voice hadn't shocked her, she wouldn't have thought herself capable of doing it.

Feeling sick and dizzy, she looked around. "Who's there?" she said, her voice sounding like a rusty nail scraping across a stone wall.

There was no reply. But wasn't there someone standing there, watching her? Further back along the tunnel, against the wall? A squat shape, blacker than the darkness? Couldn't she see it breathing? Or was it just her swimming vision that made the shadows shift and blur?

"I can see you," she tried to say, but this time the sound that emerged from her throat was barely even a croak.

They're coming for you. They'll find you.

Was that a promise or a threat? With a great effort she scrunched her legs up underneath her body and pushed down against the floor with her feet, levering herself upright. As her legs unbent, a hot, jittering pain flared in her knees, and she almost went down again, her mouth opening in a rusty scream. Desperately she gripped the stone wall at her side, her bleeding fingers with their ragged nails digging into grit. She clung on as her legs trembled, and eventually the tremors passed.

The sheer effort of standing made her gasp, each breath like an eagle's talon in her chest. Again she peered at the place where she thought the dark figure had been standing. The blackness pulsed there like a hellish heart. *Was* it a figure, small and squat, pressed up against a curving wall of rock? Or were her skittering thoughts creating images that weren't there?

At once she became aware that beneath her palm the rock was wet, and that something cold was oozing between her fingers and running down the back of her hand. She swung her head in that direction, but it was so dark in the tunnels that her hand was nothing but a vague patch of paleness on the dark stone.

Nevertheless, there was moisture here. Water! It must be running down the rock from some crevice above. She leaned her body towards it, and next moment was lapping at the back of her hand, then at the rock itself. Her tongue was fat and uncooperative, but the water flowed over it, filling her mouth, soothing her parched throat. She gulped, swallowed, not caring that the rough stone was scouring her tongue, or that she was swallowing almost as much blood and grit as water. Nor did she care that it tasted earthy; to her it was like heaven. She felt herself reviving, felt her head clearing – a little at least.

Eventually she sank to her haunches, gasping with as close to pleasure as she was going to get down here in the dark. Water dripped from her chin and lay like a cold hand on her wheezing chest, where it soaked through her pink hoodie and her favorite T-shirt with the smiling unicorn on the front. She remembered now how her best friend, Bryn, had said they should come up to look at the Devil's Throat, and how the rocks had given way at the edge of the pit and she had fallen, grabbing at the sloping sides as she slid from the light of the world above into the darkness of the world below. After sliding for some distance, she had suddenly found herself falling through space – and then she remembered nothing until she woke up, her ankle throbbing, the right knee of her jeans ripped open and the knee itself stinging and bleeding, her ribs and back aching and bruised, her clothes filthy and torn.

She couldn't have fallen far, she knew that. If she had, she'd have broken her ankle, not just sprained it. She'd slid most of the way down, and then the rocky wall must have gone vertical, like the bottom of a funnel, and she'd fallen the last...two meters? Three?

All she knew for sure was that, however far it had been, she could see no light above her when she looked up. That must have been because the wall of the shaft had been at such an angle that as she fell, the opening at the top had been obscured like the sun during an eclipse.

Imagining Bryn up there, peering anxiously down, she had shouted her friend's name, over and over – but Bryn had not replied. Had she fallen so far that Bryn couldn't hear her? Or had she been unconscious for so long that Bryn had shouted and shouted *her* name before eventually giving up and rushing off to find help?

It was scary to think she might be all alone out here, but she took comfort from the thought of Bryn returning with rescuers – men with ropes and blankets and coffee, maybe even hot chocolate. She imagined herself being strapped to a stretcher and hauled carefully up the shaft, the daylight getting brighter as she neared the top. She imagined everyone cheering as she emerged from the pit, and making a fuss of her; imagined her mother sobbing with joy and enfolding her in a hug and showering her with kisses.

These thoughts kept her going as the minutes ticked on, time stretching and stretching until she felt sure that at least an hour must have passed, and then several, and then too many to count. Although it hurt her right leg to bend it, she did so anyway, hugging her knees to her chest until the darkness around her deepened to a blackness that she assumed meant night had fallen up above, and until it became so cold that she started to shiver.

With the shivering came weeping, and then at some point she became so exhausted that she fell asleep. When she woke the cold had settled into her bones and she was hungry and thirsty. It was at least a little lighter, though, which must mean it was morning again.

Where was Bryn? Why hadn't she brought help? Could she have also met with an accident? Had she been running so fast that she had fallen into a hole, or tripped in the forest and smashed her head on a rock?

Or maybe Bryn had *meant* for this to happen? She could be spiteful and petulant at times. Could it be that secretly Bryn was jealous of her friend for being prettier and more popular than she was, and so had concocted this plan to get rid of her?

No, she couldn't – she *wouldn't* – believe that. But once the idea lodged in her head, she couldn't shake it loose. Now that she was stuck in the darkness, with no food or water and only her own thoughts for company, the craziest of ideas began to take on monstrously persuasive proportions. As time stretched further, she started to believe more and more fervently that Bryn had left her here to die, that she was never coming back. Which left only one alternative. She would have to find her own way out.

She struggled to her feet and looked around. Her surroundings were dark, but some parts seemed darker than others. Could these be tunnels? Openings? Possible escape routes? She needed to explore them patiently, methodically, but at the same time she mustn't get lost. The shaft down which she had fallen was her only link to the world above.

She shuffled towards the nearest dark patch, her body stiff. Even the smallest amount of effort made her gasp in pain. The most discomfort came from her ribs and back, which were one huge ache, and her right ankle, which was so swollen and tender that the agony that shot up her leg each time she put weight on it made her dizzy and sick.

When she eventually reached the nearest dark patch, she found that it was indeed a tunnel. As soon as she stepped into it the darkness engulfed her completely. She took a deep breath and inched along for maybe ten meters, feeling the way with the toes of her trainers, until it became so narrow that she could go no further. By the time she returned to where she had started, she was panting with exertion, her head swimming, and she needed to sit down.

She didn't know how long she spent examining the rest of the darker patches. By this point she had lost the ability to judge time, so it could have been anything from one to ten hours. Some of the patches turned out to be nothing but clots of shadow caused by the angles of the rock. Others were shallow alcoves. Yet others were actual caves, which went back five, sometimes ten meters before coming to a dead end.

A few, though, were tunnels, and these she edged down one after another. The first four or five became so narrow that after a while she could continue no further. But the one after that was more promising.

She moved along it, her hand on the wall to her right, her toes probing the way ahead. She was so exhausted by now that she had to stop every half dozen steps to lean against the wall and gasp for breath. She was heartened, though, to find that not only was this tunnel not narrowing as the others had, but that it did, in fact – judging by the way the sound of her shuffling footsteps was expanding around her – seem to be getting wider.

A little further along she came to what seemed to be a sharp right turn, and she hesitated, wondering what to do. The tunnel was impenetrably black – *so* black she couldn't even see her hand in front of her face – and try as she might to stay calm, she couldn't prevent her imagination from conjuring all sorts of horrors that might be lying in wait for her: crumbling edges of bottomless crevasses into which she might fall; jagged spikes of rock that might pierce her eyes or throat; loose boulders that might crash down on her head; nests of rats or spiders into which she might step.

For what seemed an age she hovered in an agony of indecision, wondering whether to take the right-hand turn or step forward into space and see whether the tunnel continued straight ahead. In the end she found the idea of letting go of the wall, of stepping into the unknown, too terrifying, and so she took the right-hand turn, thinking that as long as she kept in contact with the wall on her right, she could easily find her way back.

She had been inching forward for what might have been another ten or twenty minutes when she saw the light.

Halting, she stared at it, entranced. It was somewhere to her left, and it was a yellow-brown blur, roughly oval in shape. Stretching a hand towards it taught her nothing except that it was beyond her reach.

Should she move forward? If she walked in a straight line, she could easily turn and retrace her steps if the light proved to be nothing. Despite telling herself this, she was torn. The solid wall felt like a lifeline, whereas the light was something unknown. On the other hand, the light's very existence could only mean that the outside world, and possible freedom, was somewhere close by. Which meant she *had* to go for it. If she ignored chances like this she might as well curl up and die.

The moment she pushed away from the wall and moved towards the light was almost as bad as the first lurching realization – yesterday or the day before? – that the ground had given way beneath her feet. Her heart began to buck like a snared rabbit. Panic rippled through her body like a cold fizz of needles. She halted and took several shuddering breaths, clenching and unclenching her hands. Then she moved forward again, limping on her bad ankle and, as ever, probing the ground ahead with the tips of her shoes.

She counted her steps as she walked, and was mouthing, "…twelve," when the brownish blur dwindled and died.

"No!" she cried, and was instantly shocked by the way her voice echoed as if she was in a vast cavern.

She tried not to let the fizzing panic overwhelm her, tried to work out what might have happened. Maybe the light was the end of a burrow that was connected to the surface and an animal had blocked it. Or maybe a cloud had crept across the face of the sun, snuffing out the thin trickle of illumination from above.

From the blackness in front of her came a brief, deep-throated chuckle.

No! She hadn't heard that! It was just the dark and the lack of food and water that was making her hear things. Maybe the light hadn't even been there either. Maybe her own mind had created it, like one of those things people see in the desert – a mirage. She had to stay calm, had to hold it together. But as she turned to face back the way she had come, she was shaking from head to foot.

How many steps had it taken to get here from the wall? Twelve, wasn't it?

Here goes then…*one*…*two*…

She moved forward, toes tapping the ground ahead, forcing herself not to rush, not to panic. She tried to stay calm even though she was suddenly certain there was someone behind her – someone close enough that she could feel their warm breath on her neck, their fingers plucking at the sleeve of her hoodie, toying with the ends of her hair.

...eleven...twelve...

Hand raised, fingers spread, she expected to feel the rough but comforting solidness of the wall. But there was nothing. Another couple of steps then. Just a bit further forward and she would walk right into it.

But after another two steps, and then two more, the wall still wasn't there.

No! This was impossible! It couldn't have disappeared!

Another two steps...then two more...

She stopped again, trembling. That made...what? Twenty steps now? There was no way – *no way* – she couldn't have reached the wall yet. So she either mustn't have turned around far enough or she had turned around too far. Which meant that if the wall wasn't in front of her, she must be walking parallel to it – but was it on her left or her right? Was she heading back the way she had come, or going deeper into the tunnels?

New waves of panic coursed through her, cold and prickling, making her want to scream and run, to thrash her arms as if the darkness was a net tightening around her. She felt she was suffocating, that the air in the tunnel was too heavy, or too thin, and she was going to pass out.

Even though it hurt her ankle to put weight on it, she sank down to her haunches. Then she wrapped her arms around herself and began to sob, rocking back and forth. She was more scared than she'd ever been in her life. She imagined *things* all around her. Scuttling, slithering, crawling things. And she imagined that the figure that had been behind her was now standing beside her. She imagined it looking down at her without pity – because *it* could see in the dark and she couldn't.

She was going to die. She knew it. She was going to die in darkness and cold and terror. Gasping for breath, she felt pains in her chest, sharp and white, like flashes of lightning. *Let me die now*, she thought. *Let me go to somewhere peaceful and black where I don't have to think anymore.*

Her wish was granted. Her mind shut down and she disappeared. When it switched itself back on, like a phone recharging after its battery has died, she felt regret, but she also felt a little calmer – enough, at least, to climb unsteadily to her feet. She took a long, slow breath, then stretched her hands out to either side in the hope that her fingers would brush against stone.

They didn't, but neither did they touch anything unpleasant. She remembered how she had decided, before she had sunk to the ground and blacked out, that she must have got turned around, and that the wall, which she had thought was in front of her, must instead have been on her right or her left. So where should she go now? She had no idea which way she was facing. Any direction she went in could lead her back to the wall – or to another wall entirely. All she could realistically do was keep shuffling forward in the hope that eventually she would stumble across a means of escape, or at least a source of light. This might mean she'd end up heading deeper into the tunnels, further and further from safety and from the hope of ever being found. But if she stood still, which her every instinct screamed at her to do, she would surely die.

And so she began moving forward, and it was not long before what little sense of her surroundings, and of time, and of herself, that she had managed to cling to up to now, disappeared completely. She blundered through the dark, utterly disorientated, for what seemed like hours, occasionally bumping her head or scraping her limbs on unexpectedly rough surfaces that seemed to loom from nowhere. There were times when she would find a wall and follow it for a while, only to discover that the passage through which she was heading was becoming increasingly narrow until eventually it would become too tight to fit through and she would have to turn back. At other times the ground would take her downwards in a series of jagged, uneven steps, or it would suddenly slope upwards, and no matter how cautious she was, her knees or her hips would bump painfully against outcrops of rock.

Sometimes there would be so many walls around her that she would feel as if she had somehow, impossibly, become trapped in a stone box. Once she stepped into a pool of icy water that came up to her shins, and which, when she scooped some into her mouth, had a slimy consistency and tasted disgusting. Even so, she was so thirsty that she made herself swallow some of it, only to vomit it back up a while later, leaving her shrinking stomach emptier and more crampy than ever.

A few times she heard things in the darkness around her – quick, scuffling movements followed by silence. Once, she touched something on a wall that writhed beneath her hand. Another time she was certain her fingers brushed against matted fur. On another occasion she heard something breathing close by, and twice more she heard a grunting chuckle, once so close that she whirled round with a scream, instinctively shooting out a hand, which smashed into an unyielding chunk of rock with enough force to dislocate her little finger.

As she became hungrier and thirstier, her head swam, and her muscles ached, and she started to lose her balance. She fell down several times. More than once she closed her eyes and slept, certain she would never wake up, and no longer caring whether she did.

After discovering the water flowing down the rocky wall and slaking her thirst enough to partially revive herself and her memories, she quickly found herself feeling not thankful but regretful. Her physical need, her instinct to survive, had made her drink, but now she realized all she'd done was extend her hellish life a little longer.

Why couldn't she just let herself die? It was going to happen sooner or later, so she might as well get it over with. Sinking to her knees, she stared again into the blackness – and again felt certain that a figure was standing there, watching her.

But how could that be? It was so black she couldn't tell between one patch of darkness and another. Her mind must be playing tricks on her, pasting shapes and pictures on the void.

She closed her eyes, then opened them again, hoping it might help. But that only made her even more convinced that she really *could* see the faintest outlines of shapes in the darkness. She could tell, for instance, that the tunnel curved to the right just ahead, and that the ceiling sloped down on the left. And when she looked at the wall, she could see the tiniest glints and gleams of white that she knew was the flowing water she had lapped at. So where was the light coming from? Somewhere above? She raised her head, her neck feeling like a creaky hinge.

And that was when the black shape she had been certain was a figure detached itself from the wall.

She saw it out of the corner of her eye, but it was enough for her head to jerk in that direction. The black figure was now moving towards her, and although it looked shorter than an average man – not much taller than her, in fact – it also looked squat and powerful.

It's not real, she told herself, *it's not real.* But if it wasn't, then neither were the sounds it was making – its hoarse breathing, the crackle of its footsteps on the gritty ground.

Its breathing, in fact, was loud, louder than it ought to be, unless it was echoing around the rock walls. And then she realized that the sound was coming not only from in front of her, but from behind her as well.

She had barely started to turn when a bristly, rough hand snaked over her shoulder and closed around her face.

CHAPTER ONE

"Go on, mate, just one more. You know you want to."

"I don't want to. I want to lock the door, tidy up and go home."

"Aw, come on, pal, it's early yet. What do you wanna go home for? Have a drink with us. My shout."

"Sorry, we're closing."

"Five minutes. Five minutes and we'll be gone. And you'll get a free drink out of it."

"Thanks, but I don't want a drink."

"Why not? What you got against us?"

"Nothing. I just don't want a drink. I've been here since five, so I just want to finish my shift and get home."

The pissed twenty-something guy in the crumpled blue suit twisted his alcohol-slackened features into a befuddled frown. He couldn't understand why Todd, who'd been tending the busy bar of The Blue Door for the past eight hours with hardly time for a break, didn't want to keep the party going. The guy's eyes were drooping as much as his hair, which had started the evening slicked back but which now hung down like a pair of curtains, framing his fox-like face. He and his friends, two guys also in suits and two heavily made-up girls in tight dresses and high heels, had plowed through four bottles of champagne before working their way steadily through the entire cocktail menu. Their bar bill alone would double the takings for the night, a fact that Todd knew his boss, Dean, would be grateful for. But he also knew that even in these straitened times, Dean would not want to risk losing his licence by flouting the terms of his contract.

"Is this your bar?"

The speaker was the tallest of the blue-suited guy's friends. This one wore a gray suit, and had a long, lugubrious face to which a flattened nose added a suggestion of toughness.

"No, it's my boss's," Todd said patiently.

"So why are you being such a fascist?"

For the first time Todd detected an element of threat within the group. The word was like a spark that seemed to ricochet between them. Suddenly all five, the women as well as the men, seemed poised for confrontation, their body language changing subtly, their features hardening, becoming more predatory.

He flicked a glance towards the bar's exit, but their resident doormen, Joe and Darren, were standing under the awning outside, facing out into the wet London street and having a chat. He was sure they'd come running if he yelled, as would the other two bar staff still on the premises, Rick and Andrea, who were out back clearing up. Things hadn't quite reached that stage yet, though, and Todd was hoping they wouldn't. There was no point in overreacting and risk igniting what, for now, was still only a minor hassle.

Planting a friendly smile on his face, he said, "I'm not being a fascist, I'm just doing my job. I don't have the authority to serve drinks after hours. Sorry."

"Who's gonna know?" said the shorter and more made-up of the two girls.

"Yeah, it's not like Big fucking Brother's watching, is it?" said blue-suited guy.

Keeping the smile on his face, Todd said, "We don't know who's watching. Anyone in here could be a licensing inspector. And if they saw me serving drinks after hours, my friend would lose his bar."

The tall guy with the flattened nose snorted as if he thought Todd was bullshitting. The girl who'd spoken up a moment ago said, "Where you from?"

Todd looked at her a moment before answering. "Sheffield."

She and her friend sniggered, and the tall guy muttered something about Yorkshire puddings.

Ignoring them, Todd said amiably, "Look, guys, I'm really sorry, but I can't serve you and that's that. If you want another drink there's a bar round the corner called Mazzi's, which I believe is open 'til four a.m."

The blue-suited guy's eyes flashed. "Oh, you *believe*, do you? Do you know what *I* believe? I believe you're a northern cunt and this place is a fucking shithole."

Todd stayed calm. He'd seen on numerous occasions how alcohol could turn people from amiable to aggressive at the drop of a hat, and he knew that the worst response in such circumstances was to fuel the fire. "Okay," he said blandly and raised his hands in the universal calming gesture.

"That all you got, you cunt?" Blue-suit said.

"It is," said Todd.

Blue-suit eyeballed him, but Todd could tell that with nothing to bounce off, the guy's aggressiveness was already wilting. To fill the silence the third man in the group, shorter and chubbier than his companions, and obviously embarrassed by the confrontation, said, "Dunno about you lot, but I need more alcohol. Let's check out this Mazzi's place."

"Good idea," said the girl who'd been silent up to now, and to Todd's relief there were mumbles of agreement from Tall Guy and Short Girl, with all but Blue-suit turning towards the door.

"You coming, Jack?" Short Girl called over her shoulder as they moved away from the bar.

Still staring venomously at Todd, Blue-suit muttered, "In a minute."

"Come on, mate," Tall Guy said, his voice a low rumble.

Blue-suit turned and all but snarled at him. "I said in a minute. I'll see you outside."

"What you doing?" Short Girl whined.

"Going to the bog." Blue-suit turned back to face Todd. In a low, dangerous voice he said, "If that's all right with the Yorkshire pudding?"

"Sure," said Todd nonchalantly, and watched as Blue-suit pushed himself back from the bar as if he wished it was Todd he was shoving in the chest.

While Blue-suit weaved his unsteady way towards the toilets on the far side of the room, his four friends wandered outside to wait, the girls shivering in their thin jackets, Tall Guy lighting a cigarette by cupping his free hand around his match flame like a PI from a hard-boiled detective novel. It had been drizzling most of the evening, and although it had stopped now the wet streets still gleamed like dirty metal under the lights. After a mild September, the advent of October had coincided with four days of squally rain and near-arctic winds. Todd was just wondering whether to walk back to his flat after he'd closed up, or cross the road and wait for the night bus, when he heard a metallic crash, followed by another.

His first thought was that Rick and Andrea had dropped something in the kitchen, but then he saw the heads of the few customers who were still finishing their drinks swiveling towards the toilet doors.

"Shit," he muttered and ran the length of the bar, pausing only to stick his head through the kitchen door.

The dishwasher was on in there, so Rick and Andrea hadn't heard the commotion out front. They were fooling around – Rick, with his big, ginger hipster's beard, flicking a tea towel at diminutive, tattooed Andrea's legs, which were protected only by a pair of black tights that looked stitched together out of cobwebs. She was squealing at him to stop, but they both froze and looked at Todd as he lunged through the doorway.

"Get Joe and Daz," he said. "Someone's smashing up the Gents."

He was on the move again before either of them could reply, racing the last couple of meters to the end of the bar. He flipped up the hatch and ran across the now sticky wooden floor, weaving between tables towards the men's toilets.

Just before he reached them, he heard another metallic crash, then he was shoving the outer and then the inner door open. The Gents was a long, narrow room with a row of urinals and cubicles on the right and a row of sinks and mirrors on the left. Flanking the sinks were a pair of white metal hand-dryers, the first and closest of which was still attached to the wall. The second was hanging askew, and as Todd entered the room he saw Blue-suit, grunting and gasping, hair flopping over his eyes in greasy strands, trying to wrench the machine off the wall.

"Hey!" Todd shouted and ran towards Blue-suit, hoping he wouldn't slip on the tiled floor, which by this stage of the evening was slick with water and piss. Blue-suit looked up, a feral expression on his face, and with a final wrench tore the hand-dryer from the wall and heaved it in Todd's direction. Todd ducked, and the dryer sailed over his shoulder and ricocheted off a cubicle door. Next second Todd smashed into Blue-suit like a linebacker taking out an opponent, the impact causing the guy to fly back into the wall behind him.

Landing on top of Blue-suit as he slithered to the floor, Todd did his best to pin the man down. He wasn't a fighter, but at six foot he was several inches taller and probably a bit heavier than his opponent, a fact which he tried to use to his advantage.

It wasn't easy, though. Despite being small, Blue-suit was lithe and enraged by alcohol. He bucked and kicked beneath Todd, all the while unleashing a torrent of screaming abuse. "Calm down," Todd urged, "just calm down." But Blue-suit's only response was to screw up his now bright-red face and spit at Todd.

The gob of saliva hit Todd's throat and trickled down his chest beneath the collar of his T-shirt. He felt revulsion and anger, but fought the urge to give the man a slap. A second later the door burst open behind him, and suddenly the combined bulk of Darren and Joe was filling the narrow aisle to either side of him, squeezing between the sinks on one side and the cubicles on the other.

"Nice one, Todd," said Darren, a shaven-headed Black guy, whose head sprouted direct from his massive shoulders. Todd sprang back from Blue-suit, nimbly avoiding his kicking legs, as Darren and Joe – who had the rangy look of a street fighter and the birthdates of his three children tattooed on his neck – moved in, effortlessly pinioning Blue-suit's limbs, and lifting him between them as though he were a piece of light furniture.

Twenty minutes later the last of the bar's customers had left, and Todd was sitting at one of the tables nursing a cup of coffee that Andrea had made for him. In the aftermath of his encounter with Blue-suit, the stress hormones released by his body were making his stomach quiver and his legs tremble involuntarily. Because of the smashed-up hand-dryer, Todd had called the cops and Blue-suit had been taken down to the station to face a charge of criminal damage. As soon as they realized that Blue-suit had been arrested, his friends had slunk away, embarrassed and ashamed. No doubt tomorrow, once the cops had let him go, they'd be ribbing him at work and reminiscing about what a great night they'd had.

Todd sighed. He was sick of this. Sick of dealing with entitled dickheads. Sick of his sleep patterns being fucked up because he was working two jobs with incompatible hours, while trying to fit in as many auditions as his agent could get for him.

"You all right, boss?" Andrea sat down beside him, her dainty hands wrapped around a mug of hot chocolate. Todd smiled, knowing she was using the title affectionately and semi-ironically. In theory he *was* the boss because he was the senior staff member, and because Dean had told him he was in charge when Dean himself wasn't there. But Todd, Rick and Andrea worked as a team, as equals. Each of them knew exactly what needed to be done to keep things running smoothly, and Todd was thankful he never had to issue orders or pull rank.

"Fine," he said. "I was just thinking."

She sucked in a sharp breath through pursed, black-painted lips. "You don't wanna do that. It can really screw you up." She grinned. "What were you thinking about?"

With her creamy skin and huge blue eyes, she looked like a delicate china doll that had been given a Goth makeover. In the three years Todd had known her, her hair had undergone multiple transformations in color and style. She was currently sporting a flaming orange buzz cut.

"I was thinking," he said, "how long I should keep doing this before giving it up as a bad job."

"Doing what? Working the bar?"

"Not just that. All of it. Trying to make it as an actor."

"But acting's your dream."

"Yeah, but is it a fool's one?"

She took a sip of her hot chocolate. He took a sip of his coffee.

"Everyone who's ever fought against the odds must have felt like you do at one time," she said. "But some of them make it."

"Some. Not many."

"The ones who believe do. The ones who are determined and keep going."

"You really think that? That if I keep going I'll make it?"

"I think if you really believe you'll achieve your goal, then you will."

"What about talent? Doesn't that come into it?"

"You've *got* talent! Loads of talent! You're a really good actor!"

"There are lots of good actors out there."

"You've got to believe you're better than they are."

"Yeah, but how long do you keep believing that?"

"For as long as it takes."

Todd laughed softly and looked down into his coffee, as if the truth was there somewhere. Andrea nuzzled into his arm.

"What's brought all this on? Was it having to deal with those twats tonight?"

"Those and a million other twats like them. I'm just sick of...pushing against the shit, you know? I want something to happen."

"You've got to *make* it happen."

"I've been trying."

"Yeah," she said softly, "I know you have."

His legs had stopped trembling now. He took a bigger swig of his coffee. "Ignore me," he said. "It's late and I'm tired and I'm just on a bit of a downer. I'll be fine tomorrow."

They were companionably silent for a moment. Rick and Joe had headed off home and Darren was upstairs in the office, talking to Dean or maybe doing whatever paperwork needed to be done after Blue-suit's arrest. It was nearly two thirty a.m., and drizzle was forming misty haloes around the glowing heads of the streetlamps. There were still people about, though, walking past at regular intervals. London never slept.

"What would you do if you did stop acting?" Andrea said suddenly. "How would you fill the void?"

She looked genuinely concerned. Todd smiled.

"Go and work for my dad, maybe. Join him and my brother in the family firm."

She snorted. "I can't see you as a builder."

"He's not *just* a builder," said Todd. "He's the crème de la crème of builders. He only handles really big projects. Prestigious, specialist stuff."

She mimed yawning. "Yeah, I know. You've told me before. He's Mr. Moneybags. It's still boring."

He laughed. "Anyway, I wouldn't be a builder. There's a partnership there if I want it. I'd be trained to help run the business side of things."

"Oh God, it gets worse." She gripped his arm. "Please tell me you won't give up your dreams and become an office monkey. It'll erode your soul. You'd be fat and bald and playing golf every weekend by the time you're forty."

He laughed even harder at that. "No chance. But wouldn't that be an improvement on the way I look now?"

Andrea was always taking the piss out of him for looking like a 'surfer dude'. He had blond, wavy hair, which he wore long and paid little attention to, only occasionally tying it back in a bun. He had a surfer's physique too – tall and long-limbed, his arms and legs well-muscled from regular sessions on the climbing wall at his local leisure center.

As for his face, his boy-band looks were a bone of contention for him. They might get him plenty of admirers, but in acting terms Todd thought he looked too bland, too clean cut, to play the meaty roles he hankered for. "You'd be great in *Baywatch*," a girl had once told him, thinking she was paying him a compliment. Todd had laughed it off, but he'd felt depressed for days afterwards.

"You look just fine," Andrea told him now, then added, "but if you tell anyone I said that I'll deny it."

Hearing Darren's clumping footsteps descending the stairs, they hurriedly finished their drinks so Todd could stick their mugs in the dishwasher and set it going. Five minutes later the lights were off, the bar was locked up and they had all headed their separate ways.

The Blue Door was just south of Paddington, and Todd's flat, partly paid for by his parents, was in the cluster of streets between the Edgware

Road and Regent's Park, close enough to Marylebone station that he often heard the trains at night. It was no more than a fifteen-minute walk, most of it up Marylebone Road. A couple of minutes after leaving The Blue Door, the fine drizzle became a light rain, which almost immediately turned heavier, pattering on the shoulders of Todd's not-very-waterproof jacket and encouraging him to flip up the already damp hood of his hoodie.

"Thanks, mate," he muttered to a deity he didn't believe in, squinting at the night sky. Hunching his shoulders, he trudged on, focusing on nothing but the twitches of rain on the gleaming pavement ahead.

By the time he turned off Marylebone Road onto the darker, quieter streets of his neighborhood, the pedestrians, who had been out and about in still-reasonable numbers less than half an hour earlier, had now all but dispersed. Todd felt he must be the only idiot still out in the pissing rain – but as he turned onto his street, whose mature trees were barely more than silhouettes casting nets of black shadow across the road, a sharp tapping made him look up.

Through the blur of wet fringe plastered across his eyes, he saw the silhouette of a figure wavering before him. For a moment he couldn't tell what gender it was, or whether it was walking towards or away from him. It was only after pushing aside ropes of dripping hair that he realized it was a woman – a young woman judging from the swift, confident way she walked – wearing a long coat and knee-high boots.

Not wanting to alarm her, Todd hung back, so she wouldn't hear his footsteps. The Edwardian house, in which he lived in one of six flats, was a dozen or so houses along on this side of the street. At least the trees lining the pavement, their roots making the asphalt buckle and crack in places, afforded some shelter, and it was almost comforting to hear rain drumming on the leaves above his head. As he thought longingly of his snug, warm duvet, and of falling asleep to the tapping of rain against his bedroom window, he saw a tree to the right of the woman bulge and swell as she walked past. Then the bulge detached itself from the tree, split into two and converged on her.

Todd barely had time to register that the dividing patch of blackness was a pair of men, who must have been lurking behind the tree trunk, when one of them grabbed the woman – or rather the bag at her hip. The bag was attached to a strap that looped over her head, and the mugger yanked it violently enough that the woman was jerked to her right. She staggered and cried out, her ankle buckling. She might still have managed to keep her balance if the second man hadn't shot out his hands and given her a shove. As the woman went down in an untidy heap the mugger wrenched the bag free. The woman's head jerked again as the strap around her neck broke.

It all happened so quickly that the woman was on the ground before Todd had the chance to yell, "Hey!" He broke into a sprint, his feet splatting wetly on the pavement. He had no idea what he intended to do if he caught the men; he was fueled purely by indignation and outrage. His only thought was to protect the woman from further harm.

In the back of his mind, he guessed he was half-expecting the men to run away – but they didn't. Looking up at Todd's yell, they instead turned to face him, planting their feet wide and raising their arms in a 'come on then' gesture.

Alarmed, but too committed to turn back now, Todd kept running at them. The man who had grabbed the bag was the smaller of the two, so Todd focused on him. He didn't have much of a plan, apart from half-thinking that maybe he could body-slam the smaller guy, as he had body-slammed Blue-suit. If he was lucky he might even knock the man straight into his companion, with the result they would both go down like skittles.

As Todd jumped over the legs of the woman, who was still sprawled on the pavement, he saw that, like his, the heads of the two muggers were cowled by hoods. He also saw they had dark scarves wrapped around the lower part of their faces, leaving only their eyes visible, which meant there was no way he'd identify them again if he needed to.

The two men had been standing shoulder to shoulder as he approached, but as he came to within a couple of meters of them, they suddenly stepped away from one another, clearly intending to flank him. Instinctively Todd veered towards his first target, the smaller man, but in so doing he took his eyes off the second, larger man.

Raising his arms to shove the smaller man backwards, he sensed something hurtling at him on his left-hand side, and the next moment something crashed into the side of his ribcage. It felt like a sledgehammer, and it made a horrible crunching sound, like a foot stamping on gravel. He staggered, felt his knees buckling and tried desperately to keep his balance. But then he felt a shuddering impact on the left side of his head, and as the wet ground lurched up to meet him, he felt further impacts from boots or fists that were as hard as hurled rocks, thudding down on his back, his sides, his limbs.

There was no pain as yet; his adrenaline was keeping it at bay. Not even when the wet, gritty concrete sloughed a layer of skin from his palms did he feel anything. As he pedaled his legs, though, trying to scramble upright, he suddenly felt an agonizing weight crash down on his back. The searing pain in his spine flooded his head with primal terror. His legs gave way and he screamed and rolled over, curling into a ball.

The pain from the kick or the stamp on his back seemed to pulse through his body. It was so debilitating it knocked the fight out of him. He lay on the ground, hoping that if his assailants realized he was beaten they'd leave him alone – but they didn't. The blows kept coming, fast and savage, impact after impact. They rained down on him like debris from a collapsing building, homing in on his head and face, jarring his brain again and again, turning his thoughts to mush.

I'm going to die. It was a bright flash of coherence among the terror and pain. He was twenty-eight years old and after a short and unremarkable life he was going to die on a rainy London street, beaten to death by thugs. His thoughts became frantic and jumbled: he pictured his parents; his childhood home; he and his mates riding their bikes down a steep slope. He remembered drinking wine outside a St. Tropez street café with his ex-girlfriend Marianne, and the sweaty exhilaration of the mosh pit at Glasto while watching Kasabian. Here was Sarah Marshall kissing him at the school disco. Here he was delivering his two lines as a hospital orderly in an episode of *Casualty*. Here he was…here he was…here was…here…

…but suddenly there were no more thoughts.

Only blackness.

CHAPTER TWO

"Welcome back."

The voice was soft, and there was a slight accent to it that he couldn't identify. He tried to open his eyes, but his eyelids resisted. It was as if they were glued together, and for a moment he felt a flutter of panic. He took a deep breath, which hurt his chest, then he squeezed his eyes tightly shut and tried again.

This time the lids peeled slowly apart, admitting more light than he was comfortable with. In the overbright glow he saw a blurred figure looming over him. He raised his arm, which felt heavy and slow, and to his surprise felt a warm hand wrap around his outstretched fingers.

"It's okay, take it easy." That voice again. Like silk or honey. It soothed him. He relaxed, his body settling back – into what?

The harsh light lessened by degrees, and eventually he saw that the woman holding his hand was a stranger. She was young, slim, dark-haired, her feline beauty accentuated by her startlingly pale green eyes.

Captivating, Todd thought. That was the word for her.

"Hi," she said, her lips curving into a smile.

"Hi," Todd responded, and immediately realized how dry his throat was. He started to cough, then cried out as the reflexive movement awakened pain in his ribs, shoulders and neck.

"Here, here," the woman said, pouring water into a plastic cup and holding it to his lips. He gulped and swallowed, wincing because that hurt too.

"Better?"

He nodded, then wished he hadn't. It felt as if steel balls were bouncing around inside his already bruised skull.

"Try not to move too much," she said. "You were beaten up pretty bad."

"Where am I?" Todd asked, taking in the plain, clean, tastefully furnished room: window to the left, behind the woman's head, door to the right.

He knew the answer a split second before she said it: "Hospital."

"I'm guessing private," he said, and as she nodded, he added, "which means my dad's paying for this."

Despite the pain he was glad to discover his mind felt relatively clear. Already he was remembering what had happened.

"How long have I been here?"

He braced himself for the answer, worried she was going to say 'three weeks' or 'six months' or 'a year'.

Instead, to his relief, she said, "About…thirteen hours."

"So what time is it?"

She consulted her watch. "Four fifteen. In the afternoon."

He swallowed. His throat hurt. Seeing him wince, the woman lifted the plastic cup again and held it to his lips. He drank.

"So who are you?" he asked as she put the cup on the bedside table. "My private nurse?"

She chuckled, and instead of answering she rolled up the sleeve of her stylish red jacket and showed him her elbow. It had a white dressing on it.

Todd was puzzled – then suddenly he realized. "You're the woman!" he said. "The one who was mugged."

"And you're my knight in shining armor." Her smile showed a double row of very white, very even teeth.

He grunted a laugh. "Hardly. I wasn't much use. I got the shit well and truly kicked out of me."

"But you…distracted them. And you were very brave."

"I did what anyone else would have done." He knew it was a cliché, but that wasn't why she was shaking her head.

"No, I think most people would have run the other way, or at best hid and called the police. But you got right in there. I think if you hadn't…" She shuddered.

"What happened after I lost consciousness?" Todd asked.

"Some more people came. Two couples. They heard me yelling, and when they turned up the guys ran away. With my bag." She looked rueful, then shrugged.

"Are you okay? Apart from the elbow?"

"Bumps and bruises, but nothing serious. I was more shaken up than anything."

"So what's *my* list of injuries?" asked Todd. "It hurts to move, I know that, and I've got a thumping headache." All at once he remembered the agonizing weight on his back. "I'm not paralyzed, am I?"

She raised her hands to calm him. "No, you're okay. You don't have anything that won't mend. You've broken a finger, cracked a couple of ribs, you've got a concussion, and the rest is cuts and bruises. Your upper spine is bruised where they jumped on it – that's why you're wearing the neck brace."

He didn't realize he was until she mentioned it. Now he raised a hand to touch it, and noticed for the first time that the second and third fingers of his right hand were splinted together. The palm of that hand, and also the palm of his left, were covered by dressings similar to the one on the woman's elbow.

"Will I be able to play the guitar once this is healed?" he asked, holding up the hand with the splinted fingers.

She shrugged. "I don't see why not."

"That's funny," said Todd. "I couldn't before."

She rolled her eyes, then barked a surprisingly raucous laugh.

"Sorry," he said. "Bad joke. It's all I'm capable of at the moment."

"Don't apologize. A sense of humor is good. It helps the healing process."

He tried to take another deep breath. It really hurt. When his lungs inflated it felt as though his ribs were shifting, the broken ends scraping together. The thought made him feel sick.

"Are you all right?" she asked. "Do you need a painkiller?"

"Am I allowed one?"

"I don't know. I could ask someone."

He was about to shake his head, then remembered it was a bad idea. "No, it's okay. I'm hurting, but I'm not in agony, so maybe I've already got some in my system." Touched by the concern on her face, he said, "It's good of you to sit with me."

"You're my knight in shining armor, remember."

"Yeah, but...I don't even know your name."

She smiled. "It's Yrsa. Yrsa Helgerson."

"Nice name. Is that...Danish?"

She tilted her head to one side. "Yes and no."

"Well, that explains everything," he said.

"Sorry. What I mean is, yes, someone from Denmark could have this name, but I'm not from Denmark. I'm from a little island, which is actually closer to Iceland than it is to Denmark, but which is inhabited by a mix of people from different countries who have become intermingled over many generations. Our language and customs are a blend of different cultures – our names too. Which is why where I'm from is known as 'Mongrel Island'."

"Nice. So what's its real name?"

"The Icelanders called it Eldfjallaeyja, which means 'Volcano Island'." She shrugged. "The name kind of stuck."

"So *is* there a volcano on the island?"

"A dormant one. By which I mean long dormant – dead, in fact. It's actually a very peaceful place. Lots of woodland, not too many people."

"It sounds idyllic. So what brings you to smelly old London?"

Before she could reply there was a knock on the door and a nurse, bespectacled and cheerful, stuck her head in.

"Everything all right in here? Oh, you're awake, Mr. Kingston. How are you feeling?"

"A bit battered," Todd said.

She bustled in. "Well, hopefully you've slept through the worst of it. I've come to take your obs, if that's all right?"

Todd gave Yrsa a smile of apology. She rose from the chair beside his bed and said, "It's okay, I have to go anyway. But when you're better

I'd like to take you to dinner, to say thank you. We can continue this conversation then."

"That'd be great," said Todd. "Let me have your number and I'll call you."

"It's already done." She nodded towards the bedside cabinet. "I used your phone to call your parents last night, and after I'd done it, I took your number and texted you mine."

"Oh," said Todd, "okay."

She clenched her teeth and looked sheepish. "You don't mind? I don't want you to think I'm a crazy person."

He laughed, then wished he hadn't, the pain in his ribs making him grimace. "No, it's fine. I'll call you when I'm out."

"Great. And in the meantime, text me to let me know how you're doing."

"I will."

"I'll hold you to that. Well, see you for now, white knight."

"See you," said Todd.

When Yrsa had gone, the bespectacled nurse took his temperature, then wrapped a blood pressure sleeve around his arm. Catching Todd's eye, she said, "She's keen, that one."

"You think so?" said Todd.

"Would you like me to test your eyesight as well as your blood pressure? She's smitten. Keen as mustard."

Todd grunted a laugh, but secretly he was pleased.

CHAPTER THREE

"Where I come from is peaceful and picturesque, but unless you want to be a farmer or a fisherman, or maybe run a grocery store, there's nothing to do there. It's very dull."

Using her tiny fork, Yrsa loosened the oyster from its half-shell and gulped it down. Fixing Todd with her pale green eyes, she gestured at her plate. "You want one?"

Todd tried not to pull a face. "No thanks. Not my thing."

She looked amazed. "You don't like seafood?"

"I like fish. But not…" he gestured at her plate, "…slimy things."

She laughed. "Slimy things were a staple part of my childhood diet. Sorry. Is this grossing you out?"

"No," Todd lied, "you carry on. I'm happy with my soup."

In fact, his lobster bisque was too salty for his taste, but he pretended to enjoy it. Although his dad, who had started as an apprentice builder, had made a decent proportion of his fortune before either of his boys were born, neither he nor Todd's mum, Nancy, had ever cast off their thrifty working-class roots, as a result of which there had never been any wastefulness in the Kingston household. Both Todd and his elder brother, Robin, had had it drummed into them that they must always eat what was put before them, and if as kids they ever moaned about not liking something or not being hungry, they were reminded in no uncertain terms of all the poor kids who regularly went without.

Although Todd had never known what it was to be poor, that didn't mean his and Robin's parents had overindulged them. On the contrary, they'd had the same amount of pocket money, and the same number of Christmas presents, as most of the other, less well-off kids that Todd had known and grown up with. To keep their feet on the ground, he and Robin had gone to the local comprehensive too, instead of a posh private school, and if they ever wanted anything beyond their modest means they had to work for it. Todd had resented that at the time, but he was grateful now that he hadn't had a more pampered upbringing. Even though his parents gave him money towards the rent on his flat every month, Todd only took the minimum he needed to get by – and he even felt bad about that. Without his parents' subsidy, though, there was no way he'd have been able to live in London, even working two jobs, and pursue his ambition to be an actor.

Much of this Yrsa had prized out of him during pre-dinner drinks. Now he was asking her about her background. As she slurped down another oyster, he said, "So you decided to leave home and move to London?"

"I did."

"What did your parents think about that?"

"My dad didn't think anything. He died when I was five."

"I'm sorry."

"It's okay. I don't remember him very well, except as a big man with a beard. He was a fisherman and he drowned. It happens."

"What about your mum?"

"She made a fuss, but we...what's that phrase?" She put down her fork and rubbed the knuckles of her clenched fists together.

"Rubbed each other up the wrong way?"

"That's it. I was young and wanted excitement. She was old and set in her ways. I love her, but we argued a lot. If I'd stayed much longer, we'd have killed each other."

It was three weeks since Todd had been attacked. He'd been out of hospital a week, but this was the first time he'd felt well enough to socialize. He was still stiff and sore, especially his bruised back and his ribs on the left side, which were knitting together nicely but which still hurt when he took a deep breath. He'd overridden the pain barrier, though, because he'd wanted to see Yrsa – but he couldn't deny that he had been nervous. Although they'd texted back and forth over the past three weeks, he was worried that spending an evening together might lead to them realizing they had nothing in common. But so far that hadn't been the case – they'd been chatting nonstop. She was stylish and beautiful, and probably more worldly-wise than the girl-next-door types he usually went for. But she was also sparky, funny and irreverent, and unless she was putting on a show she seemed genuinely interested in Todd.

The choice of restaurant had been hers, and although it made Todd a bit uncomfortable, not only because it was more salubrious than he was used to, but also because she insisted on paying as a thank you for him putting his neck on the line for her, he soon found that – over-salty soup aside – he was thoroughly enjoying himself.

"So what made you want to come to London?" he asked.

She finished her last oyster and pushed aside her plate with a sigh of satisfaction. "Do you even need to ask? Isn't London an exciting city?"

"I suppose so."

Her eyes widened. "You suppose so? It is! It's one of the most exciting cities in the world! When I was a girl I used to watch films on our crappy black-and-white TV, and they were always set in either London or New York, and so I vowed that one day I would visit both of those places." She rapped the edge of the table with her fingertips, like an auctioneer securing a sale. "And now I'm halfway there."

"So one day you want to go to New York?"

"One day, yes. Have you been?"

"No."

"You should! Maybe we can go together."

Her enthusiasm, and the suggestion they might have some sort of future, made him laugh with delight – a response he immediately regretted as his ribs flared with pain.

"Ow," he said, pressing a hand to his side. Yrsa looked concerned. "Maybe this is too early for you?"

"No, I'm fine. The pain eases more each day. And I'd much rather be here with you than sitting at home staring at the TV. I've done too much of that lately."

She scowled. "I wish the police would catch those fuckers."

"I doubt they will," said Todd.

"If I had the chance I would break their arms and legs. I would do to them what they did to you, but much worse."

"Okay," said Todd, half-smiling. "Bit medieval."

"Wouldn't you do the same?"

"To be honest – no. I mean, it'd be great if they were caught and sentenced, but I'm not really the vengeful type."

"I am." She looked at him earnestly. "Does that make me a bad person?"

"Dunno about bad. A bit scary, maybe."

"I'm only scary to my enemies. But you're not my enemy, Todd, so you're okay."

He grinned. "Glad to hear it."

Their main courses arrived – duck breast for Todd, seared lamb medallions for Yrsa.

"This is delicious," said Todd.

"Everything is delicious here," Yrsa said, sharing the last of the merlot and then holding up the bottle. "More wine?"

"I shouldn't really. I'm not supposed to mix alcohol with my painkillers."

She puffed air dismissively through her lips. "It'll be fine. You are young and strong. And besides, we're celebrating."

"Are we?"

"Of course. We are celebrating the twist of fate that brought us together."

"The *painful* twist of fate that brought us together," Todd amended.

Yrsa laughed. "Sometimes it takes a little suffering to lead to something good. Cheers!"

They chinked glasses. As graceful and beautiful as she was, Todd liked the way that Yrsa gulped her wine, as if it was the stuff of life itself. Putting her glass down, she immediately picked up the empty bottle and waved it at the nearest waiter, who nodded.

"So how old were you when you came to London?" Todd asked between mouthfuls of duck.

"Eighteen. I came here to do an Economics degree at the University of London."

"Impressive. And what do you do now?"

"It will sound very boring to you. I'm a projects manager for a marketing company."

"That doesn't sound boring. It sounds very…grown up."

She shrugged. "It's a good job and I like it. But it's boring to talk about. Let's talk about something else. Tell me about your acting. What are the five favorite roles that you have performed?"

For Todd, the next hour or so passed in a glorious, woozy whirl. Talk of acting led to talk of movies, theater and art, which led to a conversation about the Louvre, that Yrsa had visited on a business trip to Paris last year, and then to travel in general. By the time they finished their main courses they were well on their way to demolishing a third bottle of wine and Todd felt pleasurably anesthetized – even his ribs had stopped hurting.

"Are you having a pudding?" he asked Yrsa, hoping his words weren't too slurred.

Her face lit up. "I love that word! And I love the way you say it. And in answer to your question – yes, of course! Tonight is pleasure, tomorrow I work harder at the gym. But first, I'm going to the toilet."

Todd gurgled with laughter. Maybe it was just the combination of alcohol and painkillers, but her forthrightness struck him as highly amusing. He was still chuckling even after she had put down her napkin and headed for the Ladies, and had barely stopped when his mobile started ringing.

Fumbling it from his pocket, he blinked at the screen. It took his eyes a moment to focus and then he read: *Dean Calling*.

Grinning, he pressed 'Accept'.

"Deano! How you doing?"

His friend and boss was clearly taken aback. "You sound happy."

"I'm having dinner with a beautiful woman." Todd lowered his voice. "And it's going *great*."

"Glad to hear it. This is the Danish girl, right?"

"Correct."

"And is she there now?"

"She's gone to the loo."

"Right." There was silence, then Dean said, "Look, I can call back tomorrow if it's more convenient. I don't want to spoil your evening."

"Nah, it's fine. What's up? Are you all coping without me?"

"Er...just about."

Despite his buzzing head, Todd could tell that something was wrong. "Okay," he said slowly. "But something *is* up, isn't it?"

"I'm afraid I've got some bad news for you, mate."

"Right," said Todd carefully.

"Upshot is...I've sold the bar. We're closing next week."

"What?" Todd couldn't quite take it in.

"I'm sorry, mate, I know this is a blow, but with all the closures and restrictions last year, I've been bleeding money. I know we've been doing okay recently, but with things still being dicey I just can't afford for it to happen again. So when an offer came in I decided to sell. I would have discussed it with you sooner, but you had enough on your plate."

Todd didn't know what to say, and was silent for so long that Dean eventually said, "Are you still there, mate?"

"Yeah," said Todd. "I'm...just a bit shocked."

"Yeah, I know," said Dean. "Sorry. Again. I feel bad, but I figured it was better to sell up rather than be forced out of business further down the line. Look, I'll put a good word in for you among some other bar owners I know. I'm sure you'll find something else."

Todd wasn't so sure of that – the hospitality industry was still on its uppers after the enforced closures due to Covid – but he said, "Cheers."

"I'll let you get back to your meal," Dean said. "Speak soon, okay?"

"Sure."

CHAPTER FOUR

Something's happened. I need you. How soon can you get here?

I'll come right now. What's wrong? X

Tell you when you arrive. Xxx

Sitting on the tube, Todd stared again at the text exchange between Yrsa and himself. What the hell had happened? Was it anything to do with the after-hours party at The Blue Door last night? That was the first time Yrsa had met his workmates, and in hindsight maybe it hadn't been the most ideal situation in which to introduce her to them. Dean had said they'd go out with a bang – half-price drinks for the punters and then a big fuck-off party afterwards for the staff and their friends and family. Todd had asked Yrsa along, but should have thought it through, should have realized that what was intended to be a last hurrah would degenerate into an alcohol-fueled, emotionally fraught night of tears, resentment and recriminations.

It had started to go downhill when a very pissed Andrea had cornered Todd coming out of the Gents.

"Hey," she said, putting a hand on his chest, "I want a word with you."

One glance at her eyes had been enough to tell him she was spectacularly hammered on Dean's famous Rocket Fuel Punch. "What about?"

She leaned in, engulfing him in alcohol fumes. "Your so-called girlfriend."

"Yrsa? What about her?"

"I don't like her. And neither should you."

Todd glanced into the throng of partygoers, and saw Yrsa on the far side of the room, holding a blue cocktail and speaking to a woman he didn't know.

"Oh yeah? Why's that?"

"She's a hard-nosed bitch. She doesn't understand what it means to lose a job. She thinks something like this doesn't matter. She thinks this is a shitty job and shitty jobs are easy to find. But they're not. Are they, Todd?"

"She told you this? That this was a shitty job?"

Andrea's nod made her head look as if it was loose and about to fall off. "Yup. She said the bar closing was a good thing. I don't like her, Todd. I don't think she's right for you."

Although Andrea treated him like a mate, Todd had often wondered whether her feelings for him ran deeper. Sometimes he thought that maybe they did, and other times he wondered if it was just his male ego telling him that a girl being friendly automatically meant she fancied him.

As if reading his mind, Andrea said, "I love you, Todd, but not in a girlfriend-boyfriend way. I jus' want you to be careful. You will be careful, won't you?"

"I will," he said.

Later in the evening he had broached the subject with Yrsa. She had rolled her eyes.

"Forgive me, Todd, I know she's your friend, but that girl has a problem."

"What kind of problem?" Todd asked.

"She has a major chip on her shoulder. She was upset about the closure, and I tried to console her, to tell her that maybe this was an opportunity for all of you to realize your full potential." She shook her head. "But she took it the wrong way. I think maybe your friend Andrea has very small dreams."

"It's okay not to have big dreams," Todd said.

Yrsa looked as if he had disappointed her, then she shrugged. "Maybe. I guess there will always be little people and big people. That's how we maintain a balance."

Todd bridled. "Andrea's not a little person. You don't have to be mega successful to be happy."

Again Yrsa looked doubtful, then she relented. "You're right. I'm being unfair. Do you think I should apologize to her?"

"I think she's too pissed and too maudlin to listen just now."

"Another time then," said Yrsa.

The incident had left Todd feeling conflicted and he was glad when the party finally began to wind down. Lying in bed later, unable to sleep, he had been surprised at how unsettled the evening had made him. The prickliness between Yrsa and Andrea had made him think how tricky it might be to fit Yrsa into his existing life. Although he pursued his acting dream doggedly, in all other respects he was a laid-back guy who lived a relatively bohemian lifestyle, a guy who hung out with 'arty types' and 'alternatives', as his brother Robin called them.

Yrsa, though, wasn't like that. She was driven, ambitious and forthright. Ordinarily he wouldn't have let that bother him, would simply have gone with the flow and let things work themselves out, but somehow it seemed different this time. It wasn't just that Todd liked Yrsa and wanted this to work, it was also because he sensed change coming, and no matter how much he told himself to relax and let things take their natural course, that worried him.

And now there was this. *Something's happened.* What did that mean?

Had Yrsa's glimpse into Todd's life made her realize the two of them were incompatible? But if so, why ask him to come to her flat, which he'd only visited briefly before? Why not arrange to meet him on neutral ground?

Well, he'd know soon enough. The tube was slowing as it approached Islington. He stood up from his seat as the darkness of the tunnel was replaced by the brightly lit tube station, the faces of those crowding the platform whipping by. As soon as he had passed through the barrier and was out in the open air again, striding along Islington's busy high street, he texted her: *Just arrived at Angel. With you in 5 xx*

He received no reply, which didn't help his mood, and by the time he arrived at her apartment block he was sweating with anxiety. She lived beyond the big Waterstones on the corner, on a street filled mostly with restaurants, cafés and shops selling high-end home furnishings and designer fashions, behind a portcullis-like electronic gate that filled the stone arch into which it was set. Beside the gate was a keypad with twelve numbered buttons and an intercom grille below it. Todd pressed 9 and after a moment the grille crackled at him as a prelude to Yrsa's distorted voice speaking his name.

"Yeah, it's me," he said.

The gate's electronic lock disengaged with a buzz and a click.

Todd pushed the gate open, which automatically swung shut behind him, then walked through the arch into a spotless courtyard with a fountain in the middle. On the far side of the courtyard was Yrsa's apartment block, a white-stoned building that resembled a boutique hotel. On his left was a residents-only café and an exclusive supermarket, and on his right a fitness center with its own gym, spa and swimming pool.

The door of the apartment block was unlocked, but just inside was an ash-wood desk, behind which sat a concierge in an immaculate blue uniform. He was a young Indian guy whose shaven head had ruler-straight boundary lines, and who looked as if he spent most of his downtime in the gym next door. Despite his muscles, his smile was relaxed and friendly.

"You're Miss Helgerson's friend, right?"

"I am," said Todd. "Well remembered."

"Photographic," the concierge said, tapping the side of his skull, then swiveled a leather-bound visitor's book around on the desk. "Just scribble your autograph and you can go up."

There was a lift on his right, but Todd, full of nervous energy, bounded up the spiral staircase in the middle of the open-plan entrance hall. Yrsa lived on the third floor and by the time he reached her flat he was panting. He paused to catch his breath, then raised a hand to knock, but before he could do so the door opened.

Yrsa's appearance shocked him – though only because he wasn't used to seeing her look anything less than immaculate. With sleep-rumpled hair, no makeup, and wearing nothing but blue pajamas and gray bed socks, she looked younger and more vulnerable than he'd ever seen her before. It was a sight he found almost heartbreakingly endearing – though he'd never have told her that; she'd probably have punched him.

"Hey," he said softly. "You okay?"

She said nothing for a moment. Then her bottom lip quivered, and tears began to run down her cheeks.

"Hey," Todd said again and stepped inside, wrapping his arms around her. She clung to him and he kissed the top of her head. They stood like that for fifteen seconds, then Todd heard a door open on Yrsa's floor, so he pushed the door shut behind him with his foot. As it clicked he asked, "You want to tell me what's happened?"

She drew a shuddering breath and looked up into his face. "My mother died."

"Oh shit," said Todd. "I'm really sorry, Yrsa."

She took his hand. "Let's sit down. I need to sit down. I need coffee too."

She led him along the landing and into the big sitting room on the right. An airy room with a pale wood floor, it was bathed in light from the picture window dominating the far end. This window led onto a balcony overlooking a lush, well-tended garden that even this late in the year was vibrant with color.

Letting go of his hand, Yrsa crossed to her squishy brown sofa and flopped onto it, wrapping herself in a duvet. The TV in the corner was on, the sound muted to a murmur. On screen a male comedian and a female newsreader were breaking eggs into a pan, watched over by an enthusiastic celebrity chef.

"You want to talk about it?" Todd asked, perching himself on the end of the sofa next to Yrsa's sock-clad feet.

"Coffee first," she said, sounding tired. "Would you make it?"

"Sure."

It took Todd a minute to figure out how her fancy coffee maker worked, and to decide which of her dozen or so types of coffee to use, but eventually he carried two steaming giant-sized coffee cups through to the sitting room and handed one to her.

"Thanks." She took a sip, closed her eyes and sighed. "Perfect. We should get married."

"What?" said Todd, startled.

She regarded him under heavy eyelids. "Sorry. My feeble attempt at a joke. I meant because you make such good coffee..."

"Oh, right."

She turned and stared unseeingly at the TV, where the enthusiastic celebrity chef was now chopping garlic at superfast speed. Todd was wondering whether to give her another prompt when she said, "I got the call this morning. Seven a.m. Not a good way to wake up."

"No," he said. "What happened?"

"She had an accident. She was outside and she fell. Broke her leg. It's thought she passed out and died of hypothermia."

"Oh, hell. That's awful."

"Yes, it is," said Yrsa, and although she didn't break down, tears began spilling from her eyes again.

He put down his coffee cup, shuffled across and held her. "How old was she?"

"Sixty-one."

"That's not old."

"No. She was a strong woman. Fit. She was a farmer."

"Will you go back for the funeral?"

"Yes. As soon as I can get a flight."

"How long will you be gone?"

"I don't know. As long as it takes. Will you miss me?"

"'Course I will."

She put a hand on his stomach, at first on top of his T-shirt, and then, when she had tugged the T-shirt up, on his bare flesh, her fingertips stroking the fine hairs around his belly button. Her hand slipped lower, into the waistband of his jeans. Though his cock began to stiffen, Todd tensed.

"What are you doing?"

Her voice was low, a little raspy. "I want you to make love to me."

His cock responded, his heart beat faster – but he said, "Are you sure? Your mum's just died."

"That's why." She sounded fervent, almost irritable. "I need to feel alive."

She yanked at his belt, unzipped his jeans, then slid her fingers beneath the hem of his boxers and curled her fingers around his penis. Todd groaned and pulled her pajama top over her head, leaning forward and kissing her shoulders, her breasts, his tongue flicking across her nipples.

Then they were shoving the duvet aside, pulling more and more frantically at each other's clothes. When they were naked, she put her hands on his chest, dipped her head and took his cock in her mouth. Todd gasped and involuntarily thrust his hips upwards, pushing his cock deeper between her lips.

Their lovemaking was intense, almost desperate. When Yrsa came she screamed and punched the back of the sofa next to Todd's head, as though enraged. As they hadn't paused to allow Todd to put on a condom, he pulled out just before he came and ejaculated over the side of the sofa, onto the crumpled duvet on the floor.

"You beast," Yrsa said, panting and laughing. "I'll have to get that dry cleaned now."

Pleasurable ripples coursing through his body, a cocktail of chemicals zinging through his brain, Todd began to giggle. It bubbled out of him as the two of them lay in a tangle of sweaty limbs, and only subsided when their thumping hearts began to slow.

For several minutes, bathed in a contented afterglow, neither of them moved. Then Yrsa said, "You could come with me."

Todd was feeling drowsy. "Hmm?"

"When I go home next week, you could come too."

Todd's ribs and back were aching again now as the endorphins in his system ebbed. He shuffled upright beneath Yrsa's weight. "Would you want me to?"

"Yes!" she said emphatically. "I'd love you there with me, Todd. You'd be such a comfort. But what about your job? And your auditions?"

"I don't have any auditions lined up right now," he said. "And I'm sure I could get more time off from the store if I needed it."

"So you'll come?"

"I think I just did," he replied, grinning.

She slapped his belly, then her face became serious again. "*Will* you come?"

Todd looked at her, and in that moment, as she waited anxiously for his response, her eyes hooded and her mouth half-open, he didn't think he had ever seen anyone more beautiful. Cupping her chin, he leaned forward and kissed her.

"If you really want me to," he said, "then I will."

CHAPTER FIVE

"Wow, look!" cried Todd. "Dolphins!"

He was standing at the railings on the port side of the boat they'd hired to take them to Eldfjallaeyja. They'd flown to Hornafjordur Airport on Iceland's east coast on Monday morning, and from there had caught a charter flight to a small island whose name Todd had forgotten as soon as Yrsa had spoken it. The boat they were on now looked like a decommissioned fishing vessel – or maybe it was still used for fishing and the skipper just made money on the side transporting passengers between islands. Yrsa had told Todd that Eldfjallaeyja was around twenty-five miles from the island their charter plane had touched down on, and that the journey would take anything from forty-five minutes to an hour depending on the mood of the sea.

To Todd the Atlantic seemed choppy, the boat rising over the foam-tipped swells then slapping down and hurling up plumes of spray, which were thrown back by the wind, peppering his face with icy kisses. Some passengers, he guessed, might have spent the crossing puking up, but he found the roiling motion of the boat exhilarating. Yrsa too seemed perfectly at home – in fact, she seemed at one with the sea, her dark hair whipping about her head like Medusa's snakes, her green eyes sparkling like flecks of the ocean itself. They had been going for twenty-five minutes when Todd noticed the sleek gray shapes keeping pace with the boat. There were seven or eight of them, and they moved in undulating arcs, speeding through the water. When he pointed them out to Yrsa, she rose from her seat in the center of the deck and joined him at the railings.

"They're porpoises," she said. "Their heads are a different shape to dolphins, and their dorsal fins aren't as curved. See?"

"Dolphins or porpoises, they're still cool."

She smiled. "We get many of them around here. Whales too. Minke largely, but also humpbacks, blue whales, sometimes Orcas."

"I'd love to see a whale in its natural habitat," said Todd.

"Hang around here long enough and you will."

Ten minutes later came their first glimpse of Eldfjallaeyja, little more than a smudged black line on the horizon. As they drew closer the island seemed to rise slowly from the sea, as if waking from a long sleep. Todd's first impression was that it was forbiddingly dark and craggy, the hump at its center like the arched back of some vast beast.

"I can see why it's known as Volcano Island," he said and glanced at Yrsa. Her expression was hard to read, her eyes staring ahead, mouth set in a terse line. He reached for her hand, and at first it was like a dead thing; it remained hanging by her side, unresponsive. Then her fingers curled around his and squeezed.

"How does it feel to be coming home?" he asked.

In a voice as emotionless as her expression, she said, "It's like I've never been away."

As the boat lurched towards the island, Todd realized Eldfjallaeyja wasn't quite as bleak as it had first appeared. The top half of the island might be craggy and mountainous, but the bottom half was thick with vegetation, forests of pine and spruce expanding outwards from the focal point of the harbor, in whose gray seas a couple dozen fishing boats bobbed.

Despite the murky sky the harbor looked picturesque from a distance, but the glamor faded to shabbiness the closer they got. The boats were mostly old, rusty, salt-scoured and slimy with seaweed at the waterline. The rocks that littered the shore were blotched with a whitish mold. The buildings clustered close to the shoreline were squat, their wooden walls blackened and warped by the sea, their roofs afflicted with more of the whitish mold. The jetty they were approaching was barnacled and strewn with debris – broken lobster pots and filthy lengths of old rope.

There were a dozen or so people working on the decks of boats. A couple of them raised their heads to glance at the approaching vessel before returning to what they were doing. One man, though, standing on the deck of a rust-streaked vessel called *Bryndis*, seemed to take more than a passing interest. Wearing a brown, leathery smock and a matching hat whose low brim threw his white-bearded face into shadow, the man peered at them intently, perhaps even balefully. Todd stared back at him, but the man didn't move, and after a few moments it was Todd who looked away.

Turning to Yrsa, he saw she was staring at the fisherman as intently as he was staring at them. "Do you know him?"

She nodded briefly. "It's Einar Guolaugsson. He was a friend of my father's."

"You think he recognizes you?"

"I imagine so."

"He doesn't seem to like you much."

"That doesn't surprise me." She fixed Todd with a gaze that was almost as intent as the one she had given the fisherman. "You'll find that the people here are not over-friendly."

"Why's that?"

She nodded almost disdainfully at the approaching harbor. "This place is dying on its arse. The older generation blame the younger ones for moving away. They think we're betraying our heritage."

"Do they have a point?"

Her lips curled in a sneer. "Fifty years ago the main industries here were fishing, farming, and hunting for fox and seal. But the foxes and seals are now almost extinct, and fish stocks are low in these waters. As for farming, it's subsistence-level only these days. People no longer farm to make a profit, but simply to live."

"Is that what your mum was doing?"

Yrsa nodded. "Exhausting, back-breaking work, and for what? Just to survive." She glared at the old fisherman again, and as if speaking directly to him, she said, "So what's the point in that, huh? There's nothing noble in it."

The putt-putting of the boat's engine slowed as they moved alongside the jetty. The ruddy-faced skipper, who had not spoken a word to them the entire journey, suddenly appeared on deck, hurried to the side of the boat, and leaned over to grab one of the mooring posts as they drifted into port. He secured the boat, then gave them a curt nod, his signal that they should disembark. Todd grabbed his rucksack and Yrsa's suitcase and swung them onto the jetty, before clambering onto it himself and extending a hand to Yrsa.

As soon as they were standing on dry land – or rather, on wood spongy with seawater – the skipper began to untie the rope, clearly eager to return home. Yrsa spoke to him in the local language and the skipper responded in blunt monosyllables. Yrsa scowled and released what sounded like a stream of invective, whereupon the skipper sighed and responded in a fuller, more contrite manner. Yrsa took out her phone and tapped at the screen, clearly taking note of what he was saying. When he was done, she muttered what Todd took to be a curt thank you and turned away. By the time the little boat's engine had cleared its throat and spluttered back to life, Yrsa was striding away, her phone to her ear.

Todd picked up the bags and scurried after her. Flanked by fishing boats, he kept his gaze averted from the locals, sensing it wasn't just the white-bearded man, Einar whatshisname, who was staring at them now. Whether the scrutiny was curious or hostile – or whether the men were simply ogling Yrsa because she was a beautiful woman – he had no wish to find out. He waited until Yrsa had finished her call, by which time they were almost at the end of the jetty, and then he asked, "What was all that about?"

"I've booked us a cab. It's five miles to my mother's house from here."

"They have a taxi service on the island?"

"They run a car from the hotel. It should be here in five minutes."

It was more like ten when a battered orange Volvo slunk into view. The driver, pudgy and unshaven with deep-set eyes, was wearing a horrible green and yellow sweater with frayed cuffs. He peered unhappily out of the driver's-side window as they walked up the stony causeway towards the car, though Todd realized as they drew closer that his attention was fixed on Yrsa.

"You have a lot of fans here," he muttered uneasily.

Yrsa made a sound in her throat that wasn't quite a laugh. Reaching the car, she pulled open the driver's door, releasing a fug of cigarette smoke and body odor.

"Hello, Filippus," she said.

The man, Filippus, said something in the local language, his voice raspy as if he'd been shouting a lot.

"Why do you think?" Yrsa responded. "My mother died."

Filippus said something else, though his eyes flickered away as he spoke, as if disconcerted by her direct gaze.

A flash of anger crossed Yrsa's face and, still speaking in English, she said, "Of course I care. You don't have to live in someone's pocket to prove you love them."

Before Filippus could reply she slammed the door shut and rolled her eyes at Todd. "See what I mean?" Then she crossed in front of the car, opened the passenger door and slid inside.

Todd opened the back door on the driver's side and heaved their bags in, pushing them along the seat so there was room for him. The inside of the car was grubby, the seats worn and stained, the footwells littered with small stones, clumps of dried mud, assorted food wrappers and what looked like a half-eaten bagel or doughnut with green mold growing on it.

Grimacing, he got in, the stale smell enveloping him. Yrsa was talking sharply to Filippus in his own language, and he was grunting in reply, his shoulders hunched as if her proximity bothered him. The islander turned the Volvo's ignition key, rousing its guttural engine to life, and drove away from the harbor. Todd had no idea whether the attention of the old fisherman and his colleagues was still fixed on them, but by the way the hair prickled on the back of his scalp he felt that it was.

Once the harbor was behind them he started to relax, even though the Volvo's engine was straining as it crawled up the gravelly slope flanked by scrub-covered hills. The car labored for half a mile or so, then the grinding engine began to ease as the road dipped into a more populated landscape. At first the blocky houses, most painted white with small windows and steep red or brown roofs, were widely spaced, each surrounded by several acres of undulating land on which sheep grazed. Gradually, however, the houses drew closer together, and suddenly they were entering what Todd guessed must be Eldfjallaeyja's main population center.

It wasn't much to look at. In fact, it seemed pretty run-down and depressing. The road running through the center of town was no better than the one they had followed from the harbor, though at least here faded road markings, pavement and traffic lights gave a *semblance* of order and formality. The buildings, packed together as if for warmth, were shabby and spartan, bereft of color, decoration or individuality. Todd saw no cafés, no fancy stores, no eye-catching signs or attractively illuminated windows. Hemmed in by the tall, dark trees of the surrounding forests, the town, comprising maybe a dozen streets and a couple of hundred buildings, seemed to cower in shame, or embarrassment, or perhaps even fear.

Within minutes they were through the town and out the other side. The road began to climb again, and the Volvo, accordingly, groaned in protest. Todd looked out of the window as they cut through alternating areas of pine forest and open grassland characterized by rocky formations blotched with lichens and mosses. After a mile or so the upward slope leveled out once more, and suddenly they were rattling along a gentle downhill gradient, the forest, which had been pressing in on both sides, taking a step back, retreating to border yet another area of undulating scrubby grassland.

In the distance, on their left, he saw another of the white-painted houses. It was set back from the road in a dip or hollow, and so gave the impression it was slowly sinking into the ground. A second or two after he'd noticed it, Yrsa twisted to look at him. "We're almost here. That's my mother's house."

Todd blinked. "That's where you were brought up?"

"Yes. I was born there and lived there until I was eighteen."

Ten meters from the house the car pulled onto the grassy verge. Yrsa and Filippus exchanged a few words, then Yrsa paid him and got out.

Todd was about to follow when, in the central driver's mirror, he saw the islander staring at him. He could see only the man's eyes, so it was impossible to read his full expression, but the piercing look Filippus had fixed him with made him shiver.

"Is something wrong?" he asked, trying to sound casual.

In response, Filippus moved his head deliberately from side to side, though whether he was replying in the negative or trying to deliver some kind of warning Todd had no idea.

CHAPTER SIX

"He was a barrel of laughs," said Todd, watching the orange Volvo fade into the distance.

Yrsa pulled a sour face. "He's a loser, like most people on this island."

She clumped down the stony slope to the front door of the squat little house. Like many of the buildings Todd had seen here, it was painted white, though clearly hadn't had a fresh coat for a long time. The stone walls were grayed by the elements, and splotched with moss and lichen, which resembled tumorous growths. The clustered outbuildings, beside which a muddy gray-green Land Rover was parked, were in an even worse state. Their walls missing planks, their roofs patched with odd lengths of timber and rusty squares of corrugated iron, they looked as though they hadn't been used in years. Yet from them drifted the dank odor of saturated straw and the musky scent of not-long-departed livestock.

The farmyard was a sea of mud, and at the back of the property, no more than thirty meters from the house, was a rickety wooden fence, beyond which a forest of straggly pine trees pushed right up to the boundary line. The trees were so tall they cast the yard and buildings into shadow. Even now, in the middle of the day, this was a grim and gloomy place. God knew what it would be like at night – though Todd had a feeling he would soon find out.

"I can't believe you grew up here," he said.

Yrsa's features were pinched and terse. "You see now why I was so eager to get away?"

"Are you okay?" he asked. "Being back, I mean?"

"Of course," she said, stepping up to the front door.

She turned the handle and the door opened. Todd raised his eyebrows. "Did you know it would be unlocked?"

She smirked at him. "Of course. This is not London. There are no serial killers or burglars here."

Todd laughed nervously and followed her in with the bags. Before stepping over the threshold, he glanced again at the black, silent trees beyond the flimsy boundary fence, and an involuntary shudder passed through him.

The interior of the house was as poky as he had been expecting. The ceilings were low, the corridors narrow, the rooms small. Yet although the floors were dark with ingrained dirt, the place was clean and tidy. Its aura of shabbiness was due purely to the fact that its fixtures and fittings were decades old, and had suffered much wear and tear over the years. The walls in the sitting room were covered with faux-wood paneling; the kitchen units were of cheap white Formica, frayed and chipped at the edges; the fabric on the furniture was faded; and the lighting throughout the house was 1970s ugly.

In terms of technology the most modern appliance was a microwave oven perched on a kitchen counter, next to a fat fridge that bloomed with rust at each of its rounded corners. As Yrsa showed him around, Todd felt his spirits, which had already been low, sinking further. The thought of living here alone, and of trying to keep a farm going as age crept up on you, filled him with despair. He wanted to ask Yrsa how, in all conscience, she could have permitted her mother to live like this, but he was here to offer support, not accuse her of negligence. Besides, he hadn't known the old woman. For all he knew she could have been a harridan, fiercely independent and tough as old boots.

"I'll show you my room," she said, though there was no eagerness or nostalgia in her voice. She led him out of the kitchen and back along the hallway, made narrow by the cramped wooden staircase on their left. The foot of the staircase was beside the front door, where Todd had dumped their bags. He scooped them up and followed her up the creaking stairs.

The staircase was not just cramped but steep too. A narrow landing curved back on itself at the top, leading off from which were four doors. The first was a tiny bathroom, the floor coated with gray linoleum that was curled at the edges and stained with age. The grouting between the tiles around the sink and bath was discolored and pin mold bloomed like an inverted starscape on the ceiling.

Yrsa's old room was the fourth and final one at the far end of the landing. Its walls clad in more of the faux-wood paneling, it had a sloping ceiling on its outer edge and a small window beneath the eaves that overlooked the muddy yard and the forest beyond. From here the trees resembled a ragged black curtain through which occasional chinks of milky light gleamed. The bed was a single, whose mattress, beneath its layers of thick, dusty blankets, looked lumpy.

"We can both squeeze in here or we can use the double bed in my mother's room," Yrsa said. She glanced at him as though reading his thoughts. "Either way I'll wash the bedding first."

From the way Yrsa had described her mother's death it didn't sound as if she had expired in bed, but Todd didn't like the thought of sleeping there all the same.

"Let's stay in here," he said. "It'll be cozy. I bet the nights get cold in these parts."

"They do," she said, and shot him another look he couldn't fathom.

While Todd unrolled his clothes from his rucksack and transferred them onto the shelves of a musty-smelling closet, Yrsa stripped the bedding from her childhood bed and carried it downstairs, with the promise that while she was in the kitchen she would make a pot of tea. It wasn't until Todd was done with his task that he realized how gloomy the room had become. Glancing at the small, square window, he saw that the sky above the forest was now blotchy with clouds that resembled bruises on white skin. He crossed to the light switch beside the door, clicking it down with the half-expectation that nothing would happen. However, the room was immediately bathed in a yellowish glow that reminded him of old teeth.

Immediately after switching the light on, he heard a faint growling sound. At first he thought it must be the old washing machine downstairs, juddering as it entered its spin cycle. But then, as the sound briefly increased in pitch before ebbing and dying to silence, he realized what it really was: an engine. His first thought was that Yrsa was driving away in the muddy Land Rover and leaving him alone in her dead mother's house. He hurried to the window and peered out, and was relieved to see the Land Rover still parked where it had been when they'd arrived. He crossed the room again, opened the bedroom door – and heard the front door creak open at the bottom of the stairs.

Then he heard a rustle of clothing and heavy footsteps as someone entered the house. Without calling a greeting, the newcomer clumped along the wooden floor of the downstairs hallway, towards the kitchen. Feeling a surge of alarm, Todd rushed along the upstairs landing and down the stairs. By the time he turned into the hallway, the intruder was out of sight, which meant they must already be in the kitchen. From that direction Todd heard voices – the first a low rumble, the second, which belonged to Yrsa, strident with fear or anger. He broke into a run and entered the kitchen panting with stress and exertion. His first impression was that a black-bearded giant was looming over Yrsa's cowering form.

Then he realized she wasn't cowering, but crouched in front of the open door of a soot-caked stove in the corner of the room. And she wasn't afraid of the man looming over her, but scowling at him, as if he'd annoyed her.

The man was maybe six-foot-five, a few inches taller than Todd, his natural bulkiness made bulkier by his chunky, patterned sweater and thick waterproof jacket. As Todd stepped into the room the man turned, and Todd saw the weathered face of a man in his thirties, whose thick black beard was streaked with white.

"You must be Todd," the man said in excellent English.

"I am," replied Todd, glancing at Yrsa.

Straightening up, she sighed, rubbed her sooty hands together, then gestured towards the man.

"Todd," she said, "this is my brother, Sven."

CHAPTER SEVEN

Trying to hide his surprise, Todd crossed the room, extending his hand. "Yrsa never told me she had a brother."

Sven shot his sister a dark look. "That doesn't surprise me."

Yrsa rolled her eyes. "Don't start."

Todd's hands were not small, but they were dainty compared to Sven's bear-like paws. Sven was no macho man, though. He didn't crush Todd's hand to make a point.

"Well, it's good to meet you anyway," Todd said, hoping a little friendliness would cut through the tension.

"You too," Sven said, giving him an appraising look.

"Sven is here to take me to see my mother," Yrsa said, before adding, "whether I want to or not."

"Your mother?" Todd said, startled, then realized what she must mean.

"She is laid in her box in Gunnar Hjaltason's back room," Sven said. "Tomorrow the box will be sealed. This is our last chance to say goodbye."

When Todd looked at Yrsa, she sighed. "Of course I'll go," she said, as if he had suggested otherwise. Turning back to her brother, she added, "I don't like your assumptions about me, that's all."

"I make no assumptions," Sven said.

"Your manner then. You come here telling me it's my duty to see my mother in her coffin, that it's the decent thing."

"It is."

"But you give no consideration to the fact that perhaps I wish to remember her as she was – full of life."

Sven snorted. "You had no interest in her while she was alive. No interest in her and no love for her either."

"That's not true."

"When did you last write to her? Every time I saw her, she told me she had heard nothing from you."

Yrsa looked defiant. "If she had email it would have been easier. If she had a phone even."

"Don't blame our mother for your shortcomings."

Instead of responding to her brother, Yrsa turned to Todd. "I'm sorry about this. I know it must be embarrassing for you."

In truth, Todd *did* feel awkward, but he said, "I know this is none of my business, but...would your mum want to see you both arguing like this? Wouldn't it be better to just...get on, in honor of her memory?"

Sven glared so fiercely at Todd that for a moment Todd thought the older man was going to punch him. Then Sven's hunched shoulders fell and he muttered, "Let's go if we're going."

"I'll take the Land Rover if it's roadworthy," Yrsa said. "Then you won't have to bring me back afterwards."

Sven glowered at her a moment longer, then said, "I'll see you there then," before stomping out of the house.

As soon as he'd gone, Yrsa gave another deep sigh. "I'm sorry about that."

Todd shrugged. "Families."

"I warned you this is the way of things here, didn't I? These people are so entrenched in their tiny world."

"They're *your* people, aren't they?" said Todd.

"In name only. I feel no kinship with them."

She waved a hand, which Todd had come to know was her way of dismissing a subject she no longer felt inclined to pursue, then crossed to a row of hooks on the wall by the back door.

From one of the hooks hung a set of car keys attached to a scuffed and dirty fob. Yrsa lifted it down.

"You can either come with me or wait here," she said. "Your choice."

Todd hesitated. "Do you want me to come?"

"Like I said, it's your choice."

She was still clearly smarting from the encounter with her brother. Despite her seeming indifference, though, Todd knew she'd been grateful of his support so far, and he suspected that beneath her tough exterior she was more vulnerable than she was letting on. Added to which he didn't fancy the idea of being left in a dead woman's house in the middle of nowhere as darkness fell.

"I'll come," he said.

He half-expected a smile of gratitude, but her stony expression didn't alter. "Whatever you like."

They barely spoke on the drive back to town, though this was partly because the Land Rover's engine filled the boneshaker of a vehicle with a guttural roar to go along with a pungent smell of manure, petrol and wet dog. As they rattled along, the colors of the land slowly deepened to grays and blacks, and the shapes of trees and rocks became less distinct.

Looking at the sky, Todd saw stars glinting like ice crystals. "You okay?" he asked eventually, shouting above the engine.

"Fine."

"When did you last see your brother?"

"Eighteen months ago, maybe."

"Is it that long since you've been home?"

The look she flashed him was venomous. "So you think I'm a bad daughter too?"

"No. I was just asking a question." As gently as the engine's racket would allow, he added, "I'm on your side, you know."

Her expression softened. "I know. Sorry."

They pulled into a space behind a dark pickup, in front of a building on the town's main street. Most of the premises here seemed to be either administration offices or retail outlets of some kind, though few had window displays or even signs promoting their services.

The undertaker's – if this was it – was a case in point. To Todd it looked like every other building here. It was at the end of a row, a wide entranceway beside it leading to a spacious area at the back. In the dimming light, as he and Yrsa got out of the car, their breath frosting in the cooling air, Todd made out the shapes of several vehicles parked back there.

The interior of the building was dingy, and not much warmer than outside. The room they stepped into was lit only by a couple of shaded lamps on corner tables, whose meager illumination made it impossible to tell whether the unadorned walls had been painted off-white or a pale shade of gray. There was a large desk, on which were scattered several sheets of paperwork, and a pair of wooden chairs, which were currently occupied by Sven and a small, bald man with a bushy white beard.

As Yrsa and Todd stepped over the threshold the small man rose to his feet and approached them. Holding out his hand, he spoke to Yrsa in her own language. Although Todd didn't understand the words, he guessed from the man's tone and the deferential way he dipped his head that he was offering his condolences. Yrsa answered him, then, reverting to English, said, "This is my friend, Todd. He's from London."

The man looked at Todd as if he was an interesting and exotic specimen. Holding out his hand, he said, "Good afternoon, Todd. I hope this isn't too much of a culture shock for you. We are a little insular here."

His hand was soft and warm, like a suede glove. Todd said, "Nice to meet you. And no, it's all very interesting."

"Hopefully it won't become *too* interesting," the man said, and smiled as if encouraging Todd to share the joke.

After releasing his hand, the undertaker asked Yrsa and Sven, in English, whether they were now ready to 'visit' their mother.

"Do you want me to come too?" Todd asked Yrsa.

She shook her head, suggesting with the merest raising of her eyebrows that Sven wouldn't approve. "Why don't you wait here? We won't be long."

Relieved, Todd settled back on one of the wooden chairs as Yrsa and Sven followed the undertaker through a door. Rotating his tense shoulders, he was wondering whether the man worked alone, or whether this was a family business, when a dark shape filled one of the small, square windows to the right of the door onto the street.

Startled, Todd looked up – and saw a face peering at him. It was pressed so tightly against the window that at first it appeared to be nothing but a black oval, featureless but for glints of light in its eyes. Then it moved back and Todd saw the face belonged to an old man or woman. It was glaring at him, the mouth between the fleshy jowls twisted into a hostile sneer.

The mouth opened wider, as if to harangue him – but instead of shouting, the stranger huffed a gout of breath onto the window, graying the pane. Immediately Todd saw a fingertip scrawl a symbol in the film of condensation – a circle containing a cross, like a cake divided into quarters. Before the stranger could add to the symbol – if, indeed, that was their intention – they were gone, perhaps as a reaction to Todd rising from his seat. Next moment he heard them bustling away, and sank back onto his chair, telling himself the incident had nothing to do with him.

Unsettled, he stared at the symbol, wondering what it meant. He took his phone from his pocket, googled it and found a number of possible meanings. He discovered that the Celtic Cross, or 'sun cross', was now commonly used by white supremacists as a hate symbol. One website devoted to esoteric tarot suggested that the quartered circle was the oldest known divine symbol, and as such represented everything from the four elements to the four seasons, to the four solar stations of Liber Resh: sunrise, noon, sunset and midnight. Yet another website described a cross within a circle as the symbol of Neptune; another that it represented the Spiritual Whole from which all mass, matter and life originated; another that it related to the Collective Unconscious.

Despite these suggestions, Todd couldn't help thinking that the symbol was unfinished, that the artist had been scared off before he or she could complete it, and so he delved deeper in the hope of filling the gaps.

He was looking at a website detailing protection symbols against evil spirits when he heard footsteps approaching from beyond the inner door. As hastily as a teenager ogling porn, he switched off his phone and shoved it into his pocket – though why he felt reluctant to be caught looking at such innocuous material he couldn't say.

He turned as the door opened and Yrsa emerged. If she had been upset by seeing her mother in her coffin, she didn't show it. Sven, however, was rubbing at his damp red eyes with his great paw of a hand. Seeing Todd looking at him, he turned away, embarrassed.

"Everything all right?" Todd asked Yrsa quietly.

She nodded, then turned to the undertaker, who had emerged from the corridor behind them. He, Yrsa and Sven spoke quietly for a few minutes while Todd waited. Glancing at the window, he saw the patch of condensation had faded now, though he could still faintly see the ghost of the quartered circle that had been inscribed there. Quickly he looked away, reluctant to draw anyone's attention to it.

A minute later he, Yrsa and Sven were outside, their business concluded. It had grown noticeably colder since they'd entered the building, a biting cold that made Todd hunch up his shoulders and clench his stomach muscles despite his thick jumper, woolly scarf and winter jacket. His gaze was drawn to the sky, which was almost supernaturally clear, thousands of stars standing out as brilliant pinpoints of light. He was about to say the sky here was like a high-definition plasma screen, compared to London's old analog TV picture, when Sven gave an angry roar.

Todd at first thought the big man was expelling more of his grief, but then he realized Sven was clumping towards the dark pickup in front of their Land Rover. He wondered whether whoever had drawn the symbol on the window had damaged Sven's vehicle, but then he saw a pair of small, hunched figures perched on the truck's roof.

In the twilight they looked like tiny men in long coats, their round heads tucked low into their shoulders. Todd felt a pang of superstitious fear, and then one of the 'men' rose to its full height and stretched out a pair of glossy wings.

They were birds. Big, black birds of some kind. From the size, Todd guessed they were ravens – if, indeed, ravens existed in this part of the world.

The bird that had stretched its wings lowered and folded them again, seemingly as unmoved as its companion by Sven's rage. Even when the big man ran at the vehicle waving his arms the creatures did nothing but swivel their heads to regard him.

Clumping to a halt, Sven turned towards Yrsa and barked something in their own language. From his red face and furious expression, he gave Todd the impression he thought this was somehow *her* fault.

Yrsa regarded him coldly, then snapped something in reply. She stalked forward, pushing past him, then pointed at the ravens like a schoolteacher singling out a pair of naughty schoolboys. She made a sound that startled Todd – a high, thin, ululating cry. Immediately the birds stretched their wings and took flight, and within seconds had bled into the darkness.

Twisting her head to look at Sven, she muttered something before turning disdainfully away. Sven grunted and got into his truck.

"What happened there? Why was Sven so angry?" Todd asked when she reached the Land Rover.

"He's angry because he's a superstitious savage, like the rest of them." Yrsa opened the driver's door and got into the vehicle. "Let's go."

CHAPTER EIGHT

"Let's shake things up a bit."

Todd looked up. He was sitting with his legs stretched out on the threadbare, rickety sofa in the main downstairs room, staring into the dancing flames of the fire. He'd never stayed in a place with a real fire before, and was proud of the fact he'd built it himself, first cleaning out the grate and then, following Yrsa's instructions, erecting a pyramid of split logs on top of a mound of crumpled newspaper and kindling, which he'd found in the smallest of the three outhouses.

What he hadn't mentioned to Yrsa after entering the house with his basket of logs was that, from the front door to the drafty outhouse and back, he'd felt as if someone was standing at the edge of the forest, watching him. A couple of times he'd looked over his shoulder, but had seen nothing except the motionless wall of trees, black and solid in the early evening darkness.

The fact he hadn't seen anything moving hadn't reassured him. Out in the yard the darkness beyond the bleed of light from the house's windows had been absolute. So even if something *had* been moving through the trees, it was doubtful he'd have seen it until it had crossed the yard and was only a few meters away.

Although he'd been spooked, with the curtains shut and the logs popping in the fire, he felt calm again now. The delicious aroma of stew or casserole, which Yrsa had thrown together from provisions they'd bought at the town's well-stocked general store after leaving the funeral home, only added to the sense of homeliness. It had been a long, eventful day, and Todd was now mentally bedding in for an evening of relaxation. When Yrsa appeared in the doorway, therefore, he frowned.

"What do you mean?"

She grinned wickedly. "I thought when we'd eaten we could go for a drink, ruffle a few feathers."

"Do we have to?"

Her grin became a scowl. "What's the matter? Do you want to hide away like a scared kitten?"

"Of course not. But neither do I see the point of seeking confrontation for its own sake. I just want a quiet life."

"Says the man who took on two muggers and ended up in hospital."

"Exactly. I ended up in hospital. And parts of me are still aching. I can do without experiencing that again in a hurry."

She sighed, but her mouth was still set in a determined pout. "It won't be like that. They won't kick our arses just for being here."

"How do you know?"

"I know these people. They're spineless."

Todd thought of the fishermen who'd glared at them upon their arrival. Spineless was not a word he'd have used to describe them.

"It's been a stressful day and I'm comfortable. Can't we stay here tonight?"

The muscles in her face tightened even more, narrowing her eyes. "*You* stay here. *I'm* going for a drink."

The choice that Yrsa gave Todd was really no choice at all, which was why he found himself, an hour later, sitting in the passenger seat of the Land Rover as it pulled up in front of one of the tallest and brightest-looking buildings in town. It wasn't exactly a swinging joint, but at least light was spilling from its windows, onto a pavement which looked metallic in the thinly falling rain.

As soon as Yrsa cut the engine and opened the driver's door, cold mist swirled into the vehicle, which made Todd think even more longingly of the fire they'd left dwindling back at the house. He opened his door with a groan.

"You're making old man noises," said Yrsa.

"My ribs are aching," said Todd.

Yrsa pulled a 'diddums' face. "Poor baby."

"You've changed your tune. A few weeks ago I was your knight in shining armor."

"And you still are. But you need to stop milking those injuries of yours."

"Fuck off," said Todd, but he wasn't really angry. In fact, he *was* milking it a bit. Mostly because he was tired. All the traveling and lugging bags around had taken it out of him; it was the greatest amount of exertion he'd had for a while.

With the rain had come mist, which threw the town into dismal soft focus. The drive over had been eerie, the mist swirling and coiling in the fields, the barely visible trees like a silent army of giants from some Nordic folk tale. When they were halfway between the house and the town, squat dark shapes had materialized from the murk-shrouded field on their right and slid across the road. Todd had tensed, half-imagining that malevolent entities of the forest had been conjured by the islanders to impede their progress. Yrsa, remaining composed, had gently pressed her foot on the brake, bringing the vehicle to a halt. The shapes had loomed in the headlights; the one leading the group – the largest – paused to regard them.

Todd saw the amber flash of its eyes at the same moment as he realized what the shapes were. Wild boars – a mother and her three children from the looks of it. After staring them down for a moment, the mother had continued her unhurried progress across the road, her brood trotting behind her. Seconds later the mist and the darkness had swallowed them up.

Yrsa laughed and led the way into what she had earlier described as the town's only hotel. As they stepped into a wood-paneled foyer, they were met by a surge of fuggy warmth and a swell of chatter. To their right was a curved and currently unoccupied reception desk with a wooden staircase beyond it. On the wood-paneled walls were paintings of snowy landscapes and big skies, alongside ledges on which stuffed animals were perched – an owl, a fox, what looked like a mongoose.

Yrsa marched across to the open door from beyond which the chatter was coming and stepped over the threshold. Todd, adopting what he hoped was a casually friendly expression, trailed after her.

In one of Todd's favorite movies, *An American Werewolf in London,* two American tourists enter an isolated pub called The Slaughtered Lamb and all chatter, all activity, abruptly stops. As he and Yrsa walked into the town's only bar he thought of that scene, even though the response here was not so dramatic. He was, however, aware of heads turning in their direction, of conversations faltering, of faces registering degrees of shock, surprise, wariness, distaste. Reluctant to establish eye contact with anyone, he glanced at Yrsa, and was surprised to see a smug half-smile on her face, as if she was savoring the disapproval.

She sauntered to the bar, Todd trying not to feel like an appendage as he trailed behind her. The barman, a thin guy in his twenties with a pasty expression and a scrappy ginger beard, ghosted towards them, looking nervous.

"Olav," said Yrsa. "How are you? It's been a long time."

Olav attempted a smile, but after a twitch of the lips the expression died. "Hello, Yrsa. I am well. And you?"

"My mother died," Yrsa said.

"Yes, I heard about that. I am sorry."

"Are you?"

"Of course. We all are. She was a good woman."

Yrsa regarded him a moment, and Olav's eyes flickered away. Unable to stand the tension, Todd indicated the big chiller behind Olav and asked, "What beer would you recommend?"

Before Olav could reply, Yrsa pointed at a row of bottles on whose black labels was the stylized profile of a Viking, his hair and beard flowing behind him. She reverted to her own language to make her order, whereupon Olav grabbed the beers out of the chiller and popped their tabs, vapor curling from the mouths of the bottles like lethargic genies.

"Thanks," Todd said, reaching for his beer. Olav locked eyes with him and gave a curt, though not unfriendly nod, before turning away to put Yrsa's money into the cash register.

The hotel bar was a narrow, low-ceilinged room, the bar itself stretching almost the full length of the inner wall. A row of wooden booths occupied the opposite wall, beneath an equal number of small windows positioned just above head height if sitting down. The somber lighting gave the place a cave-like feel, as did the brown décor. As Todd followed Yrsa through groups of drinkers, towards an empty booth beside an ugly gray jukebox, which was playing 'Echo Beach' by Martha and the Muffins, he was aware, despite his averted gaze, that multiple eyes were still locked on them.

By the time he slid into the booth, he felt he'd run the gauntlet. Huffing with relief, he said, "Well, that wasn't intense at all."

Yrsa sneered, though her disdain was directed at the room rather than him. "Don't be intimidated by these losers," she said, loudly enough to make Todd wince.

He tipped his bottle towards his mouth. Despite the chilliness outside, his cheeks were sizzling, which made the cold, rich earthiness of the beer more than welcome. He took three swallows in quick succession, then stole a glance around the room. Although the majority of drinkers had returned to their conversations, Todd got the impression he and Yrsa were still very much the focus of attention.

Two people in particular were making no secret of the fact. One was a heavyset old woman in bulky clothes, with frizzy gray hair and penciled-on eyebrows, who was leaning against the bar and *glaring* at Yrsa. The other was a waif-like girl in her twenties whose pale blue eyes and white-blonde hair made Todd think of overexposed photographs.

Although the younger girl's scrutiny was just as intense as the old woman's, the expression on her face suggested concern rather than anger. Oddly it was this which unnerved Todd the most, because he couldn't help feeling her anxiety was reserved for him. As soon as he established eye contact with her, however, she looked away.

"Do you know all the people in here?" Todd asked.

Yrsa shrugged. "Of course."

"Who's the old woman at the bar giving us the daggers? No, don't look!"

But it was too late. Yrsa had already swiveled on her seat and was peering through the crowd, making no attempt to be subtle.

The old woman was still glaring at them. In response Yrsa gave an exaggerated grin, then raised a hand and waved. The woman stiffened, pushing herself upright, her face twisting into a mask of undiluted hatred. Todd saw redness rushing up from her neck, mottling her saggy cheeks. He felt sure she was about to either rush towards them or collapse with a seizure. In the event, she did neither. She slammed her fist on the bar, loudly enough to turn heads, then stormed from the room, shoving people aside as she went.

Yrsa slumped back into her seat, breathless with laughter.

"Who was that?" Todd asked. He wasn't laughing. On the contrary his stomach was twisting in a sick knot.

"That was Margret Gulbransen. My mother's best friend."

"What's she got against you?"

"No doubt she thinks I abandoned my mother. You'll have to ask her at the funeral."

Todd's heart sank at the prospect. Funerals were fraught enough affairs without adding a hefty dollop of resentment and hostility to the already volatile blend of rawness and grief. But were feelings strong enough to erupt into violence? Were he and Yrsa actually in danger here? The culture and language barrier made him feel out of his depth, unable to read the situation accurately. If only he could talk to someone neutral. Sven perhaps? But how could he engineer the opportunity? He saw the defiance in Yrsa's eyes as she scanned the room. Her spirit and forthrightness had attracted him from the outset, but there were times when he wished she'd rein it in a bit.

For the next hour Todd tried to block out what was happening beyond the confines of their booth, focusing his attention on Yrsa – and also trying to keep her attention focused on him in the hope of avoiding further conflict. When he went to the bar for more drinks, he took out his phone and scrolled through his messages, so he wouldn't have to engage with his surroundings.

They were on their fourth drinks (still beer for Todd, but Yrsa had now switched to apple juice, because she was driving) when he asked, "So how was it in the funeral home? Seeing your mum?"

He asked the question tentatively, hoping he hadn't touched a raw nerve, but Yrsa merely shrugged, and almost matter-of-factly said, "I found it hard to feel anything."

"Why was that?"

"Because the body lying in the coffin wasn't her."

Todd sat up so suddenly that the room revolved around him. "What do you mean?"

She laughed. "Calm down. I mean, it *was* her, of course. But I found it hard to equate the shell with the person. It's like when you see a butterfly's..." Her eyes narrowed as she searched for the word.

"Chrysalis?"

"Yes, chrysalis. It was empty. It was just a thing. Whatever my mother's essence was...it was gone."

"So are you saying you didn't feel anything?"

"I felt confused," Yrsa replied. "No, not confused. Dislocated. Yes, that's it. It was like a dream."

"Right."

The look she gave him was penetrating. "You think I'm cold?"

"No, not cold," Todd replied, not entirely truthfully. "I just think... well, I can't imagine ever feeling like that about my parents. I'd find looking at their bodies upsetting. Just knowing they were no longer there. That they were now just..."

"Meat?" said Yrsa.

Todd winced. "A bit blunt, but...yeah."

Yrsa pursed her lips dismissively. "I lived on a farm. We had livestock. Death was a natural part of life."

"But this is your mum we're talking about, not a cow or a sheep."

"It's not so different." Abruptly she stood up. "I need to pee."

She slid out of the booth and walked away, leaving Todd feeling bewildered, unsettled. Sometimes Yrsa was passionate and caring, even vulnerable, and at other times she was like an alien – ruthless, disconnected, unpredictable. He didn't know how he felt about that, how he should react. He didn't even know whether he found that aspect of her attractive or off-putting.

"We need to talk."

The voice was thin, the words too precise to have been spoken by a native English speaker. Coming from directly behind him, it made Todd jump. He turned so quickly his back and ribs flared with pain. The pale girl with the white-blonde hair was standing there. She looked nervous, agitated; her hands were clamped together as though to anchor her body in place.

"Do we?" Todd said.

"Yes. Take this." Reaching into the pocket of her pale blue hoodie, she drew out a small square of white paper, which she thrust towards him. Todd took it automatically and started to unfold it.

"Not here. Put it away. Don't let her see it."

"Why? What's—"

"She's not who you think she is. You are not safe."

"What do you mean by—"

"Hello, Karriana."

Although the greeting was friendly enough, Todd saw the girl's eyes widen and an expression he could only describe as terror cross her face. Almost immediately she composed herself and turned.

"Hello, Yrsa."

"I hope you're not trying to steal my boyfriend?"

The girl – Karriana – laughed. "Of course not. I just came over to say hello."

"Okay."

"Karriana wanted to let me know that not everyone here is unfriendly," Todd found himself saying.

The look that Yrsa gave him was so devoid of emotion he felt an immediate need to defend what he had said, even though it was a lie. However, he resisted, holding her gaze with what he hoped was an openness that would convince her he had nothing to hide.

He was relieved when she turned her attention back to Karriana. "So how are your mother and father?"

"They're well," Karriana said. "I was sorry to hear of *your* mother. She was a nice lady."

"Yes," said Yrsa. "So what are you doing now?"

"I work with my parents. In the bakery."

"And that makes you happy?"

"Of course."

Yrsa's pause might as well have been a snort of disapproval. In the same bland voice she said, "You are an intelligent girl, Karriana. You could do much more than this with your life. Don't you wish to leave the island and see what else is out there for you?"

Karriana looked wary, as if she thought Yrsa was leading her into a trap. "No. I love it here. This is my home."

Yrsa sighed. "Okay."

Todd felt an urge to defend Karriana, to say that choosing a simple life was not necessarily a failing. He wanted to say that people found happiness in different things, and that Yrsa's choice – to break away, see the world, test her own limits – did not automatically make her a better or more fulfilled person.

He kept quiet, though, not because he was fearful of Yrsa's reaction, but because he knew she was like a dog with a bone whenever her opinion was questioned, and he often found himself defending a position he wasn't really all that invested in in the first place.

"Well, it's good to see you again," Karriana said with no conviction whatsoever.

"You too," said Yrsa with an equal lack of sincerity.

It was only now, with Karriana on the verge of saying goodbye, that Todd realized the piece of paper was still tucked into his palm. Casually he reached for his beer bottle with his left hand while sliding his right arm back until his hand was below the level of the table. He slipped the note into his pocket, then raised his now-empty hand in a wave.

"Nice to meet you," he said as Karriana walked away.

Yrsa watched her until she was out of the door, then turned back to Todd with a wolfish smile.

"One more for the road?"

CHAPTER NINE

Their first night in Yrsa's mother's house was not a restful one.

Someone came into the room when they were sleeping, slid across to the bed, and touched Todd's face, and it was only when he lurched awake that he realized he'd been dreaming.

He lay facing the door, his panting breaths matching his throbbing heart, and tried to shake off the dread-laden atmosphere of the dream. The way the amorphous figure had seemed to slide or glide across the floor was horrible and somehow malign. When he raised a hand to examine the cheek where the figure had touched him, his fingertips came away wet.

Blood? Of course not; only sweat. The nocturnal temperature beyond the bed was hovering not much above zero, but his and Yrsa's combined body heat beneath the thick blankets had created a toasty microclimate. Feeling stifled, Todd peeled the blankets back from his body, allowing in some of the frigid air from outside. He sighed as it moved across his skin like a dabbling of chilly fingers – but then the fingers reached his bladder and prodded it awake.

He groaned inwardly. He didn't want to get out of bed, but too much beer in the hotel bar meant the need to pee was suddenly urgent. He slid out lengthways so as not to rouse Yrsa, and padded across to the door. By the time he reached the poky bathroom the cold air was making him shiver. Peeing was such a relief that it made Todd sigh with pleasure. But as his bladder emptied, the dream again rose in his mind, and feeling vulnerable, he glanced nervously over his shoulder, half-expecting a figure to form out of the mass of shadows crowding the corridor behind him.

As he was still feverish with sleep, his imagination made the shadows seem to writhe with frantic movement, like a carpet of ants or beetles.

He scurried back to the bedroom and breathed a sigh of relief when he crossed the threshold and closed the door behind him. Looking across the room, he saw the light from the three-quarter moon, diffused by the thin curtains, reached no further than the bed beneath the window, and then only enough to define it as a humped black shape.

He jumped when a ghostly apparition, insubstantial as a twist of smoke, suddenly rose in front of his face, then he grinned sheepishly when he realized it was his own breath. He padded across to the bed and slid back in, shivering as he pulled the now-chilly blankets over him. Turning towards Yrsa, he shuffled across the gap between them, intending to snuggle into her back. But she wasn't as close as he'd expected her to be; she must have been crushed right up against the wall. He stretched out a hand, but all he found were rumpled bedclothes, which were cool to the touch. She wasn't there.

He sat up with a jolt. Where was she? Groping to his left, he found his mobile on the bedside table. The glowing screen showed the time: 3:47. He turned on the torch app and shone it around, half-thinking she'd be standing in a corner of the room, staring back at him.

But the room was empty. "Yrsa?" he called. He felt fully awake now. Receiving no reply, he climbed back out of bed, crossed the room, switched on the light, and turned to the battered wicker chair onto which he'd drunkenly flung his clothes. Quickly he pulled on his boxer shorts and T-shirt, then moved back across to the door and pulled it open.

Once again shadows swarmed in the corridor, but Todd punctured them with the light from his phone before striding to the switch on the wall and slapping it down. Although the light within the woven brown shade was muted, it made his eyes and head throb, reminding him he was cultivating a hangover.

Was that why Yrsa wasn't in bed? Because she'd woken up feeling ill, and had gone in search of painkillers? She'd only had a couple of beers, but even so. He crossed to the head of the stairs and peered down. The brownish darkness into which the stairs sunk swirled lazily like a whirlpool.

"Yrsa?" he called. "You down there?"

No answer. And no sounds of movement. So where could she be? His heart was thumping, though he told himself there was no reason to be worried. Maybe she'd fallen asleep while watching telly or drinking tea. He was wondering whether to go back to the bedroom and put some shoes on his freezing feet when something creaked at the foot of the stairs.

"Yrsa?" he called again, half-expecting her to emerge from the gloom. But when a second creak came, he suddenly realized what it was. The front door of the little house was ajar.

Had someone come in, or had Yrsa gone out? His anxiety building, Todd thumped downstairs. The light switch for the downstairs hall was on the wall by the front door. He clicked it, refusing to blunder about in the dark like an idiot in a horror film. Aware of how vulnerable he was in nothing but a T-shirt and boxers, he pulled the front door further open and stuck his head out. An icy breeze ruffled his blond hair and raised goosebumps on his arms.

"Yrsa?" he yelled. "You out there?"

He willed her to respond, but there was nothing.

"Yrsa, if you're out there, answer me!"

Silence.

"Fuck!"

Anxiety made him angry and he shut the front door with a bang. "Where are you?" he snarled, and stalked through the downstairs rooms of the house, slapping on lights. He longed to see her tousled head rise over the back of the settee, bad-temperedly demanding why he'd woken her at four in the morning. But the settee was unoccupied and cool to the touch. He stared into the gray ashes of the fire, wondering what to do.

There was only one choice. She wasn't in the house, so she must be outside, which meant he'd have to go and look for her. He swore again, then ran upstairs. He yanked on jeans, socks and boots, and was pulling his thick pullover over his head when it occurred to him to check that the Land Rover was still there. Rushing to the window, he yanked the curtain aside, and was relieved to see that it was, its metal frame picked out icily in the moonlight. He was about to let the curtain fall back when something beyond the vehicle snagged his attention. A flicker of light in the forest.

By the time he focused on it, it had gone. It had only lasted a second, but it was so dark out there, despite the moonlight, that it had flared like a beacon. In his mind's eye, he saw Yrsa, momentarily flicking on her torch app to see where she was going. But why was she out there? If she'd seen something she'd have woken him, wouldn't she?

He really didn't want to go outside, but he didn't have much choice. Perhaps Yrsa was sleepwalking, in which case she might injure herself, or collapse and freeze to death. Before rushing into the forest, though, he decided to try calling her. He tapped in her number and immediately heard the tinkling chimes of her ringtone. Glancing across at her old dressing table, he saw the glowing rectangle of her mobile screen, jittering as the phone vibrated. So the light he'd seen in the forest couldn't have been from her torch app. Could it have been an actual torch then, or a box of matches?

Todd hurried back downstairs and grabbed his winter jacket from the kitchen. Zipping himself into its cozy bulk did little to lessen his sense of vulnerability, though, especially when he stepped out of the house and felt the air clamp itself to his face like an icy mask. Facing the black wall of forest across the muddy yard, he remembered what Yrsa had said earlier – that there were no burglars or serial killers on the island. Todd's unease, though, came from somewhere more primal. The environment was alien to him, and therefore instinctively felt hostile. He turned on his torch app, but this close to the house the light fell short of the forest's edge. He took a deep breath and shouted, "Yrsa! Where are you?"

Nothing answered; nothing stirred; no lights flickered in the blackness. Todd crossed the yard, the mud sucking at his boots, making him heavy-legged. When the silvery light from his phone began to sidle around the first of the trees, prizing them apart, it was more disconcerting than reassuring. The meager torchlight only reminded him how much blackness there was *between* the trees, and how easy it would be for something to stay concealed until the instant it chose to emerge.

Clambering over the fence at the edge of the property, he kept his arm moving, swinging his torch beam constantly to and fro. He was doing it to give himself every chance of finding Yrsa, but also so he wouldn't be taken by surprise. Ten meters into the trees he stopped and looked back, and was gratified to see multiple points of orange-brown light. He'd switched on every light in the house before venturing outside, in the hope he could use it as a point of reference to stop himself getting lost.

He shouted Yrsa's name again, the slithering torchlight giving the trees a queasy kind of animation. As they shifted in and out of the beam they seemed to loom and sway, the shadows around them bulging and sinking. Todd moved to his right, if only because it was roughly in this direction that he'd seen the flare of light minutes earlier. He kept calling Yrsa's name, and although his voice felt flatter in here, deadened by the trees, it also seemed to carry further, the same trees acting as a barrier against the wind.

He soon got into a routine – moving forward ten meters or so, calling Yrsa's name, then looking back to check the lights of the house were still visible. All the while the beam of his torch probed the trees and foliage, but to Todd the light never seemed to penetrate deeply enough. Occasionally he jerked the beam upwards, unsettled by the rustling of overhead branches. He never saw movement up there, so he told himself it was just the wind. Or birds. Maybe squirrels.

Thinking of squirrels reminded him of the wild boar they'd seen earlier, which made him wonder what other animals might be roaming the forest at night. He was still wondering when he heard rustling in the bushes close by. His heart leaped, and he swung round, torch beam veering crazily.

In his imagination something was already leaping at him – something with claws and fangs. In reality, there was nothing – or rather, more of the same: trees, bushes, tangled undergrowth.

He moved the beam back and forth, wondering how quickly he could climb a tree if a pair of yellow eyes reflected back at him out of the darkness. Until now the glow from the house, albeit fractured like shards of a broken mirror, had given him a sense of reassurance, but suddenly he could only think how far away from safety he was. If something were stalking him, he'd have zero chance of outrunning it. But the rustling in the bushes was probably just a rabbit or a bird. In the dark and the quiet, sounds became magnified.

All the same, he felt momentarily reluctant to shout Yrsa's name again. Then it occurred to him that animals hunted by scent and movement, and generally went for prey smaller than themselves, so the bigger and more threatening he made himself, the better. So he held his phone higher and rotated his body in a circle to cover every angle. "Yrsa! Where are you?" he yelled.

Above him, a bird took fright and flapped away. Otherwise he was met with silence.

He glanced at the house again – fragments of amber light flickering like fireflies through the trees. How deep did this forest go? And how far would his voice carry? More to the point, if Yrsa *were* sleepwalking, would his calls be enough to wake her?

Realizing that his chances of finding her in the dark were low, he decided to give it ten more minutes, then head back to the house. And then what? Sit and wait? Call someone?

Suddenly he remembered Yrsa's phone charging in the bedroom. She'd have Sven's details on there, so surely his best bet would be to call him – even though waking Yrsa's brother up at four thirty a.m. was not an appealing prospect.

Recognizing that this should have been his plan from the start, Todd decided to head back. He turned to face the fractured orange glow from the distant house – and abruptly, the light from his phone went out.

For a moment fear gripped him, and then he told himself there was nothing to worry about; his phone had simply run out of battery. He started forward, hands out in front of him, and found himself hoping that not every night on the island was going to be like this. He'd probably laugh about this later, but right now his situation didn't seem very funny. If only he'd put his phone to charge before getting into bed. But he'd been pissed and knackered, and it hadn't occurred to him he'd need it before the morning. Not that it mattered. It wasn't as if—

Foliage rustled to the right of him.

He couldn't help it; he yelped in fear. Clapping a hand to his mouth, he froze, like a deer trying to magic itself into invisibility when a predator is close. He stood there for ten seconds, maybe fifteen, and then realized he couldn't stand there forever. The rustling foliage had been followed by silence, so after counting off another ten seconds in his head, he started forward again. His footsteps whispered in the undergrowth, and now, as he moved towards the light, he felt sure something was keeping pace with him. Doggedly he kept moving forward, and was grateful to see that as he got closer to the edge of the forest, the gaps between the trees were widening, and the glow from the house brightening, coalescing.

Then he was through and out, and he saw the perimeter fence ahead, the light from the house turning the wooden posts into scratchy black lines, like a child's drawing.

He half-ran, half-stumbled the last few steps, and scraped the underside of his thigh as he scrambled over the fence. He didn't care, though. If this was the only injury he was going to come away with, he'd happily take it. He jogged across the muddy yard like a marathon runner making a final effort, and gasped in relief when he reached the house.

Once inside, he leaned against the wall, laughing shakily, feeling foolish now that he was back. He scraped his boots clean on the mat, then clumped upstairs to the bedroom. He shoved open the door, and made for Yrsa's still-charging phone on the dressing table. He was reaching for it when he heard a groan from the direction of the window. He spun round, and saw the mound of blankets on the bed shifting. For a moment, as the door continued to swing open behind him, admitting an arc of brownish light, he couldn't move. Then the light reached the bed, and a figure sat up, tousled head rising from a fall of blankets.

It was Yrsa.

CHAPTER TEN

When Todd entered the bathroom, having been woken by the sound of running water, he found Yrsa sitting on the edge of the tub, her back to him. She'd rolled her pajama bottoms up and her feet were in the water, which was already brown from the mud swirling away from her skin. The pine needles she hadn't left in the bed were floating on top, and she was staring at them in bewilderment.

"My feet are filthy," she said.

"So are the bedsheets," said Todd. "We'll have to wash them again." He paused. "You don't remember what happened?"

"No." She glanced at him in confusion. "What did?"

"You sleepwalked. You went into the forest." He gestured at her feet. "At least I assume you did."

She scowled. "That's crazy. I never sleepwalked before."

"I woke up and you weren't here. I looked for you everywhere." He told her what had happened. "When I got back you were in bed. You woke up and spoke to me, but you were out of it."

"I don't remember any of that." She looked worried. "Fuck, what's happening to me?"

"Nothing," Todd said, with a reassurance he didn't feel. "You've been stressed, that's all. You've suffered a trauma. Too much pent-up adrenaline."

"I could have had an accident. My feet could have been cut to ribbons."

"But they weren't," he said soothingly. "Here, let me check." He knelt beside her, reached into the bath and took her left foot in his hands. He washed it gently, feeling for wounds. Then he did the same with her right foot.

"There. No damage done. You were lucky."

"What if it happens again?"

"Maybe we should tie you to the bed at night."

She pushed her lips out in a sultry pout, and gave an almost comedic growl of sexual arousal. Then, as quickly as it had come, the humor drained away. "Seriously, what if it *does* happen again?"

"Do you think it will?" said Todd.

"Well, I don't know, do I?"

"Can't we just lock the door?"

"If we can find a key. And if it still works after all these years."

"I'll look for one," said Todd. "And I'll make us some of that disgusting instant coffee we bought from the shop yesterday."

By the time she came downstairs he was eating toast and drinking his second cup of coffee. Yrsa was wearing a cable-knit gray sweater and skinny black jeans with zip-up boots. She'd put on makeup and tied her hair back. Her face was set and determined.

"You look like a woman who's not prepared to take any shit," said Todd.

She scowled, though not at him. "I don't like to feel I'm not in control."

Stuffing his last bite of toast into his mouth, he rose from the table. "Sit down. I'll do you some breakfast."

He put a couple of slices of rye bread into the toaster and flicked the kettle on. "I'm sure what happened was a one-off. And if not, we'll figure it out."

"How?"

"I've looked through all the drawers in here, but I couldn't find a key. So maybe we can get a couple of bolts in town? There must be a hardware store?"

"There is. But what's to stop me opening the bolts in my sleep?"

"Well...nothing, but it would be another barrier. You might open a door in your sleep, but maybe your unconscious mind wouldn't think to manipulate a couple of bolts?"

She looked unconvinced, but shrugged. Todd carried her toast and coffee to the table and set them down.

"What's the most dangerous animal on the island?" he asked.

She blinked at him. "That's a bit left field."

"Not really." He smiled sheepishly. "I heard something in the forest last night. It freaked me out. I wondered whether there were wolves on the island."

"Wolves?" She laughed.

"Well, I don't know...wild dogs, maybe. Or feral cats. I'm not exactly an expert on Nordic fauna."

Still smiling, she said, "You've already seen the most dangerous thing here."

"The wild boar, you mean?"

Her smile widened. "No, me!" She gave her full-throated, raucous laugh, which was good to hear after the tension of the past twenty-four hours.

"Ha ha, most amusing. So how dangerous *are* wild boar?"

She pulled a dismissive face. "They can be aggressive, but they mostly avoid humans. They usually only attack if they feel threatened or cornered."

"I was the one that felt threatened last night."

Now she pushed her lips out in an expression of mock-sympathy. "Aw, bless. Was my poor little city boy frightened by a bunny wabbit? Or an ickle deer?"

"Fuck off," he said, laughing. "So what's the plan today?"

"Boring stuff. Solicitor, coroner, all that. It may take a while. You can stay here if you like." She smirked. "Maybe go for a walk in the forest?"

"No, thanks. I'll come with you. Get those bolts, have a mooch around."

"I warn you, there's nothing to see."

"There'll be more than there is here."

"That's debatable." She looked at her watch. "Okay to leave in twenty minutes?"

"I'll just grab a shower."

CHAPTER ELEVEN

When he was a kid, Todd would often accompany his dad on Saturday morning trips to builders' merchants, woodyards, stone suppliers. He never particularly wanted to go, but his mum would be in town shopping, and Robin would be out with his friends, and Todd's dad would be unwilling to leave Todd home alone.

"You'd burn the bloody house down," he'd say, or, "You'd leave a tap on and flood the place." Todd never knew whether his dad *really* thought he would, or whether it was just that by being around the materials he used in his work, he hoped his youngest son might get a taste for the building game.

Much as he loved the smell of freshly cut wood, though, Todd never did get bitten by the building bug. He remembered those trips as long, boring stretches of time, during which he'd kick his heels, while his dad spent forever talking to a succession of gruff, undemonstrative men about whatever it was builders talked about.

It had been years since Todd had thought about those endless Saturday mornings spent staring vacantly at stacks of freshly cut timber and rows of ceramic tiles, but when Yrsa parked on Eldfjallaeyja's main street and told him she'd meet him back at the Land Rover in two hours, he experienced a peculiar sense of déjà vu.

If this had been London, or practically any other city or town in the UK, he'd have had no problem. He'd have done what he needed to do, then spent the rest of the time indulging himself – checking out the shops, grabbing a coffee, seeing the sights.

But here there was nothing. Just a series of drab buildings arranged in an uninspiring grid that radiated out from a long main road. As far as he could tell there were no museums or art galleries, no parks or bookshops or cafés. There was the forest, of course, which bordered the town, but after last night's adventure a stroll through the trees was even less appealing than wandering up and down the gray streets for two hours.

First things first, though. Yrsa had told him where the hardware store was, so he set off to find it. Even though a biting wind gnawed at his face like a shoal of invisible piranhas, he took his time, chin tucked into the folds of his thick scarf, gloved hands stuffed in his pockets.

Although there weren't many people around, Todd couldn't help feeling he was the main focus of attention of those who were. In his peripheral vision he saw heads turning, saw passersby stop in their tracks to regard him. He wondered whether they were just curious, or knew of his association with Yrsa. Despite what Yrsa had said, surely not *everyone* in town could harbor resentment towards her. In his experience most people were too wrapped up in their own affairs to bother with other people's. It was understandable that her homecoming had raised a ripple of interest, and he couldn't deny there was *some* bad feeling towards her. But in all likelihood, that animosity was limited to the few individuals who unfairly blamed Yrsa for her mother's death.

By the time he reached the hardware store he was glad to get out of the cold. The door was stiff, and scudded across the gritty floor with enough noise to alert the two people behind the counter. One was a round-bellied man in his thirties with a reddish beard and a black beanie pulled down to his eyebrows. The other was a woman of fifty-five or sixty with plump, ruddy skin and short, gray-blonde hair, wearing a shapeless black cardigan over a gray sweatshirt. Their large blue eyes and small, puckered mouths immediately identified them as mother and son. Looking at them, Todd couldn't help thinking they resembled seals trying to pass themselves off as humans. He smiled, but they simply stared back, their expressions unchanging.

"Hi," he said as he pulled off his gloves. "Do you speak English?"

At first he thought they weren't going to reply, but then the man nodded. "A little."

"I'm looking for bolts," Todd said, and mimed the action of sliding one into its socket. "Do you have any?"

The store was cluttered and dark, and composed of several rooms, each of which were crammed with free-standing shelves. Kitchen implements, tin buckets, heavy-duty chains and other items hung from the ceiling, and the place smelled of metal, oil, paint and wood.

The woman continued to stare as the man gestured to Todd's left. "Over there."

"Through the arch? In the next room?"

The man gave a sharp nod and grunted what sounded like, "Un."

Todd followed the man's directions, stepping behind a free-standing shelf to reach the arched entrance, which put him out of the couple's sight. He was thankful he was no longer under their scrutiny, but then he imagined them leaning down behind the counter and straightening with weapons in their hands – a lump hammer for him, a gleaming hatchet for her.

Shut up, he told himself, and stepped through the arch to run his eye over the array of locks hanging from display hooks on the pegboard wall. There were Yale locks, toggle locks, mortise locks, padlocks, and dozens more besides. There was also an impressive array of door bolts in a variety of sizes.

Todd unhooked a couple of heavy-duty steel bolts, hesitated a moment, then selected a third. He carried them to the counter and placed them on the scarred wooden surface. Neither Mum nor Junior moved, though Junior looked at the bolts, then back at Todd with an expression both unsettling and unknowable.

Starting to think that if he didn't say anything he'd still be here at closing time, Todd said, "Could I take these, please?"

Laboriously Junior reached for a barcode reader and swiped the bolts through one by one. Todd paid and left without saying goodbye, feeling two pairs of seal-like eyes boring into the back of his head. On the street again he shuddered, and then, flipping up his hood, he stalked away.

Before putting his gloves back on, he stuck his hand into his jeans pocket, intending to grab his phone and text Yrsa. But as his fingers probed for his mobile, they touched the piece of paper that Karriana had given to him.

What was it she had said? That he wasn't safe? That Yrsa wasn't who he thought she was? The look on her face when Yrsa had appeared hadn't just been resentment or hostility, but fear, maybe dread. But why? Yrsa could be fiery, but it wasn't as if she had a *violent* temper – not that he had seen evidence of, anyway. So what was it? Something that had happened in the past? Thoughtfully he drew the piece of notepaper from his pocket and unfolded it.

It contained nothing but a phone number written in blue. Todd looked at it for a moment, then came to a decision. Taking out his phone, he thumbed in the number as he walked back towards the center of town. After a moment he heard a phone ringing, then a recorded message cut in, an electronic voice speaking in a language he didn't understand. Assuming it was a standard voicemail message, Todd waited, and sure enough at the end of the message was a long beep.

"Hi," he said, "this is Todd, Yrsa Helgerson's boyfriend. You gave me your number last night. I'm in town, so just thought I'd call." After a moment he added, "I'm alone."

He glanced at the time and saw he still had over ninety minutes before he was due to meet Yrsa. He put his phone and Karriana's note back in his pocket, then pulled his gloves on and picked up his pace to keep warm, blowing his breath out in steamy plumes. He felt weird about calling Karriana; felt as though he was betraying Yrsa somehow. He was intrigued to hear what the girl had to say, though, plus he had time to kill.

His phone started ringing. After tugging his glove off again with his teeth, he pulled it from his pocket and looked at the display screen: number unknown.

"Hello?"

"Todd?" The voice was uncertain.

"That's right. Is this Karriana?"

"Yes." A hesitation. "You *are* alone, aren't you?"

"I am. So what did you want to tell me?"

"Where are you?"

"I'm on the high street, walking back towards the center. I've just been to the hardware store."

"And where's Yrsa?"

"With her brother. They're seeing the coroner and the solicitor."

"Will you meet me?"

"Can't you say what you need to say over the phone?"

"I'd prefer to meet face to face."

Todd considered asking her why, but thought he already knew. She didn't entirely trust him when he said he was alone.

"Okay," he said. "Where?"

"On your right-hand side, as you walk back to town, you will see a street called..." She said something that to Todd sounded like a jumble of letters with no shape.

"Whoa," he said. "Can you say that again slowly? Better still, can you spell it?"

She paused. Then she said, "There is a green building on the corner with white gateposts. The turning you need is directly before this. If you walk down this road a little way, past maybe five houses, you will see a playground for children. I will meet you there."

"Okay," he said. "When?"

"When you get there I will be waiting."

"Right. Well, I guess I'll see you soon then."

"Yes," she said, and rang off.

Pulling his scarf up over the lower half of his face, Todd trudged on, keeping an eye out for the green building with the white gateposts. It shouldn't be difficult to spot. This town was one of the drabbest places he'd ever seen. Everywhere was gray and black and white, with only the occasional flash of color to break it up.

He had been walking maybe ten minutes when he saw the green building on the opposite side of the road. It was on the end of a row and looked to be a business of some kind, offices maybe. He crossed the road and hurried down the side street that ran alongside the building, first glancing over his shoulder to make sure no one was watching. He felt nervous, though wasn't sure whether that was because he didn't want Yrsa to find out about his clandestine meeting, or because he was wary of Karriana's motives. What if this was some sort of trap? What if someone wanted to send Yrsa a lesson, using him as a scapegoat? He told himself he was being ridiculous, but he was still relieved when he turned into the playground Karriana had mentioned and saw her sitting alone on a wooden bench on the far side of the play area.

She was hunched over, partly concealed behind a slide. Like every other piece of equipment here – a roundabout, a climbing frame, a set of four swings, a trio of cartoonish animals on thick springs – the slide looked old and tired, its paint peeling from its rusty steps, its framework darkened and warped by the elements. As Todd raised a hand, one of the swings began to creak and sway. Empty of children, the playground, like everything else here, seemed neglected, forlorn and unloved.

Karriana was perched on the left-hand side of the bench, her hip pressed against the metal armrest, as if making room for several companions. Todd hesitated, then sat on the right-hand side, leaving a sizable gap between them.

"Hi," he said.

"Hello," she replied dully, as if out of politeness.

"So," Todd said, as the creaking swing came to rest, "what did you want to tell me?"

She shifted, as if unable to get comfortable, and looked away from him, focusing on a blue elephant whose eyes were rusty scabs.

"Why are you here?" she asked.

He frowned. "You know why. I came with Yrsa. She needed me."

The expression that rippled across her face was part disbelief, part scorn. "What did she need you for?"

"Isn't that obvious? Her mum's just died. I'm here to support her. In whatever way she needs."

Karriana shook her head. "She doesn't need your support. She doesn't need anyone's."

"What makes you think that?"

"I know. Everyone knows." Her eyes flickered and she looked directly at him for a second. "Whatever she's brought you here for, it isn't because she's…grieving. You should get away from here. Go while you can."

Todd felt himself getting angry. "Is that a threat?"

"No!" She looked startled. "I'm trying to help you."

"How? By hinting that Yrsa's dangerous? That she's going to harm me in some way?" He shook his head. "This isn't the fucking *Wicker Man*. What do you think she's going to do? Sacrifice me to some dark demon of the forest?"

She flinched. Then, in a low, urgent voice, she said, "She isn't who she says she is. She hasn't been for a long time. But we know her. Everyone here. So she's got no…influence. No power. But you're a stranger. Which means you're a…" she searched for the right phrase, "…weak link in the chain. I don't know what she's brought you here for, but it's for something. Which is why you need to go."

The anger inside Todd propelled him to his feet. "This is bollocks. You're all cracked, the lot of you. The only reason Yrsa's back is because her mum died. She wouldn't have set foot on this island otherwise."

Karriana looked at him with such desperation that Todd half-expected her to grab his jacket. "That's what she wants you to believe."

"No," Todd said. "That's the truth. But you people here are all too…deluded to realize it." He turned away. "This is a waste of time."

"Wait!" Karriana's plea was almost a sob. "Todd, please. Yrsa's mother's death wasn't an accident."

That brought Todd up short. "What?"

"Mrs. Helgerson would never have died like that." She looked desperate for him to listen.

"So what are you saying? That she was murdered?"

Instead of answering, she said, "Her death was just an excuse for Yrsa to come back, and to bring you."

Todd rubbed at his forehead with both hands as if there was an unbearable itch inside his skull. "This is like some weird, jumbled, paranoid conspiracy theory. Yrsa was with me, in *London*, when her mother died. Hundreds of miles from here."

"That makes no difference."

"Oh, for fuck's..." He controlled himself with an effort. "Of *course* it makes a difference."

"I'm not explaining this very well," Karriana said, looking miserable.

Todd barked a laugh. "No shit, Sherlock."

"It's just...if I told you all of it, from the beginning, you wouldn't believe me."

There was a part of Todd that was urging him to walk away from this – but there was another part that was intrigued, disturbed, that wanted to know more, if only to untangle the delusions in Karriana's head. More calmly than he was feeling, he said, "Why don't you try me?"

"It started when we were at school..." And then Karriana's eyes widened and a look of horror crossed her face, as if she'd suddenly had a vision of some terrible disaster.

In spite of himself, Todd shivered. "What is it?"

But already she had jumped to her feet and was sidling around the back of the bench as if using it as a barrier against him.

"I've got to go," she said, stumbling over her words. "Sorry."

Abruptly she turned and ran, refusing to stop even when he called after her.

Todd watched her go, bewildered. The girl clearly had issues. What had she seen in his face that had so terrified her?

Then it occurred to him that maybe she hadn't been looking at him, but at something *behind* him. He spun round, half-expecting to see Yrsa standing there, her face furious, accusatory.

But all he saw was a huge, black bird – a raven – perched on top of the climbing frame. The bird's head twitched and for an instant Todd swore that it was staring at him in baleful disapproval.

Then, almost casually, it stretched its glossy black wings and flew away.

CHAPTER TWELVE

"Let's get drunk."

Looking up from the fireplace, in which he was carefully building a pyramid of split logs, Todd saw Yrsa standing in the doorway, brandishing a bottle of shiraz.

"Why?" he said.

She frowned. "What sort of lame question is that? Because we're alive. Because we can. Do we need an excuse?"

Todd still felt out of sorts after his encounter with Karriana. What she had said had disturbed him, but at the same time trying to recall their conversation was like trying to subdue a snake; it slithered and coiled whenever he tried to get a grasp on it.

Had she really told him much more than she'd already hinted at in the pub? Had she actually told him anything concrete? She'd suggested that something in Yrsa's childhood had been the starting point – though for what he had no idea. She'd hinted that Yrsa had some sort of influence or power, and that his being here might lead to her wielding it in some way. She'd even implicitly accused Yrsa of having a hand in her own mother's death, despite having been hundreds of miles away in London. All the evidence pointed to the fact that Karriana had been spouting delusional bullshit. And yet, it had unsettled Todd. Unsettled him and, despite himself, made him wary.

But maybe that was Karriana's intention – to demonize Yrsa in Todd's eyes, or at least make him view her with suspicion, with the aim of...what? Isolating her?

But why? Could Karriana have some deep-seated grudge against Yrsa? Did Yrsa have some dark secret in her past? Had she done something terrible that had caused her fellow islanders to hate and fear her?

Several times that afternoon he had been on the verge of asking her, but had not quite managed to find the words. So conflicted had he been that at one point Yrsa had irritably asked him, "What is it?"

Startled, Todd had said, "What do you mean?"

"You. You keep giving me weird looks. You've obviously got something on your mind."

"No, nothing. It's just...you're different here."

"In what way?"

"I don't know. It's like...there are other dimensions to you. I can't help feeling I don't know you as well as I thought I did."

She stared at him long enough to unsettle him, then she said, "Has someone said something about me?"

He tried not to look guilty. "'Course not."

"Those imbeciles in the hardware store, perhaps?"

"They hardly said a word to me."

"Hmm." She looked away. "Promise you won't listen to gossip, Todd. Only I know how things are."

"Sure."

Now, a few hours later, he eyed the wine bottle she was holding and said, "If you really feel you *need* to get drunk, then obviously I'm not going to let you do it alone."

She gave a curt nod, and returned to the kitchen. She reappeared thirty seconds later with two full glasses.

For the next three hours, Yrsa gulped wine as though she was dying of thirst. Todd drank steadily too, to keep her company, but there was no way he could keep up with her. Whenever she drained her glass she'd refill both of theirs, but Todd's was often still at least half-full. At first he tried to get to the bottom of her strange mood, thinking her intensity, her skittishness, might be down to the meetings she'd had today.

"How did it go with the coroner?" he asked, but she only rolled her eyes.

"Why do you want to talk about that? It's boring."

"I wondered whether it had upset you, whether that was why—"

She cut him off with a snort. "God, you're so melodramatic sometimes. Don't you ever feel a need to get rat-bummed for the sheer hell of it?"

Yrsa had a repertoire of English phrases she deliberately got wrong, and 'rat-bummed' was one of them. Usually they made Todd laugh, but on this occasion he found it hard even to smile.

"I suppose so. When I'm feeling relaxed and happy. But you seem a bit..."

"What?" Her eyes flashed dangerously.

"I don't know...fanatical about it. Like you're on a suicide mission or something."

"Fuck, sometimes you're such an old nanny."

"An old nanny?"

"So stuffed up and English and proper."

"I just don't want you to be sick."

"If I'm sick, I'm sick. It will be my own fault. And it will not be a big deal."

They carried on drinking. Picking up on an earlier theme, Yrsa launched into a diatribe about the family who owned the hardware store – Todd thought they were called the Hagens, though her words were becoming too slurred to be sure – and from there she started character-assassinating the other inhabitants of Eldfjallaeyja. At first Todd tried to damp down the fire by changing the subject, but once she had started there was no stopping her. In the end he decided the best thing was to let her burn herself out by drinking herself into a stupor.

It didn't work out that way, though. Four bottles in – of which Yrsa had drunk at least three of them – she started to get not sleepy but amorous.

"I want to fuck you," she slurred, her eyes heavy-lidded. "I want to fuck you so bad."

Clumsily she yanked off her top and jeans, pulling both inside out. Now dressed only in a matching set of cream underwear, she dropped to all fours and prowled towards him, her dark hair falling forward and partially obscuring her face.

The sultry pout she gave him was intended to be provocative, but she was so drunk that Todd found it grotesque and off-putting.

"I'm not sure that's a good idea right now," he said, but she snarled at him.

"Yes 'tis. S'the best idea ever. C'mon, get your dick out. I want to see it. I want to *lick* it."

She was close enough now to reach out and squeeze his crotch. And despite the revulsion he felt, Todd couldn't prevent his rebellious cock from stirring with interest.

"Come on, Yrsa, let's not do this now," he said, but his protest was a feeble one, and he did nothing to stop her scrabbling at the fly of his jeans, or yanking down his boxers, allowing his cock to spring free.

At the sight of it she whooped like a hunter whose prey has broken from hiding.

Then she was on him.

Todd thought later that what happened next couldn't truthfully have been referred to as lovemaking. It was *fucking*, *rutting*; there was nothing tender about it. Yrsa was like an animal, snarling, clawing, frenzied. And Todd, finally finding himself aroused by her abandon, responded in kind, gripping her wrists and bending her arms behind her back as he entered her from behind, ignoring her screams as he thrust savagely into her, her face scraping repeatedly across the seat of the armchair as her head jerked forward.

When he came, the yell he unleashed was like an attack cry, by which time both of them were lathered in sweat, and grimy and bruised from their contact with the wooden floor. His body shuddered and he fell away, and as his legs turned to jelly, he was suddenly overwhelmed with a wave of horror and self-loathing.

Although Yrsa had been complicit in their coupling, he couldn't shake the feeling he'd used his superior strength to get what he'd wanted, that in effect he'd raped her. Looking at her, face down on the floor, naked and spread-eagled, his semen dribbling out of her, he felt an urge to gather up her heaving, sweat-slick body and shower her with apologies.

He started to shake, as if with cold, and was about to ask if she was okay when, with a slick and somehow snake-like grace, she drew her knees up under her body and *flowed* to her feet.

She twisted to face him, and for a moment she stood there, blinking, mouth hanging slackly open as if uncertain where she was. Her eyelids were hooded, and so dark they appeared bruised; her lips looked swollen and purple. Her eyes shifted from side to side, as though attempting to focus. Then they fastened on Todd with a look of such avidity that he felt a fresh shudder run through him.

Are you all right? The words were like rocks jammed in his throat, but he felt unable to cough them up.

Then, to his astonishment, she threw back her head and shrieked with laughter, before running – naked and with his semen still trickling down the inside of her thigh – out of the room.

"Yrsa!" Todd's voice scraped his throat as it rose up and out of him, making him cough. Feeling drained and clumsy, he scrambled to his feet. Already he could hear the new bolts he'd installed being slammed back.

Naked, his bare feet slapping the floor, he ran into the hallway, in time to see Yrsa yank the cottage door open.

"Yrsa!" he yelled again. "What are you doing? Don't go outside!"

But her only response was to give another drunken, witch-like cackle before slipping through the gap of the opening door.

Fuck! Should he go after her? How could he *not* go after her? But it was freezing outside, and the ground was muddy, and they were both naked. He hesitated, then ran back to the kitchen, grabbed his thick waterproof jacket from the hook on the wall and pulled it over his naked torso. It barely covered his genitals and left his legs completely exposed, but it would have to do. Next he pulled his boots on over his bare feet, laced them up, then ran into the living room to grab his phone from his jeans.

He knew he was using up time, that Yrsa now had a head start on him, but if she ran off, too drunk to know what she was doing, he reckoned he had a better chance of catching her if he was wearing boots and had a torch. With luck she might just be capering about in the yard, or rolling in the mud like a child – though when he exited the house, he was dismayed to find she was nowhere to be seen.

"Yrsa!" he yelled, a nightmarish sense of déjà vu sweeping over him. Last night's adventure had been bad enough, but in some ways it was even worse this time, given their nakedness and inebriation. "Yrsa, where are you!"

Another whooping cackle – but from where? He turned his body like a radar dish…and there she was, at the edge of the forest, having already scaled the fence, her body a pale glimmer against the black trees.

"Yrsa!" Todd called, running towards her. "Stay there! Don't move!"

Like a child playing a game, she simply waved, then darted away.

"*Yrsa!*" Todd yelled again, half worried, half furious. "Don't do this! Come back!"

But she didn't. And when he turned on his torch app and directed its beam at the spot where she'd been a moment before, there was no sign of her.

"Fuck's sake!" He launched himself at the fence, hyperaware of his dangling genitalia and the fact that one slip could result in…well, he didn't want to think about that.

He made it over okay, though, even if he had no time to be happy about it. Facing him was the same shitty situation he'd found himself in last night – a nocturnal hunt for his insensible girlfriend through a black, spooky forest.

"Yrsa!" he yelled. "Where the fuck are you? This isn't funny."

He half-expected to hear another mocking cackle in response, but there was nothing. He considered doing what he'd thought of doing last night: calling Sven. But last night had been different. They hadn't been naked, they hadn't been drunk. Todd knew that Yrsa would never forgive him if he and Sven (and what if Sven brought a party of villagers with him?) found her in the forest, butt-naked, pissed as a fart and with Todd's sperm running down her legs.

It would serve her right, he thought, but he still didn't seriously entertain the idea of bringing Sven in on this. He checked the battery on his mobile (forty-six percent), took his bearing by the glow from the house behind him, then started walking through the trees, the light from his phone slithering through the undergrowth. Angrily he shouted Yrsa's name, keeping a wary ear out for wild boar. Again, the trees lurched whitely from the blackness like tall figures, but this time Todd refused to let his imagination run away with him, telling himself that as long as he remained watchful, there was nothing that could hurt him here.

He walked in what he thought was a straight line until the glow from the house behind him became nothing but a firefly glimmer. Then he turned and walked in what felt like another straight line, the house-glow now winking through the trees to his left.

All the while he shouted Yrsa's name, but as time wore on, the more hopeless he began to feel. How could he find her if she refused to answer? But if he didn't find her, she might die – and that was no exaggeration. She'd drunk so much she'd have no notion of personal safety. At some point she might lie down and go to sleep, or more likely fall and slip into unconsciousness. He wondered how long a naked, unconscious human being could survive outdoors in zero degrees. He was about to google it when his head snapped up.

There was something in the trees.

He hadn't seen anything, but he'd heard it. Had it been a human voice? It had been too faint to be sure, but it hadn't sounded like the rustling of undergrowth or an animal cry.

Holding his phone out, he called Yrsa's name again.

Nothing. As if fearful of upsetting some delicate equilibrium, Todd crept forward. He wondered whether the sound he'd heard had been Yrsa calling out to him as she slipped into unconsciousness. What if she was lying nearby, half-concealed by undergrowth? Training the beam on the ground, he continued inching forward.

There! Again! The hint of a voice. Somewhere ahead of him and to his right. He glanced over his shoulder to check the glint of light from the house was still visible, then moved in the direction of the voice.

The way trees bloomed palely in the glow from his mobile, then swung aside as he passed, reminded him of an endless row of silently opening doors. Todd felt he was passing through room after shadowy room, in one of which he hoped to find the owner of the voice that was luring him.

He was close enough now to tell that the voice did belong to Yrsa. She was speaking too quietly for him to make out her words, but there was no mistaking that husky lilt he found so attractive. He assumed she was rambling drunkenly to herself, and was just about to call her name when her voice fell silent, and was answered by another.

Todd froze. An icy feverishness rippled through his body. But it wasn't due to the realization that someone else was in the forest; it was the nature of the voice itself.

It was deep, guttural and grating. It barely sounded human.

"Yrsa!"

The word was out before he could stop it. The guttural voice fell silent. And as it did, Todd got the impression that *all* sound had been suddenly sucked from the forest. He felt dread building inside him, and took a shaky step backwards. His torch wavered, causing the trees to shudder, as if with fear...

...and then something came shrieking and flapping out of the forest, and launched itself at him.

Todd shrieked too, stumbling backwards. A split second before she hit him full-on, he realized it was Yrsa, arms above her head, flesh corpse-white, breasts swinging, black hair hanging in ratty clumps.

She threw her arms around him and they both went down, Todd's phone flying out of his hand. The still-tender parts of his body – his back, his ribs – flared with pain as he hit the ground.

For a moment he thought she'd lost it, gone feral, but then she rolled away from him, and her animal shrieks dissolved into laughter.

"What the fuck?" he said angrily, pushing himself into a sitting position. He was shaking with reaction. "What the fuck was that?"

Her naked body heaving with laughter, Yrsa couldn't or wouldn't answer him. Todd rose gingerly to his feet, looked around and spotted his mobile, glimmering faintly. He retrieved it, then pointed it in the direction Yrsa had come from, the beam lancing through the darkness.

But all he saw were trees.

CHAPTER THIRTEEN

"What happened to you?"

Todd heard the stairs creaking as Yrsa descended. He looked round to see her standing in the kitchen doorway, wearing last night's knickers and a white T-shirt. Her hair was tousled and her eyes looked puffy, but otherwise she seemed none the worse for wear. There was not a mark on either her smooth-skinned legs or her exposed arms. Scowling, he said, "Show me the bottoms of your feet."

"Why?"

"Just do it."

She shrugged, turned her back on him and lifted up first one foot, then the other. Apart from picking up a little dirt from the wooden floors, they were unmarked.

"Unbelievable."

She turned back to face him. "What is?"

"Is that a serious question?"

"For fuck's sake, Todd, just tell me what you're talking about."

He was sitting at the kitchen table, his right leg propped on another chair. On the table was a bowl of warm water laced with antiseptic. Using a cloth he was bathing a graze on his knee and another on his calf. He also had a bruise on his left hip from where he'd hit the ground when Yrsa had leaped on him, and his heels were chafed raw from wearing boots without socks.

"Do you honestly not remember anything about last night?"

She gave a lascivious grin. "I remember we had very hot sex. But everything else is a blank."

"You don't remember running into the woods stark naked?"

She gaped at him. "I did not!"

"How do you think I got these injuries?"

She patted herself down. "But *I'm* fine."

"I'm so pleased," Todd said.

Looking sheepish, she took the cloth from him and gently dabbed his knee. "Did I really cause that?"

"Yes, you bloody did. That's the second night running I've wandered through the pitch-black woods, looking for you. I don't want it to become a habit."

"I'm so sorry," she said, but she was smiling.

"No, you're not. You're not even hungover. There's no fucking justice."

"I'll make you a great breakfast. How's that?"

"I won't say no – but it doesn't mean I forgive you. You're a fucking liability. No more getting trashed."

She raised her eyebrows in an *I don't know about that* expression, but said nothing.

Fifteen minutes later, as they ate pancakes and bacon, Todd said, "There's something else."

Yrsa was eating with gusto, her appetite undiminished by last night's drinking binge. "What?"

"You're going to say I imagined it."

"Imagined what?"

"Maybe I *did* imagine it."

"Just tell me!"

He described what had happened in the forest last night. He saw her eyes widen as he told her about the guttural voice he'd heard. "Who was it?"

"I was hoping you'd answer that question."

She stared at him, then frowned. "What are you accusing me of, Todd? Didn't I say I don't remember any of this? After we made love, everything is a complete blank."

"Very convenient," he mumbled, then felt bad when he saw the distress on her face.

"No! It's not! It's very *in*convenient! Do you honestly think I ran off to meet some stranger in the woods?"

"No, I just…" He groaned and sat back in his chair. All at once he felt incredibly weary. "The truth is, I don't know *what* to believe. If there *was* someone else in the woods, he didn't show himself."

All at once she sat bolt upright. "Oh my God!"

"What? Have you remembered something?"

"No, I've just thought…I was naked."

"So?"

"So that means if there *was* someone there, he saw me. Naked. What if it was a hunter or something?"

"Then he got a cheap thrill."

"Fucking hell," she groaned. "This will not help us. The people here already think of me as…"

She muttered a word that Todd didn't quite catch – something that sounded like 'vessling'.

"What's that?"

She shook her head. "Never mind, it's nothing. More stupid superstition."

"But what does it mean?"

She stuffed a forkful of pancake into her mouth. In a muffled voice she said, "It doesn't matter."

Todd sighed. He felt like slamming his fist down on the table, but instead he put his knife and fork down carefully.

"It matters to me. Ever since we've come here, you've been…"

"What?" She frowned.

"Different. Unpredictable. Volatile. It's like this place brings out some kind of…wildness in you. I'm starting to think I don't know you very well."

For a moment she looked angry, then she shook her head. "You do. It's just…it's difficult for me here."

"Would it…" He broke off, then changed his mind, deciding to say what he was thinking. "Would it be easier if I wasn't here? If I went back to London and left you to it? Maybe I'm just an added complication you don't need right now."

She looked alarmed. Her hand darted out and closed around his wrist. "No, of course not. Please don't go, Todd. I need you here. I'm sorry for…" she waved a hand, "…for all this."

She seemed genuinely contrite. Sighing he said, "What *is* it about this place? Did something happen? Either when you were young or to make you leave?"

Now her gaze flickered away. "I've already told you what the people here are like. Superstitious. Insular."

"No," he said firmly, "it's more than that. The people here are not just resentful of you, Yrsa. They're *scared* of you. And because of that they're scared of me too. Or scared *for* me maybe, I don't know."

"Like who?"

"The people in the bar on our first night. The couple in the hardware store. They looked at me as if they expected me to…pull out a gun or something. So what is it? What are you not telling me?"

She gave a deep sigh, was silent for maybe ten seconds. Then she seemed to come to a decision.

"There *is* something," she said.

"Whatever it is, you can tell me."

"And I will. But I also need to show you."

"Show me what?"

"Can you be patient for a bit longer?"

He fought down his frustration. "I suppose so, if I have to."

"It won't be for long, I promise. No more than an hour or so. But first I have to do something."

Abruptly she stood up.

"What do you have to do?" Todd asked.

"I have an errand to run. I won't be long."

"Can't I come with you?"

"It's not worth it. Finish your breakfast. By the time you've had a shower and got dressed I'll be back."

Before he could argue, she left the room. Todd contemplated going after her, but stayed put, and less than five minutes later he heard the front door open and close, then the Land Rover's engine growl into life.

An almost childlike sense of alarm swept over him, and his heart began to quicken. He listened to the engine move away from the house, and gradually fade to silence.

Although this wasn't the first time he'd been alone since being here, it was the first time he'd *felt* alone. It suddenly struck Todd how far away from home he was, and how no one knew he was here.

He'd texted his parents and Robin on Sunday to let them know he was leaving the country, but he hadn't told them the name of the island – mainly because he hadn't been able to remember it, let alone spell it. He wasn't sure whether he'd even told them what Yrsa's surname was, or where she worked, which meant that if anything happened to him...

He frowned. Why should anything happen? There was nothing to stop him texting Robin right now and telling him where he was, or even calling him – assuming he could get a signal.

He felt a measure of relief when he climbed the stairs to the bedroom where he'd left his phone charging, and saw there *was* a signal. Not much of one, but enough for him to have a chat with his brother if he wanted to.

Unplugging the phone from the charger, he glanced at the small window beyond the bed, through which morning light spilled across the white duvet and made it glow like phosphorescence. The top third of the window showed the boundary fence he had climbed over last night, caging the thin, dark trunks of the trees.

It also showed a figure standing in the trees, looking up at him.

Todd jumped as if zapped by electricity. His hand opened involuntarily and his phone slid out, landing smack on the bone of his big toe. The pain made him cry out and hop backwards, slapping a hand against the wall to steady himself. Regaining his balance, he scooped up his phone and turned back to the window, intending to take a photo of what had appeared to be either a stocky child or a squat adult.

But there was no one there. The watcher in the forest had gone.

CHAPTER FOURTEEN

True to her word, Yrsa arrived back at the house less than an hour after leaving it. Entering the living room, where Todd was sprawled on the settee, trying to look casual with a book, she asked, "Did you bring any walking boots?"

"No," he replied, "but my regular boots are pretty sturdy. Why?"

She wrinkled her nose. "They'll probably do. Come on."

She turned and headed back down the corridor. Todd went after her.

"What are we doing?"

"Going for a hike."

"Where to?"

"You'll find out when we get there. You'd better get your jacket. I'll see you outside." She pulled the front door open.

"Hang on," Todd said.

She halted. "What?"

"I'm not a child. Why all the mystery? Why can't you tell me where we're going?"

She looked momentarily irritated, but then she sighed and said, "I'm not trying to be mysterious. It's just better if I show you. Sometimes, when a thing is explained in words, it loses its power."

Todd regarded her for a long moment, then nodded. "Okay. I'll see you outside."

Yrsa was standing beside the Land Rover when Todd exited the house thirty seconds later. As he walked across to her, zipping up his jacket, she leaned into the vehicle and lifted a couple of bulky objects off the back seat, one of which she handed to him. It was a green hiking rucksack – and it looked pretty full. The rucksack she heaved onto her own back was older, and more military looking, but was equally stuffed.

As they fastened the clips and adjusted the straps, Todd asked, "Am I allowed to ask what's in these?"

"Our equipment," Yrsa said.

"What kind of equipment?"

"Ropes, harnesses, gloves, protective suits..."

Todd raised his eyebrows. "Sounds pretty hardcore."

"Don't worry," she said, "I'll look after you. You'll be quite safe with me."

He half-expected her to lead them across the yard and through the woods, but she turned the other way, up the muddy incline and onto the main road. Until now, they had turned in only one direction – towards town – but today Yrsa turned left, heading further inland. It was a cold, still day, clouds clotting the off-white sky like patches of grime on old marble. The icy air pressed against Todd's cheekbones and turned his breath to vapor, but after five minutes of brisk walking, he felt warm enough to unzip his jacket.

After trudging along the road for ten minutes, Yrsa veered left, along a track that cut through a patch of scrubland before dipping to plow a channel through an area of weirdly shaped rock formations. The further they walked, the higher the formations rose around them – or perhaps it was simply that the track was plowing an ever-deeper furrow through the earth. Their surroundings became darker and more confined as the rocks blotted out more of the sky. Just as Todd thought that the thin strip of light above them was about to be extinguished altogether, the ground sloped upwards and the strip started to widen again.

He was glad of it. It had become hard going on that part of the track that the sunshine didn't reach. The ground, solid enough before, had become boggy, the mud constantly sucking at his boots, the extra exertion it took to keep up with Yrsa – who seemed unaffected by the wetter ground – making him pant and sweat.

"Struggling there, city boy?" she said, grinning at him.

Todd tried not to let the strain show in his voice. "I'm doing fine, thanks."

"I can tell. Your red face is a good match for your blond hair."

"Fuck off," he said, making her laugh.

Conversation had been sporadic while they'd been walking. When the rock formations had started to proliferate around them, Todd had said, "These shapes are amazing. They're like something from another planet."

Yrsa had shrugged. "They've been caused by weather erosion, that's all."

"All right, Miss Blasé. But I'm sure weather erosion doesn't always produce such amazing results."

Yrsa glanced at the strangely rounded shelves of rock to her left, like a pile of fat circular cushions, gradually decreasing in size.

"I'm used to them, I suppose. This was my playground as a child."

"Did you come here with your brother?"

"Sometimes. Mostly with my best friend."

"And who was that? You haven't mentioned her. Is she still on the island?"

"We haven't been friends for a long time."

"Why not?" Todd asked, but she sighed.

"Let me do this my way, okay? You're asking too many questions."

He raised his hands. "Whatever you say. I was only making conversation."

As the ground sloped upwards, so the rock formations sank back or fell away, to be replaced by more abundant vegetation. Soon they were walking over uneven ground, liberally dotted with bushes and small trees. At one point the ground to their right became a steep descending slope tangled with undergrowth, at the bottom of which ran a fast-flowing stream from which black rocks jutted like the hunched backs of whales. Then the two sides of the valley converged and the trees thinned, the featureless sky stretching out overhead. The ground turned rocky again, and although it seemed flat, the increasing ache in Todd's thighs told him they were moving gradually uphill.

Finally, perhaps ninety minutes after they had left the house, Yrsa came to a halt. "We're here."

Todd looked around – at stunted, twisted trees; at thick, stringy undergrowth sprouting between rocks splotched with orange and white lichen.

"What's so special about this place?" he asked.

"I'll show you."

She moved right, leaping from rock to rock with the sure-footedness of a mountain goat. She stopped at a mass of fern-like bushes, and Todd assumed she was contemplating the view, perhaps searching for a particular landmark. When he hopped up beside her, though, she shot out an arm, barring him from taking another step.

"Careful," she said, and pointed at the bushes in front of them.

Todd's first thought was that there must be an animal in there – a poisonous snake, perhaps. But looking down he realized that instead of rock or dirt or undergrowth between the feathery fronds there was blackness. He frowned, not understanding – then suddenly he did.

It was a hole, a shaft, going straight down to God knew where. Instinctively he stepped back, as if the rocky ground might suddenly crumble beneath his feet.

"What the fuck?"

Yrsa eased the rucksack off her back. "Ever done any abseiling?"

He stared at her. "We're going down there?"

Already she had opened the rucksack and was pulling ropes and carabiners out of it. "We are."

Todd had done a bit of climbing, but he'd never done any caving. The thought of it made his stomach clench. "Why?"

"The sooner we get ready the sooner you'll find out."

Ten minutes later they were set to go. In his rucksack Todd had found a tightly folded caving suit, a helmet with attached headlamp, padded gloves to protect his hands from rope burn, and various items of climbing equipment – ropes, a harness, carabiners, a descender and other bits and pieces.

To his surprise Yrsa seemed to know exactly what she was doing, and as he pulled the protective suit on over his clothes and adjusted the strap on his helmet, she busied herself anchoring their ropes around a couple of nearby trees and attaching their harnesses.

"You know how this works?" she said, tapping his descender with one gloved finger.

Todd nodded. "I've done it before. You go down backwards, in an L-shape, feed the rope through here..." He talked her through the process, Yrsa nodding like a teacher encouraging a pupil.

"Okay, you've convinced me. I'll go first, and I'll shout up when I've reached the bottom. The shaft's only ten, fifteen meters long, but it's like a bent pipe. Mostly it's a gentle slope, then there's a straight drop of maybe two meters at the bottom. Okay?"

"Fine."

Yrsa switched on her headlamp, then backed towards the shaft and lowered herself down. Todd waited, taking deep breaths to try and relax, and when Yrsa called his name, her voice echoing eerily, he moved to the edge and leaned over. Through the now trampled bushes he saw a slope of gray rock, surprisingly smooth as though polished, fading gradually to blackness.

"You okay?" he shouted.

"I'm fine. I'm at the bottom. Come and join me."

He turned away from the shaft, gave his ropes a final check, then took a deep breath and backed carefully through the leafy bushes behind him.

As he had found on the few occasions he'd done this before, the first moment, when you counterintuitively step off the edge of a precipice and put your faith entirely in the equipment supporting your weight, was by far the worst. His unease was exacerbated by the cold rising from the depths of the shaft, which gave the impression he was lowering himself into icy water, and by the feathery leaves of the bushes he had lowered himself through springing back into position behind him, like a green sea closing over his head. At first, claustrophobia made the shaft appear narrower than it actually was, but once he'd got his bearings, his headlamp playing over the rocky walls, he realized he had about as much room here as he would have had in an average lift. Thus reassured, the tightness in his stomach eased, and Todd found the descent a steady, almost relaxing process.

"Welcome to the Devil's Throat," Yrsa said when he was standing beside her.

Todd grimaced. "That doesn't sound sinister at all."

Yrsa pointed at the shaft above them. "Actually, that's the Devil's Throat. This part doesn't have a name."

"The Devil's Digestive System?" Todd looked around. "So are you going to tell me why we're here?"

They were in a small cavern, the floor uneven, the ceiling a couple of meters above their heads in some areas, more like four or five in others. The jagged walls were honeycombed with passages, some of which looked big enough to walk down, others so small and narrow it seemed the only way to make progress would be to crawl on your stomach. Todd sincerely hoped Yrsa wasn't going to insist they explore one of these latter openings.

"When I was ten," Yrsa said, "I fell down here, and was in these tunnels for three days without food or water. It was quite the formative experience."

Todd gaped at her. "You're kidding me."

She rolled her eyes. "Of course I am. That's why I brought you all this way. Just to tell a stupid joke."

"But..." Todd stared at Yrsa, then at the shaft above their heads. "Okay. So...tell me what happened. How badly were you hurt?"

Yrsa shrugged. She seemed ridiculously casual about the whole thing. "I was covered in bruises, and I blacked out for a while, but I didn't have any broken bones. I was lucky, I guess."

"But the lack of food and water..."

"I suppose if I hadn't been found after three days I might not be here now. Nobody ever really talked about that side of it with me – maybe they didn't want to frighten me. I remember being very hungry for a while, then I wasn't. I was very thirsty, though, but I found some water running down a wall and swallowed as much as I could. I don't know how long I'd gone without water before then. It's all a bit jumbled in my head. Some bits I remember very clearly, but other bits are hazy or a complete blank. Like a dream."

"Wow," Todd said. "So who found you in the end?"

"I came here with my best friend, Bryn. We weren't supposed to come all the way out here. If our parents had found out, we would have been in terrible trouble. I later found out that after I fell, Bryn ran home, but she was too scared to tell anyone what had happened. When people asked her if she'd seen me, she said no, and it was only after two days that she broke down and told her mother the truth. That's when they brought a search party up here and found me more or less where we're standing now."

"So you hadn't moved in all that time?" said Todd. "You hadn't been tempted to find another way out?"

"That's the strange thing. I *did* try to find a way out. And I got horribly lost. I remember wandering around in pitch-black tunnels for hours. But somehow I found my way back here. I don't know how."

"Maybe you didn't wander as far as you thought. Or maybe all these tunnels loop back on themselves and end up back here, whichever way you go."

She gave him a pitiful look. "Don't tell me you really believe that?"

"Well…it's possible, isn't it?"

"No," she said firmly, "it's not possible. And I know for a fact it isn't the case."

"How?"

She took a deep breath. "When they finally got me out, I was so traumatized I didn't speak for a week. But apparently I didn't cry either, or show any other emotion – not that I remember this. I do remember other kids avoiding me when I went back to school, or looking at me like they were scared of me. But it was only later I found out there were rumors about me – among the adults as well as the kids. People started to say something had happened to me in the tunnels, that I'd been changed. They said the real Yrsa was dead, and that I was what they called—" She spoke a jumble of words that Todd didn't understand.

"What does that mean?"

"I'm not sure there's an English equivalent. A changeling maybe? But something dark, something with evil intent. The literal translation is 'that which stands outside'."

Her hushed voice, echoing in the caves, made him shudder. "Are you serious?"

She nodded solemnly. "You see now why I call the people here superstitious primitives?"

"But what did your mother say? Didn't she defend you?"

"Not that I remember. I think she half-believed it."

"You're kidding!"

Again Yrsa gave that casual shrug. "Whatever she thought, she was not an affectionate woman. And she didn't like attention. I think she resented me for being the cause of everyone on the island talking about us."

Todd thought back to what Karriana had said to him in the playground about Yrsa – *She isn't who she says she is… But we know her. Everyone here.* Could this be what she'd been talking about? That she believed Yrsa to be…some sort of dark entity? A changeling? His mind reeled at the notion that anyone could actually *believe* that.

"So how long did this go on for?"

"Until I left. All through my teens I was shunned. Even adults would cross the streets to avoid me."

"Seriously?"

Without smiling she said, "And a group of boys at school starting calling me a witch."

"What did you do?"

"I played up to it. I cursed them. Then one of them, the one who gave me the most trouble…he died."

Todd felt his breath lurch in his throat. "What happened?"

"He drowned. It was his own stupid fault. He went swimming at night with his friends."

"And they blamed you?"

"Of course. But they didn't bother me anymore."

Todd barked a laugh. "I bet they didn't."

"And then, when I was old enough, I left."

Her tone was matter-of-fact, her attitude almost dismissive, but Todd wondered how many scars Yrsa carried inside her, both from the experience and all that had come after. Shaking his head, he said, "You didn't have to bring me here to tell me all this. You could have just told me over a cup of tea, or a bottle of wine. It must be hard for you, coming back here. If it was me, I'd never want to come near this place ever again."

Her eyes seemed to glitter in the darkness. "No," she said, "I needed to bring you here, because I want to show you something. And to do that we have to go deeper."

Todd's mind recoiled at her words. He looked nervously at the passages that surrounded them, many of them little more than black gashes in the rock. "I'm not sure that's a good idea. What if we get lost again?"

"We won't."

"How do you know?"

"Because for the first few years after it happened, I had terrible nightmares about this place. If I hadn't decided to do something about them, I think they would have made me ill."

"So what did you do?"

"I confronted my fear. I learned how to climb, how to abseil, and then from the age of fourteen I came here again and again. And I got to know this cave system. It became as familiar to me as my own home. And the more I got to know it, the less scared I was of it."

"Did you come here alone?"

She nodded. "No one else would have come with me – not that I would have wanted them to. Of course, this meant the islanders became even more convinced that the stories were true. They thought I was coming here to be with my own people."

"Your own people?"

"The jötnar."

"The what?"

She blinked slowly. "They have many forms. You might think of them as dwarves or elves or trolls. They're said to wreak havoc, to bring chaos."

"Are you serious?"

"The islanders are. Many still think of me as a child of the jötnar."

"Fucking hell."

She smiled, but all at once she looked tired. "I dream of them. Even now I sometimes dream I'm here, in these caves, and I'm a child again, and I look up and there they are, standing in the shadows." She gave a brief shake of the head. "It's not a bad dream. Not like the nightmares I used to have. Sometimes it feels like a memory."

Todd recalled the squat figure he'd glimpsed at the edge of the forest that morning, and he suppressed a shudder. Suddenly the black gashes in the walls were not openings they might explore, but places where things might hide.

"Can we stop talking about this?" he said, trying to make his voice light. "You're freaking me out."

She gave a slow smile. "Sorry."

"What did you want to show me?"

She turned, the light from her headlamp sidling across the rocky walls. It came to rest on a black opening about two meters tall, shaped like a pointed arch – or a witch's hat.

"Follow me," she said, moving towards it. "But watch your step. The ground's uneven."

Again, Todd braced himself, expecting to find himself squeezing through an uncomfortably narrow passage, but as their joint headlamps penetrated the darkness, he realized the opening was more accommodating than it had first appeared. Once he had dipped his head to fit through the gap behind Yrsa, the ceiling sloped upwards until, within a few steps, the tunnel had widened out to the width and height of an average hotel corridor.

For several minutes they moved along it, the passage now and then curving to the left or the right, occasionally narrowing slightly before widening out again. Eventually they came to a junction with three options. Pointing to the two right-hand passages, Yrsa said, "Those are dead ends." Then, without breaking her stride, she took the passage to the left.

Such was her confidence that Todd followed her without question. And so it continued for the next twenty minutes, Yrsa never hesitating when they came to a junction, but striding confidently in one direction or another. It occurred to Todd after a while that he was completely at her mercy; if she suddenly abandoned him, he would be helpless.

"How much further?" he asked, his voice flat but echoey, reminding him of the thousands of tons of rock above and around them.

"Nearly there," Yrsa replied.

At last the passage narrowed to such an extent that Yrsa said, "We'll have to wriggle through this bit side on. But don't panic. It's only for a few meters."

Todd felt a spike of alarm. If Yrsa *was* going to abandon him – which, of course, she wasn't – now would be the ideal time to do it, while he was struggling through the gap.

He tried to keep the disquiet from showing on his face, but in the light from his headlamp he saw Yrsa frown.

"Are you okay, Todd?"

"Yeah, 'course," he said casually.

"It's okay to be scared. I'm used to this. You're not. To be scared is natural. It doesn't mean you're weak."

"I'm not scared," Todd said.

"Okay. But take my hand. We'll do this together."

She turned sideways so she could wriggle through the gap, and stretched her hand out towards him. Relieved, Todd grabbed it, trying to make his grip tight enough that she couldn't pull away, but not so tight she would guess what he was afraid of. Suddenly he thought again of the voice he had heard in the forest last night – the guttural response to Yrsa's words – and his grip tightened reflexively.

"Ow," she said.

"Sorry."

Side on, her face turned towards him, she shuffled through the gap. By the time Todd squeezed his own body into the aperture, she was almost through. He would have liked to have turned his head inward to face her, but because his left arm was stretched out, he couldn't turn far enough in that direction to prevent the headlamp on his helmet from scraping the stone wall. He was forced, therefore, to turn his head away from her, facing back the way they'd come. As the illumination from his headlamp washed back into the passage, he glimpsed a small, dark figure at the periphery of the light.

His body jerked, the stone wall scraping against his back, and he let loose a cry of pain and alarm.

Her hand still clasped in his, Yrsa said, "Are you all right, Todd? Did you hurt yourself?"

He moved his head a fraction, so the light danced across the area where he'd glimpsed the figure, and was thankful to see there was nothing there.

"I'm fine," he said. "Bumped my head."

"Just relax," she told him. "I know it's tight, but you'll get through. Take your time and don't panic."

He took a shaky breath, then eased through the gap, the front and back of his protective suit scraping – though not painfully – on the stone wall. Thirty seconds later he was standing beside Yrsa. She released his hand.

"Okay?"

"I'm good," he said, deciding not to tell her about the figure. After her story about the jötnar it would only sound like he was imagining things.

She held up her gloved hand. "I think you crushed my fingers."

"Sorry."

"I forgive you. It was in a good cause."

He looked beyond her, the light from his helmet springing into the wider space around them. "So where are we now?"

They appeared to be in a cave about the size of a large room, the walls curved and the ceiling higher than their lamplight could reach. Todd could hear dripping water, though the cave itself seemed dry. The back wall, some ten meters away, was pitted with black shadows, which he assumed were passages, though none of them looked tall enough or wide enough to crawl through.

Yrsa trudged across to the wall, which became more defined beneath the light from her headlamp. Todd saw the black clots of shadow were indeed passages, which pocked the stone like holes in Swiss cheese.

"Looks like a dead end," he said. "For us, anyway. You'd have to be a ferret to get through one of these."

"Or a child," she said meaningfully.

It took Todd a few seconds to realize what she was implying. "You're not saying you crawled through one of these holes when you were stuck down here?"

She nodded, and when she turned he was disconcerted to see a look on her face that was close to rapture. "This is what I wanted to show you. This is what I wanted to *tell you about*."

"Okay," he said, uncertain how to respond.

"Remember I said that when I was down here there were some bits I remembered vividly and other bits that were like a dream?"

He nodded.

"Okay, so at one point I somehow found this cave and came across all these openings. It was pitch black, so I must have been feeling my way, but I have a vague memory of trying a couple of passages, maybe three or four, and finding them too tight to get through. Then eventually I must have found one I could fit my body into – I was much smaller and skinnier back then."

"Weren't you scared of getting stuck?"

"I don't know. All I remember is feeling a need to go on, to find a way out. So I crawled inside and kept moving, one or two inches at a time. I was exhausted, and so hungry and thirsty that I was hallucinating, but somehow I kept going.

"How long I crawled, I don't know. But suddenly I saw light ahead of me, like stars in the sky, and I remember getting excited. I thought I'd crawled right through the rock and found my way back to the surface.

"But when I did come out, I realized I was in another cave, a *big* cave, and the walls were shining like they were full of crystals."

"Phosphorescence," Todd said, but Yrsa wafted a hand, dismissing his interruption.

"It was the first time since...well, I don't know how long, that I'd been able to see. And the first thing I saw was a ship."

"A ship?" repeated Todd, incredulous.

"A Viking ship. And it was full of treasure!"

He stared at her. "What?"

"I mean it! Jewelry, crosses, pots, little statues...all gleaming in the light."

"You were dreaming," said Todd.

Her grip on his arm became tight enough to make him wince. "No! It was there, Todd, I know it. It's still there, behind this wall. A Viking ship, full of treasure. Buried for hundreds of years."

He looked at the wall in bewilderment. "But how could it be? Didn't you tell anyone about it when they found you?"

"I did, but no one believed me. When I was found it was in another part of the cave system. I was dehydrated and feverish, and I have no idea how I got there. I told them about the ship, but they said I'd been seeing things."

"Has it ever occurred to you that maybe they were right?"

"Of course. But I know the difference between fantasy and reality. And I know in my heart that beyond these few meters of rock is a discovery of such historical and archeological significance that it will change everything." She placed a hand on the wall. "I would stake my life on it."

CHAPTER FIFTEEN

That night Todd rang Robin.

"All right, squirt? How's it going?" Robin said.

Three years older than Todd, Robin had been calling his younger brother 'squirt' ever since they were kids, and had stuck with it even though Todd now towered over him by a good four inches. Whereas Todd had inherited his looks and build from his mum's side of the family – the Sheridans were tall and willowy – Robin had his father's coloring and physique; he was stocky and dark-haired, with heavier features and a beetle brow.

Also like their dad, he was more practical than Todd, less academic. He had grown up fascinated with how things worked and fitted together. Despite their differences, though, the brothers had a great relationship. Although to Robin the acting world was baffling and alien, he was hugely supportive of Todd's ambitions, and, like their parents, took great pride in his successes, few and far between though they were.

"Yeah, okay," Todd said. "It's a bit weird here."

"Where are you again? Iceland?"

"Close. It's a little island called Eldfjallaeyja."

"Bless you."

Todd grunted a laugh.

"So how's Yrsa?" Robin asked. "When's the funeral?"

"Tomorrow. We're dreading it."

"Not surprised. I'd be worried if you were looking forward to it."

"Yeah, it's not just that. The islanders are quite…well…hostile towards Yrsa. They're a superstitious lot. They have some funny ideas."

"Sounds great. Listen, if they start building a big man out of wood, fuck off out of it as quick as you can."

"Yeah," said Todd, then hesitated before adding, "Thing is…I might have something for you here."

"What do you mean?"

"Some work," he said awkwardly. "Yrsa wants to hire you."

"To do what? Build her a holiday home?"

"No. It's something a bit different to what you normally do."

"Different how?"

Todd sighed. "Right. This is going to sound a bit mental. But hear me out."

"Go on, squirt. I'm all ears."

Haltingly, Todd told Robin about Yrsa's childhood ordeal and their expedition earlier that day. As he repeated what Yrsa had said about the Viking ship, he felt his conviction and confidence draining away. Robin was the most pragmatic of men, and to his ears Todd's story must sound delusional, like a fairy tale. By the time he stumbled to a halt, he was wishing he'd never let Yrsa persuade him to make this call.

"That's quite a story," Robin said, in a tone that Todd couldn't decide was amused, scornful, annoyed, or all three.

"Look, Rob," Todd said, lowering his voice in case Yrsa was nearby, "I know how flaky this sounds…"

"That's one word for it," Robin said.

"It's just…it's something Yrsa's carried with her for years. An itch she needs to scratch. And you should see her. She's so adamant about this that she makes it sound almost believable. I mean, what if there *is* something? What if this is another Sutton Hoo?"

"The odds of that are pretty astronomical."

"I know, but…" Todd's voice trailed into silence. He realized he had nothing more to offer, no counterargument that was even halfway convincing. Finally he said, "Aw, forget it. I know it's bonkers. And you're probably really busy…"

But then Robin said, "What exactly would Yrsa want me to do?"

Todd paused. "You mean you'd consider it?"

"I didn't say that. There are a hundred things to work out before we do anything – price for starters. But tell me what she'd expect from me."

Todd had asked Yrsa the same question. "She said she'd pay for you to come over to the island to look at the site, and she'd explain what the job involved. Then, if you were happy, she'd hope you'd come back with a drilling team and…I dunno, cut a tunnel through the wall into the cavern."

"And what if we didn't find anything?"

"Well, I suppose it would…put her mind at rest. Lay the ghost."

"And how big a team would she expect me to bring?"

"That would be up to you."

Robin was silent for a moment, then he said, "Even if it was the smallest team for the job – say, six or eight people – it would be massively expensive. I mean, as well as paying the men, we'd have to get the equipment across, there'd be food and accommodation to cover while we were there…we're talking thousands."

"I think she knows that. She's pretty well off."

"She'd have to be. Extremely."

"So…what do you think?"

"I think it's completely mental. But if she's happy to pay my way, I've got no objections to coming over there and taking a look."

"Brilliant. Okay, well, I'll talk to Yrsa and get back to you."

"You do that, squirt. And remember what I said – you see the locals building a giant wooden man, you get the next boat off the island."

CHAPTER SIXTEEN

By the time they reached the small white chapel with the red roof, Todd was wishing he had forced down some breakfast, after all.

His stomach was coiling, as though full of eels. His mouth was dry, and he felt lightheaded with nerves. He'd been hoping the funeral would be a small affair, but as Yrsa eased the Land Rover to a halt outside the white gateposts set into the stone wall, he saw that the churchyard was milling with islanders.

As in the hotel bar the other night, he was immediately aware of heads turning, of dozens of eyes regarding them. Given the occasion, he'd been hoping the locals might display a softer side to their collective nature, that Yrsa might be shown some sympathy – but Todd saw only dour, granite-like faces, inset with narrowed eyes projecting almost palpable waves of suspicion and hostility.

The appearance of Sven, emerging from the crowd and marching towards them, was almost a relief, even though the big man looked tense and uncomfortable in his shiny black suit. Yrsa, seemingly unperturbed by the attention, stepped gracefully out of the vehicle, smoothing down the gray shawl she wore around her shoulders. She had assured Todd that his dark blue mohair suit – the only one he owned – would be fine for the occasion, but Todd felt self-consciously ostentatious next to the locals in their shapeless or ill-fitting hand-me-downs. Emerging from the Land Rover, he heard Sven say tersely, "We are almost ready to begin."

As if to antagonize him, Yrsa took her time consulting her watch. "Relax. It's only seven minutes to."

Sven scowled. "All the same, we should get inside."

Falling into step behind Yrsa and her brother, Todd half-expected the islanders to part before them, to flank them on both sides and force them to run the gauntlet of their animosity. To his relief, though, the dark-clad locals began to flood into the chapel ahead of them, their sudden bustle making Todd think of dirty water swirling into a plughole.

He kept his head down as he marched up the aisle behind Yrsa and Sven, wooden pews creaking and scraping as the congregation took their seats. He only raised his head once the three of them were sitting on the front bench facing the pulpit, beside which a wicker coffin sat on a raised wooden altar.

The interior of the chapel was drab, austere – not the sort of place, Todd thought, that reflected God's eternal majesty. He didn't know what religion was practiced here, but it seemed to be one that suggested the only splendor was to be found in Heaven, and that earthly existence should be as miserable as possible.

"You okay?" he murmured to Yrsa, telling himself the surrounding rumble of conversation sounded ominous only because he didn't understand the language.

Yrsa glanced at him, then looked pointedly over her shoulder, as if defying anyone to challenge her. "I'm fine," she said.

That morning she had told Todd that half the congregation would only be there to see if she burst into flames when she set foot in the chapel. Todd had laughed, but from the defiance in her eyes it was clear she hadn't been entirely joking.

He glanced beyond her, to where Sven was sitting on her right. On *his* right was a pretty woman whose light brown hair was fashioned into French braids, and beyond *her*, two kids sat quietly – a stocky boy of about eight who took after his father, and a cute-as-a-button girl of maybe five who was clearly her mother's daughter.

Catching his eye, the woman, Sven's wife, gave Todd a friendly smile, before her attention, and Todd's too, was snagged by the scuffing sound of footsteps on the stone floor in front of them.

The priest had appeared from some hidden doorway at the back of the chapel, a thin man with crinkly red hair and a closely cropped beard streaked with gray. He was wearing ivory robes over a white cassock, and he looked over the congregation without expression, making no attempt to acknowledge the family in the front row.

Before the rumble of conversation had fully died, he began to speak in a droning voice, and continued to do so for the next twenty minutes, in a language Todd didn't understand. At one point Todd caught Yrsa's surname – Helgerson – but for the most part he sat staring at the intricate wickerwork of Yrsa's mother's coffin, his mind drifting back over the strange events of the past few days.

Throughout the ceremony Yrsa sat motionless, her back straight, her expression relaxed, her brown eyeshadow making her eyes look smoky, almost sultry. There were no hymns, no family readings, and when creaks and scuffs of movement started up behind them a few seconds after the priest had stopped talking, Todd looked up in surprise.

"Is that it?" he said quietly.

"That's it," Yrsa confirmed.

He glanced over his shoulder to see people filing out. "So what happens now?"

Given the wicker coffin and the location, he half-expected some semi-pagan ceremony – the coffin carried down to the sea, set on fire and pushed out into the waves, perhaps – but Yrsa shrugged, as though the answer was obvious. "Now we bury her."

"Just a normal burial? Like in the UK?"

"As opposed to what?"

"I don't know. Different people have different customs."

As it happened, the burial *was* pretty normal. Yrsa's mother's coffin was lowered into the ground beside the plot dedicated to her husband, who had been lost at sea, as the priest intoned more words that Todd didn't understand. The featureless burial ground behind the church was exposed to the elements, the low fence that surrounded it providing precious little shelter from the bitter wind that swooped over the distant trees, and clawed at their exposed skin.

Cold and uncomfortable as he was, Todd was at least thankful that only the immediate family was present around the grave. As the priest's drawling eulogy continued, Yrsa stood in stoic silence, her expression inscrutable, her half-open eyes fixed on a point somewhere between the rectangular hole and the dozens of stone monuments arranged in neat rows between here and the chapel. Of the seven people present, only one – Sven – was weeping, and he was doing it silently, his mouth downturned within his thick beard, his tears following the lines of his wrinkles down his ruddy cheeks. Sven's wife was holding their little girl, who was sucking her thumb, her head resting on her mother's shoulder. Glancing at Sven's son, Todd realized the boy was staring at him, his brows crinkled as though he was wondering why this stranger was here. Todd flashed the boy a quick wink, but he just stared back implacably.

When the ceremony was over and the priest had walked away, after offering a perfunctory handshake to Sven and then, after a moment's hesitation, to Yrsa, Sven's wife approached Todd. Her daughter still wrapped around her body, she said, "Hello, we haven't been introduced. I'm Gudrun."

"I'm Todd," he said. She smiled at him.

"This can't be much fun for you."

"I don't think it's much fun for anyone." Gudrun was the first person who had shown any friendliness towards him since he and Yrsa had set foot on the island, and for that reason he felt an instant connection to her. Seeing the little girl watching him warily, he said, "Hello. What's your name?"

"This is Astrid," said Gudrun. She indicated the boy, who had fallen into step beside her. "And that's Noah. Say hello to Todd, children."

Neither of them responded and she raised her eyebrows at him. "I'm sorry, they're shy. We don't get many strangers here."

"No problem," said Todd. Nodding at Sven's broad back, who was a good five meters ahead, talking quietly with Yrsa, he asked, "Is your husband okay?"

Looking at her husband, Gudrun's face flooded with affection, which Todd found oddly moving. "He was very close to his mother, and he blames himself for her death."

"Why? It was just an accident, wasn't it?"

"This is what I tell him, but he feels responsible all the same. But he is a good son." She checked herself. "He *was* a good son. He visited his mother almost every day."

"What was she like? Mrs. Helgerson?"

Her face clouded a little. "She was not the easiest of women. I understand why Yrsa went away."

"You're the first person I've met here who doesn't think Yrsa is some sort of witch."

Gudrun rolled her eyes. "I'm sorry you have seen the worst of us, Todd. But we don't all believe in fairy stories."

"That's good to know."

At that moment Astrid began to wriggle in her mother's arms.

"She must be cold," Todd said.

"And hungry. It's past her lunchtime. Will you and Yrsa be coming back to our home for some food?"

Todd raised his eyebrows. "Are we invited?"

"Of course." She said it almost fiercely.

"Thank you," Todd said, and nodded towards Yrsa, who was still talking to Sven. "I'll see what Yrsa wants to do, if that's okay."

"Of course," she said again.

Sven and Yrsa waited for them beside the now-closed door of the chapel. Sven's eyes were still red, but he seemed composed now. Gudrun touched his arm and murmured something, and he replied in a quiet voice, then kissed her head.

When he and Yrsa were back in the Land Rover, following Sven's pickup truck, Todd said, "Gudrun seems nice."

Yrsa gave him a sidelong look. "Does she?"

"Well, she was friendly towards me. And she stuck up for you." When she didn't reply, he said, "I thought you'd be glad of an ally."

"I don't know Gudrun," she said. "We're not friends."

Todd felt a flash of irritation. "That doesn't mean you have to be enemies, does it?"

"I suppose not."

"So what's wrong with making an effort while we're here – however long that may be?"

She raised her eyebrows dismissively but didn't answer. Until yesterday, Todd had assumed he and Yrsa would head back to London as soon as her mother's funeral was over, but their expedition to the caves had changed all that. Robin was arriving tomorrow, and if things developed from there it was possible they could be here for another week or two, maybe longer.

"I thought you couldn't wait to leave here," he'd said to her when she'd suggested inviting Robin to look at the site.

"I can't. But this is unfinished business. For years I've been branded a liar. Just imagine if I was proved right."

The avidity of her expression had been unsettling. "Is that all this is, then? A way of getting your revenge, of sticking it to your enemies?"

"A bit, yes," she admitted. "I can't deny I would love to see the faces of the people who dismissed me as nothing but a stupid girl." Then her face changed, a dreamy look coming into her eyes. "But it's more than that. What I saw that day has stayed with me. I suppose you might say it's haunted me. If I don't at least try to find out the truth, I'll never truly settle. I'll spend my life wondering whether I was right."

Todd could understand that, and he couldn't deny that the prospect that Yrsa *might* be right sent tingles of excitement through him. My God, if there really *was* a treasure-laden Viking ship in that cave, it would go down in history as one of the most significant archeological finds ever.

"Will you be allowed to drill through that wall, though?" he asked. "Won't you need permission?"

Yrsa had shrugged, as if the problem was of little consequence. "Strictly, the island council should be informed, but no one owns the land out there, so they don't have the power to stop me."

"That doesn't mean they might not *try*," Todd said.

Yrsa bared her teeth in a grin. "Let them."

They trailed Sven's pickup to a quiet residential street off the town's main thoroughfare, where it eventually cruised to a halt in front of a small white house. The house was of a simple design, and more or less identical to every other house in Eldfjallaeyja. Yrsa wrinkled her nose.

"The people here live such little lives."

"Maybe that's just how they like it," Todd said, feeling this was an old argument, and one he was never going to win.

Sure enough, Yrsa sneered. "Then they're idiots."

She cut the engine of the Land Rover and got out before he could respond.

Todd had half-expected to find a crowd of mourners waiting for them, and so was relieved to see the area in front of the Helgersons' house was empty. As they moved towards the house, Sven and his family leading the way, Gudrun turned and smiled.

"I think we could do with some coffee," she said.

Like the exterior, the interior of the house was modest – wooden floors, white walls, neat lines. There was no clutter, and the small, square downstairs room that they entered, although not austere, contained little that wasn't functional. Against the far wall, beyond a wooden staircase on the right, was a long trestle table covered with a white cloth. At one end was a stack of mismatched plates (Todd guessed the Helgersons' friends or neighbors must have lent them some extra crockery) and a couple of earthenware pots, one full of knives, the other of forks. The rest of the table was empty, presumably awaiting the food that would soon be piled upon it.

Sure enough, after they had taken off their coats, and the children, prompted by a few words from Sven, had scuttled upstairs with them, Gudrun said, "I'll make the coffee. Would you help me put the food out, Yrsa?"

"Sure," Yrsa muttered stiffly.

"I'll help too," said Todd.

For the next ten minutes the four of them moved between the tiny kitchen and the trestle table, carrying plates and bowls of food. If Gudrun had made all of this, Todd thought, she must have spent the whole of the previous day cooking. There were meatballs and fish dishes, beetroot and apple salad, pickled cucumbers and radishes, new potatoes, several cheeses and two different kinds of paté with dark rye bread. After setting out the buffet, the four of them drank coffee so strong it made Todd jittery, although when the first knock came on the

Helgersons' front door minutes later, he wasn't sure whether his rapid heartbeat was due to caffeine or anxiety.

As islanders arrived in a steady stream, they were greeted warmly by Sven and Gudrun, who directed them towards the buffet table. Todd had feared Yrsa might be purposely antagonistic or provocative, but instead she stood with her back against the side of the staircase, observing proceedings with the slightest trace of a smile on her otherwise implacable face. Todd couldn't help being reminded of a sleepy lioness, sated after a good meal, watching a herd of gazelle feeding placidly nearby. He fetched a plate of food that he felt too nervous to do much more than pick at, and stood close enough to her to act as her protector should she need one.

After twenty minutes or so, he put down his half-empty plate and sidled up to her, intending to ask how long she wanted to stay. But before he could open his mouth, her hand darted out and plucked at the sleeve of a tall, thin, gray-haired man who was en route to the buffet table.

The man jerked to a surprised halt and looked down at Yrsa's hand on his arm. Before he could protest, she leaned towards him and said quietly in English, "I wonder if I might have a word with you, Hakon?"

The man called Hakon looked momentarily trapped, and then licked his lips. "What about?"

Yrsa glanced at Todd, which made him realize she had spoken English for his benefit. "This is my friend, Todd," she said. "We have a proposal for you."

Hakon glanced at Todd, and although there was something like distaste on his ascetic features, Todd smiled.

"What sort of *proposal*?"

"You are, of course, familiar with the Devil's Throat and the cave system there?"

"Yes."

"We were there yesterday," Yrsa said. "We believe it warrants further investigation."

Todd tried not to look shocked that she had made him a co-instigator in her scheme. Instead, he smiled encouragingly as Hakon shot him another acid look.

"What kind of *investigation*?"

"When I was a child I spent three days in those tunnels—"

"We're all perfectly aware—"

"And when I was there I discovered something remarkable. Something I am now in a position to corroborate."

He didn't exactly roll his eyes, but his expression conveyed the same response. "You're referring to your childish—"

"How old I was is irrelevant." Her voice had become clipped. "I know what I saw and I'll prove I was right."

"I see." A thin, bitter smile touched his lips. "And how will you do that?"

"Todd's brother owns a construction company. He'll be arriving tomorrow to look at the site. The next step will be to get a team into the tunnels to drill through the wall."

Hakon jerked as if she'd slapped him. Outraged, he said, "You can't do that!"

"No one can stop me," Yrsa replied smugly.

"The council would never allow it."

"The council doesn't own those tunnels. No one does. I'm not asking your permission, Hakon. I'm letting the council know of my intentions, purely as a courtesy." She glanced at the buffet table. "I suggest you help yourself to some of those delicious herring before they're all gone."

Hakon flushed, and his hand tightened into a fist. For an awful second, Todd thought he was going to throw a punch. Instead, he hissed, "This is not the end of this matter, Miss Helgerson. You will not be allowed to do this."

Yrsa's smile was mocking. "We'll see."

"We certainly will," he said and stalked away.

Todd watched him go, then sidled up to Yrsa. "Did you do that just to wind him up?"

She blinked innocently. "Certainly not. I told him as a courtesy."

"Bollocks," said Todd. "Those tunnels are so far away from town that if you'd gone ahead without telling anyone, no one would have been any the wiser."

"And what would they have thought when your brother and his men arrived with drilling equipment? There are no secrets here, Todd."

Todd grunted. She had a point. But he still couldn't help feeling she'd deliberately stirred the pot.

"How much longer do you want to stay here?" he asked. "Do you have—"

Then something thumped into his shoulder from behind, knocking him off-balance.

Staggering sideways, Todd shot out a hand to stop himself from whacking his head on the staircase. By the time he'd regained his balance, the woman had started shouting.

It was the old woman with the painted-on eyebrows from the hotel bar – the one who Yrsa had said was her mother's best friend. She was nose to nose with Yrsa, her face red, her stubby arms waving.

What she was shouting Todd had no idea, but she was certainly going for it. The spittle flying from her mouth glittered like shoals of tiny fish as they arced across the gap between the two women.

Instead of recoiling, though, Yrsa stood her ground. She appeared calm, her arms by her sides, her body still. Perhaps it was this, or the mocking half-smile on her face, that enflamed the old woman further. Her face grew redder, her eyes wilder, her voice shriller. Assuming no one else would intervene, Todd stepped forward, hand raised placatingly.

"Let's just calm down," he said. "This is a funeral, not a football match."

Although he hadn't touched the old woman, she reacted as though he had. She swung towards him, eyes stretching so wide that her painted-on eyebrows disappeared beneath her hairline. Her mouth twisted and she screeched at him, "English pig!"

Then, to Todd's astonishment, she lunged forward, swinging her arm like a club.

He stepped back, raising his own arms defensively, and felt her fist connect, not very painfully, with his bicep. Then he glimpsed movement to his left and suddenly the old lady was reeling back, her hands flying to her face. Other hands shot from the crowd to steady her, whereupon she let out a whimpering groan and slumped forward. As her hands fell from her face, he saw four diagonal slashes, running with blood, across her right cheek.

All at once people were shouting, jostling, jabbing fingers in Yrsa's direction. When Todd looked at her, he saw the fingers of her right hand were curled into claws, and she was staring at the angry crowd not with defiance or fear, but with a glassy-eyed expression, as if she was in shock.

Fearing more violence, Todd pushed his way through to her, arriving just as Sven forced his way through the crowd and positioned himself in front of his sister. Todd assumed he was there to offer protection or support, but instead, face like thunder, he glared at Todd and growled, "What has the crazy bitch done now?"

Despite Sven's bulk, Todd felt anger flare within him. "Yrsa's not the one at fault here. That mad old woman started it. She was screaming at Yrsa, and then she attacked me."

Sven's lips curled back, his teeth very white in his black beard. He looked ready to debate the point, but instead released an exasperated huff. "Just get her out," he snarled. "We don't need this."

Todd put his arm protectively around Yrsa, who still seemed shell-shocked, and with Sven's bulk providing a barrier between themselves and the crowd, steered her towards the front door.

Before stepping outside, he turned to Sven. "This wasn't Yrsa's fault," he said firmly.

Sven stared at him, then shook his head as if Todd knew nothing. "Just go."

CHAPTER SEVENTEEN

"You sure about this?" Robin said.

He was staring at the narrow gap that Yrsa had just squeezed through, the light from his helmet dancing across the wall, as if in the hope an alternative route would magically open up for him.

"It's fine," Todd said. "You saw how easily Yrsa got through."

His elder brother gave him a deadpan look. "Yrsa's half my size."

"Well, I got through okay last time," Todd said.

Robin slapped his brother's belly hard enough to make him gasp. "You haven't got my padding. You're a fucking anorexic."

Rubbing his stomach, Todd said, "Stop moaning. I'll push and Yrsa'll pull. You'll pop out the other side like a cork from a bottle."

"Yeah, but how much will I leave behind?"

It was two days after the funeral. The previous afternoon Todd had borrowed the Land Rover and driven to the harbor to meet his brother off the boat. It was the first time either he or Yrsa had ventured out since the incident at the wake, and Todd had been nervous, his imagination in overdrive. As he drove through the town, he half-expected islanders to emerge and pelt him with missiles, or maybe force him off the road. But the town was quiet, and he made it through without incident.

Since the funeral, Todd had been expecting Sven to turn up at the house, demanding to know what had happened between his sister and the old woman, but so far there had been no word from him. Todd could understand Sven being angry, but he felt aggrieved for Yrsa, who had not been the instigator of the trouble. Immediately after arriving back at the house, Todd had tried to persuade Yrsa to ring her brother, but she had refused.

"Why should I? I've got nothing to apologize for."

"That's not how the locals will see it."

"Who gives a fuck what they think? They'll think what they want of me despite what I say."

Todd sighed. "What about Sven? Don't you care what he thinks?"

"Not really."

"I know he was angry about what happened, but that was a spur of the moment thing. I'm sure he'd give you a fair hearing."

She glared at him. "I'm not going to be put on trial by my fucking brother, Todd."

"That's not what I meant."

"Well, that's what it sounded like."

She had spent the rest of the day sleeping, which Todd took to mean she was emotionally exhausted, perhaps more upset by what had happened than she was letting on. When she emerged for the dinner Todd had prepared for them both – boar sausages, mashed potatoes, local greens and onion gravy, a proper 'stick-to-yer-ribs nosh-up', as his dad would have called it – she was calmer, even contrite, apologizing to him for snapping.

"I don't want to talk about it anymore, though," she said, "so don't ask me, okay?"

"Sure," Todd said, "if that's what you want."

At the harbor that morning, Todd had parked as far away from the fishing boats as he could, whilst still maintaining a view of the bay. He'd been relieved to see only a smattering of boats in dock, only one of which was manned, by a couple of guys who seemed to be giving the deck a thorough clean. He was relieved they paid the Land Rover no attention, although when the same boat that had brought him and Yrsa here appeared around the promontory and came chugging towards the dock, he still closed the vehicle's door as quietly as he could, so as not to draw attention to himself.

Bracing himself, he walked towards the quayside, knowing he couldn't remain unnoticed forever. Sure enough, he was halfway down the slope when he became aware of the two men turning to stare at him. A rebellious part of him wanted to call out a cheery good morning, but he knew there was no point stirring the pot.

Keeping his gaze on the approaching boat, he marched onto the jetty. As soon as he saw his brother standing on the deck of the little vessel, he raised a hand.

Robin didn't respond. He was gripping the rail at the bow of the boat as though it was a safety bar on a rollercoaster. It wasn't until the boat was ten meters away that Todd realized how deathly pale his brother was. Grinning, he called, "Pleasant voyage?"

Robin's eyes, sunk deep in their sockets, flickered in Todd's direction. Then he leaned over the side and vomited.

As soon as the boat nudged the jetty, Robin grabbed the rucksack at his feet and hurled it at Todd, who caught it cleanly. As Robin clambered up the rusty metal ladder attached to the side of the jetty, Todd put down the rucksack and stepped forward, holding out a hand. Robin glared at the hand as if he'd rather bite it than grasp it, then sighed and allowed himself to be hauled ashore.

"That was the longest fucking hour of my life," he said.

"You're not going to puke on me, are you?" said Todd.

"I ought to, as revenge for putting me through that. You owe me big time, squirt."

"Great to see you, mate," Todd said.

Robin shook his head, then gave a shaky laugh. "You little bastard. Come here."

The brothers hugged. Todd wondered what the two guys on the fishing boat were making of it. One thing was certain: news of Robin's arrival would be all round town by the evening.

Not that that was an immediate concern. For now, the priority was to get Robin's verdict on whether what Yrsa wanted was feasible. In the chilly, lamp-lit darkness, Robin took another look at the gap his brother was trying to persuade him to squeeze through, then sighed and shrugged off his rucksack.

"Why do I let you talk me into shit like this?" he muttered.

Turning sideways, he sucked in his belly and crammed himself into the gap. For the next minute he grunted and oofed, and at one point shouted, "Fucketty wank bastards!" when a fist-sized spar of rock jabbed him in the testicles. Eventually, though, he made it through, and was followed seconds later by Todd, who dragged Robin's rucksack behind him.

"That wasn't so bad, was it?" Todd said.

"Apart from being castrated, you mean?"

Todd grinned at Yrsa. "Well, you weren't planning on having any more kids, were you?"

Gingerly Robin straightened up and examined the passage-riddled wall on the opposite side of the cave. "What have we got here, then?"

Yrsa crouched and pushed her arm, shoulder deep, into a hole in the rock. "This leads to the cave I was telling you about. I crawled through one of these."

Wincing, Robin crouched beside her and directed his headlamp into the hole as Yrsa withdrew her arm.

"Jesus," he said. "You must have been as thin as a whippet." He ran his fingers around the rim of the hole, rubbing the rock. After a few moments he withdrew his hand, his fingertips covered with dark flakes. He directed his torch onto them, then brushed them off.

"What do you think?" Todd asked.

"You're right, Yrsa," Robin said, referring to a conversation they'd had the previous evening. "These are lava tubes. I'd guess this entire cave system was formed by volcanic activity. As you can see, the rock is fairly friable, which means it's got a lot of air in it."

"What sort of rock would it be?" Todd asked.

Robin shrugged. "Basalt. Pumice. Probably some other bits and pieces."

"And that's good?" said Yrsa. "That it's friable, I mean?"

"For our purposes, yeah," said Robin. "One of the biggest problems with an operation like this is accessibility – getting the equipment through some of these narrow tunnels. If this rock had been super-hard we'd have been screwed, because we'd never have been able to get the equipment we'd have needed down here. But there are smaller drills that *can* cope with this. Only problem is it may take a while to break through – and obviously the longer it takes, the more it'll cost."

"How long's a while?" Todd asked.

Robin pursed his lips. "Depends how thick this wall is, but…four, five days? A week? How long do you reckon it took you to crawl through when you were a kid, Yrsa?"

Yrsa tilted her head to one side. "My memory is very hazy. But not too long, I think. Five minutes. Perhaps ten."

Looking at the dreamy expression on Yrsa's face, it struck Todd, not for the first time, what a crazy situation they were in, and how much of a long shot this was. By her own admission, Yrsa had spent many hours wandering around in the pitch black in a state of dehydrated delirium. The likelihood, therefore, that she had seen what she remembered seeing, and that the cave she had found lay beyond this wall, was a remote one. Standing in the cave now, looking at Yrsa and Robin crouched before one of the lava tubes, Todd couldn't help thinking that Yrsa had cast some sort of spell over him – him *and* his brother. Was Robin seriously considering bringing a team of men and a bunch of equipment all the way over from England and down into these caves, based on nothing but a highly suspect childhood memory?

Then again, what did Robin have to lose? He was being paid for this, so it wouldn't matter to him one way or the other if his client was batshit crazy.

Except…

Todd knew his brother, and he knew he would never be so mercenary as to take someone's money if he thought they were pissing it down the drain. He was pragmatic, yes, and he could be blunt, even tactless. But he had integrity; he would never take on a project if he thought it wasn't going to work. Which must mean he thought there was *something* viable in this, something worth pursuing.

As if sensing Todd's scrutiny, Robin turned and looked at him. For a moment Todd felt sure his older brother was about to blink, as if emerging from a trance, and say in a bemused voice, "What the fuck are we doing here?"

Instead he pointed at the rucksack Todd was holding and said, "Pass me that, would you, squirt?"

Todd handed it over, and watched as Robin took from it a dozen or more white plastic tubes. He put these on the ground, then produced what looked like a homemade selfie stick.

Glancing at Todd, he held out his hand. "Give me your phone."

"What for?"

Robin rolled his eyes. "Just pass it here and I'll show you."

Todd hesitated, then took out his phone and handed it over. "You'd better not do anything to it."

"Because if I do you'll tell Mum?" said Robin, smiling.

"Something like that."

Chuckling, Robin slotted the phone into the top of the selfie stick, adjusting the clamp so it fit snugly. He turned the phone on, found the camera and pressed 'Record', then pushed the selfie stick, camera first, into the lava tube. Piece by piece he extended the selfie stick by screwing one plastic tube after another onto the end that was sticking out of the hole. After each new half-meter piece was added, he pushed it further into the hole until only the last couple of centimeters was poking out.

"What if one of those things snaps off?" Todd asked nervously as he watched his brother.

"Then you'll lose your phone," said Robin, deadpan.

"Why couldn't you have used your own phone?"

Robin's teeth looked very white in the light from Todd's headlamp as he grinned. "Because I didn't want to lose *my* phone."

Five minutes after Todd had seen his phone disappear into the lava tube on the end of the selfie stick, Robin was screwing on the final plastic tube. Again, he pushed all but the last two or three centimeters into the hole, waited a few seconds, and then began to draw it out again. The next five minutes he spent reversing the process, unscrewing each piece of white tubing as it emerged from the hole and placing it on the ever-growing pile beside him. Finally the selfie stick itself appeared, which Robin carefully drew from the hole. To Todd's relief his phone was still attached to the end, albeit a little grimy from its journey.

"Right, let's have a look," Robin said, detaching the phone and rewinding the ten minutes or so of video it had recorded. Todd and Yrsa leaned in as he pressed 'Play'.

There wasn't much to see – just blurry stone wall, which was mainly gradations of gray and black shadow. A regular but monotonous pattern quickly established itself: there would be five seconds of movement as the wall flashed past the camera (recorded as Robin pushed the latest extension into the hole), followed by fifteen or twenty seconds while the picture held steady (as Robin screwed on the next piece of tubing).

This went on for several minutes, until suddenly the wall seemed to recede, to fall away and be replaced by gritty blackness.

"Unless the lava tube widens out further along, this must be the cave beyond the wall," Robin murmured.

"How far?" Yrsa asked.

Robin glanced at the timer at the bottom of the screen and did a quick calculation in his head. "As we thought, around...seven, eight meters."

"Twenty, twenty-five feet," said Todd.

Robin nodded. "That's a thick old wall."

They stared at the blackness onscreen for a few seconds, then gray flashes of stone appeared again, rushing past the camera, as the stick began its return journey.

"Hold on," said Todd.

Robin glanced at him. "What?"

"I think I saw something. Just pause it and go back, will you?"

"What did you see?" Yrsa asked.

"Not sure. Just go back to when the camera breaks through into the cave."

Robin shrugged, but rewound the video. When he was at the beginning of the cave section he pressed 'Play'.

Todd frowned at the screen, not wanting to blink. What he had seen had been so fleeting, but—

"There!" he said, pointing.

"Where?" asked Robin.

"Pause it and go back. Can you play it frame by frame?"

"I didn't see anything," said Yrsa.

"Me neither," said Robin.

"Please. Just humor me."

Robin sighed. "Whatever."

He rewound the video a few seconds, then played it forward, frame by frame. Replayed in this manner the blackness didn't seem so absolute. It shifted and swirled like coils and billows of black smoke.

"Stop!" Todd snapped.

Robin hit 'Pause'.

After a moment Yrsa said, "What are we looking at?"

Todd pointed at the screen. "There. Can't you see it? Isn't that... an object?"

Robin squinted. "What are we supposed to be looking at?"

"There!" Todd said. He jabbed at the screen. "Look! That curve." He stared harder, and suddenly his eyes widened. "Oh, fuck."

"What is it?" said Yrsa.

Todd looked at her. In the light from his helmet her skin looked bone-white, but her eyes looked completely black.

"I think it's a person," he said.

CHAPTER EIGHTEEN

They'd laughed at him. Neither of them had been able to see it, and the more Todd stared, the less he could see it either. For a few seconds, while viewing the footage in the caves, he'd been sure he'd seen the curve of an arm, and maybe the suggestion of a bulbous head, but when he watched the video over again, the darkness was so thick there was nothing but shapeless swirls of gray and black.

Over the course of that evening, most of which had been occupied by a raucous and drunken meal, Todd had tried and mostly succeeded in putting the incident out of his head. Now, though, several hours later, he'd woken with the muddled conviction that the figure on his phone screen had escaped from the device and was now standing in the corner of his and Yrsa's bedroom.

He opened his eyes, and was freaked out to find he was in the same position he'd been occupying in his dream – lying on his left side, his back to Yrsa, facing the bedroom door. The duvet was pushed down to his waist and he could feel chilly air on his exposed arms and chest. The door was half open, revealing a sliver of shadowy upper landing. Had he and Yrsa left it like that when they'd flopped into bed? His memory was hazy. He'd been pretty drunk.

The rest of the room was swathed in shadow, which seemed to accumulate in clots in the corners. Todd's gaze was drawn to one of those corners. *Was* there a figure standing there?

He stared, willing the shape to move, so he could react, or to transform into something mundane as his eyes became used to the darkness. But it did neither; it remained stubbornly inscrutable. Eventually, moving slowly, he reached for his phone, which was on the bedside cabinet beside him, and drew it back to his body.

He took a deep breath, then turned on the torch app and shone it into the corner. The darkness seemed to flinch and retreat, clotting even blacker beyond the boundary of the light. To assure himself there was nothing there he moved his arm from side to side, light sweeping the walls like a mop through dirt.

When he was satisfied he and Yrsa were alone, he slid out of bed and padded across the room to close the door. He was reaching for the handle when he heard a sound. It came from the bathroom at the far end of the corridor. As he jerked up the phone, Todd saw by its light that the door was slightly ajar, a thick band of blackness around its rim.

Rob. It must be Rob. He'd got up for a piss, and the sound – a scrape or a thump – was the toilet seat clunking against the back of the cistern as he lifted it. In a moment he'd hear the splash of piss hitting water. He tilted the phone, the light pooling on the floor halfway along the landing, and waited. But the sound he'd expected didn't come. There was only silence.

No, not quite silence. There were further sounds beyond that partly open door. Shuffles and scrapes and creaks. Sounds too small to identify.

Todd thought again of the image he'd seen on his phone: the suggestion of a figure in the cavern, its head bulbous, oddly misshapen. But no. It was only Robin in the bathroom. Had to be.

But what was he doing?

Todd waited another ten seconds, urging the door to open and his brother to emerge, belly drooping over the waistband of his boxers. But the door didn't open. And whoever was in there didn't turn on the light.

A sit-down job then, Todd thought. An early-hours bowel movement. Probably best to crawl back into bed and leave Rob to it.

He didn't, though; he stayed where he was. And after a moment he directed the light beam onto the door of the room, halfway along the landing, where Robin was sleeping.

The door was closed.

If you got up to use the loo in the middle of the night, would you close your bedroom door behind you?

Maybe. But most likely not. Most likely you'd leave it partway open.

Todd flexed his toes. His feet were getting cold. Then he sighed and started walking towards the door at the end of the landing.

He kept his phone pointing at the floor, the puddle of light moving ahead of him like a faithful pet. A meter from the door, he reached out and placed his fingertips on it, as if hoping to pick up some vibration, some indication, as to who was inside.

He took a long breath. Then he said, "Rob?"

His voice cracked at the base of his throat. Self-consciously he tried again.

"Rob? You in there?"

No reply. Todd pictured the bathroom: the sink on his left beneath a wall-mounted mirror, the bath with shower attachment on the right, the toilet on the back wall, facing the door.

The bathroom light was just inside the door, on the right. A cord that dangled from the ceiling, weighed down with a piece of wood carved into the shape of a bird.

Raising his phone, pointing its beam at the door, he gave the door a sharp push.

The torch beam stretched across the door as it swung open, then spilled into the bathroom. Whoever was in there would be blinded by the light, giving Todd an advantage – and if it was only his dozy brother, sitting on the pan, then at least Todd would be nothing but a dark silhouette, and would have time to pull the door shut again before Robin knew what was happening.

As it turned out, there *was* somebody in the bathroom, but they weren't sitting on the toilet. They were much closer than that.

Yrsa was standing side on to him, hands gripping the edge of the sink on the left-hand wall. She was leaning forward, rocking back and forth, causing the floorboards to make tiny creaking sounds. She wasn't looking at Todd, but staring intently into the mirror at her own reflection.

For a moment Todd was confused. Hadn't she been in bed with him? Then he remembered he'd woken to find himself facing the door.

And he'd only assumed Yrsa was behind him because he hadn't felt her climb over him in the night.

But she must have done. And here she was. Standing in the dark, staring at herself in the mirror. Her wide eyes and blank expression made it clear she was sleepwalking again. But at least she'd stayed inside this time. She hadn't gone into the woods.

"Yrsa," he said quietly. She didn't respond. He touched her bare arm. It was cold as marble. "Yrsa."

It was his touch rather than his voice she responded to. She ceased rocking and became almost preternaturally still. For a moment Todd got the impression the flesh of her arm was squirming beneath his fingertips like a nest of worms. He flinched and jerked his hand away. Slowly her head turned towards him. She stared directly into his torch beam, though it looked as though she was staring *through* it. At him. The light, so close to her, made her face look like a doll's, white as porcelain. Her eyes, wide and unblinking, were a depthless black.

"Hey," he said softly, "it's me, Todd. You want to come back to bed?"

She stared, but didn't respond. Afraid of damaging her eyes, he lowered the torch. After a moment, he reached out again and cupped her elbow.

"Come on," he said, giving her the gentlest of tugs.

For a moment he felt resistance and then she complied. Her hands dropped from the sink and she turned towards him.

"That's it. Come back to bed."

Her eyelids fluttered. Then abruptly her knees folded beneath her and she fell.

Todd's reflexes were good. If he hadn't leaped forward and caught her she might have landed badly, or bashed her head on the sink. But instead she fell into his arms and he dropped to one knee as he took her weight. As he did so his phone was knocked from his hand. It bounced on the floor, then went skidding away towards the toilet, light looping behind it before the screen went dark.

Plunged into blackness, he held on to Yrsa's limp body, then slowly straightened with her in his arms. He carried her back to the bedroom, lowered her into bed and pulled the duvet around her, tucking it in around her cold shoulders. Once she was settled, he crossed the room again, hesitating by the open door. Should he retrieve his phone? Reluctant to let Yrsa out of his sight, he decided it could wait until morning. After closing the door, he crossed back to the bed and slid beneath the duvet. But he didn't sleep. Instead, he lay on his side, facing Yrsa, and listened to her long, deep breaths.

CHAPTER NINETEEN

Todd was driving along the main street the next morning when a woman jumped into the road.

He'd just dropped Robin off at the harbor, and was feeling jaded and hollow after his broken night's sleep. He was in the middle of an almighty yawn when the woman stepped off the pavement and lunged towards him, throwing up her hands.

If she'd been more agile, he might have hit her full-on, might even have killed her. But because she was heavy and slow and old, she was only in line with the headlight on the passenger side of the vehicle when he registered what was happening.

His reflexes may have been sluggish this morning, but he was still alert enough to twist the wheel and swerve around her, before stamping on the brake. He had an impression of the woman as a dark blur flashing by the passenger window before the Land Rover came to a screeching halt.

He sat for a moment, body tingling with reaction, hands gripping the steering wheel. But he had barely begun to recover before she was there again, thumping the passenger door, then walking around the vehicle and standing directly in front of it. Glaring at him through the windscreen, she brought two meaty fists down on the bonnet with a clanging impact. Todd gaped at her red, furious face, and groaned in recognition.

It was the old woman from the hotel bar, and the wake. He could see four raised weals on her cheek where Yrsa had clawed her. Just as before, she was yelling her head off – albeit in the local language, so he didn't understand a word.

He guessed her tirade was nothing to do with him nearly running her down, though. It was more likely she had seen him behind the wheel and had stepped into the road to force him to stop. Now that he *had* stopped, he wondered what to do next. Try to pacify her, or inform her he had no idea what she was shouting about? Alternatively he could put the Land Rover into reverse and drive around her – though as she was leaning on the bonnet, she might face-plant the pitted tarmac.

That would serve her right, but it wouldn't do his and Yrsa's tarnished reputation any good. In the end, he decided simply to wait, and hope that whatever storm was raging through her would eventually blow itself out.

She carried on ranting for another twenty seconds or so, occasionally bashing the bonnet of the Land Rover with her fists. Todd watched her in bemusement, and at last, perhaps emboldened by his lack of reaction, she stomped around the front of the vehicle and homed in on the driver's-side window.

If she expected him to wind the window down, she'd be disappointed. He saw her thrust her hand into the pocket of her greasy-looking coat, and alarm lanced through him. He pictured her pulling out a hammer, smashing the window, then swinging the weapon at his skull. His hands tightened on the steering wheel – but what she drew out of her pocket was not a weapon, but a folded sheet of paper.

Still tense, he watched her unfold it, then slam it against the window. On the sheet was a photocopied picture of a smiling, blonde-haired girl of maybe six or seven. Above the photo was a word in bold black type – TYNDUR – and below it was more text, none of which Todd understood.

He didn't need a translation to know what this was, though. Whether the photo was of a pet or a child, the format was pretty universal. It was a 'Missing' poster. But who was the child? Had she gone missing on the island? And what, exactly, was the old woman accusing him of?

Indignantly he shouted, "I don't know who that is! Why are you showing me?"

The old woman looked outraged at his response. Her rant went up a couple of notches, and the hand that wasn't holding the poster slammed against the window, as if trying to punch a hole through the glass.

"Stop that! Calm down!" Todd shouted.

But she didn't stop. She punched the window even harder.

"Fuck this," Todd said, his patience evaporating. He put the Land Rover into gear and pulled away.

Despite his anger, he did it in a slow, controlled way, aware that the woman still had her hand pressed to the window. He didn't want to spin her round, or knock her off-balance. Rather he wanted to force her to pull away, step back.

This she did, staggering only slightly, the poster she'd pressed to the glass fluttering to the ground. Glancing into his rearview mirror, Todd saw her take a few clumping steps after him, then throw her arms in the air and start yelling anew, her face a red blur as he put distance between them.

No one seemed to have witnessed the confrontation. Or if they had, they had not made their presence known. Todd wondered how the old woman, Yrsa's mother's best friend, was viewed by the other islanders. Was she voicing what others were too inhibited or afraid to express? Or was she regarded as a loose cannon, to be avoided?

Driving along the main street, he saw another of the 'Missing' posters flash by, this one attached to a lamppost. Then he saw another stapled to a straggly tree, its bottom left corner fluttering in the wind. When he saw one in the window of a building, in front of a display of freshly baked loaves, a memory sparked in his brain. Hadn't Karriana said something about working in her parents' bakery? On a whim, he pulled over to the curb.

Even if this hadn't been his destination, the aroma of sweet pastry that coiled around him as he set foot on the pavement might have enticed him inside. Pushing open the narrow door beneath an awning like an overhanging brow, he found himself in a space whose warmth, combined with its honey-colored walls and wood-paneled floor, gave the impression he was stepping into a vast, freshly baked cake. To his left, trays of buns and pastries sat on shelves behind a glass-fronted display counter. Tending the counter, in front of a wall inset with more shelves stacked with baskets of bread, were two versions of Karriana, one older than the other by maybe twenty-five years.

The older woman, clearly Karriana's mother, greeted him with a faint smile, unaware that behind her, her daughter's eyes were widening.

Todd returned the older woman's smile, then looked at the younger girl. "Hi, Karriana."

The mother blinked – then an expression crossed her face that needed no translating. She had suddenly realized who he was, and glancing at her daughter, she uttered a few terse words that sounded like a question. Karriana muttered something back, then looked at Todd again.

"Hullo."

Her tone was sullen, wary. Todd did his best to look friendly, non-confrontational. He glanced at the treats behind the glass display counter.

"Are those cinnamon buns?"

"Yes."

"Could I have two, please? Actually, make it four."

Karriana's mother watched intently as Karriana plucked a paper bag from a hook. She used a pair of tongs to transfer four buns from tray to bag.

"Anything else?"

"Yes." Todd pointed at the poster in the window. "I keep seeing those notices around town. Could you tell me who that girl is?"

Karriana's head turned to follow Todd's pointing finger. She said, "That is Märta Senvig. She is seven years old. She went missing yesterday."

"Missing how?" Todd asked. "What happened?"

Karriana's mother muttered something. Karriana glanced at her and the two of them exchanged a look that Todd couldn't fathom.

"She went into the forest to play with her friends and she hasn't been seen since."

"So she's been out all night?"

Karriana nodded.

"That's awful. I assume people are looking for her? What about the police?"

"Our police force here is small. Only three people. But yes, they are looking for her. Others too."

"I'd like to help," Todd said. "Who should I speak to?"

Karriana looked surprised. "You are not from here."

"So?" Todd said. "The more people that help the better, right?"

The silence that greeted his words was heavy. Karriana and her mother stared at him as if they couldn't work him out. Eventually Karriana said, "I suppose so, but…"

"But what?"

Todd guessed why Karriana was being evasive, and why her mother was avoiding eye contact with him. It was because he and Yrsa were suspects. In the eyes of many islanders, the little girl hadn't gone missing in the forest; she'd been abducted by the prodigal daughter and her foreign boyfriend.

As Karriana struggled to find words, Todd said, "It's okay. You don't have to explain. But I swear, neither Yrsa nor I had anything to do with this. I know people here don't like us or trust us, but believe me, we haven't done anything bad. And I really do want to help."

He paused. Karriana and her mother continued to stare at him, and eventually he held up his hands.

"Okay, if you don't think it's a good idea—"

"No!" Karriana said, so forcefully that both Todd and her mother looked at her in surprise.

Karriana's mother said something to her, her voice low and full of concern. Karriana replied quickly, causing the older woman to roll her eyes.

Turning to Todd, Karriana said, "Okay. I will go with you. I will vouch for you."

"You'd do that for me?" he said. "You believe me?"

Tentatively she said, "I would like to."

"Well…that's good," said Todd. He glanced at Karriana's mother. "But I don't want to get you into trouble. If this isn't okay with your mum—"

"Is okay," Karriana's mother said quickly.

Todd blinked. "You speak English?"

She waggled her hand in the air. "Little."

The cinnamon buns that Todd had bought were still sitting on the counter, the bag now dotted with grease. Taking out his wallet, he extracted a note and handed it to Karriana's mother. "Keep the change. And thank you."

She took the money with an abrupt nod. As Todd lifted the bag off the counter, Karriana was untying her apron.

"I'll put these in the car," he said, thinking he should call Yrsa and let her know what was happening. "See you outside in five minutes?"

Karriana nodded. "Five minutes," she said.

CHAPTER TWENTY

"Hey, it's me."

"Hi. Is everything okay? Is Robin on his way home?"

"Yeah, all fine. But listen, I'm going to be late back. A girl's gone missing. I'm going to help find her."

There was silence on the line for a long moment, then Yrsa said, "What girl?"

"Her name's Märta…something. Selig?"

"Senvig?"

"That's it. Do you know her?"

"I know her family." Todd heard her sigh. "You remember the man I spoke to at the wake? Hakon?"

"Sure, yeah."

"His full name is Hakon Senvig. He's Märta's grandfather."

"Right."

"You realize what this means?"

He did. He was way ahead of her. But he wanted to hear her say it. "What?"

"It means we'll get blamed for her disappearance. Or I will. People will have seen me talking to Hakon at my mother's wake. They already think I'm the Devil incarnate, and that I'll do anything to get what I want."

"All the more reason to offer to help find the girl, then," he said. "If I do that, maybe it'll change a few minds."

"Or maybe they'll tear you apart as soon as you show your face," Yrsa replied.

CHAPTER TWENTY-ONE

"Maybe this isn't such a good idea," said Todd.

The search for Märta Senvig was being coordinated from the chapel in which Yrsa's mother's funeral had taken place. Todd and Karriana had walked to it from the bakery, and as they turned a corner and started along the pavement on the opposite side of the road to the red-roofed building, Todd felt the same squirming sensation in his stomach as he had the last time he'd been here.

A group of men were gathered outside the open church doors, most of them huddled around a map held by a beefy, weathered-looking man in a thick gray sweater, a peaked cap pulled low over his brow. To Todd, the men looked tough, uncompromising, and the thought of approaching them and offering his services made him want to run in the opposite direction.

Karriana put a hand on his arm. "You don't have to do this. This is really not your problem."

Todd looked at her in an agony of indecision. Finally he said, "I should, though, shouldn't I? Because it's the right thing to do. The local people might not trust me, but that shouldn't matter. Not when there's a girl's life at stake."

A smile plucked at the corner of Karriana's mouth and she regarded him with approval, even respect. "I'll talk to them for you."

"You don't have to do that," said Todd, but her expression was unequivocal.

"Wait here."

She crossed the road and walked up the path towards the men. Two or three looked up idly at her approach, but it was only when she started to speak that more heads were raised. He saw her using her hands to express herself, then tensed when she gestured in his direction. Immediately faces turned towards him, and even from a distance Todd saw the expressions on them hardening. He fought down an urge to smile ingratiatingly, to raise a tentative hand in greeting. He heard a gruff voice raised in anger, saw one of the men – older than the others, with wispy white hair – flap an arm angrily, before turning away and stomping inside. Karriana had her back to Todd, so he couldn't see her face, but he sensed from her posture that she was speaking urgently, perhaps imploring the men to give him a chance.

He felt a strong urge to walk away. But he couldn't, not with the men looking at him, and not with Karriana arguing his case so passionately. He was half-hoping she would throw up her arms in defeat, stomp back to tell him his offer of help had been refused. Instead, he saw one of the men nod, another shrug; he sensed a mood of begrudging conciliation. When Karriana turned and beckoned him, he murmured, "Oh, fuck."

Forcing his legs to move, he crossed the road. The men and Karriana stood motionless as they watched him approach. Despite Karriana's efforts, most of the men were glowering. When he got within earshot, one of them barked, "So you want to help?"

Todd couldn't tell if he was being sarcastic. He nodded. "Yes. If that's okay?"

A man in a green jacket, his pasty cheeks and chin coated with a straggly growth of ginger fuzz, spat on the ground. Another man raised a cigarette to his mouth, his fingernails black as if he'd been digging with his hands.

"It's okay," came the reply, though it was Karriana who spoke. Her smile was the kind someone might give to a skittish animal.

Todd approached the knot of men slowly. The sky above the chapel was a hard white, coiling with dark clouds. The bite of cold in the air made his cheeks ache.

"What can I do?" he asked.

One of the men, young and pug-nosed, his blond hair shaved at the sides and left long on top to flap in the breeze like a ragged flag, muttered something in the local language, which the others snickered at. Karriana snapped at him, then looked back at Todd. "Sorry."

Todd shrugged. "It's okay. I didn't understand, so I wasn't offended."

No one smiled at his feeble joke. The man with the black fingernails dropped his cigarette and stamped on it. "You can tell us where she is," he said. "That will help."

Todd's heart began to bang so hard he felt it in his throat.

"I don't know where she is. Why would I?"

"Why would you?" the man said and gave a snarling laugh. As he took a step towards Todd, Karriana barked at him in her own language, but he made a dismissive gesture and snarled something back.

Another man, broad-shouldered, jeans black with grease, said in heavily accented English, "No children disappear before you come here with that…" Then he said a word that sounded like 'hex'.

Up close, the men looked even more gnarled and weathered; Todd felt effete in comparison. All the same, the accusation irked him enough to make him retort, "We came because Yrsa's mother died. We wouldn't have bothered otherwise. She didn't want to come back."

There were barked responses to his words, none of them in English. Karriana raised her hands and made what might have been an appeal for peace, but was shouted down.

"You think she loves you?" Black Fingernails said, approaching to within a few feet of Todd.

Todd sensed a trap. "What is it to you?"

As the man with the cap carefully folded his map, Black Fingernails tossed his head. "If she loves you, maybe we keep you, offer you in return for Märta." As he stalked forward, Karriana bleated another protest, but one of the men grabbed her by the elbow. Todd stepped back, unsure whether to run or stand his ground. He was raising an arm defensively when a shout rang out behind him.

He didn't know whether the single word was a name or a command, but it froze Black Fingernails in his tracks. Looking over his shoulder, Todd saw Sven marching up the church path. Behind him, taking two steps for every one of her husband's, was Gudrun.

Although his last encounter with Yrsa's brother had not been friendly, Todd felt relief wash through him. As Sven swept past with barely a glance, Gudrun caught his eye and smiled. He smiled back, and next moment she was not only standing beside him, but linking her arm through his, a show of support so unexpected he felt tears pricking his eyes. At a word from Sven, the man who had grabbed Karriana's arm released her. She snatched her arm away, then glared at the man, who had the good grace to look sheepish.

A rapid exchange between Sven and the men seemed to take the form of Sven barking out questions and the men offering responses that, judging by their voices, ranged from defensive to indignant.

"Sorry about this," Todd murmured to Gudrun. "And about the other day."

Gudrun shrugged. "It is not your fault. You are a victim of circumstance."

Eventually Sven and the men seemed to come to an understanding. There were mutters, a handshake, then the men sloped off, a couple flashing resentful looks at Todd. Sven watched them go, then walked back to Todd and Gudrun, scowling.

"You bring trouble wherever you go."

Todd felt indignant. "I only wanted to help."

"You can come with us," Gudrun said.

"You're here to search too?"

"Of course. Everybody is looking for Märta."

"What do *you* think happened to her?" Todd asked.

Gudrun shrugged. "An accident, perhaps. Or she is simply lost in the forest."

"When was she last seen?"

"Yesterday, around six fifteen." It was Sven who answered. "She went out after dinner. Her brother thought she was going to a friend's house to play. But her friends say there was no such arrangement."

"So she just wandered off?"

Sven shrugged, his bearded face inscrutable. "Who knows?"

He went into the church while Todd, Gudrun and Karriana waited outside. A few minutes later he reappeared with a photocopied map composed mainly of dark patches of forest and irregularly shaped fields. The map was divided into squares, many of which were marked with black crosses.

"These are the areas that have been searched, or that are being searched now," Sven said. He indicated a quartet of unmarked squares. "So we will look here."

"How big an area is that?" asked Todd.

"Each of these lines is four miles." Sven tapped the four sides of one of the squares.

"So four square miles," Todd said. "That's a large area for four people to cover."

"There will be others," said Gudrun. "We will keep looking until we find her."

In terms of method, the search for the missing girl was low-key, old school. There was no GPS here, no helicopters or drones to scour the area. Todd wondered if technology would be brought in from outside if things got desperate. He wondered, too, whether the search for Yrsa had been like this all those years ago; whether there had been as much concern for her welfare as there was for Märta Senvig's.

"This must bring back painful memories," he said.

Sven looked at him suspiciously. "How so?"

Surprised, Todd said, "It must have been difficult for your family when Yrsa went missing."

Sven's face cleared, as though he thought Todd had been insinuating something else. "It was. It was difficult when she came back, too."

"But at least she *did* come back," Gudrun said quickly. "And Märta will also."

Before anyone could reply there came a harsh sound, like an outburst of scornful laughter. Todd looked up and saw a pair of huge black birds launch themselves from the top of the church tower. They soared up high, described a circle in the air, then swooped towards the pine forest, the tops of whose trees formed a jagged black line, making the sky resemble a page torn from a book. Sven watched the birds balefully, Karriana with trepidation. After a moment Gudrun unlinked arms with Todd and touched her husband's shoulder.

"Let's go."

CHAPTER TWENTY-TWO

"The forest is very beautiful," Gudrun said. "It is a shame your first experience of it does not come under better circumstances."

Todd almost told her this wasn't his first experience of it, but knew it would hardly help Yrsa's reputation if he related how she had disappeared into the forest on two separate occasions. Instead, he asked, "Did you play in here when you were kids?"

"Yes," Gudrun said. "All of us. It was a wonderful playground."

"But none of us ever came here alone," said Karriana.

She had been quiet, pensive, since Sven and Gudrun had shown up. Perhaps she was just shy. Or maybe she felt bad for misreading the situation at the church – though Todd didn't blame her for that.

"In case you got lost?" he said.

"Partly that. And partly because we were afraid of the jötnar."

Gudrun laughed. Sven gave a grunt of what might have been exasperation.

"Yes, Yrsa told me about them. They're like trolls, aren't they?"

"They are a myth to frighten children," said Sven dismissively.

Gudrun looked at Todd and Karriana, raising her eyebrows as if to apologize for her husband being a grump.

A little cowed, Karriana said, "The jötnar are many things. They are not all ugly, like trolls. Some are said to be very beautiful. Like...elves or fairies."

"But they're evil?" said Todd. "Yrsa said they were creatures of chaos."

"They're complicated," Gudrun said. "Good and evil does not really exist in our folklore in the same way it does in yours. Jötnar are said to bring...unrest. Sometimes they take things just because they can."

"Like children," Karriana said quietly.

Todd thought of the figure he'd seen at the forest's edge and couldn't help shivering. He had to agree with Gudrun, though. In the daylight the forest was beautiful, the pine trees so straight and tall that the light sliced between their trunks in shafts, rather than being broken up by the leaf canopy overhead and dappling the ground, as would be the case in England. Not that one was more attractive than the other; the distribution of light was just different here, more dramatic.

"Let's spread out," said Sven. "We will cover more ground that way."

"We are also more likely to get lost," Gudrun replied, "especially as you have the map."

Sven scowled – Todd was quickly learning it was his default expression. "We can still remain within sight and earshot of one another."

"Makes sense," said Todd, though he wondered whether Sven had made the suggestion partly to curtail their conversation. Perhaps he thought talk of the jötnar was fanciful and inappropriate. Or perhaps mention of them made him apprehensive. Yrsa had called him a superstitious savage, after all.

It was decided that Sven should move left, and that Todd, because he didn't know the forest, should be third in line between Gudrun on his left and Karriana on his right. Once they were in position they set off, moving slowly and calling out Märta's name at staggered intervals. For Todd, both Gudrun and Karriana were dark, distant figures, each around twenty meters away, flitting in and out of the light, and occasionally disappearing when the foliage became thick. Even when he couldn't see them, though, he could hear their voices through the trees, thin and ghostly, sounding at times more birdlike than human. And although Sven was out of sight completely, Todd could hear his voice too, gruffer than the women's but with a peculiar flatness, as if its vitality was absorbed by the forest.

After a while the uniformity of the trees, the play of light, the slow and steady pace, the way they each took it in turns to shout Märta's name, began to have an almost hypnotic effect on Todd. Time seemed to drift away, and he felt he was in a waking dream, his mind detaching from his body and bobbing ahead of him like a balloon. The cries of his companions, the mulchy crackle of his footsteps, the shushing scrape of pine needles as the wind passed through the branches above, began to blend together into a syrupy lullaby that wrapped itself around his thoughts.

What if this isn't real? he found himself thinking. *What if I'm still in the hospital, and this is all a dream?*

He frowned as the harsh cries of crows or ravens impinged on the fantasy. Blinking, he peered ahead, where bands of radiance slanted through the darker uprights of the trees, creating an illusion of light and shadow, making it hard to grasp any sense of perspective.

He blinked again, then raised hands that felt unaccountably heavy and rubbed at his eyes. The bird cries continued, but they were transforming now, becoming less harsh, more human. Was it his companions he could hear, calling Märta's name, the word having been repeated so often that it had become meaningless? No, it seemed the sound was ahead of him, and that it was not like the cries of either birds or people, but something softer, and racked with emotion.

Sobbing. That was what he could hear. His hands dropping to his sides, he peered again into the criss-crossing patches of light and shadow, and now he could see something moving in the heart of it, within a pool of light nestled in the V of two pines that were leaning away from one another.

"Hello?" he said.

The sobbing paused. The shape shifted again, then began to elongate as it rose from the ground. Todd took another step closer, and suddenly he saw that the elongating shape was a young girl. She had been lying face down, curled up on the ground, and now she was using her arms to raise her upper body. She turned her head towards him, and beneath a straggle of blonde hair littered with leaves and pine needles, he saw the face from the 'Missing' posters, blotchy and dirt-streaked, her eyes and cheeks wet with tears.

Todd raised a hand to show he meant no harm. "Märta?"

She peered at him a moment, then sniffed and nodded.

Todd tapped his chest. "I'm Todd." And although it occurred to him that she probably didn't understand English, he added, "You're safe now."

She stared at him, uncomprehending. Todd smiled, in the hope it would put her at ease. Gently he said, "I have friends here. We've been looking for you. I'm going to call for them, okay?"

Although he got no response from the girl, he turned and shouted, "Gudrun! Sven! Karriana! I've found her! She's here!"

The girl looked so bedraggled, so exhausted, so frightened, that he wanted to put his arms around her, or at least take her hand. But he didn't want to frighten her. He had no idea what ordeal she had gone through, and there was no way he could get her to tell him. So he kept his distance, but lowered himself into a squat in the hope it would show her he was not going to leave her, and that he meant her no harm.

Gudrun was the first to reach him. She called his name, to pinpoint his position, and he called back to her, raising a hand. After a few moments he heard her approaching through the forest, the foliage yielding with soft rattles.

Turning back to Märta, he said, "That's Gudrun Helgerson. You know her?"

The girl didn't answer, but she looked in the direction Todd had pointed. That was when he noticed an arrangement of leaves on the ground close to where her head had lain, which had been formed into a kind of bowl. In the 'bowl' was an assortment of nuts and berries and twisted, pale things that might have been roots.

Is this what the girl had been eating? And if so, had she collected them herself?

Then Gudrun appeared, bursting from the undergrowth, flustered and wide-eyed. "Where is she? Is she okay?" She saw Märta, sitting beneath the tree like a wood nymph, and a myriad of emotions fluttered across her features.

Somehow, she managed to hold it together, and as she dropped to her knees in front of the girl and began to speak softly, Todd moved back, so Märta wouldn't feel crowded by the sudden appearance of all these strangers.

Karriana erupted from the undergrowth next, panting hard. She looked terrified, but when she saw Märta, with Gudrun crouching beside her, she released such a gasp of relief that she seemed to deflate.

By the time Sven joined them, Gudrun had got Märta talking. The girl's voice was low, calm, and something she said in answer to Gudrun suddenly made Karriana tense.

Todd glanced at her. "What is it?"

There was a strange look on Karriana's face. "Gudrun asked Märta what had happened to her. How she came to be here."

"And?"

Karriana took a shaky breath. "She said the little man brought her here. She said she was scared of him, but he didn't hurt her." She pointed at the bowl-shaped arrangement of leaves with its assortment of berries and nuts. "She said he looked after her and gave her food, and told her that soon she would go home."

CHAPTER TWENTY-THREE

"Here they come," Todd said.

Although he had faith that his brother knew what he was doing, Todd had lain awake the night before worrying that the boat Robin had hired to transport his men and equipment over to Eldfjallaeyja might not fit into the island's tiny harbor. He knew that Robin had organized things so they were traveling as light as possible – only three trucks and a team of eight guys, including himself – but even three trucks laden with equipment sounded too much for a narrow jetty that usually only accommodated small fishing boats.

As the boat rounded the promontory, though, Todd's fears dissipated a little. The vessel wasn't as big as he'd envisaged – it was smaller, in fact, than many of the local car ferries he remembered from family holidays in Cornwall. The three open-bed trucks were parked in a line in the middle of the deck, each covered with a brown tarpaulin.

Robin's team was mostly leaning on the railings, chatting and looking out to sea. Even from a distance Todd got the impression they were a pretty relaxed bunch, perhaps looking forward to a foreign trip, a change of scene, a job that would be more interesting than the kind of building work they usually did.

"There's Robin," Yrsa said, pointing. Snuggling into Todd, she gave a wicked grin. "Looks like he's found his sea legs."

It was true. Robin looked more at ease than he had last week, as he stood with his elbows on the top rail and his hands clasped, talking to a tall, grizzled Black man. This, Todd knew, was Dev, an old schoolmate of his dad's and the firm's oldest employee. Everyone got on with Dev; he was laid-back and amiable, the sort of man who never got ruffled and always approached problems in a measured, practical manner. Todd suspected that because of the left-field nature of the project, his dad had asked Dev to tag along and keep an eye on things.

It was three days since Märta Senvig had been found safe and well, and Todd was still uncertain whether his role in finding her was a point in his favor or a black mark against him. According to Sven, the community was divided. Some were grateful to Todd, whereas others thought it a big coincidence she'd been found by the foreign stranger, the insinuation being that he'd known where to look because the whole thing had been staged by Yrsa as either a show of power or an attempt to curry favor among the locals before the drilling operation began. Even the assurances given by Sven that Todd had had no say in what part of the forest their team had searched, and Märta's continued insistence that she had been taken and looked after by a 'little man', had failed to sway the doubters.

In light of this, Todd had been grateful that Yrsa hadn't shown any desire to show up in the local bar again to test the water, or maybe ruffle a few feathers. On the contrary, well stocked with supplies, the two of them had barely moved from the house – apart from yesterday, when Yrsa had taken Todd to view the dormant volcano after which the island was named.

The expedition had involved a trudge through thick forest and a steep climb up to the volcano's rim, but it had been worth the effort. Staring into a crater so vast and deep that all he could see beyond a certain point was blackness the size of a dozen football pitches, Todd had been struck by a sense of primal awe that had made him feel utterly insignificant by comparison.

"Ahoy there!"

The shout from the boat brought him sharply back to the present. Robin had spotted him and was facing the jetty, hand upraised. Todd waved back, Yrsa too, and some of the men responded.

Todd recognized most of them from when he'd worked for his dad to pay him back for all the financial help his parents had given him over the years. There was Andy and Amir and Jay, and the skinny guy, who looked like a rock star, his arms, hands and neck covered with tattoos, was called Sean.

Whenever Todd worked onsite, mostly doing menial stuff like digging holes, fetching and carrying tools and equipment, and making tea, the guys ribbed him mercilessly about his womanly hands and his arty-farty ways. But Todd never felt victimized or bullied. They were a good bunch and it was all just banter. His dad had always made a point of employing genuine, easygoing, hardworking guys, rather than macho dickheads.

As the boat chugged towards shore, Todd stole a glance at the dozen or so fishermen who were knocking about. To them, Robin and his men must seem like a gang impinging on a rival crew's turf, and as Todd had expected, the eyes turned in their direction were set in faces that could be described as surly. So much for his finding of Märta Senvig engendering goodwill, he thought. There was no evidence of that in the hostility radiating from these men.

The boat slid alongside the jetty, but instead of halting to let the men off, it carried on, easing up to the point where the downward slope of the concrete slipway disappeared beneath the lapping edge of the sea. Once the boat was in position, gears ground into life and a metal ramp at the vessel's stern slowly lowered into a horizontal position. By the time the ramp was level with the slipway, three of Robin's guys had climbed into the cabs of the trucks, whose rumbling engines added to the ratcheting din of the ramp and the throaty chugging of the boat's engine. When the trucks moved forward, the other guys in Robin's team clapped and cheered. Again Todd thought of how this must seem to the islanders – like a rowdy and disrespectful invasion.

As the rest of the men clambered into the trucks, Robin asked, "Where we headed?"

"Follow us," said Yrsa. "I've booked you into the local hotel. There's a place round the back where you can park."

As though relishing the silent hostility of the locals, Yrsa all but strutted back to the Land Rover. Accommodation for Robin and his team had been one of the things Todd had worried about; he'd assumed the town would close its doors to the outsiders. So when Yrsa had told him she had made the booking, he'd been astonished.

"How did you wangle that? I thought everyone hated you?"

She'd given him a wicked smile.

"They all think I'm a witch, remember, so I threatened them with black magic. Told them if they didn't do what I wanted I'd curse them all."

Even now, Todd didn't know whether she'd been joking.

CHAPTER TWENTY-FOUR

Todd was in the kitchen in his boxer shorts, moving from foot to foot on the cold floor as he made coffee, when he saw Robin's name flash up on his mobile.

"Hey," he said, "I was about to call you. How was—"

"We've got a problem," Robin said bluntly.

Although he'd been half-expecting this, Todd felt a weary slump in his guts. "What's up?"

"There's a protest at the drilling site. About fifteen locals led by an old girl who shouts a lot."

Todd had an idea who the 'old girl' might be. "What's she been saying?"

"Most of it's double Dutch to me. She's called us English pigs, though, a couple of times."

Todd sighed. He'd warned Robin they might encounter opposition from the locals, and Robin had primed his men accordingly. He'd assured Todd that while they were on the island they'd do their best to keep their heads down and not rise to provocation.

"So what's happening now?" Todd asked.

"We're keeping our distance. This isn't our battle, Todd."

To Todd's ears there seemed a hint of admonishment in his brother's voice. "'Course not. We'll be there as soon as possible."

When he told Yrsa, she sprang out of bed like a cat poked with a stick. "That fucking old bitch! I should have taken her eyes out the other day!"

Nervously Todd said, "You're not going to attack her when we get there, are you?"

She scorched him with a look. "I'm not an idiot. That would be playing her stupid game."

"So what will you do?"

Her smirk was almost as disturbing as her anger. "I'll use my womanly charms."

The first time Yrsa had shown Todd the Devil's Throat, they'd left the Land Rover behind and tramped for over an hour through mostly rocky terrain to get to it. To Todd's surprise, though, when they'd returned to the caves with Robin a few days later, they'd taken a more direct route, driving two miles along the road, then taking a left up a dirt track mostly concealed by foliage. They had lurched over horrendous potholes for a mile or so, while branches lashed the Land Rover's roof and windscreen, and finally emerged in a dirt clearing.

Bruised and nauseous, Todd had been relieved to discover that from here it had been only a half-hour tramp along mostly flat and wide forest tracks to their destination. When it dawned on him they were approaching the Devil's Throat from the rear, he had asked Yrsa, "Why didn't we come this way the other day?"

She'd given him one of her inscrutable looks, green eyes peering from beneath hooded lids which looked smoky-dark beneath the trees. "Places seem less important when they're easy to get to. I wanted you to appreciate the significance of the tunnels. I wanted you to feel you'd earned your right to see them."

The raised-eyebrow look that Robin had given him had been easy to decipher: *Figure that one out, squirt!*

When Yrsa climbed into the Land Rover today, a few minutes behind Todd, who was waiting in the passenger seat, he was surprised to see she'd brushed her hair into lustrous life, tied it back in a ponytail, and applied full makeup.

"What?" she said when he gaped at her.

"I just thought..." he gestured at his own grungy self, "...the priority would be to get up there, not worry about how we look."

She snorted. "If I turned up looking hassled, that bitch would think she'd won. First rule of business, always look in control of the situation."

"Even when you're not?" said Todd.

That grim smirk again. "That doesn't apply here."

Five minutes later, Todd braced himself as they turned off the road and started along the dirt track to the clearing. Maybe he was still bruised from the first time, but the jarring his bones took felt worse this time. He gritted his teeth, and held tightly to the door frame, and was relieved when they came to a halt.

They hadn't stopped because they'd reached the clearing, though. In front of them, filling their windscreen and framed by foliage, was the arse-end of one of Robin's trucks.

Yrsa cut the engine and hopped out of the vehicle. By the time Todd joined her, she was already speaking to Dev, who had clambered down from the vehicle in front.

"Hey, Dev," Todd said. "What's happening?"

Before Dev could respond, Yrsa was jabbing a hand towards the rear of the truck. "Those losers blocked the route ahead to stop the equipment getting through. Pathetic."

Todd looked at Dev, who was nodding. "That's about the size of it. Whether they did it deliberately to block us or because that was the only way they could get here…" he shrugged, "…who knows?"

"So what happens now?" asked Todd.

"Well, we knew the site wasn't accessible by truck and that we'd have to carry the equipment a little way, so that's not a problem; most of it's pretty light." He patted the back of the truck like it was a gigantic pet. "The tricky bit will be backing these babies up all the way to the road. But we'll make it. We'll just take it slowly."

As ever when faced with a problem, Dev was sanguine. By contrast, Yrsa was sparking with indignation. "So how much of the equipment have you managed to carry up there already?" she asked.

"Some. Not much." He shrugged again. "Not really worth stockpiling it up there if we can't get access to the site. Also, if things turn ugly and Rob and the guys have to beat a hasty retreat, we don't want to leave expensive equipment behind to get damaged."

"So they've left you to guard it?" Todd said.

"Me and Hector. We're here if the enemy launch an attack from the rear."

He looked amused, but Yrsa's face was grim. "Let's go, Todd," she said.

Dev slid his phone from his pocket. "I'll call Rob, let him know the cavalry's on the way."

Yrsa was already stalking away, pushing through the foliage at the side of the truck. Todd gave Dev a quick thumbs-up, and followed her.

Yrsa was a woman on a mission, which made the march through the forest exhausting. She seemed powered by fury, and arrived at their destination still full of righteous anger. Todd, by contrast, had unzipped his jacket and hoodie despite the chill of the day. The gray T-shirt he was wearing beneath was glued to his ribs by dark stripes of sweat.

Robin and the guys were milling around the base of the rocky slope that rose gently towards the Devil's Throat. Big Andy was sitting on the ground and bouncing small pebbles off the toe of his boot; Sean was smoking a roll-up and chatting to Amir, who had his hands stuffed in his pockets; and Jay was sitting on an upturned plastic crate against which various bits of equipment were stacked, his fingers busy with his phone.

At the sound of their approach, Robin, who had been talking to his most recent employee, a portly, red-cheeked guy in his mid-twenties called Luke, raised a weary hand, but only Todd returned the gesture; Yrsa was all business.

"Where are they?" she snapped, like a head teacher called in to deal with rebellious students.

"They're sitting in a circle around the hole."

"Okay."

She said it in such a purposeful way that Todd felt alarmed.

"What are you going to do?" he asked, scrambling after her as she marched up the slope, imagining her pushing the protestors down the shaft one by one.

"I'm going to make them leave."

"How?"

"You'll see."

With her ponytail bouncing behind her and her entourage of curious followers trailing in her wake, she reminded Todd of a female Pied

Piper. He panted hard as he tried to keep up with her, aware, not for the first time, how much fitter than him she was. Although he had no idea what she was planning, he felt his role here was to stop things getting out of hand. The presence of the shaft made him nervous. If tempers flared and things got physical, that big, gaping maw would be an accident waiting to happen.

From here, the route up to the Devil's Throat was like a trio of long, gentle steps rather than a consistent slope. It wasn't until they had crested the second of these, and were about to tackle the final uphill trudge, that they saw the protestors.

There were eight men and five women, the youngest a heavyset guy in his late twenties, who Todd thought had been among the group outside the church the other day, and the oldest Yrsa's mother's friend, Margret Gulbransen, who was stomping about like a tinpot general. Although they looked dour and hard-bitten, their thick sweaters and bulky jackets giving them an intimidating physical presence, it didn't look like they were here for the long haul. There were no banners or placards, no one-man tents or hampers of food, no real sense of permanence. Maybe, Todd thought, the best tactic might be to wait them out, move in when they'd gone. He suggested this to Yrsa, but she shook her head.

"This would only be the start of it, Todd. The people here are like rats. Leave them and they'll keep coming back. And there would be more of them each time."

"So what—" he said, but she had already turned away to continue her ascent. Sighing, he plodded after her.

"Force of nature, that one," breathed Robin, who had caught him up, and was now at his shoulder.

"Tell me about it," said Todd.

Half the protestors had been sitting down when they'd appeared, but now, having spotted Yrsa, they rose to their feet en masse.

Although most of them were physically more imposing than she was, they eyed her warily as she approached. Margret Gulbransen peeled off from the rest and stomped forward to intercept her, the weals where Yrsa had clawed her standing out proud as blood flushed her reddening cheeks.

The old woman barked something, but Yrsa ignored her. Todd tensed when Margret Gulbransen stepped directly into Yrsa's path and began to rant. She'd barely started, though, when Yrsa threw up a hand and interrupted her.

Although Yrsa's voice wasn't particularly loud, she spoke with such venomous intensity that it quickly overrode the old woman's tirade. Todd had no idea what she was saying, but within seconds he saw Margret Gulbransen at first look outraged, and then begin to bluster and stammer. Finally her eyes widened with what looked like shock, and her voice petered out. When she took another stumbling step towards Yrsa, Yrsa's body went rigid and she repeated the warding-off gesture, her arm shooting out, her hand so tightly upraised that her fingers curled back from her flat palm. Margret Gulbransen, whose complexion had turned from ruddy to a sickly gray, flinched, as if she thought Yrsa was about to slap her, and momentarily lost her balance, her left foot skidding on rubble. For a moment her and Yrsa's face-off reminded Todd of an ailing boxing champion trying to stare down a challenger who was younger, fitter, faster. When he saw the old woman's shoulders slump, he almost felt sorry for her. Yrsa's eyes bored into her for a couple more seconds, and then she strode forward, passing her by as if she wasn't there.

Without the protection of their bullish leader, the remaining protestors looked more disparate than ever. They reminded Todd of nervous sheep, unconsciously huddling together, as Yrsa marched towards them. One of them, a sixty-something Viking of a man with a nicotine-stained beard and a nose like an old potato, stepped forward. He raised his hands to either side of his shelf of a belly, and said something clearly intended to be placatory.

Yrsa walked right up to him. He was a head taller than she was, and he looked as if he could reach out with one of his shovel-like hands and remove her head from her body with a deft twist. Even so, alarm flickered in his eyes when Yrsa tilted her gaze up to meet his. Todd only knew she was speaking because he could see her lips moving, but her voice didn't even reach his ears as a low murmur. The Viking heard it, though. His shoulders tensed and he gave a brief nod. Yrsa said something else and then she turned away, like a queen dismissing a courtier.

Behind him, Todd heard one of the guys mutter, "What the fuck was that?"

And then came Sean's only half-joking reply: "Bloody witchcraft, mate."

As Yrsa walked back down to join them, the Viking was already speaking to the other protestors. Next moment they were following him meekly down the slope, refusing to meet the eyes of Robin and his men as they passed by.

Only Margret Gulbransen was still standing her ground, and as Yrsa passed her for the second time, Todd saw the old woman look up and say something. She still looked weary and shell-shocked, but she appeared to have recovered at least a little of her former defiance. Yrsa, though, simply threw back her head and barked a single dismissive laugh.

"What did you say to them?" Robin asked as Yrsa rejoined them.

She shrugged. "I simply pointed out a few home truths."

"What did *she* say to you just now?" Todd asked, nodding at the lonely figure of Margret Gulbransen.

Yrsa followed his gaze, her eyes glittering. "Her words are empty."

"But what did she *say*?"

"She said, 'This is not over.'"

CHAPTER TWENTY-FIVE

"We've bloody earned this, squirt."

"Amen to that. That was a tough day."

"Tell me about it."

Todd watched as Robin glugged half his beer in one go. The older of the Kingston boys gave a blissful gasp as he lowered the bottle, condensation running down its glass sides and pooling on the tabletop.

It was a dozen hours since the incident up at the Devil's Throat. By the time the protestors had left – a lengthy procedure, which had involved backing the Land Rover and Robin's three trucks to the top of the narrow turning to allow the locals to get their vehicles out – the drilling team was already a couple of hours behind the schedule that Robin had set for them. To try and claw back some time, Todd and Yrsa had hung around to help, and while Todd had joined Robin and his men in lugging equipment up to the cave entrance, Yrsa had set up the abseiling gear, so it would be in place when needed.

The rest of the day had been spent relaying men and equipment up and down, and into and through the caves. With Yrsa acting as guide, lights had been set up at the bottom of the shaft, and then through the tunnel network, to the point where the tunnel narrowed prior to widening into the cave containing the wall they were planning to drill through. With the lighting in place, they had lowered the drilling equipment down and transported it along the tunnels. Yrsa and Todd had squeezed through into the final cave, and the equipment had been passed through piece by piece, before being wrapped in tarpaulin and stowed in a dry corner, prior to the real work beginning the following day. Most of the guys had squeezed through the aperture one by one to take a look at the wall, though three of them – Big Andy, Luke and Hector, a stocky Greek guy with a hard pot belly – had been unable to fit through the gap. There'd been some talk of widening the aperture there and then, but by this time it was almost six p.m. Everyone was grimy, exhausted and more than ready for a shower, some food and a few beers, so it was decided to leave it until the following day.

"We can probably only have two or three guys in there at any one time anyway," Robin had said, meaning the cave, "so it'll give the others something to do while they're waiting their turn."

Dusk was falling by the time the men piled into the trucks for the journey back to town. Robin, the last to climb aboard, gave Yrsa a hug and thanked her for her help, and then he wrapped his arms around his younger brother too, dragging him into an embrace.

Before Todd could break away, Robin, his breath smelling of the bitter coffee that had sustained them through the day, put his mouth close to his younger brother's ear and breathed, "Think you can get away later?"

"Sure," Todd said. "Why?"

Robin released him from the hug, then looked over Todd's shoulder and raised a hand. Through the smile that Todd knew he must be directing towards Yrsa, who was opening the door of the Land Rover, he muttered, "Want to talk to you about Yrsa in private. Meet me in the hotel bar in a couple of hours."

Todd put off mentioning Robin's request to Yrsa for as long as possible, fearing she'd want to come too. By seven forty-five p.m., though, he knew he could delay it no longer. Wandering into the main room, where Yrsa was stretched out on the settee, tapping away on her laptop, he said, "I've just had a text from Rob, asking if I'll meet him for a beer. You don't mind, do you?"

He'd already rehearsed the scene in his head. When Yrsa suggested accompanying him, he'd pull an apologetic face and tell her he had a feeling Robin wanted to talk privately about their dad's impending retirement and how it should be handled in terms of the family business. Maybe he'd add something about how Robin was hoping Todd would eventually join him in the family firm, and how Todd would have to tactically tell him that wasn't going to happen.

As it turned out, though, he didn't need to say any of this. Yrsa glanced at him, then turned back to her laptop.

"'Course not," she said. "Tell him hi from me."

"Will do," Todd said, surprised and relieved. "I won't be late."

"Be as late as you like. I'll probably go to bed early. Love you."

"Love you too."

Todd now picked up his own beer and took a sip. The hotel bar was nowhere near as busy as it had been the last time he'd been here, and he wondered whether most of the locals were boycotting the place due to the presence of Robin and his men. Not that Robin's guys seemed bothered by the standoffishness of the natives. Like their boss, they were enjoying some downtime, clustered round a couple of tables laden with beers and snacks. Todd saw Dev, ever the diplomat, chatting amiably to a middle-aged couple at the bar. Unless the couple were here to glean information about the foreign invaders, it was heartening to see that not everyone on the island was a member of the Anti-Yrsa Society.

In the relaxed atmosphere, Todd felt the tension he'd been carrying since his arrival on Eldfjallaeyja easing a little. It was good to have his brother and the guys here. It wasn't until now that he realized how lonely he'd been, despite Yrsa's presence.

"So," he said, "what did you want to talk about?"

Robin took another swig of beer. Without preamble he said, "What the fuck happened this morning, Todd?"

Todd hesitated. He'd been expecting this, and he knew there was no point in prevaricating. Running his fingers down the sides of his bottle, creating clear lines through the condensation, he said, "To be honest, I don't know."

"It was freaky," Robin said. "I mean, I like Yrsa, don't get me wrong. She's ballsy and headstrong, but that's not a bad thing. She reminds me of Mum, to be fair. But this morning she was something else. It was like she had a weird hold over those people."

"I did hear Sean mention witchcraft," Todd admitted.

"Not only Sean. A couple of the lads were freaked out. Sorry to tell you this, squirt, but...Yrsa unsettles them."

Todd grunted a laugh. "She unsettles me too sometimes."

Robin picked up his bottle, used it to gesture towards the tables where his men were sitting. "Some of the lads are wondering what they've got themselves into here."

"What did you tell them?"

"That it was just a job and not to be so soft." He took a long swig, finishing the bottle. "Another?"

Todd had taken only a couple of sips of his own beer. "Better not. I'm driving."

"Good call. Back in a minute."

The barman was Olav, the same guy who had served them the other night. Catching Todd's eye as he watched his brother's progress to the bar, he gave a small nod of recognition. As soon as Robin sat back down, a fresh beer in his hand, he asked, "Did you talk to Yrsa about it?"

"A bit. She didn't say much."

"Did she tell you what she told that old woman?"

"The old woman's called Margret Gulbransen, and she was Yrsa's mother's best friend, believe it or not. Yrsa told me she accused Margret of using her mum's name as an excuse to...well, to be a bitch basically, and that her mum would be disgusted if she knew how Margret was stirring up hatred towards her best friend's daughter."

"Ouch," said Robin, then looked thoughtful. "Although if that *is* what Yrsa said, and I'm not saying it isn't, then the old woman's reaction seemed a bit...extreme to me. I mean, I could understand the old girl looking ashamed, but she looked...shocked. Scared even."

Todd shrugged. "I don't know what else Yrsa said to her, but she did tell me she gave Margret Gulbransen a right mouthful. Said she told her a few home truths." Feeling a need to provide a halfway acceptable explanation of the incident, he added, "When she wants to be, Yrsa can be very articulate and cutting."

"I don't doubt it," said Robin. "And what about the others?"

"What others?"

"Up at the site. Yrsa said something to them too, and they buggered off quick-smart. She twisted that big bloke round her little finger."

"She told me she threatened them with the law. Said she had some powerful legal contacts who could make things very bad for them if they intimidated any of the drilling team or damaged any of the equipment."

"And can she?"

"I've no idea. I wouldn't put it past her."

Robin laughed. "Me neither. She's a bloody powerhouse, that one. You sure you can handle her, squirt?"

His brother's words made Todd think of the Yrsa who had run naked into the forest, and had later rutted with him like a wild animal. "'Course I can."

"You don't sound very sure."

"No, I am. We get on great. It's just…things have been a bit weird since getting here."

"Weird how?"

There was a part of Todd that wanted to tell his brother everything. But he knew it wouldn't be wise to add yet more fuel to the fire. So he shrugged and said, "Just the way the locals have been towards us. You know what Yrsa thinks of them – that they're all a bunch of superstitious savages. What with that and the funeral, I can't say things have been relaxing."

"I hear you." Robin lifted his bottle and tilted it towards Todd in a salute before taking a swig. Todd took a swallow of his own beer, and felt as though he was swilling away the stale taste of his disquiet.

"So what do you want me to do?" he asked. "About Yrsa, I mean? Do you want me to keep her away from the drill site?"

"Do you think you'd be able to?"

"I can try."

"Good luck with that one." Robin smiled and drank more beer. After a moment he said, "Tell you what, though – we wouldn't normally allow civilians on building sites anyway, not without permission, not without being supervised, and not without them wearing the correct protective equipment. If ever we give tours to clients or prospective buyers, we down tools for the duration. It wouldn't do to drop a brick on a visiting dignitary's head. Now, I know how keen Yrsa is for us to drill through into that cave, so if you were to tell her that, due to health and safety regs, we'd have to stop work every time she paid us a visit..."

"She'd stay away," said Todd.

"Exactly." Robin raised his hands in apology. "Just want to make it doubly clear, though, that it's not that *I've* got anything against her. You get that, right?"

"Totally," said Todd.

Silence fell between them. Robin looked contemplative as he took another sip of beer, and Todd got the feeling he had something else on his mind. Sure enough, after placing his bottle carefully on the table, Robin said, "You know what else is a bit strange?"

"What?"

Robin grimaced, as if unsure how to put his thoughts into words. "Remember the other day, when you, me and Yrsa went into the tunnels and you said you'd seen something in the video? A figure?"

"And you laughed at me," said Todd.

"Yeah, well..." Robin looked uncomfortable. "Thing is...some of the other lads reckon they've seen and heard things too."

"Really? Who?"

Robin slid his eyes towards the tables, where his men were drinking. In a low voice he said, "Young Luke claimed he heard someone moving about in one of the side tunnels. I told him it was probably an animal – a rat or something – but he swore blind it was something bigger. And Amir said when he was setting up the lights, he saw someone out of the corner of his eye, standing further up the tunnel, watching him. He turned his head, thinking it was one of the other guys, but when the light from his helmet swung round, there was nobody there. Except..." He grunted a laugh and shook his head.

"What?" prompted Todd.

"Didn't you say the figure you thought you saw in the video was a little feller?"

"That's what it looked like," said Todd.

"Yeah, well, it's probably just a coincidence, but that's what Amir said too. He said the figure he saw was short. Like a child or a dwarf."

CHAPTER TWENTY-SIX

Like her, the Nissan Combi was old and temperamental. When she brought it to a creaking halt, it sputtered a moment before groaning to silence. The instant its engine and headlights died, the darkness closed in. Although the sky was more blue than black, and peppered with stars, what little light remained in it did not extend to the forest.

Alone in the parking area at the end of the bumpy track, Margret Gulbransen looked through the windscreen at trees so saturated with shadow they had fused into an impenetrable mass. She couldn't even see the track between them, though that wouldn't be a problem. She knew she was alone out here, which meant she could illuminate the path ahead without fear of detection. The *veksling* and her human mate – who must be either enchanted or depraved – were embedded in the home of her old friend Ása Helgerson, and the English fools the *veksling* had brought here to do her bidding were drinking themselves senseless in the hotel they had infested like cockroaches.

Margret still felt jittery from that morning's encounter with the interloper who dared call herself Ása's daughter, but she was damned if she was going to allow the creature to get her own way without resistance. When she told her friend and neighbor, Eyjólfur Hannesson, how the *veksling* had used her dark magic to crush her chest in a vise and begin to drain her life energy, his bewhiskered face had creased in doubt.

"Are you sure it wasn't just your heart, Margret?" he had said. "It was bad even before the girl came back. You know Dr. Örn told you to avoid stress and excitement."

Margret, though, knew better. "It was *her*. You can't deny her evil influence. If you have any doubt in your mind, it was that creature that put it there."

Eyjólfur had sighed and leaned forward to wrap his hand around the mug of gritty coffee that Margret had made for him, his vast belly resting in his lap. "We don't even know why she's here. Since she was a little girl she's said—"

"That thing has never been a little girl. And that story about the boat in the cave is nothing but a veil."

"A veil for what?" Eyjólfur's voice had been weary.

"Once we find out it will be too late. We mustn't let what happened today stop us. We must make our voices heard, banish her if we can."

"And how are we going to do that?"

He had sounded defeated; perhaps the *veksling* had used some dark enchantment to sap the fight from him too. "By targeting her weak spots. Driving away the underlings she relies on."

"The English, you mean?"

"Of course!"

"Again, how?"

She had narrowed her eyes. "I have ideas."

Margret massaged the spot on her breastbone that was still sore. Perhaps she did have a bad heart, but that didn't mean the *veksling* hadn't rooted out and taken advantage of that weakness. The fact that the creature had not shown its hand so blatantly, that it had used its dark magic to weaken Margret in a way that could be explained as a natural ailment, suggested it was yet vulnerable. The *veksling* had given Margret a scare, but not a permanent one. While there was still breath in her body, she would oppose it.

When she swung her legs out of the van and stood up, she was not sure whether the creak she heard came from the vehicle's suspension or her own bones. Stumping to the rear of the van, she opened the double doors and was assailed anew by the stink of rotting fish she'd grown more or less used to on the drive here. Leaning forward, she grabbed a head torch and forced it over her wiry gray curls, adjusting the headband so it was nice and tight. Then she reached for the two-wheeled sack trolley, which was lying in the back, and dragged it towards her, gasping with exertion even though the thing was made of lightweight metal.

She leaned it against the van, ragged breaths huffing from her pursed lips. Now came the hardest part. The four sixty-liter plastic barrels might only be half as tall as she was, but, brim-full of rotting fish, they were backbreakingly heavy.

With an effort, she clambered into the van and shuffled the nearest barrel towards the open doors, working with the constantly shifting weight as the contents sloshed from side to side. When the barrel was as close to the lip of the bed as she could get it, she took a renewed grip on the raised rim of the barrel's lid and tried to tilt it towards her.

At first it seemed too heavy, but she continued to heave until the barrel's contents began to shift, redistributing the weight. At last her efforts were rewarded, and she was able to tip the barrel and shove it forward, off the edge of the van bed and onto the waiting trolley. As the barrel slid down the trolley's curved back, Margret lunged for the handles. She grabbed them and bore down just as the barrel hit the flat metal bottom of the trolley. The pressure she was exerting prevented the heavy barrel from flipping the trolley over. Even so, the handles were wrenched from her hands with so much force it was like being kicked by a mule in both palms. She yelled in pain as the trolley snapped into an upright position.

For a moment the barrel teetered forward, and Margret held her breath, half-expecting it to tumble over and burst open, spilling its cargo of fish guts across the ground. But after an agonizing second it slumped back and came to rest.

She breathed a sigh of relief, her heart fluttering like a trapped moth. Suddenly she felt sick and faint, and had to sit down, her broad back sliding down the inside wall of the van. She closed her eyes momentarily, but didn't realize she'd grayed out until a sound from the forest – a rustle of leaves or the crack of a twig – made her snap back into consciousness. As she looked out of the back of the van, the light from her head torch swept the screen of trees like a feeble searchlight.

There was nothing there. The sound must have been made by some animal, which had now slunk into the darkness. Taking a deep breath, she put a hand on her chest. She felt a little better now, her heart beating at a steadier rate. It would be a struggle hauling the trolley up the hill, and not just once but four times, but Margret was determined to give it a try; anything to slow down the *veksling*'s intentions. Was it too much to hope that her actions might even upset the English invaders enough to make them abandon the task the *veksling* had employed them for? If not, perhaps she, or some of the many who agreed with her, could persuade them to leave. She knew diplomacy was not her strongpoint, that where the *veksling* was concerned she allowed her anger and her hatred to overwhelm her, but that was understandable. Ása had been her friend since childhood, and it had torn Margret apart to see how that creature had manipulated her, ground her down, and eventually, through some remote and diabolical agency, hounded her to death.

Margret had always known it would come to this, and now, after half a lifetime of waiting, she was ready for the fight. She scrambled from the van and took a grip on the handles of the trolley, wincing at the tenderness of her bruised palms. With the beam from her head torch lighting the way, she set off through the forest, wheeling the trolley ahead of her. Most of the going was relatively easy, and she hoped that on subsequent trips, when she returned with the second, third and fourth barrels, she would be able to use this part of the journey as a way of regaining her strength before the final strenuous toil uphill.

She was about halfway along the track, and had settled into a steady rhythm, when one of the trees ahead of her moved. She didn't see it clearly – she was concentrating on the ground to ensure there were no obstacles in her path – but it registered in her peripheral vision strongly enough for her to jolt to a halt, her head snapping up. Admittedly the trees flanking the track had seemed to step forward in turn as the light from her head torch had swept across them, but this movement was different. This time a part of the trunk, low to the ground, had seemed to twist towards her, and then to dart smartly back behind the tree directly in front of it. The obvious explanation was that the light had dazzled some animal, which had fled into the trees. The fact that the 'animal' had appeared to be standing upright must have been nothing but a fanciful notion.

Fanciful or not, the experience spooked her. She was suddenly overcome by the sense she was being watched. Her head darted left and right, the beam from her head torch veering about in the trees. Black, contorted shapes dipped and dodged between the trunks, refusing to be snared by the light. But they were only shadows, made darker by the contrast that the light provided. After ten seconds of mounting panic, Margret felt her angry resolve asserting itself. She had come here to make a stand against something far more fearsome than her own imagination. She refused to allow herself to be frightened by the dark, like a timid child.

Defiantly welcoming the pain in her hands as she tightened her grip on the handles, she continued on her way. The fish guts sloshed in the barrel, and the beam from her head torch bobbed along the uneven path. If dark shapes were keeping pace with her, they were simply absences of light, nothing to be alarmed about. And if the leaves and bushes occasionally rustled, it was only the wind passing through them.

Another ten minutes of stolid, focused walking brought Margret to the base of the trio of slopes that led up to the Devil's Throat. Gentle as these slopes were, she knew hauling the trolley uphill would take it out of her. But she was determined, and even if lining the Devil's Throat with rotten fish guts didn't *stop* the English invaders, it would at least make things extremely unpleasant for them. If her efforts only hampered the *veksling*'s operations for a day or two, it would be worth it.

Glancing up the slope to assess the best route, she was momentarily distracted by the sight of a large rock on her right. On a whim she left the cart where it was and cast about for a loose stone. After a few seconds of searching, she found one, and stumping over to the rock, she lowered herself gingerly to her knees and scratched a symbol into it – a circle bisected into quarters by a cross. Where the four points of the cross met the inner edge of the circle, she drew four further semi-circles, and then bisected each of the four lines radiating out from the center of the 'crossroads' with two shorter lines.

Satisfied with her handiwork, she straightened up, leaning back on her heels. Though crude, the ancient runic symbol was a protection against evil. She doubted it would stop the *veksling*, but she hoped it might give it pause, or even irk it physically – the spiritual equivalent of a nettle sting.

She tossed the stone aside, and was gritting her teeth in readiness to unbend her aching knees, when she heard rubble shift behind her.

Instinctively she twisted round, crying out as hot, wrenching pain tore up her back and into her neck, before exploding like a firework in her skull. For several seconds the pain was so bad it literally blinded her. The shifting of rubble had sounded like someone creeping up behind her, and now she imagined that 'someone' getting closer as she floundered on her hands and knees. Despite her vow not to succumb to fear, she couldn't prevent herself screeching raggedly, "Who are you? Who's there?"

Receiving no reply, she tried to slow her breathing and will the pain away. It wasn't easy, but eventually the pain began to ebb, and she was able to ease herself back into an upright position and slowly raise her head.

The light from her head torch showed her there was no one creeping up behind her, nor lurking nearby. Her sack trolley with its barrel of fish guts was standing exactly where she had left it. Grunting with effort, she heaved herself to her feet. Puffing like a weight lifter, she stood a moment, then stumped across to the trolley. Her torchlight raked the trees as she rechecked the edge of the forest, then she grabbed the handles of the trolley and began to back slowly up the slope.

Ascending one agonizing step at a time, she glanced behind her frequently, and every dozen steps or so she stopped to rest. Anxious as she was to get this over and done with, she knew she had to be both patient and dogged. It was over twenty minutes later when the vegetation started to become more plentiful, a sure sign she was nearing her destination. By now she was drenched in sweat, and wheezing like a chronic asthmatic. Turning carefully to look behind her, so as not to reawaken the pain in her spine and neck, Margret tried to plot a course through the tangle of undergrowth. Fortunately, the English had done her a favor, having trampled a route back and forth earlier that day while fetching their equipment. Speaking of which, if they had been foolish enough to leave any of that equipment on the surface, she would happily push it down the shaft along with the contents of her barrels.

When she reached the Devil's Throat, though, she saw no evidence the English had ever been there. They had clearly already lowered their equipment into the tunnels, and had even been cautious enough to remove whatever gear they'd used to descend the shaft. Breath rasping, hair a damp, frizzy mop, she dragged the trolley up the last few feet before parking it on a flat piece of ground. Releasing the handles, she slumped beside it, utterly exhausted. But despite her physical discomfort, she grinned in triumph. She had made it! One barrel down – or rather, up – three more to go.

Somewhere below her, stones clattered.

Margret froze. The sound had come from just beyond the edge of the third and final plateau, which from her current position was obscured from view. Could it be a delayed shifting of stones, made by her own feet or the wheels of the trolley? Or perhaps it was an animal, come to investigate her exertions? If so, she would frighten it away.

Brushing her hand across the ground, she found a stone that fit snugly into her fist. She drew back her arm with the intention of tossing it in the direction of the clattering sound – but then, from behind her, she heard scuffling echoes coming from the Devil's Throat itself.

The sounds could only mean one thing: something was clambering up the shaft! Her back erupted in gooseflesh as she heaved her bulk around. Even before her head torch had swung fully to illuminate the Devil's Throat, she saw a dark shape swelling out of it. When the light fell on the thing's face, her lungs seemed to clamp shut. Immediately blackness swarmed across her vision, and she felt herself dwindling. Her last sense to shut down was her hearing, which registered a scuttling approach from two directions: from the mouth of the shaft above her, and the rocky slope below.

CHAPTER TWENTY-SEVEN

"You seen the sky?" said Todd.

He was kneeling on the bed, leaning over Yrsa, his head stuck between the curtains. He ducked back into the room to see Yrsa peering at him through one sleepy eye.

"What about it?"

"It's black. Really black. Like there's going to be a thunderstorm."

She turned over, unimpressed, closing the eye again. "There probably is."

"Let's hope it won't stop the drilling."

She opened both eyes this time. "Why should it?"

"If there's a downpour it might flood the caves."

"It won't."

"How do you know?"

"I know those caves. They've never flooded. There are plenty of outlets for water to flow away."

"It'd get slippery up there, though. With all the bare rock and everything. Health and safety nightmare."

"They'll be underground. And they've got hard hats, in case they fall. What's your problem, Todd?"

"I'm just saying, that's all."

She gave a big sigh and pushed herself into a sitting position. "No, you're not. You're working your way around to saying something you think I won't like. You're as subtle as a kick."

"A brick," Todd corrected automatically.

"What?"

"The phrase is 'subtle as a brick'."

Her eyes narrowed. "I'll kick your balls very hard in a moment, and then you'll see that I'm right."

He bared his teeth in a mock grimace and cupped his hands protectively over his testicles.

"So tell me," she said.

He sighed. "It's just something Robin said in the pub. He felt a bit awkward about it. He knows this is a pet project of yours, but he said as soon as he and his guys start work, we won't be able to go down there to oversee operations. If we did, they'd have to stop drilling, in case one of us got injured, 'cos we're not covered on their insurance. He wasn't sure how you'd feel about that."

Yrsa regarded him steadily, in a way that made Todd feel she knew there was more to it. But then she smiled and shrugged.

"That's fine. If I want to go into the tunnels I'll contact Robin and make an appointment."

Todd was relieved. "You don't mind?"

"I'm not a control freak."

"That's news to me," he said, grinning.

"I really will kick you in the balls in a minute."

He leaped off the bed, and was crossing the room to the closet when someone banged loudly on the door downstairs.

"Fuck," he said, yanking the closet open. He dressed hurriedly, and was still fumbling to do up the fly buttons on his jeans when the hammering came again.

"I'm coming!"

He thumped along the landing and ran down the stairs barefoot. He opened the door to see a stocky, bearded man glowering at him. The man was wearing a black baseball cap ringed with a band of two-tone checks just above the peak, and a bulky jacket with plenty of front pockets. A walkie-talkie was attached to his left breast pocket, beneath a strip of white lettering that read 'Police' in English.

"Oh," Todd said, surprised. "Sorry, we were just..." As words deserted him, he waved a hand vaguely.

The man looked him up and down, his lip curling as his gaze alighted on Todd's long, white feet.

"Mr. Kingston?" His voice was clipped and heavily accented.

"Yes. Todd. Er…my name's Todd."

"Mr. Kingston, I'm Detective Constable Hagen. Can I come in?"

"Yeah, sure." Todd moved back hastily, swinging the door wide, and DC Hagen stepped inside, exuding cold, wintry air. Leaning awkwardly around the police officer to shut the door, Todd indicated the door to the main room. "Shall we talk in here?"

DC Hagen had been looking around, as though assessing the décor, but now he fixed Todd with a deadpan gaze. "Fine."

He was moving towards the door, Todd hovering behind him like a nervous butler, when a sharp voice said, "What are you doing here, Anders?"

Both men turned. Yrsa was descending the stairs, looking cool and stylish in a black sweater, skinny-fit jeans and black pumps. Her hair was glossy and she had even put on makeup. Todd felt like a tramp by comparison.

Until now, Todd had been so taken aback by their visitor's arrival that he hadn't had time to wonder *why* DC Hagen was here. Suddenly it occurred to him to ask, "Is this about Robin? Has something happened?"

The police officer's gaze was emotionless as a shark's. "Robin?"

"My brother. He's staying in town. He's here with some of his—"

"Yes," DC Hagen cut in, "I'm aware of your brother's arrival. No, this isn't about him. Not directly anyway."

"What do you mean, not directly?" Yrsa asked.

The corridor was narrow and dingy, which made their proximity to one another seem confrontational somehow. As though making a point, DC Hagen turned and entered the main room without answering Yrsa's question. Yrsa pursed her lips and marched in after him, Todd bringing up the rear.

The police officer strode over to the fireplace and stood in front of the charred remains in the grate, his gaze still roaming restlessly.

"Can't find what you're looking for?" Yrsa said in a challenging tone.

DC Hagen's gaze snapped back to her, and for a moment he looked contrite. "My apologies. I was thinking about the last time I was here, when..."

"When my mother died."

"Yes."

"She was found outside, wasn't she? Was she brought in here?"

DC Hagen nodded. "Yes. She was laid on the sofa and wrapped in blankets. Sven lit a fire – he was the one who found her, as I'm sure you know – but it was too late. She was gone."

Todd looked at the shabby settee and swallowed. He'd stretched out on there several times, blissfully unaware that Yrsa's dead mother had been laid out on it. As though in defiance, Yrsa walked nonchalantly over to the settee in question and sat down. Todd looked at DC Hagen to gauge his reaction. The police officer's expression was neutral.

"So are you going to tell us why you're here, or do we have to guess?"

Todd could see that Yrsa was in a bristly mood. She was clearly unintimidated by the dour police officer, who was maybe ten or fifteen years older than them. Todd was wondering whether DC Hagen might have been part of the rescue team who had found Yrsa in the tunnels as a child – perhaps he had even investigated the death of the boy who had bullied Yrsa and subsequently drowned – when the policeman said, "I understand you've had some trouble with Margret Gulbransen?"

Yrsa rolled her eyes. "What about it?"

"When was the last time you saw her?"

"Yesterday morning, up at the Devil's Throat." She smirked. "Is she still causing trouble?"

"Not exactly. She's dead."

Todd felt a physical jolt at the news. He glanced at Yrsa, but she looked as though she was determined not to react.

"What happened?" Todd asked.

"It appears she had a heart attack."

"What has that to do with us?" asked Yrsa.

"She was found up at the Devil's Throat this morning."

"Alone?" said Todd. "I mean, none of the other protestors were with her?"

"No. It was thought she went up there late last night."

"Why?"

Hagen sighed. "We can only speculate, but there was a trolley nearby, containing a barrel full of rotting fish parts. Her van was found in the parking area with three similar barrels in the back."

Abruptly Yrsa laughed. "She meant to sabotage the drilling site. Throw fish guts around, perhaps pour them down the shaft." Her laughter increased. "Silly old bitch!"

"Yrsa," Todd said, shocked. "Don't be so…I mean, she's dead."

"So? She brought it on herself. She was a mean bitch and her meanness killed her."

"What do you mean, her meanness killed her?"

"Her heart must have given out under the strain of pulling that cart all the way up to the Devil's Throat." She looked at DC Hagen. "Is that what happened?"

"It's…likely."

"But what?" said Todd. "Is there more to it? Otherwise, why would you come here?"

Hagen's eyes were dark, his face like stone. "There were marks on her body. Signs she might have been attacked."

"By who?"

Before Hagen could respond, Yrsa said, "Animals probably. There are boars in the forest, rodents, birds, foxes. If she's been lying there all night, any of those might have seen her as a tasty treat."

There was a dark, vicious humor in her voice, which Todd found distasteful. "Is it possible she was attacked by animals?" he asked.

Hagen said, "A postmortem will tell us what we need to know. But we won't get the results for a few days. In the meantime, where were you both last night?"

"I was here," said Yrsa. "All night."

"And you, Mr. Kingston?"

"I went to the hotel for a drink with my brother."

"And what time was this?"

"I got there about eight, and got back here about...eleven fifteen or so."

"And Miss Helgerson was here when you returned?"

"Yes. She was asleep in bed."

"So you didn't speak to her?"

"Not until about fifteen minutes ago. We'd only just woken up when you arrived."

"And you have only the one vehicle between you?"

"Yes. The Land Rover. Which I used to go to the hotel."

Yrsa was smiling. "So what do you think, Anders? That I used my witchy powers to change into a wolf and run fleet foot to the Devil's Throat?"

DC Hagen glared at her. "This is not a joke, Yrsa. I'm simply making inquiries. In light of your relationship with Mrs. Gulbransen, isn't that a natural thing to do?"

"Of course it is," said Yrsa, but there was a mocking smile on her face.

CHAPTER TWENTY-EIGHT

Although his ear protectors reduced the screech of the drills to little more than a dull roar, Robin could still feel their vibrations through the rock. After a delayed start, they were now into their third day of drilling and things were going well. The first day after the initial setup they'd been unable to access the site, because it had been cordoned off with police tape. Robin and his men had sat around while the island's limited force – a grumpy, bearded DC, a tall, nervous-looking young man with a prominent Adam's apple, and a girl so swamped by her uniform that she made Robin think of his own first day at school wearing clothes his mum had told him he'd grow into – had spent most of the daylight hours scouring the area for evidence.

It was ironic that by dying, Margret Gulbransen had achieved her aim of delaying the start of their operation. The men had already been unsettled by Luke's and Amir's claims they had seen and heard weird things in the tunnels, and the lack of activity only served to make them more jittery. Although the delay had ultimately been a short one, Robin had never been more grateful to get back to work. In the past forty-eight hours there had been no further setbacks, and the operation was now running pretty much like clockwork.

Most of the first day back had been spent widening the narrow passage into the inner cave to allow both men and equipment through. Since yesterday morning, two guys had been taking it in turns to man the twin pneumatic rock drills that had been subsequently set up in the cave.

Because of the rotation system, with the guys working staggered shifts, they had been able to keep at least one or both drills going almost constantly for a good twelve hours at a time. The drills were mounted on pusher legs, which gave them the appearance of upright machine guns, and they chipped away at the wall sliver by sliver, and occasionally, in the more brittle areas, chunk by chunk, halting intermittently so that staff changeovers could be made, coolant replenished and rock debris cleared away.

Luke and Big Andy were manning the drills currently – a double-pronged attack on the wall – and as far as Robin could tell, a pleasing amount of progress had been made. He had originally told Yrsa it might take four or five days, perhaps a week, to drill a big enough hole through the rock, but his thinking now was that his more optimistic projection actually looked like being closest to the mark. If they didn't make a breakthrough by the end of tomorrow, it would be the following day for sure.

He pressed his back against the wall as Amir and Hector bustled through, carrying another load of rock debris. The floor was too uneven, and some of the tunnels too narrow, to get carts through, so the debris was being shifted the old-fashioned way – two men at each end of what amounted to a canvas hammock full of rubble.

Like him, Amir and Hector were wearing yellow hard hats, tough protective overalls and steel-capped boots. Also like him, they were wearing ear protectors, which meant that conversation was at a minimum.

As Amir glanced at him, his face shiny with sweat and his eyes glittering in the wash of light from Robin's head torch, Robin gave him a thumbs-up. Amir nodded to show all was well – just as the roar of the drills was curtailed by a sharp sound like the crack of a giant whip.

As all three men froze, then turned towards the cave where the drilling was taking place, another sound pierced the sudden silence – a primal wail of human pain. Next second someone was yelling for help, the sound faint and flat through Robin's ear protectors, but by then he was already running.

He careered along the tunnels and through the widened passage, tearing the ear protectors from his head as he burst into the cave. Useful though the protectors were to drown out the ratcheting scream of the drills, they had a distancing quality, and Robin felt this would be a situation where he'd need his senses and wits about him.

He took in the scene at a glance: Luke lying on the ground, his drill in pieces beside him; Big Andy, his own drill having been switched off but still standing upright, crouched over him, trying both to calm and restrain him.

No, not restrain him. It was only on second glance that Robin saw the blood. Against the dull blue of Luke's overalls it looked black – and there was a lot of it. It seemed to cover the left side of Luke's torso from his armpit to his hip, and it was beneath him too, a widening pool spreading across the rocky floor. It looked as though Luke had slipped on a pool of oil and fallen on his arse.

Seeing the blood made Robin realize that Big Andy was pressing his gloved hands to the wound, or wounds, in Luke's body, to stem the flow. Luke's face was twisted in agony, and looked chalky white in the light from Big Andy's headlamp. By contrast, Andy's bearded face was flushed and sweaty with panic. He was gibbering at Luke, telling him he was going to be all right.

"Holy fuck!" said a voice behind Robin. It was Hector. He and Amir had abandoned their hammock of rubble and were crowding into the cave behind Robin, their combined bulk filling the doorway. Thinking quickly, Robin said, "You two, go back, dump your load, and bring the sheet back here. We'll need to carry Luke out." As both men nodded and ran back the way they had come, he shouted after them, "And dump it somewhere where we won't have to climb over it."

That done, he rushed over to the corner of the cave where they had stashed the first-aid box, then hurried back to where Luke was lying. Dropping to his knees beside Andy, he said breathlessly, "What happened?"

"Drill head must have sheared off...I didn't really see... It all happened so fast..."

Sweat was running down Andy's fat cheeks, and his eyes were rolling; he looked as though he was hyperventilating.

"Deep breaths," Robin said, already tearing open the first-aid box. "He'll be all right."

Secretly he was thinking that things looked bad, and that there was nothing in the first aid box bulky enough, or absorbent enough, to stem the flow of blood. Pulling out bandages, unraveling them and wadding them into a ball, he said, "Where's all this blood coming from?"

Andy pointed. "His side...just under the ribs." He took a huge breath. "Drill head must have flown back...sliced through him..."

Luke was groaning softly now, his eyes fluttering, his lips very pale. Now that Andy had pointed it out, Robin saw the gash in Luke's overalls – cut as neatly as if with a pair of shears – and the equally neat gash in his flesh beneath. Something was bulging out of the gash (muscle, fat, intestines?) and the blood was still gushing, like water.

Robin pressed the wad of bandages against the wound, and almost immediately saw the mass of white gauze turn red, felt the material become slick, then sodden, beneath his hands.

How many pints of blood in a human body? Eight? Ten? How much could you lose and still survive? Robin didn't know, but every second that passed here was vital. Twisting his head he shouted, "Where's that fucking—"

But here was Amir, dragging the canvas sheet. Hector was behind him, holding his end clear of the floor.

"Lay it down as close to him as you can," Robin said. "I'll keep the pressure on this and you three lift him onto it. Quickly but carefully."

Robin concentrated on pressing the now-sopping wad of blood-soaked bandage against Luke's side while Hector and Amir dropped the sheet and flanked him. Together, the four of them maneuvred Luke's now-limp body onto the canvas sheet. As they did, there was an almighty rumbling from above, which seemed to reverberate through the stone walls of the cave.

Amir's voice was hushed and scared. "What the fuck was that?"

Robin remembered how black and brooding the sky had become these past few days.

"Just thunder," he said.

CHAPTER TWENTY-NINE

The crash of thunder rattled the little house so much that Todd thought it was an earthquake. He gripped the edge of the kitchen table and watched the picture on the screen of his laptop flicker and strobe a moment before settling.

"Shit, did you hear that?" he shouted, realizing what a dumb question it was the instant it was out of his mouth. "It sounded like it was right above us."

Before Yrsa, who was upstairs, could respond, there was a flash like a camera going off, followed by a vast whooshing noise. Instinctively he hunched his shoulders, his fingertips going white as he gripped the table even tighter. Then the whooshing became a hammering, as if a thousand small drums were being pummeled simultaneously. When Todd looked up at the window, he saw the glass rippling with curtains of rain, the world beyond dark and distorted by the sudden torrential downpour.

The storm had been threatening to break for several days, brooding clouds massing overhead like an invasion force. Yesterday, he and Yrsa had driven to the unpopulated western coast of the island, where the gray, rubbly shore was mostly inaccessible beneath jagged cliffs you'd need abseiling gear to reach. They'd huddled on the cliff top in the brutally aggressive wind, Yrsa's dark hair thrashing around her face, and watched the slate-gray ocean raging below.

"It's like something alive," Todd had shouted. "Alive and trying to get at us."

"It *is* alive," Yrsa had replied. "And it will still be here long after we're dead and gone."

By 'we', Todd hadn't been sure whether she meant the two of them, or humankind in general. Before he could ask, there'd been a growl of thunder, followed almost immediately by a flash of lightning on the horizon, like a thin, jagged crack in the windowpane of reality.

Todd had expected rain then, but it hadn't come. The storm had remained far out at sea, visible only as dirty streaks on the horizon. Since then there had been further distant rumbles of thunder, but it hadn't amounted to anything.

Until now.

He was still looking at the rain, mesmerized by its sinewy writhing on the glass, when Yrsa burst into the room. He hadn't heard her come downstairs; her footsteps must have been absorbed by the rain. She had a huge grin on her face, and her eyes were wide and bright, like a child excited by the arrival of the ice-cream man.

"It's happened!" she said. "It's here!"

Todd couldn't help grinning along with her; her glee was infectious. "It certainly is."

"I have to greet it," she said.

"What do you—" Todd began, but she had already ducked out of the room and was heading back down the narrow corridor towards the front door.

"Hey!" Todd said. He stood up and went after her. By the time he exited the kitchen, she had already reached the front door and was pulling it open.

"Yrsa!" Todd cried, as if it wasn't rain out there but a pack of wolves.

The rain and wind rushed into the house like something alive. Yrsa had pulled the door no more than a few inches open when the elements slammed against it, shoving it so hard she was forced to let go of the handle and take a rapid step back. As the door smashed against the wall and rain sluiced over her like the jet from a sprinkler, she arched her back and raised her face to it, welcoming it like an anointment.

"Yrsa, don't—" Todd cried, but she plunged outside, into the rain, before he could complete his sentence. He'd taken no more than a step along the rain-swept corridor after her when his mobile started to ring.

He was tempted to ignore it, but conditioning made him yank the phone from his pocket with an exasperated huff.

'Robin Calling' his screen informed him. Thumbing 'Accept', he said, "What's up?"

"Something's happened."

Only two words, but the strain in his brother's voice caused Todd's stomach to clench with dread. To a background of faint, joyous whoops from Yrsa, he said, "What do you mean?"

Brokenly, breathlessly, Robin explained.

"Fuck," Todd breathed. "So how's Luke now?"

"He's being operated on as we speak. I only hope the facilities here are up to it."

"I'm sure they will be. There must be fishing accidents all the time…"

"Yeah," Robin said, unconvinced.

"I'll come down."

"You don't have to."

"I want to. You wouldn't even be here if it wasn't for us. Luke wouldn't, I mean."

"Do you know where it is?"

"I'll find it. See you soon."

He hesitated a moment – he could still hear Yrsa whooping outside – then hurried back to the kitchen and grabbed the Land Rover keys off the hook. He stuffed them into his pocket, then dragged on his coat and ran back along the corridor. He flipped up the hood as he stepped into the squall of rain that was swirling into the house, but the vicious wind immediately yanked it down again.

Fuck it, he thought as sheets of rain drenched him as effectively as if he'd been doused with a bucket of water. Ducking his head, he exited the house.

Something white was cavorting in the mud of the yard, stark against the trees. When he squinted into the driving rain, he was astonished to see that Yrsa had stripped naked and was splashing around like a child, head thrown back, arms in the air, hair trailing down her back like a black length of rope.

"Yrsa! What the fuck!" he yelled, anger boiling inside him.

She only laughed at him, which made him angrier still.

"There's been an accident," he shouted. "One of Robin's men has been hurt in the cave. Maybe badly." When she didn't respond, he added with a kind of vicious relish, knowing how much she wanted her childhood claims to be vindicated, "They've had to stop the drilling."

But even this didn't goad a reaction from her. She continued to dance, arms and head thrown back, laughing as if the rain had come at the end of a long and devastating drought.

Torn between attending to Yrsa or supporting his brother, Todd stood for a moment in the lashing rain, watching his girlfriend's antics with a sense of despairing disbelief. Then, water running down his face and plastering his clothes to his body, he splashed across to the Land Rover, got in, and drove away.

CHAPTER THIRTY

The hospital on Eldfjallaeyja was the same inside and out – gray and functional. Todd wouldn't have known it was a hospital if Karriana hadn't given him directions. The seething bewilderment he felt at Yrsa's behavior had filled his head all the way into town, and it was only as he was driving along the rain-lashed main street that he realized he had no idea where he was going. He stopped outside the bakery, where raindrops the size of golf balls were bouncing off the awning. Dragging his hood over his damp hair, which thanks to the hot, stale air that huffed from the Land Rover's heater had now stopped dripping, he splashed across the pavement and shoved the shop door open. He was adopting the smile he'd intended for Karriana when he realized the only person attending the counter was a large man whose round, florid face blended almost seamlessly with his ginger beard. The man's beady eyes were not unlike the currants embedded in the buns occupying several rows of a tray behind the glass-fronted display counter. Modifying his smile, Todd said, "Hi."

The man allowed a beat of silence to fill the air before his lips twitched in his bland face. "Yes?"

"Is Karriana about at all?"

"Why?"

Todd was wondering whether describing himself as her friend would get her into trouble when she appeared behind the man, who Todd assumed was her father, as though she'd been there all the time.

"I was in the back and I heard your voice," she said. "Hello, Todd. How are you?"

"I'm...well, not so great actually. I came in to find out whether you could direct me to the hospital."

The man didn't react, but Karriana's eyebrows lifted in alarm. "Are you ill?"

"Not me. Someone I know has had an accident."

"Not Yrsa?"

Was he only imagining the hint of eagerness in her voice? Todd pictured Yrsa as he had left her, cavorting naked in the rain, and shook his head. "No, one of the men working for my brother. He had an accident in the tunnels. A drill snapped and cut him badly."

Now the man did react. His eyes narrowed and, turning to Karriana, he muttered something. His words were quick, his voice breathless, and Todd got the impression he was warning her about something.

Karriana's response was brief and snappy. Rolling her eyes, she said to Todd, "I'm very sorry to hear that. I hope he will be all right. The hospital is very close."

Her directions were precise and accurate, and three minutes later Todd was striding up to a semicircular desk manned by a middle-aged woman wearing a blue cardigan over a stiff white nurse's tunic.

"Excuse me, do you speak English?"

"Yes," she replied, as though it pained her to admit it.

"An English man was brought in here with an injury to his side."

"Yes," she repeated with equal reluctance.

"Do you—" and then his conscious mind caught up with what he'd already seen in his peripheral vision – Robin slumped in a chair in the waiting area.

"Never mind," he said, rounding the desk and striding towards his brother. Robin was leaning forward, hands clenched between his knees. Todd was wondering whether he was praying when Robin, sensing him approaching, glanced up.

"Hey," Todd said as his brother rose from his seat.

Robin looked tired, but not distraught. "Hey. Thanks for coming, squirt."

"As if I wouldn't. How is he?"

"Out of surgery. The doctor said it went well. We should be able to see him soon."

"That's good. So it was just a freak accident?"

"Totally," said Robin, sinking down into his seat again. Todd sat beside him, the chair's gray vinyl cushion only marginally less cold than its thin metal frame. "Drill head must've been faulty. Those things never shatter like that." He shook his head, scowling in anger.

"So how bad are his injuries?"

"A chunk of metal went through his side. Doctor said it was like being hit by a spear fired from a cannon. Luckily it wasn't more central. If it had been, he'd've been a goner."

Apart from the woman at the desk, Todd and Robin were the only people in the reception area. With its pale blue walls and gray floors, Eldfjallaeyja's hospital felt like a giant, hollowed-out iceberg. The chilly décor and the damp clamminess of his clothes beneath his thick coat combined to make Todd shiver.

He thought again of Yrsa, cavorting in the downpour, and hoped she was okay. In some ways, though, he was glad she wasn't here. She was so obsessed with breaking through the wall and vindicating herself in the eyes of her fellow islanders, he doubted whether she'd have been able to resist asking Robin how much Luke's accident might delay the drilling.

He wondered what would happen if they didn't find anything. Presumably they'd leave with the minimum of fuss and head back to London. Secretly, Todd hoped this would be the case. Although he felt disloyal for wishing disappointment on his girlfriend, he thought if they *did* find treasure behind that wall it would only open up a whole new can of worms. Not only would it prolong their stay here, but he could foresee ownership claims becoming volatile and entangled. Would the treasure belong to the finder or the island authorities? He was about to ask Robin whether there was a coffee machine around here when he heard the clack of approaching footsteps.

The two of them turned towards the one corridor that led deeper into the building and saw a thin, balding man ambling towards them, a monobrow seemingly perched on the crossbar of his dark-framed spectacles like a furry black caterpillar. The hem of the man's unbuttoned white coat flapped around the knees of his brown suit, and the grim look on his face made Todd's stomach tighten. As the doctor moved closer, Robin jumped to his feet.

"Your friend has been transferred to the ward," the doctor said in a thin, clipped voice. "You can see him now."

Robin's relief was palpable. "Which ward is he in?"

"Ward one. Follow the corridor to the end and turn left."

They found ward one without difficulty, and pushed through a pair of heavy, gray swing doors into a functional, cheerless room, four beds along each wall, each bed surrounded by a metal frame from which hung a privacy curtain that looked woven from cobwebs. There were small, high windows above the beds along the left-hand wall, beyond which the incessant rain resembled gray static. Only two of the beds were occupied, and one of those occupants was concealed within a cocoon of curtain. The other, in the second bed on the left, was Luke.

He was lying on his back, his shoulders bare, a pale blue blanket pulled up to just beneath his throat. Todd expected him to be hooked up to various monitors, but he wasn't. He just looked to be asleep.

Although Luke was more or less the same age as Todd, in this situation he looked young and vulnerable. As the brothers approached his bed, Todd became aware of movement to the left of the swing doors, and realized there was a nurses' station there, tucked into the corner of the room. He turned to see a heavily built woman of about thirty with corn-colored hair heading in their direction, as if to intercept them.

Todd was so used to being treated with hostility by the locals that the warmth of her smile startled him. "Hello," she said, "you are friends of Luke, yes?"

Robin nodded. "I'm his boss and this is my brother, Todd."

"But we're also his friends," Todd added.

"Luke is sleeping now," the nurse said unnecessarily, "but he will wake soon."

"Is it okay to sit with him for a while?" Todd asked.

"Of course."

There was a plastic chair beside each bed. As Robin sat in the one next to Luke's bed, Todd grabbed the one allocated to the next bed along. As he set it down with a quiet clunk, Luke stirred, his brow crinkling in pain or confusion, lips parting with a soft pop.

Robin leaned forward. "You're all right there, Luke," he murmured. "You're in bed and everything's fine."

Luke grunted, then moaned. He scrunched up his face as if having a bad dream.

"Do you think we should get the nurse?" Todd said. She had now returned to the nurse's station.

"In a minute, maybe." Addressing Luke again, Robin said, "It's Robin, mate. You've had a bit of an accident, but you're fine. You're in hospital, but you're being well looked after. Todd is here too."

Robin looked at Todd, nodding as if encouraging him to speak. Todd barely knew Luke, but said, "Er...hi, Luke. Yeah, like my brother says, you'll be fine."

Luke groaned again, then uttered a weak, inarticulate cry. Todd glanced across at the nurse's station and saw the nurse raise her head. When he turned back, he saw Luke alternately raising and lowering his eyebrows as if struggling to open his eyes. Luke swallowed, licked his lips. Then he began talking.

His voice was a low mumble, and at first Todd thought he was spouting gibberish, perhaps still too affected by the anesthetic to form words. Then he caught a word he'd heard before, and the effect of it was like a shock going through him.

Leaning against Robin, he craned forward, tilting his head so his ear was directly above Luke's mouth.

"What are you doing?" Robin said.

"I'm trying to listen. What did he just say?"

"Nothing. He's talking rubbish."

"No. *Listen.* He said it again."

"Said what again?"

"Jötnar."

Robin looked at Todd as if he'd lost his mind. "What's that supposed to mean?"

"Shh, listen. Get the nurse."

"Why?"

"Just get her."

Robin sighed, but made a beckoning gesture in the direction of the nurse's station. A few seconds later she was beside them.

"Is something wrong?"

Todd was still leaning over Luke, but now he stepped back so the nurse could take his place.

"I know this sounds mad, but I think Luke's speaking in your language. Will you listen?"

The nurse looked surprised, but complied, leaning forward and tilting her head, as Todd had done. Robin looked at his brother in exasperation. "What are you on about? Luke doesn't speak…whatever language they speak here."

"I know," Todd said, "but I definitely heard him say jötnar. More than once."

"So you said. But what's it mean?"

"It's a…creature from Nordic folklore. Like a troll." He looked at his brother meaningfully. "Remember what Amir said he saw in the caves? A small figure. Like a child or a dwarf."

Robin still looked exasperated, but now he looked unsettled too. Before he could respond, the nurse murmured, "This is very strange."

"What's he saying?" Todd asked. "I was right, wasn't I? He is speaking in your language."

She straightened up. "Yes he is. But it's a…how do you say? Old version of it. Not modern. Like the language you read in old books."

"But how is that possible?" Robin asked.

Todd shrugged, turning back to the nurse. "So what is he actually saying? I thought I heard him mention the jötnar."

"Yes, you are right. The language he speaks is hard to understand, even for me, but he keeps saying the same thing. He says 'the jötnar are coming.'"

CHAPTER THIRTY-ONE

Jay was miserable.

He didn't know why the drilling site needed guarding, especially not on a night like this, when anyone would be mad to come traipsing out here in the pouring rain, but Robin had been insistent. He didn't know whether the old woman's death would kill the protests stone dead, or whether it would whip the locals into an even greater fervor of resentment, but he'd said the last thing they needed was for the drilling site to be 'compromised', and so he'd proposed a rota of round-the-clock surveillance.

All their names had been written on bits of paper – including Robin's – and drawn out of Amir's baseball cap, to determine the order in which they'd fulfil their night watchman duties. Tonight should have been Luke's turn – and with the storm finally breaking, Jay hadn't envied him. But then Luke had had his accident and been rushed to hospital, and guess which poor sod's name had been next on the list? Yep, *this* guy.

A one-man tent had been erected on flat ground, half a dozen meters from the entrance to the Devil's Throat, and fitted out with blankets, a sleeping bag that Sean had told him was a proper mountaineer's one, and a little gas stove, along with tea, coffee, sugar, powdered milk, soup, bread, biscuits and a gallon container of water. It was cozy enough, he supposed, especially with rain clattering on the canvas roof, but Jay still couldn't help feeling hard done by. After three days the inside of the tent smelled of Sean's roll-ups and Big Andy's sweaty feet, and why did it have to throw it down on the very night *he* was on duty? He might be okay now, but he'd get soaked when he ventured out for his nightly piss. And because of the sudden change of plan necessitated by Luke's accident, he'd left his Kindle at the hotel, which meant his intention to while away the hours when it was his turn by losing himself in the latest Lee Child had been well and truly scuppered. All he had to amuse himself with was his phone, which had less than twenty-five percent battery. He was scrolling through photos of himself with Elaine and their two-year-old son, Hugo, and wishing longingly he was back home in Ealing, when something brushed against the side of the tent.

Jay jumped so violently that he dropped his phone. He turned to where the sound had come from, and saw a shadow darken the canvas for a moment – or thought he did. One of the lads had said there were wild boars on the island, which could be vicious if roused. Meeting one of those would be bad enough – but out here, alone in the dark and miles from anywhere, Jay wasn't thinking of wild boars.

He was thinking of serial killers.

The lads would laugh if they knew – but it was easy to laugh when you were sitting in a cozy hotel bar with a beer in your hand and your mates around you. He'd defy any of them not to be spooked in his situation, even though both Sean and Big Andy, whose names had been first out of the hat, had insisted they'd enjoyed the peace and quiet during their stints on watch, and had slept like babies.

For ten seconds, maybe fifteen, after hearing the sound and seeing the shadow, Jay sat motionless, afraid to move or even breathe. But all he heard was the rain, like a million finger-taps on the outside of the tent, and eventually he released the long, slow breath he'd been holding in his lungs.

He picked up his phone, dropped it into the pocket of his waterproof, and shuffled on his knees towards the entrance, all at once horribly aware that the only thing separating him from whatever was outside (*which would be nothing*) was a semicircular zip.

He reached for the zip, then paused. If there *was* something out there, would it hear the unmeshing of the metal teeth over the battering rain? If it was a serial killer, of course, it wouldn't matter. It – and he could only think of whatever might be out there in terms of *it* – would already be aware of the tent, and probably of the fact he was inside it. But if it was something else (*a monster*), it might not become aware of him until he showed himself, whereupon it might rush at him with the single-minded ferocity of a killer shark.

His fingers felt numb as they closed over the tab of the zip. He thought of Elaine. He thought of Hugo. He wished their smiling faces would give him strength, but all it did was make him long more desperately than ever to be home. He wanted to hold his boy. He wanted to smell Elaine's hair. He wanted the clamor of London, not the dislocating weirdness of this shitty island.

Gritting his teeth, he tugged at the zip. Each tiny click of the metal teeth felt like a sound that would attract a predator. Logic told him that a meter from the tent the sound would be drowned out by the rain. But it didn't help.

Eventually he'd raised the zip high enough to create a flap to look out of. Pinching the corner of the flap between his thumb and forefinger, Jay carefully lifted it.

A low, deep, rumbling growl from outside the tent made Jay jerk back, letting go of the flap. His heart hammered so ferociously he could feel it in his throat. But then his brain caught up and he released a short, hard burp of laughter.

Thunder. That was all that was. Like the indigestion of the gods, it had been grumbling all day. There had even been flashes of lightning, though most of them had looked far away, maybe out at sea. Composing himself, he took hold of the flap again and lifted it. When nothing happened, he cautiously leaned forward and peeked out.

The entrance to the tent was facing the Devil's Throat, although from this angle, and in this darkness, the shaft could not be seen. The only indication it was there was that the foliage around it had been trampled flat. The ground between the tent and the shaft was mostly rock, and in the pouring rain it gleamed black, like polished obsidian. Although he didn't have a panoramic view of his surroundings, Jay was relieved to see neither a machete-wielding figure standing in the rain, nor a wild boar with vicious-looking tusks and black, mean eyes.

At the lack of an immediate threat, his racing heart slowed a little. But then two of the stubby bushes just beyond the Devil's Throat suddenly stirred into life, uprooted themselves, and came shambling towards him.

If he'd been able to, Jay might have screamed. But he was so scared he could do nothing – couldn't find the breath to make a sound, couldn't even let go of the tent flap, which was screwed tightly in his fist. When the 'bushes' reached the lip of the Devil's Throat, Jay expected them to circle it and keep shambling in his direction. But instead, the first of the 'bushes' leaned forward and seemed to slide into the hole in the ground, disappearing from view. A moment later the second 'bush' did the same.

For several seconds, Jay could only gape at the place where the 'bushes' had disappeared. He was still terrified, but already his mind was trying to make sense of what he'd seen. Had the 'bushes' been animals that had fallen down the shaft? He could have sworn they'd risen from the ground and stood upright on two feet, like people or apes, but maybe he'd been mistaken?

All at once he started to shake, though not from the cold. On the contrary, his body felt unbearably hot in its thick layers of clothing, and his head started to swim. The tent suddenly seemed claustrophobic, stifling. If he didn't get out, he might pass out, maybe even suffocate. He reached for the zip and pulled it all the way up.

Now the tent flap gaped. Then the wind caught it, making it thrash back and forth like the wing of a trapped bird. A muscular breeze, accompanied by flurries of rain, flailed at Jay. The rain stung his skin as he scrambled out of the tent. Within seconds his hair was soaked and dripping. Mini streams of water ran down the rock slope. From outside, the tent looked precarious, as though it could be washed away at any moment. Jay again looked towards the Devil's Throat. There was no sign of movement around it. Had the black shapes fallen or clambered all the way down the shaft, or were they perched just under the rim, like spiders beneath a toilet seat?

That last thought sent another shudder through him. He took a few steps towards the shaft, craning his neck in an attempt to see into it. There was movement all around it, but it was only the rain, bouncing off the ground, battering foliage into submission.

His clothes were drenched now. Thunder rumbled again. He couldn't stay here. Maybe he should call Dev, ask to be picked up. But the rain was so torrential it would fritz his phone as soon as he took it from his pocket. His best bet would be to find shelter in the forest and call from there. He was picking his way down the slope, glancing frequently over his shoulder, when he heard the whispering.

It was hoarse and wordless, and seemed to float eerily up from the depths of the shaft. Gripped by panic, Jay began to run down the slope. The rocks were wet and slippery, and he knew that if he fell, he would likely break his leg or neck, and there would be nobody to help him. But fear had him now, and so he kept running. And he didn't stop until he was all the way through the forest and out the other side.

CHAPTER THIRTY-TWO

Thump...thump...thump...

At first Karriana thought she was dreaming. Then, drifting awake, she heard the thrashing of rain against the house, and thought the wind must have torn something loose – the awning at the front of the shop, maybe.

Still groggy, she sat up, pushing aside the heavy duvet. Rubbing her face, she tried to pinpoint the source of the slow, rhythmic thumping. It didn't sound like it was coming from outside, or even from downstairs. It sounded much closer.

What time was it? She grabbed her phone and lit up the screen. Four twenty-seven a.m. Still too early for her father to start the day's baking, even though the sound was like someone punching a big wad of dough.

As another flurry of rain hit the house, she tensed. Winter storms were not uncommon, but this one was earlier and more violent than usual. Of course, many were claiming that Yrsa Helgerson was responsible. They were saying the drilling at the caves, Margret Gulbransen's death and the storm, which had enclosed the island like a shroud, were all connected.

Did Karriana believe that? She didn't know. She was scared of Yrsa, and thought there was something weird about her, but she didn't know how much of that stemmed from the ideas embedded in her as a child. Seeing Yrsa that first night in the bar had been a shock – she hadn't even known her old classmate was back until that moment. Seeing Todd with Yrsa, she'd acted on impulse, feeling an urge to warn him about who he was with, or at least let him know what people here believed about her.

Now, looking back, she felt a little embarrassed. She liked to think she was more rational than the more superstitious members of their community – of whom, admittedly, there were many. All she could say in her defense was that the beliefs of a lifetime were hard to shake. And there *was* still a part of her that thought Yrsa was...unnatural. She couldn't deny that fact.

A further barrage of rain rattled the window, accompanied by a rumbling roll of thunder. And still, underpinning the storm, was the sound that had woken her – *thump...thump...thump* – like a distant drumbeat.

Planting her feet on the floor, she stood up. Her thin nightshirt provided little protection from the cold, which was why she kept her thick shawl and fur-lined moccasins on the chair beside her bed. She stepped into the moccasins and dragged the shawl around her shoulders, then moved towards the door, rain hitting the window like buckshot as she passed.

She considered pausing to look out of the window, but didn't – she was pretty sure now that the thumping was somewhere in the flat. Could it be the plumbing? An air block in a pipe? It was possible, but the sound seemed too regular for that. Too deliberate.

Nervous, she hesitated before opening the door. All at once she remembered the raven alighting on the climbing frame behind Todd the day she had met him in the park. Caught up in her childhood beliefs, she'd imagined Yrsa watching her through the raven's eyes. And now she was experiencing a similar sensation. It wasn't that she thought Yrsa was the cause of the thumping, but she had a bad feeling about it all the same. Her instinct was to dive back into bed and pull the duvet over her head. But instead she made herself open the door and step into the corridor.

The flat above the bakery, where Karriana had lived all her life, comprised a long hallway with five doors leading off it, and a central staircase in the right-hand wall, which led down to another door that opened into the bakery below. The hallway was windowless, so they always left the bathroom light on at night and the door ajar. In the gloom beyond the light that spilled from the bathroom, Karriana saw her father. He was standing in the hallway in a pair of blue boxer shorts, his hairy belly, as big as any pregnant woman's, spilling over his waistband. He was facing the section of wall between the living room and the bedroom he shared with Karriana's mother, and he was deliberately slamming his forehead against the wall over and over.

Thump...thump...thump...

Karriana could see a dark, football-sized stain on the wall in front of his head. In the gloom the stain was black, but Karriana knew if she turned on the corridor light, the stain would magically become a bright, shocking red.

She staggered against the wall as the strength drained out of her legs, but not before screaming, "Dad, don't!"

Miraculously her plea worked. Her dad stopped head-butting the wall and became motionless. For several seconds he stood there, rounded shoulders hunched, meaty arms hanging down, his big, sausage-fingered hands open and relaxed. Then, slowly, he turned his head towards her. And now Karriana saw the wet, dark stain on his forehead, trickles from which were running down the sides of his nose and over his lips. If it wasn't for his beard, the trickles would be dripping off his chin and spattering onto his fat belly, but instead they were accumulating in his beard, turning it dark and shiny.

"Dad," Karriana whispered again. She tried to say more, but shock had jammed the words in her throat.

Karriana's father opened his mouth, and at first Karriana thought he was about to speak. But then his face went slack, his knees buckled and he crumpled forward, hitting the floor of the hallway as gracelessly as a sack of meat.

CHAPTER THIRTY-THREE

"Hi, Rob. You okay?"

Todd was surprised, and a little alarmed, to see his brother standing on the doorstep. Robin looked cowed by the rain, shoulders hunched inside his thick coat, hands buried in his pockets. The funnel-like hood threw his face partly into shadow, though Todd knew the darkness around Robin's eyes was due more to tiredness and stress.

"Could do with some decent coffee," Robin said, his voice drained of energy.

"Couldn't we all?" Todd stepped back, dragging the door further open. "Come in. You been at the hospital all night?"

"Not all night. Got back to the hotel about…three?"

"Is Luke okay?" Todd asked as Robin peeled off his dripping coat and wiped his wet boots on the mat. He was still wondering why his brother had come here, why he hadn't just called, as he usually did.

"He's fine. Just sleeping."

"No more…weird outbursts?"

"Not while I was there."

Possible explanations for Luke 'speaking in tongues' at the hospital had been circling in Todd's mind all night, but none of them made any sense. For now he was going with the possibility that Luke's subconscious had soaked up bits of the local language, and had chosen to jettison them while he was semiconscious.

"So what brings you here?" Todd asked.

"Wanted to talk to you both about something. Thought I'd do it face to face."

Todd heard alarm bells ringing in his head. "You're not pulling the plug, are you?"

Robin rubbed his jowls as if to massage some vitality back into them, his hands rasping on stubble. "No, I'm not pulling the plug. At least… hopefully it won't come to that. Mostly I just came for a change of scene. Things are a bit…intense back at the hotel."

"Because of Luke?"

"And something else." He gestured towards the kitchen. "What about that coffee? And where's Yrsa?"

"I'm right here."

She emerged from the kitchen as the two men moved towards it. Todd wondered how much she'd heard of their conversation, and felt guilty, even though they hadn't been talking about her. He hadn't told her about the 'speaking in tongues' incident, and still wasn't exactly sure why. Maybe because Yrsa had been at the center of most of the weirdness that had occurred since they had arrived here, and he'd felt reluctant to feed the fire?

Since he'd got back from the hospital yesterday, he and Yrsa had barely spoken. He hadn't known what he'd find when he arrived back – some elfin sprite of the forest, perhaps, feral and mud-spattered – but in fact she had been asleep on the settee her mother's corpse had been laid out on, dressed in her night things and wrapped in a thick, woolen blanket, having clearly had a bath or shower.

"Hi, Yrsa," Robin said. "How are you?"

"Better than you by the looks of things. Come through. Coffee's on."

Five minutes later they were sitting around the kitchen table, steaming mugs in front of them. Robin wrapped both hands around his, as if desperate for its warmth. When he raised it to his mouth, his eyes closed in ecstasy.

"Could do with this on an intravenous drip."

"So what did you want to talk about?" asked Todd.

Robin sighed and told them about the phone call he had received from Jay early that morning. "He was in a panic. Freaking out. Claimed to have seen strange figures up at the drilling site."

Todd suppressed a shudder and glanced at Yrsa. She was staring at Robin, her green-eyed stare intense.

"Strange how?" Todd asked.

Robin shrugged. "Ask me, he was imagining things because of what Amir said earlier in the week. Jay said the figures were small, like dwarves. But when I tried to pin him down, he admitted he hadn't actually seen them close up. It was dark and pissing it down." He swigged more coffee. "Probably just shadows."

"So what's the problem?" asked Yrsa guardedly.

"The problem is that it may slow the operation down a bit. Jay wants to go home, as do a couple of the other guys, and of course Luke's in hospital. The rest of us could carry on, but it would be at a reduced capacity. We've got enough spare parts to repair the damaged drill, but we'd be lacking in manpower. It's knackering working in those tunnels, and a reduced workforce would only be able to do about half the hours. In an ideal situation I'd send home the men who want to go and get replacements in, but with this weather..."

He didn't need to elaborate. The rain sounded like waves crashing down on the house. There had been times, during the night, when Todd had thought the entire building was about to be ripped from its foundations and sent swirling through the sky like Dorothy's house in *The Wizard of Oz*. Todd had reached the stage where he wished they could *all* go back to London and leave the weirdness behind, but he knew that, like it or not, they were stuck here for the foreseeable. He nodded in sympathy with his brother, but Yrsa was frowning.

"But you're the boss, Robin," she said. "Or am I wrong about that?"

Robin might have been stressed and exhausted, but he still had enough about him to give Yrsa one of his 'don't piss me off' faces.

"Of course I'm the boss," he said sharply. "But if you're going to suggest I crack a whip over this, you clearly don't know how to read people. The men were jittery enough before Luke got injured, and what Jay claims he saw last night has only made things worse. I've already asked a lot of these blokes. They're in a hostile environment, they're out of their comfort zones..."

"They're being paid well," said Yrsa.

"They'd get paid almost as much if they went back to London and worked for Dad." He held up his hands, as if to forestall an argument. "All I'm saying is that some of them are starting to think this job is not worth the 'hassle bonus' they're getting."

"But they're already here," Yrsa said, "so they might as well be working. If they weren't, what else would they do, except sit around and wait for the storm to settle, so they could all go home?"

"Do you want to tell them that?" said Robin.

Todd looked at Yrsa. "Would it be so bad if the work took longer than originally scheduled? I mean, yes, it would be a pain because we'd have to stay longer, but if it's just—"

"I want this job completed as soon as possible," Yrsa said. "I've waited many years for this."

"Exactly. So a few more days—"

"No, Todd!" She raised a hand, then swung back to Robin. "Tell the men if they're willing to work, I will pay them double from now until however long it takes to break through."

Robin raised his eyebrows. "Are you sure you can afford that?"

"I want this done."

For a few seconds the only sound in the room was the rain flailing at the house.

"I'd need that in writing," Robin said. "And I still can't guarantee all the men will agree to it."

"Those who do will be rewarded," Yrsa said. "You have my word."

CHAPTER THIRTY-FOUR

What the fuck is happening? Anders Hagen thought, putting down the phone. *Has the town gone mad?*

He was alone in the tiny police station that served the island. His colleagues, Erik and Pálína, were out on separate calls. Erik was following up a report that Gunnar Haraldsson had gone crazy and was running around in his underwear in the torrential rain, using a mallet to bash in the brains of whichever of his pigs he could catch, while his wife and children cowered inside the house, and Pálína was investigating claims of a domestic disturbance at the Nilsen home.

On the rare occasions when violent incidents *had* been reported on Eldfjallaeyja – and these usually took the form of drunken punch-ups or family squabbles – at least two officers, and sometimes all three, had gone to investigate. Often this wasn't because they expected to run into danger, but simply because it gave them something to do. Crime on the island was rare, and certain offenses – burglary, robbery, sexual assault, murder – were nonexistent, so most of the time there wasn't enough work to go round. Even so, traditions died hard here, and the Council had long ago decided that in a 'worst-case scenario', three law enforcement officers would be the optimal number needed to maintain order. It was how it had always been, and it was probably how it always would be.

Whilst Hagen was not sure whether the past twenty-four hours could be termed a 'worst-case scenario', they were certainly the busiest he had known in his twenty-odd years as a police officer, and probably the busiest that any law enforcement officer on Eldfjallaeyja had *ever* known. Oddly, it was as though the deluge of rain, which still assailed the island, had presaged an altogether different kind of deluge – one of disturbing and bizarre incidents.

In many ways, though, Hagen thought that recent events, connected or not, could be traced back even further, to before the storm – to Ása Helgerson's death a couple of weeks ago. After Ása's death had come the disappearance of little Märta Senvig, and then Margret Gulbransen had died up at the Devil's Throat – and although the postmortem had confirmed the old woman had expired of heart failure, there were still aspects of the case that bothered Anders.

Following this had been the accident in the tunnels, where the young Englishman had been injured. And the common thread that seemed to connect all of these incidents, albeit tenuously, was Yrsa Helgerson. In his mind, Anders saw Yrsa's mocking smile and her intense green eyes. He heard her joking about killing Margret Gulbransen – 'the old bitch' – under the light of the midnight moon.

He had been a young officer at the time of Yrsa's childhood disappearance, and remembered her subsequent rescue from the caves very well. He was naturally aware of the stories about Yrsa, and knew how her return had sent ripples of unease through the community. And yes, the links between Yrsa and the island's recent troubles were certainly there; they couldn't be denied. And yet, and yet…

He sighed. Even now he wasn't sure how much he was being influenced by gossip and superstition. Some of the locals were even adamant that Yrsa had conjured up the storm, for God's sake. And he had no doubt that the blame for all that had happened since – several outbreaks of violence; at least three mental breakdowns; half a dozen reports of dead or missing livestock – would be laid squarely at her door. If he wasn't careful, he would have a witch hunt on his hands.

Looking at the hand that had just placed the phone in its receiver, Anders saw that it was shaking. Lack of sleep could account for some of that, but mostly it was down to adrenaline and stress. He had just received a call from Sverrir Stefánsson, who lived on one of the island's most remote farms, telling him that his aged father, Ásgeir, had seen intruders prowling around – intruders who the agitated old man described as 'little people'. Stories of trolls, of jötnar, were part of local folklore. But to Anders' knowledge, this was the third such sighting in the past dozen hours. He rationalized it by telling himself the idea had been planted by Märta Senvig, who insisted a 'little man' had looked after her while she'd been lost in the forest. Even so, three unrelated sightings in such a short time was not just unusual, it was downright *weird*, and it only added to the sense of dislocation that Anders was feeling, the sense of… he hesitated, then decided to admit it.

The sense of impending doom.

CHAPTER THIRTY-FIVE

This must be what it's like to be a ghost, Todd thought.

For the past two days he and Yrsa had been indoors, doing nothing very much. The unrelenting barrage of rain clattering against the house had made him feel almost cozy at first, especially with a log fire crackling merrily in the grate. But now it just made him feel trapped.

With the internet signal too spotty to access social media or YouTube or Netflix, Todd had passed most of his time cooking and eating, sleeping more than usual, and reading listlessly. A week ago he would have expected Yrsa and him to have spent at least part of their enforced isolation having sex, but something about the dreariness of the rain seemed to have dampened their libidos, as well as giving Todd an almost constant, low-level headache. Thanks to Yrsa's offer to double the wages of the drilling team, all of Robin's men – bar Luke, who was still in hospital – had agreed to go back to work, including Jay, who had previously vowed never to set foot near the Devil's Throat again. As a result, Yrsa had spent most of *her* time – at least in Todd's eyes – hovering by the phone, waiting for it to ring.

Robin had assured them that news of a breakthrough should come within seventy-two hours, maybe less, so surely they wouldn't be waiting *much* longer. Sitting at the kitchen table, Todd drained his sixth or seventh mug of tea that day, and then, groaning like an old man, carried it across to the kitchen sink and stared out at the yard as he rinsed it out.

It was a quagmire out there, although the camber of the land meant neither the house nor the outbuildings were at risk of flooding. He could see streams of water snaking through the mud, heading towards the black spiky mass of the forest. The streams reminded him of veins, which fed the forest's dark, beating heart. Certainly, thanks to the wind and rain, the place seemed full of life – tree branches waving, bushes thrashing, leaves twitching like myriad nerves.

A moment later it felt like his own nerves were twitching in sympathy, the side of his right thigh vibrating like a trapped wasp. It was his phone, which he slid out of his pocket. When he saw the words 'Robin Calling…' his heart beat a little faster.

"Hey, Rob," he said, and was answered by his brother's muffled voice, which Todd imagined fighting its way through tons of compacted rock and lashing sheets of rain to reach him.

"We're through."

Todd glanced behind him, expecting Yrsa to be there, but the kitchen was empty. "What can you see?"

There were thick, rustling sounds now, as if Robin was speaking to him from inside a sleeping bag.

"None of us have looked. We think the honor should go to Yrsa, if the two of you want to come out here. If not, we'll just—"

"We'll come," Todd said, knowing Yrsa would insist upon it. "We'll be with you within the hour."

In fact, they were at the entrance to the Devil's Throat in less than forty minutes, Yrsa having insisted on jogging, if not running, through the forest and up the rocky slope to their destination, once Todd had parked the Land Rover. Although the ground was like a swamp in places, and the rocks slick and treacherous, she refused to slow down, as a result of which Todd was gasping and pouring with sweat inside his thick, hooded raincoat and heavy waterproof over-trousers by the time they arrived.

As he bent double, hands on knees, wondering whether to puke or simply pass out, Yrsa ran up to the lip of the Devil's Throat and peered down the shaft. Straightening up, Todd noticed that just over the rise to their left was a yellow one-man tent, clinging to the slope like a limpet on a rock. No sooner had he seen it than the semicircular zip on its side began to rise, and a moment later the opening gave birth to a blue, inflated figure with a bulbous head. When the figure had emerged, it straightened up, and Todd saw Robin's face peering from the depths of the funnel-like hood.

Even before the two brothers could greet one another, Yrsa was homing in on Robin, her right hand, white and dripping like that of a corpse fished from a river, reaching for the orange straps of the abseiling harness he wore over his waterproofs.

"We need to get down there now," she said. "I want to go first."

Taking a step back, Robin grabbed Yrsa's wrist, much to her evident outrage.

"You can go first on one condition," he replied. "Which is that when you touch bottom, you wait for us, you don't go off on your own. If you fail to do that, you'll be banned from any further descents. I mean it, Yrsa. I'm not having any more accidents."

For a moment Todd thought she was going to lash out, as she had done at her mother's wake when Margret Gulbransen got too close and personal. Then, just as quickly, she relaxed. Todd expected resentment, but her voice was surprisingly compliant.

"Of course."

Robin released her wrist, and both of them drew their hands back warily. "I know you're excited," he said. "Believe me, I am too, and I don't have anything like the emotional investment in this that you do. But we need to do this by the book. Which means taking care. Okay?"

"Absolutely," said Yrsa sweetly.

Despite her assurances, Todd was not sure whether Yrsa *would* play it by the book. He was relieved, therefore, when, having descended the shaft first, she was dutifully waiting for him when he reached the bottom. Abseiling down had been like descending through a giant shower, the rain pattering off his helmet and ricocheting off the surrounding walls. As soon as his feet touched firm rock and he had unclipped himself from the ropes, he stepped out of the tube of rain and shook himself like a dog. Peeling off his wet coat, he looked around, his helmet light dancing across the walls.

"You were right about the tunnels," he said.

Yrsa was looking back up the shaft, her right leg jiggling with pent-up energy. "Huh?"

"You said they wouldn't flood because there were a lot of outlets for the water to drain away. And you were right, the water's just running into cracks in the rock. It's not even pooling anywhere. Where do you think it's draining away to? The sea?"

Yrsa glanced briefly down. "I don't know. Maybe."

Todd had a mental image of the island at the center of a world of water – of countless gallons beneath it, and countless gallons above, raining down from the sky. He thought of the forests and fields soaking it up like a giant sponge, and for a moment he felt small and vulnerable. He wondered how much the sea level would have to rise before the island disappeared beneath its surface.

He put the thought from his mind as the meager light spilling down the shaft abruptly darkened. A minute later Robin was beside them, unclipping himself, and peeling off his dripping waterproof. He shook it out and draped it over a rock, then turned to Todd and Yrsa.

"Right, let's go and see what's what."

The route through the tunnels, with Robin leading the way, Yrsa behind him, and Todd bringing up the rear, was beginning to seem almost familiar.

"Where's everybody else?" Todd asked, his voice echoing.

"Fighting over front row seats for the great unveiling," Robin replied.

Sure enough, as they neared the now-widened gap into the final cave, snippets of conversation, made ghostly by acoustics, came floating back to them. Aware that within minutes Yrsa's dream would be either realized or shattered, Todd gave her shoulder a reassuring squeeze. The muscles beneath his fingers felt knotted, unyielding, and she failed to react to his touch. Leaning close to her, he murmured, "You okay?"

Again, she didn't immediately respond. Then she gave a slow nod. "Fine."

The three of them entered the cave. As they did, faces turned towards them, starkly white under the conjoined light from the helmet lamps. To Todd, most of the men looked wary, uncertain, though Dev, seemingly as relaxed as ever, nodded and smiled.

Most of the men were in a group to their left, their backs against the wall. Todd was sure it was simply to give him, Yrsa and Robin room to maneuvre, but the impression they gave was that they were fearful of the porthole-sized opening on the far side of the cave, beyond which only blackness was visible.

Robin unclipped a heavy-duty torch from his toolbelt and handed it to Yrsa.

"It's only right you should be first to see what's on the other side," he said. He turned and grinned at the men, as if attempting to lighten the mood. "That's assuming none of you have already had a peek."

The men shook their heads, a couple of them vehemently. "No, boss," Hector muttered. "No way," said Sean, folding his arms tightly.

Holding the torch, Yrsa approached the hole. When she thumbed the button inset into the torch's rubber grip, a dazzling white beam, significantly brighter than the one from her helmet lamp, bleached the wall in front of her. As Yrsa leaned forward and directed the beam towards the hole, Todd tensed.

For several long seconds she remained frozen in place, and the men were frozen with her, their eyes fixed on her slight frame. Todd could hear nothing but the far-off rush of water – unless that was the sound of his heart pumping blood through his veins. Within the cave there was not a scuff, not a sigh, not a rustle of clothing. It was Robin who finally broke the silence. "Well? What can you see?"

Yrsa turned slowly, and Todd expected her face to be either alight with rapture or slack with disappointment. Her expression, though, was neutral. Flipping the torch round so its beam was pointing at her torso, she offered it not to Robin, but to Todd.

"Tell me what *you* think, Todd," she said.

He took the torch from her and bent forward to peer into the hole. As Yrsa had done, he brought the torch up level with his face, the rubber resting against his cheekbone, and followed the beam with his eyes as it leaped ahead of him.

At first he wasn't sure what he was looking at. Neither could he get any real sense of perspective. His only impression was of shapes and textures, angles, shadows, different gradations of black and gray. He narrowed his eyes, as if that might help focus his vision. And maybe it did, because suddenly he realized he was looking into a space – perhaps a vast space – and that to the far left, at the point where the torch beam started to fade, there was the suggestion of…what? A curving structure of some kind? Could it be…?

Straightening up, he turned to Yrsa, his heart beating faster. He licked his lips and said, "I think it might be wood. Something made of wood."

Now there was rapture on her face, albeit still contained for the time being. Behind him he was aware of a collective murmur, like a sigh or a groan. Then Robin was beside him.

"Let's see."

Todd stepped aside as Robin took his place, his protective suit rustling like dry skin as he bent forward, torch level with the side of his head. His face was a mask of concentration, brow furrowed, lips pursed. Then he said, "I think you may be right. We could be on to something here."

Todd looked again at Yrsa, whose face still held that expression of restrained wonder. "Holy fuck," he murmured.

Robin stepped back from the hole, switched the torch off and clipped it back to his belt. Suddenly he was all business.

"Who's on drill duty?" he asked, turning to the men.

"That'd be me," Big Andy replied, though he didn't sound that eager to admit it.

"Right. Everybody else out. Head down to the canteen. Amir, will you make Todd and Yrsa a cuppa?"

Amir nodded. "Sure."

"Canteen?" Todd asked Robin as the men filed out.

"Joke. It's more of an alcove. But there's everything there you could wish for, as long as all you wish for is tea, coffee and biscuits. I'll let you know when we've made a hole big enough to crawl through."

"How long will that be?" Yrsa asked.

"An hour? Two at the most."

The next hour passed slowly, all of them sitting around, slurping tea, chomping biscuits. There wasn't much chitchat, and not only because the ratcheting screech of the drill provided a constant background noise. Todd wondered whether the guys were simply being reserved because of Yrsa's presence, whether they were reining in their bawdy banter so as not to offend her. He didn't think so, though; instead he got the feeling they were wary of her. Once or twice he noticed uneasy glances cast in her direction.

If Yrsa was aware of their disquiet, she showed no sign. For the most part, she sat quietly, her slender hands wrapped around a large red mug. When Todd asked her how she was feeling, she barely glanced at him. "I'm fine. But I'd rather not talk right now if you don't mind."

It was ten minutes over the hour when the drilling stopped. At first there was little reaction. The drilling had stopped a few times already, only to resume moments later. This time, though, fifteen seconds passed, then another fifteen. Dev put his mug down on the trestle table that had been set up along the back wall. "This could be it," he said.

As Yrsa rose slowly, Todd saw the guys looking at each other. None looked particularly happy. He wondered whether their disquiet was rubbing off on him, or whether his sudden unease was down to some other factor. Filling the silence, he heard the sound of approaching footsteps that were both rapid and urgent. Every head turned to the arch leading into the main tunnel as Big Andy's bulky frame appeared.

Andy was sweating and covered in grimy dust. His protective goggles had been pushed up onto his forehead, and there were clean circles around his eyes, giving him the appearance of a jowly racoon in negative. As a dozen headlamp beams homed in on him, he threw up an arm.

"Bloody hell, guys!"

There was a smattering of apologies. The light dimmed as hands rose to cover helmet lamps.

"I hope you've brought good news," Dev said amiably.

Still blinking from the glare, Andy nodded. "We're through."

They were the same words Rob had used on the phone. Todd felt a sudden jab of disquiet at the thought of his brother waiting alone by the opening into the inner cave.

"What did you see when you broke through?" he asked.

Big Andy shrugged. "Too much dust to see anything."

"We'll find out what's in there soon enough," Dev said, striding past Big Andy and heading down the tunnel that led back to the drill site. Yrsa was so close to his heels she was in danger of stamping on them. Todd hurried after her.

The dust from the drilling had not yet settled, and as they got closer to the drill site, it grew thicker, coiling in the beams of their helmet lights. Todd could taste its grittiness in the back of his throat. When they entered the cave, the light seemed pearly, opalescent with it. Todd looked around, and at first couldn't see Robin. Wondering if he'd been unable to resist crawling through the waist-high arch in the wall, he shouted his brother's name.

"Here, squirt," said a voice to his left. Todd turned to see Robin sitting against the wall, facing the newly widened opening.

Todd grinned in relief. "You managed to resist the temptation, then?"

"It was tricky, but I have a will of iron," Robin said dryly.

By contrast, Yrsa clearly couldn't wait to see what was on the other side. Even as the others were still filing into the cave, she rushed across to the opening and dropped to her hands and knees. Robin was quickly there too, reaching out as if to haul her back by the scruff of her neck, though he didn't actually touch her.

"You can't go first," he said. "Sorry, Yrsa, but we've got to stick to the regs. We don't know what's in there."

She didn't protest. After a cursory look, she shuffled backwards, then rose to her feet, clapping dust from her hands.

"What did you see?" Todd asked.

"Something big," she said, eyes shining with barely supressed excitement.

Before he could ask her to elaborate, Robin said, "We'll check what's in there, and then we'll take more lights through if necessary. I'll go first. Yrsa, you're behind me, but stick close once we're on the other side. We need to exercise caution here – understand?"

"I'm not a little girl," she said.

Robin regarded her steadily. "It's not a criticism. I know what this means to you. But I also know how easy it can be to get carried away." Before she could respond, he continued, "Todd, you're behind Yrsa, and Dev, you're at the back."

Dev rolled his eyes. "Story of my life. Always the arse-end of the donkey."

"Right, here we go," Robin said, as chuckles rippled around the cave, and dropping to all fours, he shuffled forward, his helmet light brightening in the confined space, forming a dusty yellow halo around him. Yrsa crawled in after him, followed by Todd.

What struck Todd as he shuffled forward, Yrsa's rump wiggling just in front of him, was that the tunnel was no more than three or four meters from entrance to exit. The first time they'd brought Robin here, and he'd measured the distance with his selfie stick and all that white tubing, this wall had been a good seven or eight meters thick.

Clearly Robin's team hadn't just drilled *through* the wall, then, but had thinned it out too, shearing off layer after layer of rock, as if carving slices from a block of cheese. Todd was sure his brother knew what he was doing, but it still made him nervous to think the wall was now half as thin as it had been. He hoped the thinning-out process hadn't made it brittle enough to collapse. As he crawled out of the other end of the tunnel and stood up, he put his hand on his chest and took several deep breaths, fighting down a tingling sense of claustrophobia.

At least the air seemed less dusty here, which seemed to confirm the sense they'd had, peering through from the other side, that this was a considerably bigger space than the cave they'd come from. The light from their helmets disappeared into the gloom, and when Todd looked up, he saw nothing but a brownish fog, which gradually tapered into darkness.

"Bit parky," Dev said, rubbing his arms as he stood up.

Robin cocked his head to one side. "Listen to that."

He was referring to the distant but unmistakable rush of water.

"What is it?" said Todd. "Underground river?"

"Could be. Let's hope it's not about to burst its banks with all this rain."

"Can we focus on what we came here for?" said Yrsa with obvious impatience.

"Remember what I said about caution," said Robin. "Let's get the lay of the land."

He unclipped the torch at his belt and switched it on. Almost immediately its powerful beam was joined by another, shining from an identical torch in Dev's hand. Methodically the two men examined their surroundings, the twin beams roaming across the walls, the floor, before crawling upwards. The jagged, uneven ceiling was so high above their heads that even now much of it remained hidden in blackness and shadows.

"Floor looks solid enough," said Dev. "No obvious shafts or cracks."

"Stick close behind me," said Robin, the harsh white light from his torch pushing aside the murk and gloom as he moved forward.

As the twin beams homed in on what appeared to be a vast, possibly wooden structure on the far side of the cavern, Todd had to admit that, despite Yrsa's conviction, he had secretly expected her dreams to be shattered today. In truth, he had believed that what she'd claimed to be vivid childhood memories had been feverish hallucinations brought on by stress and dehydration.

But now he wasn't sure. Although he couldn't see it clearly, there was *some* kind of massive structure against the far wall. *Could* it be a Viking longship? If so, it would be like something out of a fairy tale, almost impossible to accept. How, for instance, could such a thing have ended up here?

"Holy Moses," breathed Dev, for once shaken out of his sanguine state.

As Robin had been shining his torch around, trying to get some idea of the size and shape of the cavern, Dev had moved ahead, and was now standing about fifteen meters closer to the structure, his torchlight roaming across it. Todd could see illuminated curves of what certainly appeared to be wood rising from the misty darkness, but it was only as he moved closer that he started to get any sense of the structure's true shape. His first thought was that it was partly embedded in the rock. Could lava from an eruption have trapped the longship and solidified around it? His half-baked theory lasted only as long as it took for Robin to add his torchlight to Dev's, whereupon the real truth was revealed.

"Fuck me," Robin said. "Is that a tree?"

It was. Incredible as it seemed, the 'structure' was not a longship at all, but a vast, leafless tree, the girth of its trunk at least a dozen meters, maybe more. It sprouted directly from the rock beneath their feet, and its branches, starting a meter or so above their heads, erupted upwards and outwards in all directions, many coiling up the wall behind it, others stretching into the shadowy cavern.

"How the fuck did this thing grow here?" Robin said. "How is it even alive?"

"Maybe it's not alive," said Dev. "Maybe it got trapped in lava and petrified, like that lot in Pompeii."

"It's not petrified," said Todd. "That's definitely wood, not rock."

Robin crouched down, directing his torch beam at the tree's base. The rock there had fused around much of the bark, but he pointed out several areas where blackness showed between roots that had thrust their way from beneath the ground like tentacles.

"They're like boggart holes," Todd said.

Dev looked puzzled. "*What* holes?"

"When we were kids," said Robin, "our parents would sometimes take us to Richmond Park, and whenever we saw a burrow under a tree, our dad would tell us it was a boggart hole."

"What's a boggart?" asked Dev.

"It's a...troll-type thing. An ugly little monster that lives underground."

"Like the thing Amir says he saw in the tunnels?"

Todd and Robin looked at him. Dryly Robin said, "Yeah, thanks for that."

Todd was wondering how likely it was that the tree was still alive, perhaps nourished by the underground water source they could hear rumbling beneath them, when he suddenly remembered Yrsa. Remarkable though the tree was, it wasn't the treasure-laden longship she'd hoped to find, and he wondered how she was feeling about that. He turned to see her standing a few meters away, gazing up at the tree with wide eyes.

"You okay?" he said. "I know this isn't what you were hoping for."

But she didn't seem disappointed. She seemed…entranced. Still gazing upwards, she murmured a word he didn't catch, one filled with sibilants.

"What's that, darling?" asked Dev, turning around.

Yrsa lowered her gaze slowly, looking first at Dev, then Robin, then Todd.

"Yggdrasil," she said quietly. "The tree at the end of the world."

CHAPTER THIRTY-SIX

Most people seemed to resent the newcomers, but Celine Sundby didn't mind them at all. In fact, she liked seeing a few new faces on the island; she thought it injected a bit of energy into the community. And the few she had met, who had visited the hospital to see how their friend Luke was doing, had all been very polite and friendly. Not arrogant and rude, and certainly not drunk most of the time, as some claimed.

She particularly liked Robin, Luke's boss, who seemed genuinely worried about his young employee. Robin had thanked her with real sincerity for looking after Luke, and Celine hadn't known what to say, except, "It's my job." Robin had replied that you could do your job without being kind, but that kindness was the choice she had made, and they were all grateful for that. Celine had blushed and smiled and shrugged, and the man who had come with Robin on that occasion, an older man with dark skin and deep, brown, gentle eyes, had smiled at her, and told her she was 'a little diamond'.

Celine had liked that. A little diamond. She particularly liked the 'little' part, because she wasn't little and never had been. She had a job that kept her on her feet, and she was always dieting, yet still her mother harangued her about how she needed to lose weight, and how she would never find a husband if she didn't.

What Celine hadn't told her mother, though – what she was dreading telling her – was that she didn't *want* to find a husband on the island. The thought of being tied to Eldfjallaeyja for life horrified her. Secretly she envied and admired Yrsa Helgerson for breaking away, and making a new and exciting life for herself. Celine wanted to do the same thing – not in London, of course; she wasn't brave enough to venture *quite* so far from home. But she had plans to go to

Norway, where her family was from originally. Dreamed of settling in Oslo – getting a job in a hospital there, and finding a flat, and starting a new cosmopolitan existence, with new friends and new experiences. Just thinking of the potential opportunities made her giddy with anticipation.

This time next year, she often thought, as she secretly looked for nursing jobs on her glitchy old laptop. *This time next year I'll be living in Aker Brygge or Frogner or Bislett.* Was it a pipe dream? No, she told herself firmly. She *would* do it one day. In fact, not one day – soon. She would do it *soon*. She was just waiting for—

Her train of thought was interrupted by screaming.

As she banged down her mug beside the computer into which she'd been inputting patient data, she realized what had jolted her from her reverie wasn't the sound of one patient screaming, but a whole chorus of wails and groans and cries of distress. It was as if every patient in the hospital had suddenly woken up in terrible pain, or been stricken by the same nightmare.

What was happening? Was it something to do with the storm? Although essential, the hospital on Eldfjallaeyja had never been a hive of activity. Before today, the greatest number of patients occupying the couple of dozen hospital beds was five, maybe six. But in the last twenty-four hours the sick and wounded had been flooding in, the majority of them victims of assaults, self-inflicted wounds, bizarre accidents. At last count only two beds were still unoccupied, and if the current trend continued it wouldn't be long before she and her colleagues – a grand total of four doctors, six nurses (including herself), and six ancillary staff – would be turning people away. As it was, they were already rushed off their feet, with Celine only able to grab her first coffee for maybe five hours thanks to a momentary lull in what had otherwise been an intensely busy shift.

Already, though, it seemed the lull was over – and with a vengeance. Casting a fleeting look of regret at the mug she'd managed to take only two sips from, she hurried from the nurses' station back out into the ward to see what the commotion was about.

Looking around, though, she could see no immediate reason for the outbreak of mass distress. The screamer was a middle-aged woman – Klara Nilsen – who had been stamped on, then beaten unconscious by her husband, Egil. It was an incident that had shocked Celine, because the Nilsens had always seemed such a loving couple, with Egil, who was now in police custody, a gentle and devoted husband.

Distressed as Klara was, however, she didn't appear to require any further medical attention. Watching Agnetha, the youngest of Celine's colleagues, doing her best to calm the injured woman, Celine recalled her thought of moments before – that it was as if every patient in the ward had been plucked from sleep by the same distressing nightmare. Certainly Klara's screams were not those of someone in pain, but of someone who had woken in fear and distress. It was possible the trauma of her ordeal had finally hit home, but in Celine's experience the emotional repercussions of such experiences tended to bubble to the surface gradually, seeping out like poison from a wound.

Scanning the rest of the patients, she saw similar results from one bed to the next. The outpouring seemed emotional rather than physical; no one was bleeding, or vomiting, or doubled over in agony. The only anomalous behavior came from Luke, the Englishman, who was still sleeping peacefully.

Celine's gaze was sliding away from Luke when the young Englishman's body, suddenly and shockingly, bent like a bow, his mid-section rising into the air. For a couple of seconds his body was so rigid that only his heels and the back of his head were pressed into the mattress. Then his body abruptly relaxed and he crashed back onto the bed.

Even as Celine was rushing across to him, it happened again. His body jerked, then rose into an arch, heels and head supporting the upward curve of his body. As the sheet and blanket slid away from him, and his hospital gown rode up over his thighs, Celine saw the muscles in his legs bulge and tighten. His teeth were clenched, his eyes wide open and glaring at the ceiling. Despite this, she suspected he was still unconscious and unaware.

Remembering her training for when a patient had a seizure – clear the area around them of anything hard or sharp – she shoved the chunky bedside cabinet aside, then placed a hand gently on Luke's stomach. His abs felt as hard as rock, and for a moment she had an unreasoning fear that his spine might snap under the pressure. Then, to her relief, his muscles abruptly relaxed, as before, and with an involuntary groan, he slumped onto the bed.

Immediately she leaned over him, slid her hands around his hip and shoulder and attempted to lever him gently onto one side. Around her the other patients were still wailing and sobbing, but she was barely aware of it now; it was nothing but background noise. As she altered his position, she was gratified to see that he appeared to be breathing freely. His face had relaxed and his eyes had closed – but as she straightened up, his eyes opened again and he looked at her.

Such was the intensity of his gaze that Celine took an involuntary step back. "Luke?" she said. And then she asked, "Are you okay? Can you see me?"

Luke's lips parted. Then, just as before, he began to speak, or more accurately to babble, in what sounded like an old Nordic dialect, his voice gruff and sibilant, the words rushing over one another as they flowed out of him.

"I don't…" Celine said, but his only response was to speak faster, more urgently, drowning out her words. His face reddened and the intensity of his gaze redoubled, as if he was desperate to make her understand. He gripped her arm, pulling her closer; she attempted to extricate herself, but he only squeezed tighter.

"Luke," she said calmly. "You're hurting me. Let go."

He stared at her beseechingly, and then he spoke a word that she recognized and understood. He said it twice, forcing it out as if his life depended on it, before slumping back, exhausted.

The word resounded in her head as his eyes drifted closed.

"Ragnarök," he had said. "Ragnarök."

CHAPTER THIRTY-SEVEN

Karriana was heartily sick of the softly beeping machines around her father's bed. She knew they were monitoring his vital signs, which was a good thing, but being constantly reminded of his heart rate, blood pressure and everything else was making her paranoid. For her, the readings were an indicator of how many things could go wrong with the human body.

Of course, there was already a lot wrong with her dad's body, or more specifically his head, though they were problems he had brought on himself. There were certain words and phrases she had become very familiar with over the past couple of days – 'intracranial hemorrhage', 'edema', 'medial prefrontal cortex injury'. She knew in great detail *what* was wrong with him, and what the ongoing effects might be should he recover – motor weakness, personality changes, memory loss, difficulty in concentrating or problem-solving – but what she didn't know was *why* he'd done what he'd done. One day soon she hoped he might be able to tell her, though she was also aware that, depending on how things panned out here, it was a question that might *never* be answered.

But she tried not to think about that for now. Tried to remain positive for herself and her mum. She felt wrung out, her world flipped upside down, but compared to her mum she was a tower of strength. By damaging himself, her dad had damaged her mum as well, and there was a part of Karriana that hated him for that. In the space of just two days, her mum had become colorless, cadaverous. It was as though the hospital, with its bland walls and clinical lighting, was a vampiric entity that was slowly draining her life essence. It didn't help that her mum had barely eaten, barely slept, barely spoken, since her dad's admittance to hospital. All she'd done was stare at her husband, and hold his hand, in the process becoming increasingly more hunched and crone-like.

Looking at her watch for the thousandth time that day, Karriana saw it was seven minutes to four. At four o'clock she would get up and walk the familiar route through several featureless corridors to the reception area. There she would buy herself and her mum muddy coffees from the drinks machine, and she would treat herself to a chocolate bar from the snack dispenser.

She was greatly looking forward to this little indulgence, and the fact of it depressed her no end. Is this what her life had become now? An endless vigil at her father's sickbed, with her only bit of daily pleasure a brief infusion of sugary sweetness?

She wondered how long it would go on. Dr. Tofte, who had operated on her father, had been able to offer them no time frame. "Could be days, could be weeks, could be months," he had said with a shrug. Karriana had nodded, but her mind had been reeling. It had seemed insensitive to broach the subject with her mum, but she couldn't help wondering what would become of the bakery, of their livelihood. Even if Dad recovered, how long would it be – if ever – before he could bake again? If he couldn't return to work, was it possible she could take on his mantle while Mum worked in the shop? But then who would look after her dad, and how much would it cost? Wherever she looked, all she saw were problems, obstacles, uncertainties.

We'll get through it, she thought, knowing her faith wasn't really faith at all, but blind hope. She looked at her watch again. Three minutes to four. Soon be time for chocolate, and chocolate always made things—

Beyond the curtains that were pulled around the bed, something started happening.

Suddenly all the other patients in the ward began to cry out, in what sounded like anguish or fear. Alarmed, Karriana jumped to her feet, turning to face the thin gray curtain that enshrouded them. Her heart hammered at the prospect of what might be beyond it. Given recent events, it didn't seem so far-fetched to imagine an intruder striding into the ward, armed with a gun or a knife. She reached out to pull the curtain aside, then hesitated, fearful of exposing her family to danger. The gray curtain might be a flimsy barrier, but still…why risk drawing attention to themselves? If there *was* some madman out there, out of sight might also mean—

"Karri!"

Her mum's voice was sharp, urgent. Karriana spun back round to tell her to be quiet. Of all the times to—

Then she saw that her dad's eyes were open, and he was staring at her.

From his expression, he didn't seem to know where he was. There was a blankness there, but there was also a sort of…ferocity. As if he felt under threat and was prepared to defend himself. Ignoring the cries from beyond the gray curtain for the moment, Karriana took a step towards the bed. A brief snippet of the conversation she'd had with Dr. Tofte flashed through her mind:

When you say personality changes, you don't mean he'll be…aggressive, do you?

It's too early to say.

But he might?

Well, it's best not to speculate at this stage.

"Dad?" she said.

He didn't respond. Just continued to stare at her. Her mum, meanwhile, clutched her husband's limp hand in both of hers, and for the first time in days she looked radiant.

"Dad?" Karriana repeated. "Can you hear me? Do you know who I am?"

Her mother frowned. "Well, of course he can hear you. He's not deaf, Karri. He just needs a bit of—"

Her dad sat up.

He did it suddenly, mechanically. Although this was her dad, Karriana felt fear ripple through her. Having taken a step towards the bed, she now took a hurried step back.

"Mum," she said, "be careful."

But her mother was too overcome by the miracle of her husband's resurrection to show caution.

"Oh, Leif!" she cried. "You've come back to us! I knew you would! It's me. It's your Tuva!"

Leif seemed unmoved by his wife's joy. Nor did he respond to his name. His attention remained fixed on Karriana, and now he was not just staring, but *glaring* at her.

She took another step back, which brought her into contact with the gray curtain. It draped itself about her shoulders.

"Mum," Karriana said nervously, "I don't think Dad's properly awake. I don't think he knows where he is."

Her mother's only response was to clasp her husband's hand even tighter and gaze adoringly into his wide, red-bearded face. "He will in a minute. Won't you, Leif? You just need time to come to."

In one fluid motion, her dad swung his legs from the bed. He dragged the sheets and blankets with him, which came untucked on the far side and spilled onto the floor next to his wife's chair.

"Oh dear, Leif, see what you've done," Karriana's mother said. She let go of his hand and leaned sideways in her chair, directly in front of his rigidly seated body, to pick up the bundle of bedding. Almost casually, his eyes still fixed on Karriana, Leif took his wife's outstretched arm in both hands, and twisted it sharply, his hands moving in opposite directions. There was a hideous crack, and Karriana's mother gave a short, awful screech. Instantly her face drained of color and she tumbled onto the floor among the bedding, her mouth gaping in pain and shock.

Karriana stared in disbelief at her mother's forearm, which was bent at a horrible angle. Already there was blood spurting from a ragged gash in her skin where her broken bone had punctured it like a splintered stick. Her father stood up so abruptly that the electrodes stuck to his chest popped free, and the tube attached to the cannula in the crook of his elbow tore away. Karriana blundered back into the gray curtain, which enfolded her like a vast web.

Panicking, she clawed at it, tearing it from the plastic rings that held it in place. Hurling it aside, she again turned to face her dad, who was now stepping forward, directly onto his wife's body.

"Dad, no!" Karriana screamed, but he didn't hesitate. His foot came down on his wife's back, as if he was unaware she was even there. She grunted as he crushed her into the floor, her unbroken left arm flailing to smack against the leg of the hospital bed.

Karriana yelled, "Get off her!" but he was already stepping forward, off her body. Half-twisting as she backed away from him, she shouted, "Somebody help!"

Focused on her dad, who was lurching towards her like Frankenstein's monster, she had only a peripheral impression of other patients trying to rise from their beds, and of hospital staff attempting to calm them. In response to her cries, Dr. Tofte and another man, who might have been a hospital orderly, rushed forward to waylay her father. Dr. Tofte held up his hands in a placatory manner, while the orderly took her father's arm, speaking in a soothing voice.

With what appeared to be superhuman strength, however, her dad wrenched the orderly's hand off his arm and cast it aside. Then, before either the orderly or Dr. Tofte could react, he shot out his arms, grabbed the heads of the two men and smashed them together. Even as they slid to the ground, Karriana's father stepped between them, hands reaching for his daughter.

Casting a final agonized look at her mother, who was still floundering among blood-soaked bedding beside her father's hospital bed, Karriana turned and ran.

CHAPTER THIRTY-EIGHT

For the first time in his career, Anders Hagen felt completely out of his depth.

Although he, Erik and Pálína had tried their best to cope with the situation, Anders had to admit that what had started as a spate of bizarre and disturbing incidents had now escalated into an epidemic beyond their control. It was as if some higher power was punishing the islanders for avoiding the virus that had ravaged the rest of the world a few years ago, by now visiting a more lethal virus upon them – one that addled people's brains, making them delusional and violent. Until a couple of days ago, Anders had been hoping the incidents were an anomaly, a kind of mass hysteria that would eventually die down. But now the hospital was full of people who had either harmed themselves or who had been harmed by others (often by loved ones, who had flipped for no apparent reason), and, as a consequence, the four cells in the local station, which most of the time stood empty, were full too – crammed beyond capacity, in fact, and mostly with offenders who needed psychiatric help that was not available.

Admitting a need for help and conveying that need to the people who could provide it, though, were two very different things. Although Eldfjallaeyja was an independent nation, an agreement had been made in the dim and distant past that, in the event of an emergency, the islanders could call on their nearest neighbor of significant size, Iceland, for aid and assistance. Such action required the Council's approval, and several times that day, while rushing between call-outs, Anders had tried to contact various Council members to recommend they act on the agreement. But each time, he had failed to get through. The island's phone network had been down since yesterday due to the storm, and now the mobile network was fucked too – for the past few hours, Anders had been getting the 'No Service' signal on his phone whenever he had tried to use it. To add insult to injury, radio contact with his colleagues was now also kaput, the airwaves full of wall-to-wall static. This effectively meant he was in limbo – they all were. If there were further incidents on the island requiring police investigation and intervention, there was no way of finding out about them.

Sitting in his car, rain hammering on the roof with a force that felt capable of stripping flesh from bones, Anders assessed the problem. Assuming the communication blackout was widespread, his only option was to head back to the station and hope his colleagues had had the same idea. Once there he'd liaise with them and try to formulate a game plan.

Contact with the outside world would have to wait until the storm abated, but in the meantime they could at least ensure the rest of the community was okay. Although it would be labor intensive, Anders was thinking in terms of door-to-door patrols, the three of them establishing a route to cover every occupied part of the island. If possible, he'd prefer Erik and Pálína to stick together, work as a pair. He knew he was a sexist old dinosaur, but given recent events, he didn't want Pálína visiting some of the more remote homesteads on her own. He knew she was tough and courageous, despite her slight frame, yet what had previously seemed like a community made placid by its insularity suddenly felt like the Wild West.

He knew what they'd say to his suggestion. They'd counter his argument that they were young and inexperienced by mentioning his age, and the fact that he was carrying a few extra pounds, which meant neither his speed nor his reflexes were as good as theirs. And they'd have a point – the bite mark on his hand was proof of that – but when it came down to it, he was the boss, and the final decision would be his.

Thinking of his injured hand seemed to awaken a pulse of pain within it, and he flexed it experimentally. The bite, eight distinct teeth marks, four on the back of his hand, four on the palm, were clustered between his thumb and wrist. At least they'd stopped bleeding, though the flesh around them was swelling as the bruises came out. Anders only hoped that whatever had sent old Arne Ström crazy was not infectious, and that he wasn't now destined to turn into a ravening madman himself. No sooner had the thought entered his head than he was dismissing it. *Of course* that wasn't what was happening here; such things only existed in those horror films Pálína liked.

The call-out to Arne's place was the last one he'd received before static had engulfed the airwaves. Marianne Jensen, who manned the phone at the station, had radioed to say that the eighty-odd-year-old man, who lived alone at Svart Rokk farm, had been spotted by Pétur Sigurdsson and his son when they were out in their SUV checking their livestock. Arne had been walking along the side of the road, buck naked in the lashing rain. When Pétur had stopped to speak to him, Arne had hooted like an owl, bashed several times on the side of the vehicle with a clenched fist, then climbed over a nearby fence and capered across a field. Pétur had shouted after him, imploring him to come back, but the old man had ignored him, and had eventually disappeared within the seething curtains of rain. The Sigurdssons said the only consolation was that Arne appeared to be heading back home – so that was where Anders had gone.

Svart Rokk farm lay at the bottom of a long zigzagging road, which eventually crossed a river. Most of the year, the river flowed so gently that the water resembled a mirror full of sky, but when Anders reached it, it was as turbulent as a white-water run, and so high that waves crashed against the side of the wooden bridge that spanned it, spray cascading across the rain-darkened planks like shards of glass.

Glancing into the tempestuous waters, Anders shuddered. If Arne had attempted to cross that on his way home and been swept into the water, there'd be no hope for him. Gritting his teeth, he drove slowly over the bridge, his visibility reduced to zero by the side swipes of frothing water. Five minutes later he pulled up in Arne Ström's mud bath of a front yard.

Even before leaving the vehicle, he'd seen the farmhouse door open and banging in the wind. Donning his already drenched waterproofs, he tramped through the mud, bent almost double, and entered the house.

After wiping his feet on the mat, he closed the door and shouted Arne's name. He paused to listen, but received no reply – and then he spotted muddy prints, made by someone walking barefoot, trailing up the stairs.

He followed the steps to the bathroom, the chipped and flaking door to which was slightly ajar.

"Arne," he called. "It's me, Anders. Are you okay?"

When he received no answer, he started to push the door open – then heard rapid footsteps behind him.

Turning, he was confusedly aware of a stringy figure, all bony limbs, bared teeth and swinging genitals, scuttling along the landing. Then Arne's long, veined hands shot out, hitting Anders in the chest.

It wasn't a forceful shove, but Anders, who had half-spun round, had been off-balance. He fell backwards, his back slamming into the bathroom door, which flew open behind him. To add insult to injury, the toilet caught him a glancing blow on the side of his head as he went down.

Black shapes jittering in his vision, he was aware of Arne looming over him. He didn't realize he'd raised his right hand in defense, though, until he felt the flesh at the base of his thumb enclosed in hot, slobbery wetness, followed by a clamping pain that made him cry out.

For a split second he felt panic, as though the pain, which was slicing through both sides of his hand, would meet in the middle, and that when it did it would take his entire thumb with it. Then the pressure – if not the pain – was gone. The old man, belying his age and infirmity, darted out the door and down the stairs, thudding footsteps growing fainter.

Shocked, relieved, faintly embarrassed, blood dripping from his fingers onto the floor, Anders would dearly have liked to have stayed where he was for a few minutes, to recover. But he couldn't. As a police officer, his duty was to protect the individuals under his care. And Arne Ström, despite appearances to the contrary, needed his protection. Vigorous though he seemed, he was still a frail old man, and even fully clothed would not last long outside. So Anders heaved himself to his feet and blundered after his attacker, clenched fist seeping blood held protectively against his abdomen.

Try as he might, though, he'd been unable to find Arne. He'd searched on foot, shouting his name at regular intervals, and then in his car, driving slowly around the area. Knowing Arne was out there somewhere, naked and vulnerable, had been agonizing, but what else could he do? He couldn't call for backup, and it was pointless driving around aimlessly, so eventually, reluctantly, he'd admitted defeat, drenched and despondent.

And now he was heading back to the station, guilt, concern and an awful sense of failure grinding in his belly. He hadn't felt this useless since Linnea had left him eleven years ago. Although she had been the love of his life, he'd been spectacularly bad at marriage, and their inability to have children had only exacerbated the problem. But at least their parting currently provided him with the only source of comfort he could glean from this shit show, in that he knew she was now safe and happy in Denmark with her new husband, and not anxiously awaiting his return in the little home they had once shared. There was something to be said for only having yourself to worry about, even if it did make for a lonely existence. Hunched forward over the steering wheel, peering through a slithering screen of water at a world of blurred, constantly fracturing shapes, he wondered whether he would ever see Linnea again. The possibility that he wouldn't filled him with sadness.

It took him fifty minutes to complete a journey that would normally have taken twenty. By the time he pulled up outside the station, he had a pounding headache, and his injured hand was so swollen that the slightest movement sent pain shooting up his arm.

He was pleased, though, to see that Pálína's car was here. He parked his own beside it, then switched the engine off and sat back, closing his eyes for a moment. He felt sweaty and nauseous, but he didn't think he had a fever. And despite his headache, he wasn't having strange ideas, or experiencing murderous impulses – so at least that was something.

Trying to put his still-wet waterproofs on with one hand proved an impossible task, so after struggling for a minute or so, he hurled them angrily into the passenger footwell and decided to make a dash for it. Bracing himself, he threw open the car door and stepped out. The rain swooped at him immediately, drenching him. He ran through it, head down, and burst through the station doorway into the entrance vestibule. Two meters in front of him an inquiry window in the wall, a screen of toughened glass, separated the station staff from the public – although in his two-decades-plus of employment, such a level of protection had never been necessary. To the right of the window was a door with a keypad beside it. Anders tapped a four-digit code into the keypad and the door opened with a wasp-like buzz.

The office beyond was high-ceilinged, bright and airy. It was occupied by four desks – one each for him, Erik, Pálína and Marianne. Marianne's desk, on the far left, was the biggest and most cluttered, not only because she was responsible for fielding phone calls and passing on information when they were out on patrol, but because she was the station's office administrator. Marianne was a stout, no-nonsense woman in her seventies, with a stern face that could sometimes crinkle into a disarmingly warm smile. Years before, she had been Anders' maths teacher at secondary school, and he had been terrified of her. When she retired, the Council had offered her the admin job on a part-time basis. Although Anders hadn't initially liked the idea of renewing his acquaintanceship with her, soon he had not only come to accept that her organizational skills made their lives a lot easier, but he actually liked – if not loved – her. In many ways she became a substitute for the mother he lost to cancer when he was fifteen.

He expected her to be sitting at her desk when he walked in. Usually she'd be on the phone, or hunched over her computer, spectacles perched on her forehead. Today, though, there was no sign of her; the office was empty.

Maybe she'd gone home, having realized that with nothing working, there was no point hanging around? That was possible, but it wasn't the sort of thing she'd do, not without telling anyone.

Equally strange was the fact that Pálína wasn't here, even though her car was outside. He guessed she could be taking a leak, or checking on the prisoners in the basement. As he raked a hand through his wet hair, it occurred to him that something looked off about Marianne's workstation. He tried to work out what it was – and suddenly realized that the chunky police radio that was usually propped on its charging port next to her computer was not there.

Then he saw the leg sticking out from behind her desk.

Thick-ankled, varicose-veined, clad in a brown stocking and a browner woman's brogue, he had no doubt who it belonged to.

"Marianne!" he yelled, rushing across, slapping a hand on the edge of her desk as he circled it. Sure enough, there she was, and as soon as he saw her, he reeled back. Now he could see where the police radio had gone. The heavy, brick-shaped device was buried in the shattered eye socket of Marianne Jensen's very dead face.

Her one remaining eye stared at him in frozen indignation, and her mouth hung open as if she was about to reprimand him for running in the corridor. Along with the ruin of her left eye, her face was battered and bruised, her gray hair soaked red from the blood she was lying in.

Anders had seen some terrible things in his time, not least the bodies of fishermen dredged from the sea, but this was Marianne, who he'd known since childhood, and his reaction was an almost primal sense of horror. Even so, he remained mindful of not contaminating the crime scene as he wheeled away, his gorge rising. Staggering across to Erik's desk, he grabbed the metal waste bin and vomited into it.

His stomach heaved three more times before it was empty, after which he began shaking with cold and shock. Taking a deep breath, he crossed to the water cooler and poured himself a paper cone of water. He sipped it slowly as he tried to pull his fragmented thoughts together.

Who had killed Marianne? Could someone infected with whatever sickness was sweeping the island have got into the station? But how had the killer found out the door code? Unless…could it have been a prisoner? And if so, was the killer still in the station? And where the fuck was Pálína?

He pictured his young officer being held hostage, wondered if she had a knife to her throat at this very moment.

Or maybe she's lying dead somewhere like Marianne. The thought crept out before he could stop it. He glanced at the door leading to the cells.

He imagined the killer crouched on the other side, and drawing his baton awkwardly from his belt with his left hand, he tiptoed to the door and put his ear against it. All he could hear was the *drip...drip...* of water from his clothes onto the carpet, like a sonar blip signaling his whereabouts.

He listened hard for a minute or more, but the silence held. Should he open the door quietly or burst through, baton swinging? With his right hand out of action, he thought the cautious approach might be best. Tucking the baton under his right armpit, he eased down the handle. Grabbing the baton as soon as his left hand was free, he shoved the door open with his body and stepped through. His heart pounded, and his eyes darted everywhere, but the corridor was empty.

There were two doors in the left-hand wall, male and female toilets, both closed. The doors had spring-operated door closers rather than handles, so they would close automatically behind whoever was entering or leaving. Pushing open the first door, to the women's toilet, with his left shoulder, he stepped inside. The room was empty, as was the men's toilet next door. That left only the basement. Was Marianne's killer down there? It was more likely he'd have already escaped into the rain, but he had to check it out.

Like the door into the office, the basement door was opened via a keypad. Again tucking his baton beneath his right armpit, Anders reached for it with his left hand – and froze.

There were smeared, red fingerprints on buttons 2, 6, 7 and 9 – the four numbers of the code needed to access the cell area.

Looking closer, Anders saw there was also a smear of blood on the cream-colored wall below the keypad, and also on the door handle. So the killer *had* come back this way. But why? Anders knew the only way to unlock the cells was by using one of two sets of identical keys. One set he carried with him. The other was in the top right-hand drawer of his desk.

Dread crawling through him, he stabbed at the four-digit code, grimacing at the thought that he was getting Marianne's blood on his finger. As the door clicked open, he wiped the finger on his wet trousers, then grabbed his baton. Nudging the door open with his foot, he sidled around it.

Ahead of him a set of uncarpeted stairs led down. At the bottom stood a figure, looking up at him. Although he'd been preparing himself for an encounter, the figure's sudden motionless presence was so unexpected that his body jerked, sending pain shooting up his injured hand into his arm.

Even as the pain dissipated, he recognized the figure. It was Pálína. His relief that she was alive and seemingly unharmed was mixed with disquiet. Why was she standing there, staring at him?

"Pálína," he said, "are you okay?"

Her only response was to sway slightly from side to side, like a cornstalk in a breeze, giving him the odd impression that she had been somehow unbalanced by his words.

When she didn't reply he tried again. "Is everything all right here, Pálína?"

She shifted more significantly this time, lifting a foot and placing it on the step in front of her. As she did so, something jangled.

Anders saw that the spare keys to the cells were dangling from her right hand. The main light source in the basement corridor came from behind her, the staircase shadowy enough that her body was mostly in silhouette, her features barely discernible. However, there was enough light to see that her hand was smeared with some dark, slick substance to which the wash of backlight lent a crimson halo.

"Oh, Pálína," he murmured. "What's been happening here?"

Finally she spoke.

Her voice was low, gruff, monotonous. The language she spoke contained words he half-understood, but the dialect was odd, and the full meaning of what she was saying was lost on him. He felt fear prickling his body. This wasn't Pálína. Or rather, Pálína wasn't herself. Whatever this illness, this infection was, it had hold of her.

Which, although Anders didn't want to believe it, probably meant that Pálína had killed Marianne.

She took another step. Then another. And now there were shadows massing behind her, sounds of movement. He imagined her going from cell to cell, unlocking their doors one by one, swinging them open. He considered trying to appeal to her, but when she took another step, it brought her close enough for him to see her eyes, and realize it was not Pálína he would be appealing to.

He turned and ran.

Reaching the door into the corridor, he wasted precious seconds trying to scrabble at the keypad with the baton in his hand, before taking a breath, tucking the baton beneath his throbbing right arm and trying again. By the time he pulled the door open, he felt that Pálína and the prisoners were right at his back, but he retained the presence of mind to take a step back so he could open the door wide enough to pass through.

Making it into the corridor, he leaned his weight against the door, hearing it click and lock behind him. Then he staggered towards the door at the end of the corridor, the one that led back to the office, where Marianne lay in a congealing pool of her own blood.

He was six paces from the door when it opened and Erik stepped through.

"Erik!" Anders gasped, stumbling towards him. "Get back! We've got to get away!"

But Erik simply stood there, and Anders felt a flash of irritation. His deputy had always been a bit slow on the uptake.

"Erik, turn round!" Anders yelled. But then he saw the expression on Erik's face and he halted abruptly. "Oh, Erik," he muttered. "Not you too."

Behind him, the door to the basement clicked open. Anders spun as Pálína stepped into the corridor, many bodies behind her. Anders was exhausted, terrified, soaking wet, injured, but he raised his baton, determined to fight for his life.

CHAPTER THIRTY-NINE

"What does that mean?" Todd said.

Yrsa was freaking him out. She looked like she was high on something, face filled with awe, as if the world was full of wonders. All at once, and not for the first time, Todd found himself longing for his old life – the grime and noise of London, the everyday stress of bills and auditions and tube cancellations.

Yrsa gave him a slow smile. A *knowing* smile.

"Poor Todd," she said. "You've played your part well."

Robin and Dev looked at him questioningly. Todd felt guilty in spite of himself, though it emerged as irritation.

"What do you mean? What part? What are you talking about?"

Still smiling, she said, "I selected you right from the start. You were young, handsome, single. Yrsa liked you. And you had *connections*."

She looked pointedly at Robin, who looked confused. "What's she on about, squirt?"

Suspicion was creeping through Todd's head, all the odd occurrences since they had arrived here coming together to form a picture. For now the picture was blurred, incomplete, but he had a feeling that when it came into focus it would be awful to look upon.

"Why are you talking about yourself in the third person?" he said. "Are you saying you're *not* Yrsa?"

She laughed, then pouted and lowered her eyelids, giving him a coquettish look.

Angrily Robin said, "Of *course* she's bloody Yrsa! We can all see she is."

But Todd shook his head. "No, Rob, I don't think she is."

Robin gave a snort of disbelief. Calmly Dev said, "You saying there's something wrong with her, Todd? Up here?" He tapped his forehead. "Split personality? Schizophrenia?"

"I'm not sure it's even that," Todd said.

"What the fuck is it then?" demanded Robin.

"I think she's what the islanders have been saying she is for years," said Todd. "An imposter. A changeling. Or that's what she thinks she is, anyway."

"A what?" said Robin.

But before Todd could answer, Yrsa gave a bark of dismissive laughter. "*Changeling?*" she said. "*Please!*"

"What would you call yourself then?" Todd asked.

That knowing smile again. "I'm a passenger." Then she checked herself. "No. I'm the driver. Though mostly I sit in the background, allow the car to run on automatic."

Robin rolled his eyes. "This is crazy."

Todd stared at Yrsa, mind racing. Could this really be happening? Was this an honest-to-god case of possession? He'd heard about such things, but nowadays real-life cases were believed to be rooted in mental health issues, not devils and evil spirits.

"You mean you allow the real Yrsa to show through sometimes—"

"Most of the time. It's easier that way."

"But sometimes you take over. To…what?"

"To manipulate events. To manipulate you." Her smile now was smug.

"Okay," said Todd, as if this was a rational conversation. "So why do you do that?"

She regarded him with a wry smirk, as if he was a pet dog, or a child.

"I was trapped here. I was trapped for a long time. In this chamber, behind that wall. I was held, restrained, by what you would probably think of as a magic spell." She gave a mocking laugh, as if scornful of their limited minds. "And when little Yrsa found me, a small part of me latched on to her and hitched a ride back."

"A small part?" said Todd. "Are you saying that most of you was still stuck here?"

"Once the girl was mine, I knew it would be only a matter of time before someone would release me."

"Just by knocking that wall down?" Todd pointed at the tunnel they'd crawled through.

Yrsa's smirk was beginning to irritate him. She said, "That will only be the start of it."

"The start of what? Of breaking the spell?"

Robin looked at Todd with incredulity.

"You're as bad as she is," he said. "You don't honestly believe this load of cock, do you?"

"*She* does," Dev said quietly. "Look at her."

Robin, though, shook his head. "I thought you two met when she got mugged?"

"We did," said Todd.

"And I arranged it," said Yrsa. "I found the men. I paid them to attack Yrsa. I made sure she was in the right place at the right time, so that you, gallant knight, would come to her rescue. And poor Yrsa knew nothing about any of it."

"We could have died," Todd said. "Either of us. What if something had gone wrong?"

Yrsa flashed him a look, her eyes alight with savage glee. "That's what makes life so *interesting*, isn't it?"

Dev half-raised a hand. "Can I ask a question?"

Yrsa inclined her head.

"What are you?" Dev said. "You say you're inside Yrsa, controlling her? But what do you claim to be exactly? A demon? An evil spirit?"

Yrsa scoffed. "I am the herald of the gods."

"Yeah, 'course you are," said Robin heavily.

Yrsa gave him an amused look. Then, slowly, she raised her arms.

As she did, the rumbling of water from beneath their feet gradually increased in volume. All three men looked at each other in disbelief.

"What the fuck's happening?" Robin said, looking down at the ground.

Todd could feel it too. A trembling beneath him. As it increased, so the roar of water became louder, more defined. He imagined the days of torrential rain slowly saturating the island, filling up every underground cave and tunnel, and then, with nowhere else to go, being forced up through thousands of cracks and fissures. He looked again at the 'boggart holes' around the tree, at the dozens of minute fractures running like veins through the rock. Then he looked at Yrsa, who was standing with arms upraised, a gleeful look on her face.

Could she *really* be doing this? Drawing the water up from below, controlling the elemental forces of the earth? It was a crazy notion, but right here, right now, he was prepared to believe anything.

One thing he *was* sure of was that they were in terrible danger. Grabbing the sleeve of Robin's baggy protective suit, he gave it a yank, encouraging him to move.

"Come on!" he yelled, raising his voice above the roar of what sounded like an approaching tsunami. "We need to get out of here!"

Robin had been staring at Yrsa with furious disbelief, but now he blinked, then began loping back across the cavern towards the arch in the wall.

Indicating Yrsa, Dev said, "What about her?"

"You go. I'll speak to her."

"No time for chat. We could carry her between us."

Todd shook his head. "Better if I do it alone."

Dev looked uncertain, but said, "Okay. But drag her out if you have to. And if you're not right behind me, I'm coming back for you."

"I'd expect nothing less," said Todd.

Dev clapped him on the side of the arm, then took off after Robin. Stepping towards Yrsa, Todd said gently, "Come on, Yrsa. We need to go."

Yrsa was still smiling, but it no longer looked like a human expression. It looked like a mask whose lips had been stretched by wires. "There's no escape for any of you, Todd," she said matter-of-factly.

"Come on, Yrsa, fight that thing inside you. We can both escape if we go now."

Mouth still stretched in a ghastly grin, she said, "I can't expect you to understand. It's time, Todd. Time for the world to split open and the true gods to rise again."

The ground was really shaking now. Todd was half-crouched, hands held out as if balancing on a surfboard. Preferring even now to regard Yrsa's words as the ravings of a crazy person, he said, "We need to go *now*, Yrsa. If you won't walk out with me, I'll carry you. I mean it."

Her only response was to tilt her head, to look not at Todd, but over his shoulder, in the direction of the vast tree. "Look, Todd," she said.

Despite himself, Todd glanced over his shoulder. He saw movement at the base of the tree, where the darkness within the 'boggart holes' seemed to be squirming.

Water? The first upward surge, brimming and about to spill over? No, the darkness wasn't moving like water. It seemed more solid, more purposeful. Animals, then? Rats trying to outrun the flood?

Before Todd's disbelieving eyes, the first lump of darkness emerged from the hollow beneath the tree, then unsteadily unfolded itself, rose upright until it was standing on two stout legs.

It was a man. Squat, hunched, deformed, no more than three feet tall – but a man all the same. No sooner had one emerged than another hauled itself out of another hollow close by. Then a third, reaching up from a thick black crevice in the rocky ground to grasp a tentacle-like root and drag itself into the gloomy half-light, like a dead thing rising from a grave.

The light from Todd's head torch illuminated faces that were lumpy, misshapen, the brows thick and ridged, the eyes low, almost on the cheeks, and inset with pupils that were nothing but black horizontal slits, like the eyes of goats. The small men were snuffling and grunting, like moles after a long period of hibernation. One of them opened a cavernous mouth, and Todd saw boar-like tusks curling upwards.

Jötnar, he thought.

"If they become aware of you, they'll kill you," Yrsa said pragmatically.

The thought of that, of the jötnar becoming aware of him, overwhelmed Todd with terror.

He spun away and ran.

CHAPTER FORTY

Todd couldn't tell how much the cavern was shaking and how much of it was his own fear. As he focused on the arch into the next cave, all he knew was that he was staggering like a drunk. The air was filled with dust and a rising bellow that, for all he knew, might have been the awakening roar of the gods. Beyond the simple instinct to survive, his mind reeled with the impossibility of what was happening. But that was something he would have to come to terms with later – if he got the chance.

Reaching the arch, he dived into it, ducking his head to avoid smashing his helmet light on the low ceiling. Every instinct screamed at him to rise to his feet and run, but he couldn't in here. Even a stooping crouch would cause his back to scrape against rock.

The tunnel was only a few meters long, but knowing what was behind him made his crawl through it seem interminable. The light from his helmet bounced crazily around the walls; his vision shivered out of focus, unless it was the rock vibrating under the pressure of water rushing up through the cave system. Shoulders and elbows scraping rock, feet scrabbling, he felt as if the walls were closing in. Then, with a whoop of gritty air, he was out, the darkness expanding around him.

He was alone in the cave, the drill that had carved out the passage standing abandoned on his right. But beyond the opening on the opposite wall came the rustles, thumps and half-coherent cries of movement. No doubt encouraged by Robin and Dev, everyone was running. Staggering upright, Todd followed them. Just before entering the tunnel leading back to the Devil's Throat, he glanced behind him.

Could he see movement in the man-made tunnel, or was his jittering lamplight creating an illusion of eager activity? Either way, he had all the impetus he needed to push on. He plunged into the tunnel ahead, his lamplight flowing across the rocky walls and uneven ground. Using his hands on the walls to propel himself along, he quickly fell into a steady rhythm. He had been going for several minutes when he saw a figure filling the tunnel ahead. Whoever was at the rear of Robin's group was moving considerably slower than he was.

"Faster!" Todd yelled, appalled at the thought of having to slow down. His voice bounced off the rock, the echoes seeming to mock his panic. The figure in front of him glanced over his shoulder, and Todd saw Big Andy's scared face.

"Don't stop! Keep going!" he screamed. "There's something behind us!"

His words galvanized the big man, who put on such a spurt of speed that he disappeared from view. However, plowing onwards, Todd was dismayed seconds later to discover that Andy had simply rounded a curve and that his broad back was filling the tunnel once more – and Todd was now even closer to him than ever.

"*Faster, Andy!*" he yelled, his voice a frantic screech.

Andy tried, but within seconds Todd was right on his heels. Although panic was crackling through him like electricity, Todd resisted the urge to shove Andy along, afraid that the big guy might lose his balance and fall. Trying to adjust to Andy's slower pace, Todd glanced behind him again. His helmet beam was blurred with dust, reducing visibility to a few meters, but did he see pinpoints of light, like the reflected eyes of cats, winking in the darkness?

Ahead of him, there came a shifting of rock and Andy cried out. Todd's head whipped round to see Andy stumble, thump the left-hand wall with his shoulder, then thankfully regain his balance. Instinctively Todd stooped to grab the chunk of rock that Andy had stepped on. Half-twisting, he lobbed it into the darkness behind him. He was reassured to hear the crack of rock on rock, followed by a smattering of smaller sounds as the rock bounced a couple of times, then settled. If the jötnar *were* in pursuit, they were clearly still some way back. Facing front again, he eventually saw the narrow tunnel ahead of Andy open out, and beyond that a vertical shaft of light fizzing with rain.

It was daylight, pouring in through the Devil's Throat. The ground beneath it was slick, and appeared to be sparking, as water pummeled it. Around the haze of moisture, Todd was aware of busy movement and the flash of headlamps. The dripping, empty harness they'd used to lower themselves in here was twitching in the downpour. As Todd overtook Andy, who had staggered out of the tunnel and was now bent double, gasping, to the left of the tunnel entrance, he saw Dev buckle himself into the harness as rain pounded his head and shoulders, surrounding him with an effervescent halo. When Dev was done, he tugged on the rope that stretched into the shaft above, then started to haul himself up. Todd reached Robin just as Dev's toes disappeared around the kink in the shaft above.

Robin looked at Todd, then beyond him. "Where's Yrsa? Didn't you bring her?"

"Couldn't," Todd gasped. "Things started coming out of the ground."

"What things?"

"Creatures. Men. Though not human. I think they might be coming this way."

As before, Robin looked furious – his default response to dealing with the inexplicable. "Not human? This is fucking cracked, Todd. Get a grip."

Even so, he glanced uneasily at the tunnel from which Todd had emerged. Big Andy was still leaning against the wall to the left of it, trying to catch his breath.

"I know what I saw," Todd said. Fear was making him angry now too.

He wanted to add that Robin would find out the truth soon enough – but really, he hoped he wouldn't. He'd happily settle for them all getting out of here, even if it meant his brother ripping the piss out of him later for imagining things.

"Just don't tell the others," Robin said, reducing his voice to a hiss that matched the rain. "They're spooked enough as it is."

Todd was about to reply when Jay said, "What the fuck's that?"

With a sense of dread, Todd turned. Jay was a few meters away, looking at the opening Todd had emerged from. Amir, Sean and Hector, who had been watching Dev rise slowly (too slowly) up the shaft, turned too. The light from their headlamps washed over Andy, making the sweat on his cheeks and forehead gleam like plastic. Andy's tree-trunk legs straightened, and his head turned towards the dark opening to his right. Todd realized the big guy must have heard what Jay had also heard – a scrabble of movement from the tunnel.

He peered into the opening, which was shaped like a crooked witch's hat. Through the brownish light, he saw what he thought he had seen earlier – the reflective flash of eyes in the darkness.

"Andy," he said urgently, "get away from—"

Before he could finish his sentence, a shape emerged from the opening, its speed belying its squat bulkiness, and thrust a long pole in Andy's direction.

No, not a pole, Todd realized, as Andy let out a pig-like squeal, *a spear*, crudely fashioned, though horribly effective. Todd glimpsed its metal point flashing in the light before it entered the side of Andy's leg.

As Andy collapsed, and blood gushed from the wound and sprayed across the rocky ground, all hell broke loose. Around Todd, the men began to yell in fear and fury. Robin, Sean and Hector rushed forward to help or defend Andy, while Amir and Jay dropped back, horrified by what they'd seen. The creature that had emerged from the tunnel wrenched its spear from Andy's leg, provoking another screech of pain, then swung round to face them. It raised its head, and made a terrifying chattering noise, that seemed full of savage, berserk fury.

Whether it was the creature's bizarre attack cry, the first sight of its bestial, tusked face, or the fact that three other dark, squat shapes were now emerging from the opening, Robin, Sean and Hector's surge forward suddenly faltered. Hector raised his hands as if to deny the nightmarish sight, and Robin almost tripped over Sean, who had come to an abrupt halt in front of him.

Todd remained where he'd been standing when Andy had been attacked, on the edge of the beam of light and rain spilling into the cavern from above. Partly he was shocked into immobility, and partly he instinctively knew it was pointless trying to oppose the jötnar, because, like apes, their strength and savagery would far outstrip his, or any human's.

This was confirmed when the creature that had speared Andy darted across to the fallen man, grabbed his flailing arm, and dragged his frantically struggling body across the rocky ground and into the blackness of the tunnel. Within seconds all that was left to remind them that Andy had been there was an abattoir-smear of blood across the rock.

As Sean clapped his tattooed hands to his head and cried, "Fuck!" Robin lurched forward, as though confronting drunken thugs in a pub. "Give him back, you freaks!" he yelled, sounding terrified rather than aggressive.

In response, one of the jötnar swung round to face Robin. This creature had baggy, slate-colored skin and bulging, misaligned eyes, its right one so low it gave the impression of having oozed from its socket and down its cheek. It was only when the creature raised its stubby arms that Todd realized it was holding a kind of crossbow.

"Rob, look out!" Todd yelled, a fraction of a second before a zizzing *snap* accompanied a slim black projectile, which sliced through the air.

Robin's half-turn at Todd's warning saved his life. Instead of ripping through his chest, the bolt passed through the sleeve of his heavy protective suit, shattering his upper arm and tearing away a lump of flesh.

Robin bellowed in pain and clamped his right hand to his left arm, from which blood was now pouring like water. Even in the flat light from his helmet, Todd saw his brother's face turn a deathly shade of white. Next moment, Robin's eyelids fluttered and his legs turned boneless beneath him. Todd winced as his brother's head hit the ground as he folded, though consoled himself that the crack of impact was the plastic helmet, and not Robin's skull, meeting the rock.

Things were now happening too rapidly for Todd to keep track of. As he scrambled across to his brother, he sensed movement halfway up the wall to his left. He saw a flash of yellow eyes reflected in his helmet lamp, and realized that more jötnar were emerging from cracks and crevices, some of them ten or fifteen meters above the ground.

Like ants pouring from a nest, he thought, and then he had his hands in his brother's armpits and was dragging Robin towards the shaft. As he scrambled backwards, he tried to focus on his immediate task, and blot out not only the noise and movement around him, but also his terror of getting a spear or a crossbow bolt through his head.

Hearing a pattering sound on his helmet, he looked up. Immediately he felt the sting of rain on his face, and was blinded by light pouring into his eyes. Twisting in the light, he saw something dark and stringy, which he realized was the dangling harness. Dev must have made it out of the Devil's Throat and sent it back down. After laying his brother gently down, Todd rose to his feet and reached for it. He spent the next couple of minutes manipulating Robin's deadweight into the harness, doggedly securing clips and making the checks that had been drummed into them: grigri, ropeman, roller carabiner...ensuring the ropes were in place to create the 2:1 pulley that would bear their weight and enable them to ascend to the surface.

He wondered briefly whether the pulley would take the weight of them both, and whether he would be able to hold on with nothing but a foot loop and his own benumbed grip on the wet ropes. But it was a moot point; they had no choice. Once Robin was in position, dangling from the harness, head lolling to one side, Todd slipped his foot into the loop beside Robin's leg and hauled himself up beside him. As he pulled the rope through the pulley to begin their ascent, he glanced back into the cavern, wondering why, after the crossbow attack, he and Robin had been left unmolested by the jötnar. What he saw was both reassuring and horrifying.

The reassurance came from the fact that the cavern was empty of life. The drumming of rain on Todd's helmet had blotted out all other sounds for the past couple of minutes, and so he was relieved to discover that the jötnar were now gone, having presumably retreated into the crevices from which they had emerged. Horrifying, however, was the realization that Robin's men had gone too – all but two of them.

These two were lying on the ground, so dark and still that when the light from his helmet passed over them, he initially thought they were humped areas of the rocky floor. Then his beam alighted on what appeared to be a large white egg among the undulations of rock. Todd tilted his head to lower the angle of the light – and saw Hector's bulging-eyed face staring at him.

He jerked so violently that he almost lost his grip on the wet rope. The expression on Hector's face was hideous; with his mouth yawning open, he seemed to be screaming in enraged silence. But it was only when Todd scanned the ground to the right of Hector's face that he realized the full and awful truth.

What he had taken for a humped rock was Hector's crumpled body. It was lying several meters from his severed head, limbs sprawled like those of a broken mannequin. The ground beneath the body was painted in shiny maroon blood. Todd could see more blood pooled in the palm of one of Hector's hands, fingers curled inward like a dead crab on its back.

The rain on Todd's helmet felt like the mad clattering of his own thoughts. For a long, scary moment after seeing Hector's violated corpse he struggled to draw breath; his head began to swim and he thought he would fall from the rope and pass out. Closing his eyes, he clung on, and was eventually able to suck air in through his mouth. Gratified to feel his lungs respond, he opened his eyes again and turned his head, directing his lamp beam, slowly and with reluctance, in the direction of the other hunched form.

He couldn't see a face this time, but its general stature and size told him that it was Amir. Amir, who had reported seeing little men in the tunnels, and had now been butchered by one. Amir's dad worked for London Transport, and he had three older sisters. Todd felt ashamed that he knew little else about him. He remembered, though, that a couple of summers ago, when Todd had worked on one of his dad's sites to earn some extra money, Amir had one day brought in some vegetable samosas that his mum had made, which he'd shared among the men, and which had been delicious.

As for the others – Jay and Sean, Andy of course – there was no sign. He could only presume the jötnar had taken them. But why those three? Why had Amir and Hector been killed (because they'd resisted, because they'd got in the way?) and he and Robin spared?

The only person who might be able to provide an answer was Yrsa – or whatever now occupied her body – but Todd would be more than happy if he never saw her/it again. Turning from the sprawled remains of his dad's employees – men who had come here because of him, and had died a long way from home – he began to haul on the rope that would carry him and Robin up to the surface.

CHAPTER FORTY-ONE

Through the rain, Karriana ran.

The world – her little part of it, at least – had become a place of madness. Something was happening to people's minds, making them crazy. They were a bit like the zombies on *The Walking Dead*, except they were still alive. They were mindless, blank-faced, moving as if their bodies were not their own. And they were violent. For some reason they had an urge to hurt people who were not like them. She had seen several instances of that in the hospital, before she had got out.

It wasn't just the sick who'd been affected either. Although they'd been the first to succumb, all of them responding to some kind of signal and rising from their beds, it hadn't been long before the majority of staff had started to go the same way, their eyes glazing over, their movements becoming puppet-like.

Worried that some kind of gas or poison had been released in the hospital, Karriana had decided to get out before it affected her too. And in truth, she had felt – and *still* felt – lightheaded, unable to think straight, but she told herself that was just stress, and that even if it wasn't, a good blast of wind and rain would clear her head.

Outside now, without her coat, her only instinct was to head for home. The rain was torrential, the wind propelling it like an endless torrent of icy arrows. She was drenched, shivering from the pit of her stomach, and trying to repress the urge to burst into messy, howling tears at what she'd seen and experienced.

On foot, it usually took about twelve minutes to get home from the hospital, but the buffeting wind, which made her stagger, and which caused her hair to whip around her face, was slowing her to at least half her normal pace. The streets leading away from the hospital, although empty of people, were strewn with debris – pine needles, twigs, branches. Some of the smaller pieces were not only swirling and flying through the air, but hitting her with stinging slaps that made her cry out in pain, and that she knew would leave scratches, cuts, weals.

The image of her father casually breaking her mother's arm, and then just as casually stamping on her back, kept rising to the forefront of her mind. Again, she pushed it away, trying instead to focus on what she would do when she got home. First, she'd ring the police, tell them what was happening at the hospital, if they didn't already know. Then she'd treat herself to a hot bath, dry clothes, coffee.

After that...she had no idea. She didn't dare think beyond the immediate future. Head down, she struggled on, throwing up her arm as a small branch hurtled towards her face. As the branch hit her elbow, igniting a flare of pain, she heard a bang of impact somewhere to her right.

She was passing a row of houses on a residential road off the high street, and at first thought a falling branch had maybe landed on the roof of a car. She turned to squint in that direction, through eyes blurred by rain, and saw something large and dark rushing towards her.

Fear leaped inside her, and she blinked frantically. The dark blur became a man – bulky and bearded, wearing a dark sweater and greasy-looking waterproof trousers. His feet were bare, but he seemed oblivious to the fact he was trampling on sharp stones and twigs as he targeted her in a lumbering run. Behind him the door to his home was wrenched open by the wind, then slammed back against the wall of the hallway, with the same bang that had first drawn her attention. Karriana had time only to register that the man was someone she recognized, Bjarne Haugen, who owned one of the island's many fishing boats, before he barged into her so forcefully that her feet left the ground, and she flew into the road.

She landed hard on her hip, the impact jarring the breath from her body. For a moment she could only lie where she had fallen as pain swamped her senses. Then, as awareness came back to her, she heard herself gasping for breath above the pummeling roar of rain, and then the scrabbling, wet sound of movement close by.

Her survival instincts kicked in, and she rolled onto her side to face whatever was making the sound. She saw Bjarne Haugen lying on his stomach a few meters away. He must have bounced off her, and ended up sprawling in the road himself. But although his trousers were torn open at the knee, and blood was seeping through the material, he was now flopping and fumbling back to life, his eyes blank but fixed on her. Then, as though animated by some frenzied force, he raised himself onto his palms and toes, and scuttled forward.

It was a horrible, inhuman movement. Like watching a spider that had suddenly found itself in control of a human body. In that instant, Karriana knew that whatever was infecting many of her fellow islanders was not confined to the hospital.

With a yelp of terror and revulsion, she pressed her heels into the road and propelled herself backwards. Her hip felt full of broken glass and her left leg was enfeebled by a numbing ache, but the sudden surge of adrenaline enabled her to rise to her feet.

Adrenaline, though, had its limits. If Karriana had been able to twist and run, she might have got away. But when she turned, putting her weight on her left leg, a spasm of pain shot through her hip, and her leg almost buckled beneath her. She yelled, staggered – and Bjarne Haugen's meaty hand closed around her ankle.

The sudden brake on her momentum unbalanced her even more, and she went down again, her hands and knees hitting the road. As a child she had done this many times – lost her balance, scraped her palms, barked her knees, and bounced back up within seconds. Now, the impact jolted through her, the pain in her injured hip flaring up worse than ever. She gasped, like a runner collapsing after a marathon. She'd be all right in a moment – but she didn't *have* a moment. As she floundered, Bjarne Haugen, who was twice her size and weight, flipped her onto her back, then sat astride her chest, his hands reaching for her throat.

Karriana battered at his wrists but he was relentless. His thick-fingered hands closed around her neck and began to squeeze. When Karriana felt his thumbs pressing into her throat with a force she feared would crush bones and cartilage like thin plastic, she began to thrash in panic – but still Haugen didn't let go. He bore down, determined to squeeze the life out of her, even though he was staring off into the middle distance, a slightly bemused look on his face. He was muttering to himself, too, though all Karriana could hear was the pounding of blood inside her skull, which felt close to bursting.

Desperately her hands scrabbled at the ground on either side of her. Her fingers encountered sodden pine needles and wet twigs, and then they brushed against something more substantial. She clutched at the object, a length of gnarled, rain-slicked wood as thick as a broom handle. Gripping it in sheer desperation, she put all her remaining strength into swinging it up and round in an arc, aiming for Haugen's head.

What she was grasping turned out to be a small branch torn from a tree – perhaps even the one that had struck her elbow earlier. She whacked Haugen in the side of his bearded face with the leafy end, and although it did no more than scratch his cheek, it diverted his attention enough for him to loosen the grip on her throat.

In that precious moment she sucked in a breath that felt like inhaling a bruise, and flipped the tree branch round in her hand, almost fumbling and dropping it. Now it was the splintered end that was pointing towards his face. Before today, Karriana would never have thought herself capable of stabbing someone, but her urge to survive was strong, so it was with real intent that she brought the branch up and round, towards Haugen's head.

The makeshift weapon, just as his hands were tightening around her throat once again, struck him below the cheekbone. The torn-off end of the branch, as sharp as a steel blade, punctured the skin as if it were dough. The impact snapped Haugen's head to the right, and the momentum of the blow caused Karriana to drag the branch down, towards Haugen's chin. Through the rain streaming into her eyes, she saw a ragged, vertical rip open in her attacker's face, saw blood erupt from the gash with such force that within seconds it was dripping off his beard and onto her own face. Once again she felt Haugen's grip on her bruised throat loosen, but still she couldn't move; even now his considerable weight bore down on her chest.

Yanking the branch free, she drew her arm back, then pistoned it forward again, once more aiming towards the side of his skull. More by accident than design, the sharp, jagged point entered Haugen's left ear and buried itself several inches into his head, its progress only halted when it impacted with something hard, possibly bone, which caused the branch to snap in two.

Now Haugen had a sheared-off length of splintered wood sticking out of his ear, around which blood was squirting onto his shoulder and down his arm. Eyes flickering, he turned his head to his left, as if expecting to see a bird hovering there, pecking at him. Through the gash in his cheek, Karriana could see Haugen's clenched teeth, the sight so unreal it looked like a horror movie prosthetic. Even now, his expression was unchanged; he seemed oblivious to the pain. Clearly, though, her attack had disabled his ability to function, because she felt his grip around her throat slacken. Next moment, he rolled off her, slumping onto his side. As his head hit the ground with a thump, driving the length of splintered branch even deeper into his ear, Karriana flinched, her stomach lurching with nausea.

Her throat was so bruised and painful that not only could she barely move her head, but it still felt as though Haugen's fat fingers were squeezing her throat – the sensation so vivid she had to bring her own trembling hands up to her neck to check there was nothing there. Rolling onto her side, then pushing herself shakily to her feet, she kept a wary eye on her attacker, half-expecting him to clamber upright and come for her again. But he remained where he was, his right foot jerking in an involuntary spasm, as if the force that was driving him was urging him to stand up. Horribly, Haugen's face wore an expression of disinterest, considering the damage done to it. His right eye was open and staring straight ahead, while the lid of his left eye was drooping, as if he was offering her a secretive wink.

Drenched, filthy, and plastered in pine needles, Karriana backed away. To her left Haugen's door banged again as the wind slammed it back against the wall of his hallway. Glancing across, she wondered where his wife and teenage son were. The thought that he might have done to them what he had tried to do to her was awful – but worse still was the prospect of them suddenly emerging from the house with similarly murderous intentions.

Although she knew that what Haugen had tried to do to her was not his fault, she found it hard to feel anything but grateful that she had managed to overcome him. Grateful, but also terrified at the prospect that everyone on Eldfjallaeyja was now under the influence of whatever had gripped the island.

But no. *She* was okay. Which meant surely there must be others?

Her head like a heavy boulder balanced on a neck so tender it felt like a swollen lump of pain, she cast one more nervous glance at Haugen's twitching body, and then she staggered away.

CHAPTER FORTY-TWO

In her dream, Gudrun was talking to her father.

He was sitting at the dining table in their old family home, leaning forward, hands clasped together. He was a thin man with grizzled hair, and eyes that had looked red-rimmed for as long as she could remember, as if he cried a lot, or suffered from allergies.

In the dream, Gudrun knew she had a husband and children, and yet it didn't seem strange to her that she had just come home from school, and was delighted to see her father sitting there. Dropping her school bag on the floor, she said, "Hello, Poppa. I thought you'd died of that thing."

The old man nodded sagely. "Alzheimer's," he said, voicing the word she hadn't mentioned in case it upset him. "I got better."

"That's great," she said. "When did you get back?"

"Just today. I wanted to surprise you when you came home from school."

Although Gudrun had not been expecting to see her father, in her strange dream-logic she suddenly realized that the only reason she'd gone to school, then come back to the house she'd not set foot in since it had been sold after her mother's death, was so that her father wouldn't be waiting here, wondering where she was. Placing her hand over his – and yes, it was solid and warm, which proved this was real! – she said, "We don't live here anymore, Poppa. And I'm married now with two children. Why don't you come back with me to meet them?"

Her father shook his head. "I can't. I have to wait for your mother."

Gudrun knew her mother was dead, but sensing that her father's mind was still in a fragile state, she said, "I'll leave her a note," whilst secretly she thought: *I'll keep pretending Momma's alive. Poppa will never know.*

She reached for a pen on the other side of the table, but then was distracted by a wasp that stung her throat. When she put her hand up to the sting, though, there was nothing there.

"Did you see that?" she asked her father. "I think it was a wasp."

"I offer this life so the gods may awaken," her father said, speaking in her daughter's voice.

This came as such a shock that Gudrun jerked awake.

Her brain processed several things as her eyes opened. The first was the quality of light in the room, which was minimal, shadowy. Yet although it was dark, she knew it wasn't nighttime. It felt more like… late afternoon, maybe early evening, and most of the darkness came from the fact that the curtains were closed.

When her eyes flickered towards the window, she saw this was the case, a grayish light seeping through the rectangular curtain. Almost simultaneously she remembered why she was lying on the bed. She'd started getting one of her migraines around four p.m., or at least the aura that preceded a migraine, and so she'd come upstairs to lie down, knowing that if she rested in darkness for a while she could sometimes nip the migraine in the bud. And it seemed to have worked, for although she felt groggy, her vision had now cleared.

She listened to the rain battering the window, and for a few seconds watched the squirming of vague gray shapes – rivulets of water running down the glass – through the thin, pale material. Then, thinking she ought to get up and help Sven with the children, she looked away from the window and turned her head towards the door.

As she did, two things happened:

The wasp from her dream stung her on the side of her neck again.

Someone held a piece of glass in front of her face.

She thought it might be a mirror. She got the impression of light flashing off a reflective surface. But as she brought a hand up to touch the place on her neck where the wasp had stung her, her perspective shifted, and she suddenly realized what she was really looking at:

The blade of a very large knife.

And what had stung her wasn't a wasp, but the tip of the blade, which was pressed so tightly against her neck that it had broken the skin.

Despite the shock, Gudrun had the presence of mind to freeze. She instantly realized that any attempt to scramble clear of the knife would likely result in the blade slashing her throat. Aware that the tip was uncomfortably close to her jugular vein, she shifted her gaze from the knife to the person holding it, moving only her eyes. Her throat clicked with a soft gasp when she saw that it was Astrid.

The knife, which Gudrun now realized was the carving knife from the kitchen, which she or Sven often used to carve meat, looked huge and obscenely wrong in her daughter's tiny hands. Astrid had both of those hands wrapped around the hilt, and her arms were upraised, the knife pointing vertically down with its tip pressed against Gudrun's throat. Gudrun could see that Astrid's eyes were wide open but glassy, and that her face was expressionless.

Oh, my God, Gudrun thought, *is she sleepwalking?*

Astrid clearly didn't know what she was doing. So what would be the best thing here? Shoot out a hand, shove Astrid away from her? But she didn't want her little girl to fall and bang her head. Added to which, she was holding a knife, for God's sake! Who knew where that might end up?

Gudrun thought briefly about speaking to her daughter, trying to wake her, but just as quickly she dismissed that idea. The shock and disorientation might startle Astrid, cause her to jerk her arms down suddenly.

No, the best option, the safest option, would be for Gudrun to raise her left hand slowly, then grip Astrid's two hands tightly and ease them up, making room for her to scoot out from under the blade. And just in case Astrid woke with a jolt, Gudrun would keep her own hand locked into place while she twisted her body out of the way. She knew it would be a tricky maneuver, but she thought she could do it. Keeping her eyes on Astrid's unseeing face, alert for any change in her expression, she slowly began to raise her left hand...

At that moment the bedroom door opened and Noah walked in.

Gudrun's eyes flicked across to her son, and what she saw made her freeze. Noah too was holding a big knife – the serrated one they used to cut bread – but the blade of his was smeared with blood. And there was blood too – fresh and dark, and far too much of it – on his hands, and all over his green and gray *Jurassic Park* hoodie. It was spattered up the sleeves, and half-obscuring the picture of the velociraptor on the front, and there were even speckles and streaks of blood on the right side of his face.

Gudrun's mouth opened and she made a noise – a breathy whimper, which was all that her throat could produce. She thought of Sven, and dread seized her like paralysis. She looked at Noah's blood-speckled face, and saw that his eyes were as glassy and unseeing as his sister's.

Noah's entrance seemed to act as a cue for Astrid to speak. In a low, mumbling voice that did not sound like her at all, she repeated the words Gudrun had heard in her dream:

"I offer this life so the gods may awaken."

Then she pushed the knife firmly down into her mother's throat.

CHAPTER FORTY-THREE

Jay was in Hell.

What was happening was so far beyond his comprehension that he almost felt he was having an out-of-body experience. At the same time, he was terrified to the point where he believed the intensity of the emotion might kill him. His heart was not just racing but trying to *batter* its way out of his chest. Because of this he felt lightheaded, his vision swimming and blurring, making him feel he was on the verge of passing out.

In some ways he wished he *would* pass out – anything to escape this reality. Simultaneously, the thought of leaving himself vulnerable to whatever these monsters were planning to do was making him hyperventilate with panic. Crying and sweating, often dry-retching with terror, he had been trussed with a thick, vine-like rope and was now being carried through the tunnels by one of the…he could only think of them as *trolls*.

Whatever these things were, they were horrific. Short, broad-shouldered and barrel-chested, with massive, spade-like hands. Their faces were hideous, their features jumbled together, their leering, rubbery mouths so wide they stretched almost to their ears. And they had *tusks* – gray and twisted like ram's horns! And they *stank*! Jay had never smelled rotting human flesh, but he imagined this was what it must smell like. The things gave off a throat-clogging musk of rotting corpses mixed with something fishy and fecal.

Beneath the terror, Jay felt an overwhelming sense of regret and resentment. After what had happened during his night shift a few days ago, he had wanted to go home, but had been persuaded to stay by Yrsa, who had offered them all double wages to finish the job. Even then he'd been unsure, but Amir had said he might as well stick it out. And now here he was, captured by trolls, along with Andy, who he'd seen stabbed with a spear and dragged into the tunnel ahead of him. As for everyone else – Robin, Todd, Dev, Hector, Sean and Amir himself – Jay didn't know *where* they were. Hopefully at least some of them had escaped and were on their way to get help.

It had been chaos back in the cave. Lots of shouting, and running about, and Jay was pretty sure there had been some fighting too, but he didn't know how much – those things had been carrying weapons, for fuck's sake, whereas he and his mates had nothing but rocks and fists. Scared shitless and realizing they were outnumbered and outgunned, Jay had tried to hide in an alcove, but one of those things had come in after him, snuffling like a hog rooting out truffles, its eyes shining with a sick yellow light. It had grabbed him and thrown him over its shoulder, as if he weighed less than a rag doll. Then it had scampered across the cave like an ape and carried him back into the tunnels, where it had trussed him up. And Jay, able to make out nothing but random movements in the shadows as he had jolted up and down on the thing's shoulder, had screamed for help, and had begged the thing to let him go, but no one had helped him. He had no idea whether the thing even understood what he was saying.

And now they were back in the cave where they had been drilling all week. Jay still didn't know what was in the bigger cave that lay beyond the crawl space they had carved through the wall. Maybe a whole community of these creatures – descendants of old miners, perhaps, who had made a home for themselves down here?

Had Yrsa known about these things? And where was she now? Dead? Captured? His thoughts tumbled together in his racing mind. The only ones that remained constant, rooted at the heart of him, were of Elaine and Hugo. What would they be doing at this moment? Shopping? Eating? Visiting friends? Feeding the ducks in the park? Jay didn't even know what time it was in England right now. Here in this stinking cave, with the only light coming from the lamp on his helmet, his life in London felt like nothing but a lovely dream he had once had. His memories of Elaine and Hugo gave him comfort, but also induced in him a desperate craving. *Please let me live through this*, he begged silently. *Please let me see them again.*

Grunting like an animal, the 'troll' stumped up to the waist-high tunnel drilled through the rock and shrugged Jay from its shoulder as if he was an old carpet. It dumped him unceremoniously on the ground, ignoring his agonized gasp as his spine hit the rock with a bruising impact that sent a starburst of pain into his skull.

Any hope Jay might have had that the creature would disappear up the tunnel and leave him was dashed when his captor grabbed the meter or so of rope left dangling when it had tied his feet together. Looping the loose end around its own ankle, it plunged into the tunnel like a rat into its lair, dragging Jay, feet first, behind it.

Jay tensed his muscles and gritted his teeth as he was dragged through the tunnel at speed, his buttocks, back and elbows taking most of the jolting impact. He did his best to hold his head above the floor, though still took a couple of shuddering cracks to the back of his plastic helmet.

The journey, though, was brief, and although Jay was hurting in a dozen places by the time they emerged from the tunnel, one small mercy was that the lamp on his helmet was still working.

Or was it a mercy? Because as the 'troll' straightened up and plucked at the rope around its ankle with its thick fingers, the light from Jay's helmet flashed on multiple pairs of eyes, peering back at him from the shadows.

Oh, fuck. There were *dozens* of the things in here, and they were at all levels, many of them perched on jagged promontories or stone ledges, or wedged into cracks and crevices in the walls. Some were even on the move, clambering up and down and across the walls like expert climbers, nimble and quick despite their thick limbs and gnarled bodies.

If the creatures were making any sounds, Jay couldn't hear them, because the constant roar of water, the volume of which had been increasing during their journey through the tunnels, was so all-encompassing that he felt as though they were right on top of some subterranean water volcano, which was about to erupt.

He had only a few seconds to register all this before he found himself on the move again. Having untied the rope from around its own ankle, the 'troll' grabbed the dangling end and began to plod across the rocky floor of the cavern, dragging Jay in its wake as if he were a toy truck being pulled along by a child.

Once again he gasped and grunted in pain as his body scraped across a rocky, uneven floor, and once again his protests were ignored. He was dragged across to where a fire, enclosed within a circle of rocks, filled the cavern with a flickering, shadowy effulgence. What Jay saw in its glow, combined with the light from his helmet lamp, filled him with a fresh wave of terror and dread.

On the far side of the cavern, sprouting from the rocky ground and spreading up and across the back wall, was a leafless, multi-limbed tree. Around the roots of the tree, like macabre fruit that had dropped from its branches, were crouched more of the 'trolls', their eyes shining in their firelit faces. Standing on a hump of rock, like a natural dais, about six meters in front of the tree, was Yrsa. She had shed her protective suit and helmet and looked diminutive against the backdrop of the vast trunk and its twining sprawl of limbs. She looked calm and relaxed, head slightly raised, arms hanging by her sides. But her face was blank as if she'd been hypnotized, her eyes wide and unfocused.

All of this was terrifying enough, but even worse was the sight of Andy and Sean lying on the ground to Yrsa's right. Andy was face down in a pool of his own blood, runnels of which had trickled along sloping rocks into cracks and crevices. He was still alive but in a bad way, whimpering and panting as his body heaved. He made Jay think of some large, placid animal from a wildlife documentary, savaged by predators and left to die on the plains.

Sean was also on his front, his feet tied together and his arms lashed to his sides, as Jay's were. In contrast to the bigger man, he was thrashing like a beached fish in his efforts to escape. He was yelling too, his face puce with rage, but his words were lost amid the roaring tumult of water. Jay was dragged forward until he was lying next to Sean, and then the 'troll' that had brought him here threw down the rope, stumped forward and flipped him over so that, like his companions, he was lying on his front.

Jay started shivering from head to foot, his teeth chattering uncontrollably, but it wasn't from the cold. He knew something awful was about to happen, and that it was extremely unlikely help would arrive in time, if at all. He was going to die here, in this impossible place among these impossible creatures, and he would never know why. Never would he set foot in his homeland again, or see his beautiful wife, or watch his son grow up. At the crushing realization of this, he dry-retched, his stomach feeling as though it was turning itself inside out, and then he started to cry.

Through the blur of tears, he saw one of the 'trolls' detach itself from its place within the tangled roots of the tree and clomp towards him. This 'troll' was holding something that flashed in the dancing light of the fire – some sort of blade, as long as a machete.

Everything let go inside Jay, his bladder, his bowels, and like Sean he began to writhe and thrash in a futile attempt to burst free from his bonds. He tried to scream, but his voice was locked inside him, and although it seemed to tear his throat to shreds, he could produce nothing but a thin, high-pitched wheeze.

When the 'troll' stomped over to Andy, stood astride his back and raised the machete-like blade, Jay wanted to look away. He wanted to, but he couldn't.

It was only after the 'troll' had cut away Andy's clothes, sliced deeply into his back, either side of his spine, and started to yank Andy's ribs out through the slashes it had made, its actions accompanied by the snapping of bones and Andy's hideous screams of agony, that Jay was finally able to shut his eyes. Deranged by terror, and frantic to escape the torment that was Andy's last moments, and that was destined to be his too, he raised his head as high as he could from the ground and slammed his forehead back into the rock. Sickeningly dazed, blinded by blood, but still conscious, he did it again. Then again. Again. Again.

By the time the 'troll' had finished with Andy and was moving towards Sean, Jay was mercifully unconscious. He knew nothing more.

CHAPTER FORTY-FOUR

The top of the Devil's Throat – a circle of boiling gray clouds through which rain poured – was visible only when Todd and Robin had ascended the majority of the forty-five-degree slope that inclined towards the surface. It was a gruelling ascent for Todd, as he had to rely almost entirely on the strength in his arms, no longer able to anchor himself and push up with his feet on the sloping wall.

If he had been alone, it would have been fine, but with the added weight of his unconscious brother to contend with, his biceps were screaming for mercy by the time the opening was within reach. He was only a few meters below it when the rain-lashed patch of murky daylight was partially obscured by the silhouette of a bulbous head. At first, Todd thought the jötnar had got here ahead of him. Then a voice, loud enough to be heard above the rattle of rain on his helmet, said, "That you, Todd?"

Relief surged through Todd. "Yes," he shouted back. "Me and Rob. But he's injured. Unconscious."

"You're nearly at the top, son," Dev yelled, his head – helmeted and hooded – bobbing in encouragement. "Just a few more feet."

Seconds later, Todd's head rose above ground level, the sideswiping wind hurling a barrage of rain into his face. As he squeezed his eyes shut, he felt strong hands grab him and haul him out. For a few seconds he sprawled on his back on the rocky ground, rain forming little streams around him as it poured downhill. Then, groaning, he rolled onto his hands and knees, before rising groggily to his feet. Looking across at the Devil's Throat, he saw Dev lying on his front, reaching into the shaft with both arms. Todd staggered forward to help, and between them they managed to drag Robin out.

Todd switched off his helmet lamp, then shielded his brother's face from the driving rain while Dev, his fingers wet and numb, divested Robin of the sodden harness. The left side of Robin's protective suit was drenched in blood, despite the diluting effect of the rain. By contrast his hands and face were an almost luminous white, the wet gleam of rain giving his skin the look and consistency of cod fillets in a supermarket cooler. Once Dev had freed Robin from the harness, the ropes of which were also stained red, he threw the whole dripping mass back down the shaft for whoever might need it next. Then he unzipped the unconscious man's protective suit as far as his breastbone and pushed his hand inside to check for a heartbeat.

Todd held his breath, fearful of seeing Dev's frown deepen into something more ominous.

Neither man had spoken since Dev had hauled Todd out of the shaft, but now, unable to bear the suspense any longer, Todd asked, "Is he okay?"

"Heartbeat's faint, but it's there," Dev said. His gaze flickered to the shaft. "What happened down there?"

"We were attacked."

"By who?"

Todd hesitated. "Cave dwellers."

Dev was generally unflappable, but now he almost growled in frustration. "Cave dwellers? What's that supposed to mean?"

"I don't know," said Todd, reluctant to mention and explain the word *jötnar*. "Little men. Dwarves maybe. Very hostile. And very strong." He indicated his brother. "Will Rob be all right?"

Dev puffed out his cheeks. "We'll have to carry him to the truck, then drive to the hospital. Whoever else is down there will have to—"

"I don't think anyone else is coming up," Todd said quickly.

Dev's eyes widened. "You serious?"

Todd felt a thickening in his throat, and a hot, trembling rush rise up through his body. He let it all out in a long sigh. "Yeah, sorry."

"Fuck," Dev breathed. Then he was all business. Jumping to his feet, he nodded towards the one-man tent still clinging to the hillside several meters away. A steady stream of water was flowing against and around it, as though it was a boulder jutting from a river.

"Back in a sec," he said, and splashed across the sloping ground. Reaching the tent, he braced himself against the water flowing around his boots, then unzipped the entrance flap and ducked inside. He reappeared seconds later with a sleeping bag, which he unzipped all the way to the bottom as he crossed back to Todd and Robin. Laying the already soaked bag on the ground next to Robin's unconscious form, he said, "We'll put him on this to carry him down. It'll be easier than holding his arms and legs, and he'll lose less blood this way."

The two men carefully picked up Robin and shifted him over to the sleeping bag. Immediately blood from Robin's arm starting seeping into the quilted material, a slowly expanding stain that looked black against the bright blue nylon. Grabbing a handful of each corner, Todd and Dev lifted the bag and made their way carefully downhill. Within a minute, the muscles in Todd's arms were aching again, and sweat was trickling out of his helmet and down his face to blend with the scything rain. But he gritted his teeth and clung on, knowing that for his brother this could be the difference between life and death.

The trudge back through the forest was draining, and seemed interminable. Exhausted, drenched to the skin, and with the mud sucking at his boots with each shuffling step, Todd focused simply on putting one foot in front of the other. The trees on either side flickered by like a film clip on endless repeat. The only soundtrack was the amorphous roar of the torrential rain.

So completely did Todd retreat into himself that Dev had to shout his name three times before it penetrated his consciousness. Finally he looked up, blinking. "What?"

"I said have you got the keys?"

"What keys?"

"To the Land Rover. Didn't you hear a word I said?"

"Sorry, no."

Dev took a deep breath. "I said it would be better to take the Land Rover instead of one of the trucks, because it's faster and we can lay

Rob on the back seat. But that would depend who's got the keys – you or Yrsa."

Todd thought back to when they'd arrived here. So much had happened since, it seemed like days ago. Vaguely he recalled Yrsa being skittish at the news they'd broken through into the other cave, and how he'd insisted on driving.

The corner of the sleeping bag still screwed into his fist, he tapped the hip pocket of his jacket with his elbow and heard a metallic jangle.

"I've got them."

"Come on then."

Looking around, Todd was surprised to see they had made it through the forest and were now standing parallel with the last line of trees, on the edge of the turning circle where the vehicles were parked. As they trudged past the two trucks towards the Land Rover, Todd hoped the tires of the smaller vehicle would have the gripping power to get them through what was now a mud bath in which pools of water twitched with rain. Reaching the Land Rover, their boots and lower legs caked with mud, Todd said, "I'll have to lay Rob down to get the keys out."

Dev shook his head. "Give him to me. I can take his weight for a minute."

With the dripping sleeping bag cocooning him, the two men heaved Robin's body into Dev's arms. As Robin's position altered, he stirred a little. His mouth opened as though he was tasting the rain on his lips, and a frown of pain or disquiet etched itself into his forehead.

The knowledge that his brother was still hanging on gave Todd a burst of energy. Retrieving the keys, he opened the driver's door, then reached in and unlocked the back door on the driver's side.

Together, he and Dev laid Robin as gently as they could across the back seat, though not gently enough to stop Robin moaning, as if having a bad dream. That done, they climbed into the front of the vehicle, Todd sitting with a squelch in the driver's seat.

As he stamped the mud from his boots, Dev groaned, his head tipping back on the headrest.

"You okay?" Todd asked.

Dev looked weary. The whites of his eyes were the color of old ivory. "I'll be fine. Let's just get Rob to hospital. He's the one we have to worry about."

Todd turned on the engine, then put the vehicle into first. "Cross your fingers," he said, easing down on the accelerator while slowly releasing the clutch.

The back wheels spun in the mud for a second or two, then the Land Rover lurched forward. It crawled and bumped and occasionally slid across the circle of mud, but within thirty seconds they were on the track – still muddy but not as swamp-like – heading towards the main road. The windscreen wipers, going at full tilt, tried their best to cope with the deluge, but the landscape through the glass was still a slithering mass of distorted, monochromatic shapes.

Todd's shoulders relaxed slightly when they reached the end of the narrow side-track. With the hedges – long smears of black through the curtains of rain – hemming them in, and the overarching foliage thrashing at the car, he had felt under siege. But lurching out of the tunnel of vegetation was like bursting from darkness into light.

Even so, the murky sky still churned with clouds, and the teeming rain still bounced off the road and transformed the surrounding fields into wetlands from which bedraggled foliage sprouted. But as Todd drove towards town, the Land Rover picking up speed, he couldn't help but feel a thread of hope worming its way through the black weight of dread inside him.

And then he saw the people.

At first he thought his mind was conjuring figures from the kaleidoscopic patterns made by the onslaught of rain on the windscreen. He leaned forward, narrowing his eyes as if that might help him see better. A few hundred meters ahead, blocking the road, was a dark wave, an approaching mass, composed of bobbing heads, moving limbs. Still, he continued to drive steadily towards them, until Dev quietly said, "Slow down, Todd."

Todd did so and the vehicle dwindled to a crawl. The hammering of rain seemed to double in volume as the engine's throaty growl dropped to a purr.

Todd and Dev watched the approaching mass for a few more seconds, and then Todd said wonderingly, "What are they doing here?"

"Beats me, son." Although his voice was calm, Dev said, "I don't mind admitting I am seriously out of my comfort zone."

As the crowd drew closer, Todd was able to pick out details, despite the warping effect of the rain. What he could see he didn't like. He didn't like at all.

Pressed together like a herd, the crowd of fifty or more was comprised of islanders of all ages, from small children to hobbling pensioners. Despite their proximity to one another, there seemed to be no communication between them; every one of them looked to be in some sort of trance, their eyes unfocused, many of their mouths hanging open. Eerily, not one of them seemed to be affected by the pouring rain. No one was hunched against the elements, and there was no evidence of coats or hats, gloves or scarves. They all looked as if they had walked out of their homes, just as they were, at some given signal. One old man was wearing nothing but pajama bottoms; one portly, middle-aged woman wore only a bra and a pair of high-waisted pants that held in at least some of her stomach fat. Like this woman and the old man, some people were barefoot, others wore only sandals or slippers. Several of the women, and a couple of the men, had long hair plastered across their faces by the rain, but they made no attempt to push it aside, even though it must have been obscuring their vision.

"There's something wrong with them," Todd said.

Dev nodded. "I'm with you on that, son."

"So what should we do?"

For a moment Dev didn't answer. Then, in his characteristically calm voice, he said, "We can't just drive through 'em, and our priority is to get Rob to hospital, so I say we wait here."

"Seriously?" said Todd, nervousness making his voice waver into a higher register.

"For now – why not? They look like they're heading somewhere, so if we just sit tight, maybe they'll—"

Abruptly he halted. Several of the islanders at the front of the crowd had suddenly broken into a shambling run. They hadn't looked up, or shown any awareness of the vehicle's presence; they had simply started running towards it. Then, like sheep, others started running, then yet more behind them. And within five seconds of the first runners breaking away from the crowd, the entire mob was pounding towards them.

"Reverse!" Dev snapped, glancing into the rearview mirror to check the road behind them was clear.

"Where to?" Todd yelled, slamming the vehicle into gear.

"Just do it!" Dev shouted. "Drive fast but straight. We'll work the rest out later."

When the Land Rover started to reverse, the nearest runners were no more than twenty meters away. That distance stretched as they sped backwards, but it was only when they had put a good hundred meters between themselves and the running crowd that Todd said, "What now? We can't just keep reversing forever."

"Just a bit further, round this bend – not too fast. In a minute you should be able to do a three-point turn. Then maybe we can find an alterna— *Todd, stop!*"

Todd almost jumped out of his seat, but instinctively stamped on the brake. As the wheels locked and they were hurled back against their seats – including Robin, who let out a semiconscious cry of pain – the Land Rover slewed in an arc across the wet road. Todd had caught only a glimpse of what had made Dev yell out his warning – two hunched figures perched on a toppled tree they had presumably dragged into the road – before the image in the rearview mirror was swept away.

It wasn't until they slammed to a stop that Todd's heartbeat seemed to catch up with him. His pulse was throbbing so hard he could feel it through his hands, which were still gripping the steering wheel. Through the dissolving windscreen, which the sweeping wipers constantly, though fleetingly, reformed, Todd saw a patch of wet road and one of the waterlogged fields that were flanking it. But he didn't realize the

Land Rover had spun round ninety degrees until Dev said, "Those little buggers are coming this way."

Todd glanced past him and saw the two jötnar loping towards them, their dark forms smearing and fracturing through the rain-lashed glass of the passenger window. Looking out of the driver's window, he saw the first of the running islanders rounding the bend some seventy or eighty meters away.

"We're trapped!" he yelled. "They're coming at us from both sides."

"Only one way to go then," said Dev. "Straight ahead."

Todd was appalled. Straight ahead meant crossing a narrow ditch, then descending a short slope into a boggy field.

"We'll never make it!"

"Got to try," said Dev, and nodded at the approaching islanders. "With that tree in the way, the only other option is to smash through that lot."

"Fuck!" Todd shouted, but already he was revving the engine. Reckless though it was, he knew Dev was right. There *was* no other alternative.

Slamming the vehicle into gear, he released the clutch and floored the accelerator. As the Land Rover shot forward, Todd let out a wordless yell – a scream not only of terror, but of defiance, rage, injustice. When the front wheels hit the raised lip of the meter-wide ditch between road and field, the Land Rover was going at close to forty miles an hour. There was a lurch that jolted Todd from his seat and locked his seat belt painfully across his shoulder, and then they were airborne.

Todd braced himself, and gasped as the front wheels hit the top of the downward slope edging the field with such force he felt sure the vehicle would either crumple or flip over. But it did neither of those things. It hit the ground with a jarring crunch, then sprang back up whilst still maintaining its forward momentum. Todd yelled again – not exactly a whoop of triumph, more a cry of sheer relief. He fought with the steering wheel as they surged into a field that had now become a shallow lake.

How shallow was the question. Although the remnants of rain-battered crops straggled from the newly formed lake's surface, it was impossible to predict the water's depth. Todd could only hope they would be able to make it across to where a stretch of forest rose up like a blurred black wall.

Another question to consider was whether the forest was a good place to aim for, but that was one he and Dev would have to think about later. Todd was acting on instinct, and in his mind, trees equaled a place in which they could hide. If they were lucky, there might even be a route through the forest, or alongside it, that would lead them back to town.

"Whoa!" Dev said as water sprayed up on both sides of the car. "If you're not careful, you'll flood the engine."

Todd glanced into the rearview mirror. "No choice," he said. "They're still coming."

It was true. Although the view through the back window was distorted by rain, they could still see dark shapes dropping from the road and doggedly pursuing them across the flooded field.

Gritting his teeth, Todd kept going, though he forced himself, against his instincts, to slow to twenty miles an hour, hoping that if he maintained a steady speed he might save the engine, while still extending the distance between themselves and their pursuers. Despite feeling as if they were crawling, the engine was roaring throatily as if under great strain. They managed to make it two-thirds of the way across, the water still spraying in arcs on either side of the vehicle, when suddenly the speedometer started to sink.

"We're slowing down!" he shouted.

"Could be water in the engine," said Dev, "or maybe the wheels are getting bogged down in the mud. Put your foot down, see what happens."

Todd did, forcing himself to depress the accelerator gently rather than stamping on it. The Land Rover roared and picked up speed again – but not for long. After a few seconds the speedometer began to sink once more, and now the engine was rattling and misfiring.

"Put your foot *right* down," Dev said grimly. "Keep the revs up."

Todd pushed his foot all the way down, and again, with a throaty, wheezing grumble – *a death rattle*, Todd thought – the vehicle surged forward another few meters. But then, abruptly, it gave an almost apologetic cough and died, and suddenly the Land Rover was entirely without power. Alarm spiking through him, Todd tried turning off the engine and turning it on again. There was no response.

"It's no use," Dev said as Todd tried a third time. He was already unclipping his seat belt. "We'll have to leg it."

Todd glanced at the rearview mirror. Without the wipers to sweep away the rain, the back windscreen resembled an abstract painting in monochrome, making it impossible to tell how close their pursuers were.

"What about Rob?" said Todd.

"We'll carry him. We've got a good lead on that lot behind us. We'll be all right."

Despite the circumstances, Todd found Dev's optimism reassuring enough to waylay the panic inside him. They would only get out of this if they kept their wits about them and focused on what they were doing.

Briefly clenching his hands to stop them shaking, he unclipped his seat belt and opened the car door. Instantly rain lashed at him like a barrage of tiny needles, and he had to shove the door hard to keep it open as the wind tried to slam it on his legs. He paused, seeing only water beneath him, then jumped down. Mud bubbled up through the water, flooding his boots as his feet sank to a depth of at least ten inches. Afraid that if he stayed still he might sink further, he pulled his left foot from the mud with a *schlurpp!* sound, and turned to the rear door.

Now, through the lashing rain, he had a clearer sight of their pursuers. He was relieved to see that not only were they still some distance away, but their progress through the boggy field was labored. Several of the islanders had slipped and fallen, and were now floundering in the muddy water, unable to regain their feet. There was even one, a child, lying face down, arms out in a cruciform shape, unmoving. It was horrifying that no one was helping the child, and what made Todd feel doubly awful was knowing that, if he wanted to stay alive, he could do nothing to help either. Sickened, he turned away, pulled his right foot from the mud with as much effort as it had taken to extract his left, then lurched forward and grabbed the handle of the rear door.

He pulled it open to find that Dev had already opened the door on the passenger side, grabbed Robin under his armpits, and was now hauling him out. To make it easier for Dev, Todd scrambled onto the back seat, grabbed the soles of Robin's boots, and pushed his brother ahead of him. When Robin was out, Todd jumped down beside Dev, who was supporting his brother's weight.

"Get his left arm over your shoulders and your arms under his left leg," Dev said, panting. "We'll carry him in a sitting position. Easiest way."

Although it might have been the *easiest* way, it certainly wasn't easy. Even without the burden of Robin's body, crossing the quagmire was like trudging through a field of hungry mouths, eager to swallow them. Add to that the rain, which was so fierce it was like being bombarded by thousands of small stones. After a few minutes, Todd again found the muscles he'd strained climbing out of the Devil's Throat and carrying Robin through the forest singing with pain.

Despite the physical strain, however, they had no choice but to keep going. Doubled over, his arms wrapped round his brother's leg, which felt as heavy as a tree trunk, Todd resisted the urge to look back. It would only have wasted time, and possibly unbalanced them. As it was, both he and Dev slipped several times as they splashed along, and once Dev went down on one knee, which almost caused them to topple sideways into the mud.

Finally, however, Todd became aware that the water was getting shallower as the field sloped gently upwards. Raising his head to squint into the flailing rain, he was thankful to see the wall of trees was now less than ten meters away.

Grateful though he was to reach the trees, they were an unprepossessing sight. Having soaked up more water than was good for them, their drooping branches gave them a cowed, defeated look, and their black, slimy-looking trunks gave the impression they were rotting from within.

Glancing at Todd, rain running down his face and dripping from his chin, Dev said, "We need somewhere to hide."

Todd shook his head, water flying from the rat-tails of hair hanging down under his helmet. "I don't think that's a good idea. We need to keep moving. I've a feeling those things won't stop looking for us until they find us."

He meant the jötnar, but realized he could have been referring to the islanders.

"If we keep moving, they'll catch us eventually. We're going slower than they are."

Todd felt bitterness rise in him. "So we're fucked either way."

"Not necessarily. If we can find a place to hide, I'll stay with Rob while you fetch help. It's only a few miles to town. If you're quick you can be back within two hours."

Todd thought that was a pretty optimistic estimation, but that wasn't his main concern. "And what if everyone in town has turned into a...a zombie psycho?"

"Then we *are* fucked," Dev said laconically. "But let's not assume the worst *just* yet."

They plunged into the forest, following a random route in the hope of losing their pursuers. Although boggy, the ground was choked with pine needles, twigs and small branches, which meant it was easier to make progress here than it had been wading across the flooded field. After fifteen minutes, Todd glanced up through the canopy of thrashing branches, and got the impression the sky was dark not only because of the storm clouds blanketing the island.

"What time is it?" he asked.

"Haven't you got a watch?"

Todd gave the older man a look. "I'm twenty-five, Dev. I look at my phone if I want to know the time. But I can't get to it right now, not without putting Rob down."

Dev looked up, squinting into the rain, against which the trees offered minimal protection. "It's been a strange sort of day, so I've lost track of time. But it's definitely late afternoon. Maybe five?"

Despite everything, Todd gave a snort of laughter.

"What?"

"'A strange sort of day.' Understatement of the century."

Dev smiled without humor. "You know me. I like to keep things in perspective."

Todd was about to reply when Robin groaned and muttered something.

"Rob?" Todd said, but his brother had already slipped back into unconsciousness. Sighing, Todd said, "We ought to find somewhere for you and Rob to hide sooner rather than later. If I'm going for help, I'd like to be out of the forest before dark, otherwise I could spend the whole night wandering around."

Although he had the lamp on his helmet, he knew that using it would be a bad idea. He also knew, but didn't want to say, that because of the haphazard route they had taken, he didn't know whether he'd be able to negotiate a safe route out of the forest even *with* sufficient light. He knew he had to, for Robin's sake. But needing to do something and actually doing it were two different things.

They trudged on, looking for a suitable hiding place. Eventually the ground became rocky, some of the outcrops rising to six or eight meters tall. Making their way along one of the passages between them, Dev said, "What about there?"

He was pointing at a triangular patch of shadow at the base of two huge rocks that were leaning together like drunks.

"Can you take Rob's weight while I check it out?" said Todd.

"Sure."

They carefully leaned Robin against a rock wall, Dev wrapping his arms around him to keep him upright. Blood was still seeping from Robin's arm, but it was impossible to tell how much he was losing; as soon as it appeared, the rain washed it away.

Todd crouched in front of the triangular crevice, placed his hands against the wet rock and leaned forward.

"It's a little cave," he said. "It seems to go back quite a way."

"Will we be able to fit?" asked Dev.

"I think so."

They maneuvered Robin into the cave, Dev tucking his arms under the unconscious man's armpits and backing through the opening in a shuffling crouch, Todd taking the weight of his brother's feet. Eventually Robin was all the way inside, and all Todd could see of him were his legs below the knees. Dev was completely concealed in the darkness, though Todd could hear him moving about.

"You all right in there?"

"Not too bad," Dev said. "It's actually quite dry. Hang on."

Todd could tell from the way Robin's legs tilted beneath his hands that Dev had laid his brother down. He lowered Robin's legs to the ground just as the triangular patch of darkness was filled with yellow light.

Dev had turned his helmet lamp on, which threw the rest of him into silhouette. As he looked around, examining his surroundings, the light dimmed and brightened, shadows rising and sinking across the walls and ceiling.

"Not a bad little bolthole," he said. "I think we'll be all right here for a while."

"I'll find some branches to cover the entrance."

"Good idea. But don't make it too obvious. And don't take too long about it. You need to be off."

Plenty of twigs and branches had been stripped from the trees by the wind, and it didn't take Todd long to make a stack tall enough to conceal the gap between the rocks from prying eyes. Assessing his handiwork, he was pleased with the effect. The stack of debris looked haphazard enough to have accumulated there naturally rather than having been carefully placed. As long as Dev and Robin kept quiet, it was unlikely they'd be found.

"Right then," Dev said, his voice muffled behind the makeshift barricade, "you'd better go."

"Suppose I'd better," said Todd – yet now the time had come, he felt reluctant to leave. It wasn't just the thought of being alone that scared him, but the awareness he might never see his brother alive again. Even if he *did* manage to return with help, would it be soon enough for Robin? Agonizing though that prospect was, one thing was certain: the longer he waited, the slimmer were Robin's chances of survival.

As if sensing his indecision, Dev called, "Stay lucky, son. And don't worry. I'll look after him."

"I know you will," Todd said. He hesitated a moment, then added, "Listen, Dev, if Rob should wake up, can you tell him…"

But words failed him. He and Robin were close, but the men in his family had never been able to fully express their feelings for one another.

Dev, though, said, "'Course I will, son. I'll tell him exactly what he needs to hear."

"Thanks." Todd took a deep breath, listening to the rain drumming on his helmet. Glancing up, he saw the sky had darkened yet further. "See you then."

CHAPTER FORTY-FIVE

The bodies of the three men hung from the branches of Yggdrasil, the great tree at the end of the world. The men had been killed in the ritual manner, the flesh either side of their spines sliced open, their ribs and lungs wrenched out through the gashes in their backs to form rudimentary wings. Writhing in agony, choking to death in their own blood, they had been hoisted up, their arms stretched into a cruciform shape and bound to the branches of the sacred tree. Their blood, spilling hot and red into the many fissures that had opened in the rock below, had nourished the gods, who even now were preparing to re-establish dominion over the world of men.

The herald inside the woman known as Yrsa, who for many years had been manipulating events in the woman's life without her knowledge – events that had led to this glorious moment – looked upon its work with satisfaction. The herald thanked the men for their sacrifice, even though their deaths were an honor for which they were unworthy.

Three had been chosen because three was the sacred number. Each sacrifice had been offered in exchange for a gift that would be bestowed upon the gods at the time of their re-emergence. The first sacrifice imbued them with harmony; the second, wisdom; the third, understanding. In the days to come, more gifts would follow. Each human life that was snuffed out would be another trinket, another coin, another glittering bauble to add to the ever-swelling treasure house of the divine.

Beneath the herald's feet, the rising rumble of water had crescendoed into a screeching roar. It was as if the gates of the underworld had been thrown open, releasing the tormented wailings of the eternally damned. The floor of the cave that housed the great tree was splitting; chunks of rock were breaking from the walls and ceiling and falling all around the herald's diminutive human body. Yet although the jötnar, servants of the gods, had scattered, their presence required elsewhere, the herald remained, standing calmly amid the swirling dust and the flying splinters of rock, an expression of rapture on its borrowed face.

As the screeching reached its climax, the herald slowly raised its arms. The gods had been summoned and they had come. In the next moment the fissured rock floor burst open in a thousand places, and water erupted upwards with shattering force.

CHAPTER FORTY-SIX

Growing up, Todd and Robin had lived with their parents in a big house on a new-build estate on the outskirts of Richmond. Their cul-de-sac had been full of young families, and as a kid Todd had loved the mass games of hide-and-seek that he, Robin, and many of the neighborhood kids had played on summer and autumn evenings.

The games from mid-September to the end of October, with crisp autumn leaves on the ground and a smoky, pre-Halloween chill in the air, had been the best, with the murk and shadows adding an extra *frisson* to proceedings. If hiding, you became jumpy at the prospect of seekers looming out of the darkness and grabbing you; if seeking, you were wary of hiders bursting from patches of gloom behind hedges or cars, often with blood-curdling shrieks to make you jump out of your skin, and racing you to the lamppost at the end of the street that served as 'home'.

At the end of such games, when Mum called them in for bath and bedtime, Todd and Robin would return to the house, grinning and sweaty and jittery with adrenaline. Looking back on those autumnal games years later, he had never failed to regard them as among the happiest memories of his childhood. To him, they were perfect examples of times when he was delirious with excitement and fear, yet completely absorbed in the moment. As an adult, he'd often wondered whether he would ever feel quite so alive again.

Well, now he did. But instead of delicious dread, what gripped him during *this* game of hide-and-seek was a sensation of utter terror.

It had been forty minutes or more since he had said goodbye to Dev, and during that time the sky had darkened still further. Looking up, he saw only two colors – the solid black of the leafy canopy, and the bruised denim-blue of the sky between the leaves.

There was a little more definition at ground level – but not much. Although the rocks were several shades of gray, and the tree trunks and bushes mostly black, the incessant rain, as well as imbuing the forest with a twitching simulacrum of life, blurred the edges of things, giving Todd the impression he was viewing the landscape through spectacles with scratched and clouded lenses.

There was something else the rain did, too – it obliterated the sound of everything but itself. All Todd could hear as he crept through the forest was the battering hiss of water. If pursuers were nearby, foliage rustling as they moved through it, he couldn't hear them. Moving from tree to tree in what he hoped was a route that would lead him to the edge of the forest, he felt profoundly deaf and mostly blind.

He was initially reassured by the thought that his pursuers would have the same problems as him – but then he remembered the jötnar. He didn't know exactly what the creatures were, but he *did* know they were cave dwellers – so wasn't it likely their night senses were heightened? He had seen their eyes shining with an amber glow in the tunnels, which might mean they could see in the dark as easily as he could see in daylight. The prospect was terrifying, but he couldn't let it slow him down. If he didn't make it back with help, he would effectively be signing his brother's death warrant.

Up to now, he hadn't seen another soul in the forest. But his hope their pursuers had given up the chase was dashed minutes later. Skirting a tall bush, Todd saw what appeared to be a tree trunk about five meters ahead of him move. Instantly he dropped to a crouch, tucking his head into his hunched shoulders in the hope he would look like a piece of foliage. He peered intently at the place where he thought he'd seen movement, his heart thumping so hard that the darkness in front of him seemed to be pulsating. He took a deep breath, closed his eyes, then opened them again. The shadowy shapes settled, stilled. And now he saw that something *was* moving. Not a tree trunk, but something that had stepped out from *behind* a tree trunk, and was now crossing the ground in front of him.

It was short, less than five feet high, and at first Todd was terrified it might be one of the jötnar. But looking again, he saw it was a little taller, a little slimmer than the troll-like creatures he'd seen, and also it moved differently.

A child, then – but that was still no reason to relax. In some ways it was actually worse, because if a possessed child attacked him, he'd have to defend himself – but to what extent? He was sure their pursuers were no longer in control of their own minds, which made them just as much victims as he, Robin and Dev. So, if Todd were to injure an attacker, he wouldn't be hurting the real enemy, but simply the man, woman or child they had possessed.

His thoughts turned to Yrsa, the ultimate victim of whatever force or entity was present in the caves. What was it the thing controlling her had said? That it was the herald of the gods? The tragedy of his and Yrsa's relationship, the knowledge the whole thing had been manipulated from the start, filled him with desolation, but he couldn't succumb to that now. He had to stay alive, keep fighting. Maybe later, when he, Robin and Dev were safely back in London, there would be time for tears.

He watched the small figure cross the stretch of marshy ground in front of him and disappear into the blackness of the trees. He wished again that he could hear it, that he could be sure it had moved away. He waited thirty seconds, then rose to his feet. He took a step forward – and immediately another figure stepped from behind a tree.

This second figure was taller, and from its bulk and shape Todd was pretty sure it was a man. Instead of ducking down and drawing attention to himself, he froze, feeling horribly exposed and vulnerable. He was appalled to see the figure freeze too, as if it had suddenly become aware of his presence.

For a moment Todd and the figure simply stood there, as if playing a game of 'statues'. Todd felt as if the rain, drumming on his helmet and the heavy, protective material of his coat, would be bound to give him away. But that was just his paranoia. What sounded like a clattering racket to him would be lost in the hissing roar of the deluge. He saw the figure turn its head, and then its entire body, towards him – but again, his imagination was simply providing him with a worst-case scenario. In the dark it was actually impossible to tell whether the figure was turning towards him or not.

Apparently not, because a moment later the figure resumed its previous course. Todd watched it cross the patch of ground just as the child had done, and disappear into the blackness of the trees.

A long breath shuddered out of him. How many more of their pursuers were wandering aimlessly through the forest? He felt like an avatar in a computer game, whose aim was to stay alive by avoiding the monsters. He could only hope the majority of the mob had given up the chase. Failing that, he had to hope the forest was big enough and dark enough for him to avoid detection.

Wary of a third figure appearing from behind the same tree, Todd crept towards it in a semi-crouch, then took a huge breath and lunged across the boggy patch of ground beside it. Nothing hurled itself at him, and seconds later he was pressed against the slimy trunk of another tree on the far side of the clearing, gasping with relief.

He moved on, eyes darting everywhere. On all sides there was movement – vegetation jerking as it was battered by rain. He'd been going another ten or fifteen minutes when he glimpsed a black, bulky shape shambling or lurching in the darkness to his left. But when he turned his head, there was nothing there. A few minutes after that, some distance away, he glimpsed what he was convinced were the eyes of a jötnar – a flash of yellow lights, like two flaring matches. Again, though, when he focused on what he'd seen subliminally, nothing but blackness met his gaze.

His mind was now in overdrive. He started to think there *had* been a jötnar there, and it was now homing in on him like a torpedo, its squat body plowing through the foliage. The thought panicked him, and for the next thirty seconds he plunged through the mire, like an animal startled by a predator. Eventually, panting hard, he sank to the wet ground between a bush and a tree, knees under his chin, arms wrapped tightly around his bent legs. Shivering, he sensed danger all around him: slithering shadows; looming patches of blackness that might form into grasping figures. But when several minutes passed, and nothing happened, he thought: *Get up and get fucking moving. Keep going for Rob.*

He rose to his feet and plodded on, creeping from tree to tree. Every second he expected jötnar to drop from the branches, to surround him, their eyes glowing a sick, soft yellow. Maybe the only reason they hadn't done so was because they were toying with him, savoring the hunt. And maybe, to fully relish his despair, they would wait until he was on the edge of the forest before springing their trap.

Attempting to push these thoughts aside, he looked up, palm shielding his face from the stinging rain, and realized he could no longer distinguish the canopy of trees from the night sky; it was now one impenetrable expanse of black. It felt like the middle of the night, but Todd knew it couldn't be any later than seven thirty p.m., eight at most. So if he could make it to town by nine, he could be back here with help by nine thirty, and Robin could be tucked up in a hospital bed by ten. That process, that chain of events, seemed unattainable right now – but if he kept going, if he had luck on his side, then maybe it—

The figure came out of nowhere.

One second Todd was trudging forward, weaving between trees and bushes, trying to maintain what he hoped was a straight line through the lashing rain, and the next the black shape was lunging at him, closing with him, grabbing at his throat, his face.

Todd stumbled backwards, too shocked to do anything but flail wildly and defensively. He'd been as watchful as he could, but robbed of his most crucial senses, every step had been a gamble. He'd got this far largely through luck, and now that luck had run out. As his attacker slashed at him, fingers hooked into claws, Todd jerked his head back – and felt something hard impact with the back of his skull. Instantly, despite his helmet, fireworks exploded across his vision. *There's two of them*, he thought. And then someone yanked the forest floor out from under his feet as though it was a soggy carpet, and he went down.

He fell in stages, staggering on wobbly legs and fighting against it every step of the way. When he hit the boggy ground, he didn't particularly hurt himself, his bulky clothing cushioning him from the worst of the impact. Instinctively he rolled aside as his assailant lurched into the space he'd occupied a moment earlier. And then he did something he might not have done if he'd been thinking straight. He reached up and turned on his helmet light.

Instantly he realized two things. The first was that he hadn't been struck from behind by a second attacker, but had simply whacked his head on a tree. And the second was that his assailant was an old woman in a sodden gray housedress that was clinging to her scrawny frame like a shroud.

Illuminated by the beam from his helmet, the woman looked like a specter, her staring eyes cataracted by the harsh light, the fish-white flesh of her face veined with rain-flattened strands of white hair. Her mouth hung open in an idiot yawn, and her arms stretched towards him, skeletal fingers clawing at the air. Looking down, Todd saw that her stick-thin legs and naked feet were scratched and bleeding.

In other circumstances he would have felt sorry for her, but right now she was terrifying. As she jerked towards him, he reached up and clicked off his helmet light once again. As soon as he'd turned it on, he'd realized it was a stupid thing to do. If there *were* jötnar in the area, they were surely now all converging on him like sharks with the scent of chum in their nostrils.

He rolled again, the boggy ground squelching beneath him, then rose to his feet. He felt heavy and awkward in his wet clothes, and by the time he was upright, the old woman – an emaciated silhouette in the darkness – was no more than a couple of meters away.

But Todd felt better equipped to avoid her now. He realized the only reason she had managed to attack him in the first place was because he had walked straight into her. Now he knew where she was, he could see that her movements were slow, hampered by infirmity. Slipping behind a tree, he sidled around the side of it and splashed away, taking lunging strides, like an astronaut on the moon's surface.

Although the clatter of rain was as much an advantage as a disadvantage, Todd again found himself wishing it wasn't drowning out all other sound. He was sure he could move a lot faster than the old woman, but he would still have found it more comforting if he could hear the sounds of pursuit receding behind him. As it was, the itch between his shoulder blades persisted until a stabbing pain in his side forced him to press a hand to the bulky clothing over his ribs and duck behind a tree. Gasping, he peeked around the trunk, back in the direction from which he'd come. Overlapping sheets of rain lent the blackness the restlessness of ceaseless motion, but none of it looked purposeful enough to constitute a threat.

He allowed himself a minute of long, deep breaths before moving on. The old woman might not be fast, but he had no doubt she'd be dogged, her frail body propelled by whatever force was controlling her. There was always a chance she might collapse with exhaustion before catching up with him, but he wouldn't wish that on her. For the next ten or fifteen minutes he blundered on, his stitch nagging at him like an old wound, until he eventually became aware that something about the darkness – its texture, its nature – was subtly changing.

He slowed, and again sought the shelter of a tree, eyes narrowing as he tried to make sense of what he was seeing. Until now, the darkness had felt…enclosed, confined, but now it seemed to stretch out before him. Could it be that he was almost at the edge of the forest? But if so, which edge? Warily he left the shelter of the tree and moved towards what he sensed rather than saw was an open patch of ground directly ahead.

It quickly became apparent that his instincts were right – he *was* at the edge of the forest. Beyond the last of the thinning trees was a blank expanse that he was sure was a field, with nothing to mark its border except a trio of dark posts, or standing stones, which were almost indistinguishable from the darkness beyond them. Looking around, fighting the urge to switch on his helmet lamp for a few seconds to confirm he was alone, he hurried towards the posts. He was no more than six or seven meters from them when first one, and then the others, turned towards him.

Fuck! They weren't posts; they were *people*. How could he have been so stupid? He had assumed, because they were motionless, that they were inanimate objects, but now he guessed the reason they'd been so still was because, having come to the edge of the forest, they'd simply switched themselves off like machines. The alternative, that they had been waiting for him, was too creepy to contemplate, because how could they have known he would emerge here – unless the reason the forest had been so sparsely populated was because possessed islanders had stationed themselves at every potential exit point?

The figures were not just turning now, but moving towards him with purpose. Clumsy with fear, Todd turned back towards the trees, his left foot slithering from under him and almost spilling him onto his arse. Regaining his balance, he staggered towards what now seemed the relative safety of the forest. But he had taken no more than a few steps when several nearby tree trunks swelled, before birthing smaller versions of themselves.

More people, more possessed islanders, emerging from the darkness. When they too began to move towards him, he realized the only way he could go was sideways. But turning first right, then left, he saw figures materializing from every direction, some of them only distinguishable by the fizzing halo of rain around their upper bodies as it bounced off their shoulders and heads.

He was trapped, his pursuers closing in. Spinning back towards the three figures he had mistaken for posts or upright stones, he decided his only chance was to rush them, try to barge his way through. Although it was difficult to be sure in the darkness, he thought the one on the right of the group looked the slimmest and lightest of the three. He gathered himself to fight for his life – and then the world tore itself apart behind him.

Instead of running, Todd *threw* himself forward, arms outstretched, like a diver plunging into a pool. The ground was so wet and muddy that he slid several meters before coming to a halt, whereupon he twisted to look over his shoulder.

What he saw, on the horizon to his right, beyond the field and the road and the forest, was a vast, silvery cloud rising into the night sky. At first he thought it was smoke – *glittering* smoke, radioactivity perhaps – and then it struck him what it really was.

Water. A vast, powerful geyser of water. It had erupted out of the ground with such force that it had torn the rocky hillside apart as if it were paper. The geyser was now coiling, billowing, rising majestically above the island, clashing with the torrential rain and creating a colossal scintillating wall that even now was shedding parts of itself, great arcs falling to earth in crashing waves and spreading in all directions over the already flooded land. To Todd, the island resembled a boat that had sprung a leak. He remembered the subterranean roaring in the cave and thought of Yrsa. Then he wondered how long it would take before everything was engulfed.

Distracted by the eruption, it was several seconds before he remembered he was facing a more imminent threat. Scrambling to his feet in the slippery mud, he quickly realized his pursuers had not only been distracted by the eruption too, but had been affected by it far more profoundly. Looking around, he saw them turn away from him and shuffle in the direction of the still-surging geyser, as if drawn by some irresistible signal. The three he had mistaken for posts or standing stones even walked right past him, as if he wasn't there.

Todd again glanced at the source of their fascination, and for a split second he had the impression of a shape within the towering column of water. It was a nightmarish face comprising curved horns and multiple eyes, rising from a body whose bloated bulk was alive with a coiling, thrashing motion, like a swarm of eels in a feeding frenzy.

Then he blinked, and the monstrous vision collapsed, the frothing shapes becoming shapeless once more. Turning away, seizing his chance, Todd set off in a loping, splashing run across the field he hoped would eventually connect with the road back to town. For now, the field was a black, ankle-deep lake, but he wondered how long it would take for the water level to rise if the 'geyser' continued to gush at its present rate. How long, for that matter, would it take for the water to flood the cave where Robin and Dev were hiding?

Exhausted to the point of collapse, but aware he was now involved in an ever more desperate race against time, Todd pushed on through the darkness.

CHAPTER FORTY-SEVEN

Despite the hammering of rain on the roof, Karriana heard the island being torn apart from several miles away.

Curled in the womb-like security of her bed, it registered as a prolonged rumble, like a distant earthquake. She raised her head briefly, wondering what was happening. But despite the painkillers she had taken, her throat and neck still felt bruised and swollen, and within seconds she lowered her head back to the welcoming support of her pillow. She closed her eyes, but couldn't fully lose herself in sleep, because every time she started to drift, an image of what she wanted to forget bobbed into her mind – Bjarne Haugen, the man she had killed, the side of his face hanging off and a spar of splintered wood jutting from his ear.

He was not the only person who had approached her with murderous intent on her way home – but he was the only one who had caught her. After almost being strangled by Haugen, Karriana had kept her distance from everyone else she had come across. In truth, the streets had been quiet, which was not surprising given the weather, but the few people Karriana *had* seen had set her alarm bells ringing. As with Haugen and her dad, there had been something vacant about them. It was as if they were sleepwalking, or drugged.

One such group, who had shuffled past while she'd been crouching behind a car opposite the bakery, had numbered half a dozen people, among which had been Seia Heikkinen and her son Cedrik, who ran the hardware store, and Óskar Kristinsson, who had given Todd a hard time outside the church the other day. Karriana had emerged and started to cross the street only when the group was out of sight. She had been so relieved to have almost made it home that she didn't notice she had company. Registering movement at the periphery of her vision, she froze and, because of her painful neck, swung her body in that direction. Standing in the center of the road, about twenty meters away, was a small, dark-haired girl.

Like everyone else, the girl, who was about six years old, and who Karriana had seen in the bakery with her mother and knew was called Lotti, had been soaking wet, her thin cotton pajamas, covered with cartoon cats and birds, plastered to her body. Her hair hung in two dripping braids either side of her face, and her bare feet were dirty and plastered with pine needles. With dismay, Karriana saw that Lotti's eyes had that familiar glazed look, and her mouth was hanging open.

For a moment Karriana and Lotti stood and stared at each other, the small girl tilting her head to one side as if she was sizing up a potential opponent. Moving her arm slowly, Karriana unsnapped the fastener on her jacket pocket and slid her wet hand inside. Locating the key to the bakery with the tips of her fingers, she took a cautious step forward. She'd calculated it was only fifteen steps, twenty at most, to the bakery door, though the road was perilously wet, rain bouncing up off the tarmac and the treacherously smooth flagstones of the pavement.

The reaction from Lotti to Karriana's forward step was instantaneous. Her expression unchanging, her arms still hanging by her sides, she began to run towards Karriana.

Although Karriana had been expecting it, she still found the child's emotionless intent utterly terrifying. As soon as Lotti started to run, Karriana did too, her body galvanized by a fresh rush of adrenaline, which caused the grinding pain in her hip to temporarily disappear.

Karriana was bigger and faster than the little girl, and when she reached the door, thankfully without losing her footing on the slippery ground, she still had a good twenty-meter lead over her pursuer. Trying not to think of Lotti running up behind her, she pushed the key into the lock and turned it. The latch disengaged, and Karriana shoved the door open, at the same time pulling back on the key to release it. There was a moment of panic when the key seemed to stick, maybe because it was wet, but then it slid free. Slipping through the door, Karriana turned to push it shut again, and saw that Lotti, still running, was about to leap from the road onto the curb of the pavement, no more than three meters away. Karriana slammed the door, and a second later heard a shuddering thump as the child's body hit the wood on the other side.

Karriana gave a little scream and jumped back, but the door was sturdy and the girl couldn't have weighed more than twenty kilos. She half-expected Lotti to attack the door frenziedly, but after the initial thump of her body impacting with the wood, there was silence.

Karriana remained crouched for twenty or thirty seconds, and then, keeping an eye on the big display window that was a mass of slithering gray, sidled across to the door behind the counter and slipped through it. Although the hallway beyond was gloomy, Karriana left the light off, scared of attracting attention to herself. Beyond the hallway was the big kitchen with its vast ovens where her father did all the baking. Karriana crossed to the door that led up a narrow, curving staircase to the flat where she had lived with her parents all her life.

It was the reality of being alone in a place that normally felt familiar and safe that caused her emotions to finally overwhelm her. All the grief, fear and shock she'd been holding at bay came pouring forth, and hot, messy tears streamed down her face as she sank onto the bottom step, wails of distress wrenching their way out of her guts.

How long she sat there she wasn't sure, but at last she dragged herself up the stairs, took a handful of painkillers and crawled into bed, suddenly incapable of anything more. And there she stayed, haunted by the memories of the past few hours, shifting fitfully between consciousness and unconsciousness, until she was dragged into brief wakefulness by a noise that sounded like a distant earthquake or explosion.

Although she wondered what the noise was, she could summon up neither the energy nor the interest to investigate. It struck her, though, that the distant rumble had come from the direction in which all the 'infected' had been heading – out of town, towards the unpopulated north of the island. Lying sleepless and exhausted, she wondered if the two things were connected. She was still wondering as she slipped back into a fitful doze. It was the sound of the world cracking in two that startled her fully awake.

Body rigid, fists clenched, heart beating hard, she blinked into the gloom, wondering what time it was. All she knew was that it was as dark now as when she had fallen asleep. She wondered what had woken her. She had the sense she'd heard a sharp crack, like something buckling that had been under great strain. But was that real, or just part of some now-forgotten dream? She listened hard, but heard nothing except the hissing patter of rain. Then her ears re-attuned, and she suddenly realized that part of the rainfall was *inside the room!*

She sat up, only remembering her injuries when a pain like a collar tightening around a bruise made her gasp. She paused, then gingerly tried again. Although her neck still hurt, the pain was manageable if she didn't make any sudden moves. From an upright position, the sound she had heard seemed different, more of a gritty sifting that made her think of sand rather than rain.

Reaching for her phone, which she'd placed on her bedside table, she switched on the torch and shone it in front of her.

"Holy fuck," she muttered.

Karriana was not a girl who swore much, but on this occasion the sight warranted it. There was a wide black crack extending all the way up the wall of her bedroom and partway across the ceiling. Dusty rubble was sifting from the ceiling crack and pattering on her dressing table and wooden floor. Already both were coated with a fine film, and more dust was swirling in the light from her torch.

Eyes wide, she got slowly out of bed. What was happening? First the storm, then everyone going crazy, and now the island itself seemed to be breaking apart.

So maybe the sound she'd heard *had* been an earthquake? Or maybe the dormant volcano was not so dormant, after all? Could the way people were behaving be due to atmospheric pressure affecting their brains? Or could there be something in the rain? Some chemical? Maybe this was all an experiment by the Russians or the Chinese? Maybe they were testing some new weapon, a drug that made people psychotic? And maybe she was one of a small proportion who were immune?

She knew this sounded crazy, and yet viewed from the inside it seemed not only halfway feasible, but, in a strange way, even kind of reassuring. At least it was an explanation she could work with.

Whatever the truth, though, she was sure of one thing: crawling under her duvet and hoping all this madness would be over when she woke up was not the best approach. Maybe she should get off the island. But how? As far as she could see, the only way was to head down to the harbor and commandeer one of the fishing boats.

In these conditions it was a bonkers plan, but it was the only one she had. At least if she left the island she'd have a *chance* of survival, whereas if she stayed here, she'd likely die along with everyone else.

As if to confirm this, there was another sudden crack, which made her neck flare with a pain that shot into her skull as she flinched. Narrowing her eyes, she again directed her torch at the opposite wall, and was horrified to see that several horizontal cracks had now branched off from the main one, which looked wider than before. Even more alarming, more cracks had opened in the ceiling too, which was now sagging a little.

That decided it. She had to get out. Crossing to the wardrobe to drag out warm, dry clothes (she had dumped her wet ones on the floor before crawling into bed), she glanced out of her bedroom window.

Her room was directly above the main entrance to the bakery, with a view over the main street. The rain-distorted image through the glass made her gasp in shock. Last time she'd looked, the street had been rain-lashed, excess rainwater flowing along the gutters and gurgling into the drains. But now it was a lake from which buildings jutted, the road and pavements hidden beneath dark, churning water that looked ankle (perhaps even shin) deep. The surface of this newly formed lake reflected the glow from the miraculously still-working streetlamps as a kaleidoscope of luminous shards.

Looking closer, she saw that several areas of the 'lake' were bubbling like hot springs. Could the water be hot? Could there be things *living* in there? Then she realized that the road, like her wall, must have cracked open, and that water was actually bubbling up from underneath, perhaps even from the seabed itself.

Behind her, more rubble sifted down, pattering on the floor. Hurriedly Karriana got dressed, dragging on several layers – she'd certainly need the extra protection once she was at sea. Her boots and her big 'waterproof' coat were still damp, inside and out, but that couldn't be helped. Once she was ready, she clomped into the kitchen and swallowed several more painkillers before shoving the rest into her coat pocket. Her water bottle and a few hastily grabbed snacks were distributed among her other pockets, and then she went downstairs.

Peeking around the door into the bakery itself, Karriana saw that the floor was awash with water that had seeped in through whatever gaps it could find. Additionally, the big display window was cracked like her bedroom wall, a slanting black line dividing the huge sheet of glass from top to bottom. Apart from the rain, she could see no indication of movement through it, and so she crossed quickly to the main door, listened a moment, then pulled it open.

Instantly standing water sluiced in like an incoming tide, and she screwed up her eyes as a sheet of rain hit her like a jet from a hosepipe. Blinking, she saw items drifting by in the shallow river that the main street had become – a bicycle, a display board, and what appeared to be a large tarpaulin, or perhaps an awning torn from a storefront.

Across the street, several buildings appeared to be sagging, or otherwise crooked, and quite a number of windows were broken, curtains flapping like frantic appeals for help. Turning her head gingerly from left to right, she was relieved to see that at least the street appeared to be empty of people.

Nevertheless, she remained watchful as she waded out of the bakery and set off down the street, keeping close to the storefronts. She saw more devastation as she splashed through water which came to just above her ankles. One flat-roofed building on the opposite side of the road had caved in completely, like a cardboard box crushed by a giant foot, and others were showing signs of structural damage. The further she walked, the more debris she saw, some of which swirled around her boots. There were wooden boards and chunks of masonry, branches, twigs and shrubs, twisted chunks of metal, children's toys, items of clothing, bedding, cushions, food packaging, broken furniture, and dozens of other items.

Head down, eyes darting everywhere, she forged through, hoping that when she reached the harbor, she wouldn't find the boats capsized, or wrecked by the storm, or scattered to the four winds. All she needed was one vessel sturdy enough to carry her to safety. Once she was in calmer waters, she could make her way towards one of the islands that were sprinkled like seeds off Iceland's east coast, or even radio for help.

Then it struck her: how could she operate a boat without a key to start the engine? She cursed herself for not thinking of that before. Although Eldfjallaeyja was a law-abiding place – or had been before everyone went crazy – it would be pushing her luck to assume that some of the boat owners had left their keys on board.

So what could she do? Immediately it came to her: Bjarne Haugen. *He* had a boat. And chances were, he kept the keys in his house. Which Karriana knew for a fact was open and probably empty.

But could she face going back there? Could she face seeing his body again, which was now no doubt lying half-submerged in the floodwaters, if it hadn't been carried away?

Her stomach rolled at the thought, but she knew she couldn't let her squeamishness deter her, not when her life was at stake. It would be ironic if she died simply because she couldn't bring herself to look at the corpse of a man she'd been forced to kill to save herself.

Sighing, she looked up and down the street again. She was almost parallel with the intersection that led to the road where Haugen lived – *used to live*. To reach it, she'd have to move into the open and splash across the road – avoiding the areas where the water was bubbling like a witch's cauldron, of course.

She felt nervous as she moved away from the buildings she'd been pressing against for safety, and couldn't help but feel relieved when crowds of assailants didn't suddenly come screeching out of hiding.

She splashed across the road, stepping over small items and skirting around larger ones. As she neared the buildings on the north side of the street, she could see how much closer they were to collapse than their counterparts on the opposite side. She wondered why, but then noticed that the water was more turbulent here – there were more areas where it was bubbling and churning, which she guessed meant the ground had cracked or given way. Directly in front of the building that had collapsed was what looked like a whirlpool, water spinning and frothing, as if a sinkhole had opened beneath it.

She paused as a four-meter-long pine branch, its needles clumped with mud, drifted past, turning slowly in the current. As she waited to cross behind it, she became aware of a roaring behind her, first blending with the hissing of rain, and then rising above it.

Alarmed, but unable to twist her head because of her swollen neck, she had to turn her entire body ponderously towards the sound. Horrified, she saw a battered open-bed truck bearing down on her. It was approaching at speed, water spraying in glittering arcs from its wheels. Occasionally it slewed to one side or the other to avoid floating debris. The driver, hunched over the wheel, was nothing but a silhouette.

Panicked, Karriana turned too quickly, and pain shot through her neck. Dragging her leading foot out of the water, she leaped over the trailing end of the tree branch. Although the truck was still thirty meters away, and would be easy to dodge if it continued in a straight line, her fear was that the driver might be one of the infected, intent on running her down. Looking for a barrier between herself and the vehicle, she spotted a low wall in front of a white-painted building about eight meters away. If she could only make it in time…

Gathering herself, she leaped over the branch. When her right foot came down on the far side of it, her trailing foot was still in midair, her body off-balance – which would have been fine if she'd had a solid landing.

What she hadn't seen, though, was that a smaller branch, attached to the main branch and thick with pine needles, was entirely submerged.

Her foot came down on it, and immediately twisted beneath her. Thrown off-kilter, she fell forward, instinctively raising her hands to break her fall. She landed heavily, filthy water splashing her face, blinding her.

As she spluttered and floundered, all she could hear was the guttural bellow of the truck's engine, like the roar of a predator swooping on its prey.

CHAPTER FORTY-EIGHT

Robin's breathing changed at the same time as water started to creep into the cave.

Although the two things were not related, both were worrying. It was Robin's breathing that Dev became aware of first. In the darkness, he had lost track of time, not least because, exhausted and with nothing to stimulate his senses, he had been dozing intermittently. Snapping awake for the third or fourth time, he suddenly realized he had no idea how long it had been since Todd had gone for help. His phone, which he shielded with his cupped hand so its light couldn't be seen outside, told him it was eight seventeen p.m., but that meant nothing, because he hadn't checked the time when Todd had left. If he'd been able to, Dev would have called him to see how he was doing, but the last few times he'd looked there'd been no service.

Whenever he had faced a crisis in his life, and there'd been a fair few in his sixty-three years, Dev's philosophy had been: *What can be done to improve this situation?* On this occasion, though, he'd known the best thing he could realistically do was sit tight. With Robin injured and unconscious, the only way not to get caught by the crazy people was to hide from them, and wait for Todd to come back.

But now that Robin's breathing was giving him cause for concern, he was aware he might have to rethink.

Calm as ever, he sat in the darkness and considered the alternatives. The best-case scenario would be for Todd to turn up in the next few minutes with medical aid and transport. Second-best would be for Robin to wake up and feel well enough to stagger through the forest under his own steam.

Of these two, the best-case scenario was actually the more likely to happen. Dev thought there was little chance of Robin recovering without medical help. The younger man had lost a lot of blood, and as far as Dev knew, he was still losing it. Laying a hand on Robin's chest, Dev was concerned by the way his ribcage was rising and falling so shallowly and fitfully. Leaning over so his ear was close to Robin's mouth, he heard his friend making little gasping noises, each one separated by a silence of three or four seconds.

It didn't sound good, and by the time another fifteen minutes had passed, it sounded even worse. First, the gasps had become wheezes. Then the wheezes had become more erratic, more guttural. Hoping the sound – which was loud in the confined space – could not be heard from outside, Dev located Robin's limp hand, and squeezed it. He was alarmed, but not altogether surprised, to find it was freezing cold. Sighing, he laid the hand down gently and leaned back against the cave wall.

The first dead man Dev had ever seen had been his Grampa Roy. Dev had been nine years old, and his Grampa had been somewhere in his sixties. Grampa Roy had been a committed smoker all his life – Capstan Full Strength. Dev's mum told Dev that because of his smoking, Grampa Roy had a disease called arteriosclerosis, and it was so bad that it had stopped the blood flowing into one of his legs, as a result of which that leg had developed gangrene and had been cut off.

All of this had been nightmare fuel for young Dev, and when he had been taken by his mum to visit Grampa Roy in hospital, he had been terrified 1) that Grampa Roy's severed leg would be propped in a corner of his hospital room, green and rotting, and 2) that at some point Grampa Roy would whip back his bed covers and show Dev his bloody stump.

None of those things had happened, for which Dev had felt mightily thankful. In fact, Grampa had been in no fit state to whip back the covers of his bed even if he had wanted to. He had been asleep the whole time Dev was there, sitting by his bedside, next to his mum, who had rocked back and forth and wept loud, snotty tears into a big white handkerchief. Dev might only have been nine, but he had instinctively known that Grampa Roy was not long for the world. The old man – *not so old really*, Dev thought now – looked small and shrunken, his brown skin withered and dry and somehow chalky, as if white powder had been rubbed into its cracks and crevices. Grampa's mouth had been open, and his breathing, erratic and halting as Robin's was now, had sounded both wet and rusty, as though he was choking on something.

"Why is Grampa breathing like that?" Dev had asked.

His mum had blown her nose loudly, then looked at him with wet-rimmed, bloodshot eyes. "It's 'cos he's dying, sugar. That's his death-rattle you can hear."

Death-rattle. To nine-year-old Dev it sounded like an actual thing. He imagined that something like a hard, ridged worm had crawled into Grampa's throat, and was now curled up in there, suffocating him.

"Can't you get it out?" Dev had asked.

"No, sugar. We can't do nothing for Grampa Roy now. He'll be meeting the angels very soon."

Since that night, Dev had heard a couple more death-rattles. One had come from his mum, who had introduced him to the phrase. She had lived to a good age, but in the end a stroke had got her, and then, for good measure, a virus she'd contracted in hospital had carried her away before she'd had a chance to regain consciousness. And the other had come from his big brother, Jordan, who had died of pancreatic cancer five years ago, after leaving it too long to get treated.

And now Robin makes four, Dev thought, listening to the younger man's phlegmy, guttural breathing. He didn't know if there was any way back from this – he wasn't a doctor – but he did know that if Robin was left untreated for much longer, he'd die.

Groaning, Dev adjusted his position in the cramped cave, stretching his legs towards where he knew the entrance to be. To his surprise, the heels of his boots did not encounter hard earth, as he'd expected, but splashed into what felt like several inches of water. Maneuvering his body round in the tight space, he crawled forward, feeling with his hands. For a few feet the ground was hard earth, and then suddenly his hand slid into water, up to the wrist. It was like crawling blindfold across a beach and suddenly reaching the sea.

Tentatively he stretched his arm out, but only confirmed what he already knew – that the further he reached, the deeper the water became. He knew the interior of the cave sloped gently upwards from the entrance, so it wasn't surprising that the water got deeper, but what alarmed him was how quickly the forest must have flooded in the short time he and Robin had been in here. Yes, it had been raining torrentially, and yes, the ground had been boggy underfoot – even ankle-deep or higher in low-lying areas – but that had been after several days of incessant rain. There was no way the water level should have risen so dramatically in just a few hours, unless something had happened – a river bursting its banks, say.

But there wasn't a river nearby, was there? Wasn't the island composed mostly of pine forests and farmland, which sloped up to the dormant volcano at its center? If so, there was no way the forest should have flooded so quickly. So what the hell was happening?

Whatever it was, one thing was certain: they couldn't stay here. If they did, the water would just keep creeping in and eventually would reach the back of the cave and they'd drown. Given its current level, it must be at least knee-high, if not thigh-high, in the forest. The thought of carrying Robin's unconscious body through God knew how many miles of possibly still rising floodwater was beyond daunting. Looked at objectively, it seemed like a complete non-starter.

But Dev didn't have the luxury of objectivity. This wasn't a puzzle to ponder over, it was a problem he had to deal with *now*. And the only practical way to do it was to take it one step at a time. First priority was to get them out of the cave. And so, crawling back to Robin, he activated the torch app on his phone, shone it into his friend's face, and gave him a gentle shake.

"Rob, mate," he muttered. "Wake up."

He didn't expect to rouse Robin, but he was hoping he might get at least *some* reaction to either his voice or the glare of light – a groan, a movement of the head, a flicker of the eyelids. But there was nothing.

Robin was clearly sinking fast, his link to this life so gossamer-thin that Dev was afraid the slightest disruption might snap it completely.

But it couldn't be helped. Although trying to save Robin might kill him, it was still his only realistic chance of survival. Consoling himself with the thought that at least Robin was blissfully unaware of what was happening, Dev patted his friend gently on the chest and said, "Come on, old mate. We need to go."

Switching off his torch app and shoving his phone back into his pocket, he shuffled down the length of Robin's body. Tucking one of Robin's feet under each of his armpits, Dev wrapped his arms around his friend's legs and started to crawl backwards towards the cave entrance, dragging the younger man behind him. He knew his feet had reached the water when he felt the coldness of it through the toes of his boots. He paused briefly to prepare himself, then carried on, the water creeping over his shins and calves, then his knees and thighs.

It was like being slowly encased in ice; it chilled his flesh, but at first it didn't penetrate the thick material of his protective suit. Then, inevitably, it found the narrow gaps between ankle cuffs and boots and started to seep in. He gasped at its coldness, but had no choice but to keep going. The water spread like hypothermia over his stomach and back, before sidling up his arms. By the time he reached the cave entrance, only his shoulders and head were still above the water's surface.

Trying not to bump his head on the sloping roof, he maneuvered himself around so that he was at Robin's side as he guided him out, and able to hold his head and face clear of the water. Even with his body immersed in water that was bone-numbingly cold, Robin didn't stir. Slowly, awkwardly, scraping his back several times against the jagged rock wall, Dev guided himself and his friend out through the cave's narrow entrance.

It was almost as dark outside the cave as it was inside, and so Dev only realized he was beyond its womb-like confines when, to add insult to injury, the still-falling rain started to hammer at his head and shoulders. He swore, and as soon as Robin's body was clear of the cave entrance, he tilted it upright, so that the rain wasn't lashing directly at the younger man's face.

Looking around, Dev saw only the vaguest impression of trees and rocks, the sky like dense oil swirling overhead. He was aware branches were waving in the wind only because there was a vague sense of restlessness to the blackness.

As he'd guessed, the water was thigh-high, and appeared to be not stagnant like a pond, but flowing like a river. But in which direction? Downhill presumably. But from where to where? Acutely aware that time was of the essence, not just for Robin, but also for him (he was a sixty-three-year-old man faced with the very real dangers of exhaustion and hypothermia, not to mention the attention of any half-crazed pursuers who might still be around), he knew that whatever decisions he made in the next few minutes had to be the right ones.

Ignoring the temptation to strike out immediately, he forced himself, once he'd heaved Robin onto his shoulder in a fireman's lift, to recall what he knew of the layout of the land. He pictured their flight through the forest, trying to remember the twists and turns they'd made to evade their pursuers before discovering the cave. He tried to mentally draw a map of the route in his head, imagined looking down on the land as if he was a bird hovering high above it. Finally, once he was satisfied that the decision he was about to make was the best one he *could* make under the circumstances, he set off.

He moved neither with the flow of the water, nor against it, but cut through it in a sideways, crablike motion. Even so, he tried to keep the oncoming water at his back as much as possible, so it pushed against his butt and flowed around him.

It was hard going, especially as the water was full of small branches and clumps of foliage, which frequently bumped against him, but he knew it would have been a hell of a lot harder if the water was flowing towards him. Being unexpectedly jabbed in the arse might be irritating, but being whacked in the stomach or groin with the pointy end of a branch would be a damn sight worse. It would have been different if he could have seen what was coming, and taken evasive action, but it was so dark that the water and whatever was swirling in it was nothing but a mass of black.

Tempted though he was to move quickly, the ground beneath the water was slippery and uneven, and so Dev forced himself to progress with the utmost care. He knew that testing the ground with his toe before taking each step was a tortuously slow process, but he also knew that recklessness or haste would lead to accidents, which in his case could literally be the difference between life and death.

Although he itched to use the torch on his phone, he resisted the temptation. Any light would be seen for miles around, and would act as a beacon to any crazies still in the vicinity. The floodwater and the unceasing rain might be unpleasant, but at least they provided camouflage through which he could creep undetected. Hunched beneath Robin's weight, which was increasing the more saturated Robin's clothes became, Dev inched doggedly on, trying to block out his physical discomfort and the sense of futility that hovered at the edge of his thoughts like a cloud of gnats on a hot day.

It was unlikely he would have described the state of mind he managed to attain during this process as Zen-like, but when a hand brushed against his leg in the water some minutes later, he snapped to a state of alertness as if woken from a trance.

Looking around him, he saw nothing. Had he really felt a hand, or was it more likely a clump of vegetation, or even a drowned animal? He stood motionless for ten seconds or so, and then, using his free left hand, he cautiously patted and prodded at the water beside him. Every moment he half-expected a hand to rise from the murk and close tightly around his wrist, but as far as he could tell there was nothing there.

Imagined it, he told himself firmly, and moved on.

Since leaving the cave, he had become used to encountering trees in the dark. To avoid walking into them, he had been sweeping his left hand slowly back and forth. Trying to put the 'hand' incident out of his mind, Dev now slipped back into his established routine – probing forward with his right foot, sweeping the darkness ahead with his left hand. Three or four minutes later, as his fingers brushed across the spongy roughness of yet another tree trunk, an obstruction just under the surface thumped into his upper thigh, making him gasp and bringing him to a halt.

His immediate assumption was that the object was part of the tree, most likely a low branch. Lowering his hand to the water, he touched the thing he'd collided with – and recoiled.

It was a human foot – or at least, that was what it felt like. Fighting his natural revulsion, he again lowered his hand towards the water to re-examine what he'd touched.

There! Bobbing on the surface. Something that felt like a smooth hunk of meat. The fact it wasn't moving, that it didn't respond to the brush of his fingers, should have been a relief, but it wasn't. Dev had never been squeamish, but now his stomach tightened as his every instinct urged him to flee. But Dev was not a creature of instinct. He had always relied on calm logic, had always believed in the phrase 'forewarned is forearmed'.

And so, resisting the impulse to snatch his hand back again, he gingerly examined the object.

And yes, it *was* a foot. And furthermore, it was attached to a leg that appeared to be clad in a pair of sodden trousers made of some flimsy, slippery material. Silk maybe.

Edging forward along the length of the leg, Dev's hand traveled cautiously up the body. He felt a thigh, a hip, another leg, the bottom of a light jacket or shirt, made of the same filmy material as the trousers.

A picture formed in his mind. The shape and slightness of the body, and the thin, flimsy clothing (silk pajamas?) suggested this was a young woman, perhaps even a child. Dev's guess was that she was dead (drowned?), and that her body had washed up here and become entangled in the low branches of this tree.

Further examination would confirm or disprove his theory, but Dev had no wish to touch the dead girl's face, or hair, or even her upper body. Not so much because it would disturb him, but because it would feel like a violation of her privacy, her dignity.

Releasing a long breath, he stepped back, uncomfortably aware of her foot bumping once more against his leg. He found himself rubbing the palm of his hand across the sodden fabric of his protective suit, as if fearful of contagion. Again, he thought about using the torch on his phone, just to confirm his discovery, but resisted the impulse. He assumed the girl had been one of his pursuers and had died as the result of some accident.

To avoid further contact with the body, which was snagged on the right-hand side of the tree, Dev sidled around the left side of the trunk. He had taken no more than a couple of steps in that direction when, to his shock and astonishment, Robin suddenly jerked to life and threw himself forward, flipping off Dev's shoulder like a salmon and plunging into the water behind him.

Dev was caught so off-guard that his body was wrenched sideways. Boots slithering on the spongy ground, he stumbled, arms pinwheeling as he tried to stay upright. He might have managed it if one of Robin's trailing feet had not caught him on the side of his face as he flew past. Half-blinded by the blow, Dev staggered, then fell backwards, the filthy water closing over his head.

For an awful moment he thought hands were pressing down on his chest and limbs – but then he realized it was simply the weight of his sodden clothes. Fighting the urge to panic, he dug his heels into the soft earth beneath him, and pushed himself up into a sitting position.

He gasped as his head broke the surface, water streaming down his face. He took in a couple of lungfuls of air, then rose unsteadily to his feet.

He still didn't know what had happened. It was as if Robin had suddenly been shocked awake, and, not knowing where he was, had hurled himself forward in panic. But considering the state he had been in, where could that energy have come from? Baffled, Dev turned in the darkness, the drag of water against his legs making his movements sluggish. He couldn't see or hear anything except the rain. Not caring who might hear him, he shouted, "Rob? You there?"

No answer. Nothing but the frenzied clatter of rain. Dev felt exhaustion sweeping over him, but waded forward, plunging his hands into the water.

It was hopeless. Having stumbled and fallen, Dev had no idea which way he was facing. With the water flowing fast around him, the chances of finding Robin, alive or dead, were remote.

Then his fingers bumped against what felt like a booted foot.

It was bobbing in the water to his right, and having touched it once, he lunged and grabbed the boot by its heel, feeling the heavily ridged tread of the sole against his palm. Exultant but fearful, he dragged it towards him, able to tell from its weight that it was still attached to its owner's body. He could tell, too, that the body was lying face down, and so he frantically grabbed handfuls of its clothing as he hauled it in, desperate to reach the head and lift the face clear of the water.

Wrapping his arms around the torso and rolling the body over, though, Dev encountered something he wasn't expecting. His hand bumped against a gnarled pole of what felt like wood, sticking up at an angle. Puzzled, his hand slipped down the pole, and then his guts clenched. The pole was the shaft of a spear or harpoon – and it was embedded in Robin's back!

Even as nausea rose up in him, Dev realized what had happened. Robin had been hit in the back by a projectile going at such force that it had wrenched his body from Dev's shoulder. Even now unwilling to believe his friend might be dead, Dev reached beyond the projecting shaft, grabbed the shoulder of Robin's jacket, and hauled his head clear of the water. With his other hand he cupped Robin's face, aware of its waterlogged weight, the rubbery texture of Robin's skin, his open, drooling mouth. Dev lowered his head to the younger man's face.

"Rob," he muttered, "Rob, Rob." He kept speaking his name, as if doing so could resurrect him.

"He's gone," said a voice from the rain. "Soon you will all be gone. You must offer up your lives, so the gods may live."

Dev's strangled cry was the closest he'd ever come to a scream. He twisted so violently that he almost slipped and went under the water again. It was only his desire to keep Robin's face clear of the surface, despite what the voice had said, that kept him standing. Legs shaking, clutching Robin to him, he yelled, "Who are you? Why are you doing this?"

Even now, in extremis, he knew how plaintive and childlike his questions were. He saw something flare in the darkness ahead – a flame, a match. He flinched, thinking it was close to his face; in the blackness he had no sense of perspective.

Then another flame ignited, somewhere to the right, and then, despite the still-bucketing rain, a third. And now it was as if a stage that had been in darkness was slowly coming to life. And when Dev saw what was surrounding him, he immediately wished for the darkness to return.

In the water, floating and bobbing, were a dozen or more corpses. Among them were an old woman in a white nightgown, and a small girl in pink pajamas. Most of the bodies were face down, but here and there he saw white, wet faces, rain drumming into their open eyes and gaping mouths.

Undoubtedly these people had been among the mob who had chased them into the forest. But what had killed them? Had the sudden flood taken them by surprise? Then he remembered what the voice had just said to him, about how everyone must offer up their lives, and he wondered whether these people had drowned themselves in an act of self-sacrifice. Tearing his eyes from the dead, still clinging to Robin's skewered body, Dev again raised his gaze into the trees.

Impossibly, given the unrelenting downpour, three torches were blazing up there. Each was gripped in the clawed hand of one of the ape-like creatures he had glimpsed back on the road. *Cave dwellers*, Todd had called them, and as Dev's gaze flickered from tree to tree, he saw that the torchbearers were not alone. There were dozens of the creatures up there, their hunched forms clinging to the thicker branches and the tall, thin trunks of the pines.

Was it one of these creatures who had spoken? They looked so brutish that he found that hard to believe. He was sure the voice he had heard, distorted by the clatter of rain, had been female.

A suspicion forming in his mind, he shouted, "Who are you? Why don't you show yourself?"

There was laughter above him.

"You know who I am."

Up there. Perched on a branch high above. A form that looked slimmer, slighter, than the others. It was outside the range of the torches, so it was nothing but an impression.

"Yrsa?" he said.

The laughter came again, and now it sounded darker, more unpleasant. "Not anymore."

Her voice sounded…wrong somehow. Sludgy. Clogged. Forced through vocal cords that no longer worked properly.

"You don't sound too good," he said defiantly.

"This vessel too has given up the spark it contained. I continue to use it out of convenience." There was the slightest of pauses and then the voice said, "Now you too shall offer yourself to the gods."

Dev was aware of a shifting in the trees above him. Some of the creatures seemed to be holding objects other than torches. He thought of the spear that had severed the thin thread tethering Robin to this life, and he thought fleetingly of turning away, plunging beneath the water and swimming for his life. But he knew it was pointless. And besides, he didn't want to die like Robin, with a spear in his back.

Face full of defiance, he stared up into the trees.

CHAPTER FORTY-NINE

Lying on the ground, spitting dirty water, Karriana turned as quickly as her injured neck would allow. She glimpsed the startled face of the truck driver through the rain-speckled windscreen, and then she saw him twist the steering wheel to the left. Immediately the truck slewed in that direction, missing her trailing foot by no more than a meter. The truck skidded, tilted, surged forward on its two left-side wheels for a couple of seconds, and then crashed over onto its side.

The crunching impact as it hit the tarmac, despite the cushion of water, made Karriana flinch and instinctively hunch up her shoulders, which sent a fresh spasm of pain through her neck. Her head throbbed and her vision went fuzzy for a few seconds. When the pain passed, she rose gingerly to her feet.

Dripping wet, she looked across at the truck, which, although on its side, didn't appear to have sustained much damage. She couldn't see the driver's side, though, which for all she knew could have crumpled like a Coke can. She recalled the startled look on the driver's face, and the way he had deliberately twisted the wheel to avoid her. Surely that was proof he was normal like her – not infected, like the majority of islanders. Splashing across the street as quickly as she could, she circled the front of the truck, then squatted to peer through the windscreen, fearful of what she might see.

The windscreen had been wrecked, and now resembled a piece of twisted, heavily scarred plastic that still clung to one side of the warped frame. Unfortunately, it hadn't peeled far enough away on the driver's side for Karriana to see into the cab, and so she grabbed what looked like a wooden gatepost from a tangle of debris that was floating past and used it to bash the mangled windscreen aside. Now she could see the driver, and although it was dark, she realized with a jolt that she recognized him. He was slumped against the side window, which was cracked in multiple places but not broken. His eyes were closed and she could see blood in his blond hair where it rested against the glass.

Scrambling closer, murky water swirling around the toppled truck and splashing against her knees, she leaned into the cab through the now glassless windscreen and touched the driver's shoulder.

"Todd," she called, "can you hear me? Todd, wake up!"

Relief washed through her when he groaned and stirred. Speaking his name again, she was delighted to see his eyes flicker open. He stared at her a moment, then groggily said, "Hi."

"How do you feel?" she asked. "Are you hurt?"

He licked his lips, grimaced. "My head."

"You bumped it on the window," she said, hoping that was all he'd done. "Do you hurt anywhere else?"

"Don't think so."

"Can you crawl out to me? You'll have to undo your seat belt."

"I'll try."

She saw him fumbling at the seat belt with shaking hands and leaned forward to help him. Together they managed to unclip the belt, whereupon gravity caused Todd's body to slump down until his shoulder and face were pressed against the driver's window. Water was seeping into the cab now, though not enough for it to be a problem. Karriana noticed that Todd's body was twisted at the waist, his thighs pinned between the edge of the seat and the steering wheel. Hoping his legs and feet were neither trapped nor injured, she said, "Todd, can you move your legs? Can you pull them out from under the steering wheel?"

He sighed, like a drunk man who had to be persuaded to take his boots off before climbing into bed, and tried to wriggle free. It was clear, though, that he didn't have much room to maneuver, and that he was still too woozy to put much strength and coordination into his efforts.

"Hold on," Karriana said, and crawled through the flowing water, until her entire upper body was through the windscreen and inside the cab.

It took several minutes of pushing, pulling and grunting in the confined space before Todd's legs were finally free. As he slid them sideways and up, so they were stretched above his head along the length of the scuffed front seat, Karri was relieved to see he had sustained no obvious injuries.

"Shuffle round so you've got your back to me," she said.

He did so, slowly and awkwardly, and eventually she was able to slide her hands under his armpits. As he pushed with his feet against the long front seat – now upstanding like a scuffed leather column in the toppled cab – she pulled him out, inch by inch, the strain on her shoulder muscles sending fresh pulses of pain into her head and neck.

At last, the heels of Todd's boots bumped over the twisted rim of the windscreen and the two of them were free of the cab. Karriana pulled him clear of the truck completely, and then, exhausted and aching, she sat in the ankle-deep water, like a child in a paddling pool, with Todd's upper body slumped dazedly across her legs. If this was a movie, the petrol tank would explode and the truck would go up in flames at this point, to emphasize their narrow escape. But the truck merely remained on its side like a ruptured tin box, water swirling around it.

Water swirled around Karriana's and Todd's slumped bodies too, but for maybe fifteen seconds, Karriana was too weary to do anything about it. Finally, though, she patted him on the shoulder. "You're getting heavy."

"Sorry." He still sounded drunk.

"Can you stand?"

His eyes opened sleepily, then closed again as rain fell into them. "Dunno."

"Could you try? We're taking a risk, staying out here so long. Another group of infected people could come by at any moment."

That snagged his attention. His eyes squinted open once more. "Infected?" he murmured.

"That's what I call them."

He sat up with an effort, Karriana pushing him from behind. Groaning, he rubbed his head. "I feel dizzy."

"Just a mild concussion," she said, hoping she was right. "It will pass."

As he leaned forward as if about to be sick, Karriana stood up and looked both ways along the street. Relieved to see no one about, she turned back to Todd. Beads of blood were oozing from the left side of his scalp, which, as soon as they appeared, were diluted by rain.

"Your head's bleeding," she said.

"Is it bad?"

"It doesn't look too bad. Do you mind if I see? I'll be gentle."

"Go for it."

Kneeling in the water beside him, she carefully parted the wet strands of hair. Sure enough, there was a gash in his scalp, but it wasn't deep and there was no glass or metal sticking in it.

"You must have cut your head when the truck turned over. It's bleeding, but it looks worse than it is."

"So I'll live?"

"As long as the monsters don't get us."

Neither of them laughed at that.

Rising again to her feet, Karriana held out a wet hand. "There's a pharmacy a few doors away. We can find a bandage or something. Do you think you can stand up now?"

He enclosed her small hand in his larger one. "I'll try. Head still hurts like a bastard, though."

Suddenly she remembered the painkillers she'd brought with her, and produced them from her pocket.

"Take a couple of these."

Unquestioningly he popped a couple of tablets from the blister pack and put them in his mouth. "Got any water?"

She pointed at the sky, then smiled and passed him her water bottle.

Splashing across to the pharmacy, Karriana cupped her hands over her eyes and peered through the front window. The floor was awash, the water glinting with reflected light in the darkness, but as far as she could tell the place was empty. Even so, she pushed the door inwards with caution, allowing more water to flood into the store. Before entering, she said to Todd, "Will you be able to run if someone comes?"

His face was so pale it looked luminous in the lamplight, but he gave her a thin smile. "Only one way to find out."

They went inside, Karriana grateful that the rain battering the building would mask any sounds they might make. Against the wall by the long counter was a plastic chair – a place for older residents to sit while they waited for their prescriptions. Karriana instructed Todd to rest there while she looked around. As he leaned back, closing his eyes, she checked out the shelves. Eventually she waded across to him, arms laden with ointments, bandages, dressings and more painkillers. She dumped everything on the counter, then pulled several other items she had found from her coat pockets.

"Two energy bars and an energy drink," she said. "You're not allergic to nuts, are you?"

"I wasn't this morning," he said. "Thanks." He peeled the wrapper off one of the bars and chewed stolidly as Karriana prepared the dressing and bandages. When he'd eaten both bars, he reached for the energy drink, which was in a bright red can with a heavily muscled cartoon rabbit on it. Todd raised his eyebrows at Karriana, then popped the tab and took four long swallows.

"Cherry flavor," he said when he came up for air.

"Nice?" said Karriana.

"Disgusting. But at least now I'm as strong as a rabbit."

Despite the situation, she chuckled. As she tended to his head wound, she said, "So why were you driving a stolen truck?"

"How do you know it was stolen?"

"I'm pretty sure I recognized it. Doesn't it belong to Lukas Frifelt? He owns a farm not far from the Helgerson place. A little closer to town."

Todd shrugged. "No idea what the owner's called. You're right about the farm, though. I found the truck in the farmyard with the keys in the ignition. There was no one around, so I borrowed it. I was desperate."

"Why were you desperate?"

"My brother's badly hurt. I left him in the forest, so I could come here and find help. There were people after us."

"Infected people?"

"Yes. But I don't think they're infected. Not by any…virus or anything."

"What then?"

"They're under some kind of influence. You might say they're possessed."

Having cleaned and put ointment and a dressing on his wound, Karriana paused in the act of winding a bandage around his head. "Possessed? By what?"

Todd released a long sigh. "It sounds mad, but there's something in the tunnels. Some kind of…entity, or creature, or power. I think it's been trapped down there, imprisoned maybe, for years, centuries even. You were right about Yrsa, by the way. As a child she got stuck in there, crawled through a lava tube to where the thing was, and…I don't know…it got into her head somehow, and it's been manipulating her ever since. And now she's manipulated me…"

He went silent then, and Karriana saw the hurt and confusion on his face. She tied off the bandage and squeezed his shoulder.

"None of this is your fault, Todd."

"Isn't it?"

"No! How were you to know? How could you possibly guess that any of this would happen?"

"It doesn't change the fact that people have died…"

"None of this is your fault," she repeated.

"Thanks," he said, but he didn't look convinced.

To stop him dwelling on his guilt, Karriana said, "So you came here to find help?"

He grimaced. "And failed. I went to the police station and found two dead people. Murdered. It was the same at the hospital. Doors wide open and nothing but corpses inside." He looked at her with haunted eyes. "I think it's a mass sacrifice. To bring the old gods back. That's what Yrsa said. The possessed all went up to the caves to offer themselves, not that they had any choice – they were drawn there like sheep. But whatever had been trapped down there caused some sort of eruption, not of lava but of water, and drowned them all. Meanwhile, whoever the possessed found on their way to the caves, who hadn't fallen under the influence…"

"They killed," said Karriana.

"Yeah. I guess the more death there is, the stronger the gods get."

Karriana indicated the stuff on the counter. "Can you get all that into your pockets?"

"I guess so. Why?"

"We need to get off the island. My plan was to go down to the harbor, take a boat."

"In this weather?"

"What choice do we have?"

Todd shook his head. "I can't leave Rob. He's still in the forest."

"You can't help him either. Our best option is to take a boat and sail to the next island. It's less than an hour away, and it's bigger than Eldfjallaeyja. You can call for help from there."

Todd looked torn by indecision, but eventually nodded. "I guess you're right. I hate leaving him, though."

"You're not leaving him. You're giving him the best chance of survival."

"It doesn't feel that way."

"Well, it is that way," she said firmly. "The last time I saw my parents was at the hospital. My mother was badly injured, hurt by my father, who was one of…" She faltered, then said, "One of the possessed. But that doesn't mean I'm giving up on them – either of them. I won't until I know for sure."

Todd nodded, but avoided her eyes.

"So are you ready to go?" she said.

"I am."

"Come on then."

They splashed back into the street, which was still deserted, and turned left. Although he had only been to and from the harbor a couple of times by car, Todd's recollection was that it was about a mile and a half away from here, and that once you left the main street of the town behind, it was mostly downhill.

If the water was flowing fast, as it almost certainly would be, that might be a problem. He didn't want to be swept downhill with the rest of the debris. Judging by the size of some of the branches drifting past them, not to mention items like bicycles, furniture and chunks of masonry, he wouldn't fancy their chances if they got caught among it all, especially in the darkness.

He said as much to Karriana, who looked thoughtful. Eventually she said, "If the main route becomes too dangerous, we can move into the fields, where the water will be better…" She swirled her hand round, searching for the correct English word.

"Distributed?" he suggested.

"Yes, distributed. Spread out. It will be slow, but at least it will be calmer there."

He nodded. "I was hoping I'd done tramping through fields of water, but I suppose you're right."

"Before we do that, though," she said, looking apologetic, "we must take a small detour."

"Must we? Why?"

She told him briefly about her confrontation with Bjarne Haugen, and about needing the keys to his boat, which she was sure would be in his house.

"Can't we just…hot-wire the engine or something?" Todd said.

She gave him a dubious look. "Is this something you know how to do?"

"Well…no."

"Me neither. I'm sorry for the extra time, but I think this is the best way."

Todd sighed, thinking of Robin, but after a moment he nodded. "Okay. Let's get it done."

They waited until the water flowing down the center of the main street was relatively clear of debris, and then they waded across. Karriana pointed out the areas where water was churning and frothing, and also the larger 'whirlpool' in front of the partially collapsed building.

"There were areas like this in the fields I came through," Todd said. "The water was bubbling up like the ground had sprung a leak."

They trudged up the side street towards Haugen's house, through water that was flowing down a slight incline towards them. Although it wasn't exactly gushing, wading against it was hard going, and by the time they reached the top, they were panting with exertion.

At least no one's about, Todd thought, but a few minutes later, as he and Karriana turned onto the street where Bjarne Haugen had lived, they both froze at the sight of a figure flailing towards them through the water flowing along the road.

The figure was lying full-length in the fast-moving stream, and Todd's first thought was that it was so eager to get at them it had hurled itself forward in order to scythe through the water like a shark. He took such a hasty step back that he felt his foot skid from under him. He threw out his arms for balance, but was only stopped from falling by Karriana, who grabbed his right arm.

"It's okay, Todd," she shouted. "She can't hurt us. Look."

Todd looked again, and realized that the figure was not propelling itself after all. Rather, it was being carried along, just another piece of flotsam, its limbs waving only because the eddies and currents created by the water's momentum were pushing them to and fro.

As the corpse drifted towards them, they stepped aside almost out of deference, like bystanders watching a funeral cortege. Up close, they saw that the body was that of a stout, middle-aged woman, wearing a green cardigan that billowed around her like a fishing net. The woman was on her front, her hair a dark, seaweedy froth between her outflung arms, but as she drew level with them, the water spun her over, briefly revealing her face.

Karriana's gasp of distress emerged as an almost disapproving, "Oh!" Todd screwed up his face and turned his head aside, as if at an appalling smell.

Something was sticking out of the woman's left eye socket, which was nothing but a ragged black hole. Todd only caught a glimpse of the object, but thought it was a plastic toothbrush. The woman's mouth was wide open, as though in a silent scream of outrage. Then the corpse was past, turning slowly in the current as it washed down the street.

Shocked into silence by the sight, the two of them plodded on. They said nothing for the next couple of minutes, until Karriana pointed at a house whose front door was wide open, pinned back against the wall of a narrow hallway by floodwater.

"That's Haugen's house." She looked at the water flowing around them, her expression wary. "His body is gone."

"Washed away," said Todd.

"I hope so."

He looked at her. "You definitely killed him?"

She hesitated, then said, "He could not have survived his injuries."

"Well, then. He's probably halfway to the sea by now, if not in it."

"Yes," said Karriana, not altogether convincingly.

"So where would these keys be?" Todd asked.

"My father keeps our keys on hooks in the kitchen. Maybe Haugen does the same?"

"Sounds like a plan. Do you know where the kitchen would be?"

"My friend Hilda lives further up this street...lived. So I know these houses. The kitchen is at the back."

"Do you want to wait here while I look?"

"No. We should go together. Splitting up is always a bad idea in movies."

He smiled. "Good call."

They splashed across the road, pausing to allow a plastic recycling bin to float past. As they waited, they heard a screeching caw from above, and Todd made out the shape of a large bird, black against the storm-laden sky. It circled them several times before wheeling away. Karriana shielded her eyes to track its progress until it had disappeared over the jagged tops of the distant pine trees.

"Hey," he said softly, seeing the anxiety on her face and remembering their meeting in the playground, "it's nothing. Just a raven."

Rainwater trickling down her cheeks like tears, she said, "Let's do this quickly."

He led the way through the shin-high water to the open front door. The hallway beyond was dark, so he pulled his phone from his pocket and activated the torch app. Like everything else in his pockets, his phone was wet, but Todd was relieved to see the thin white beam of light shine out from it as strongly as ever. He moved the beam across the walls and ceiling of the hallway, alert for movement. There was a staircase on the left, leading up into darkness, and two doors on the right-hand wall, which they would have to pass to reach the door at the far end, which Karriana had said would open into the kitchen. Of the two right-hand doors, the second was closed, but the nearest was ajar, the gap wide enough to slip through.

Todd peered hard at that gap for several seconds, trying to convince himself there was nothing ominous about it. In his experience, the possessed were not thinking beings. They weren't wily and cunning; they didn't set traps. The door was ajar simply because it had been left that way, and because the water inside the house was not flowing strongly enough to push it any further open.

In fact, the water in the house was not flowing at all. It looked as still and murky as a swamp. When he shone his torch onto its surface, it reflected a circle of white light back at him. He knew the impression it gave of depth was an illusion, and that when he stepped over the threshold he wouldn't plunge into water deep enough to close over his head. Even so, he moved forward tentatively, testing the floor with his toe before putting his weight on it.

Nearing the door that was standing ajar, he tried not to think how his body was weighed down by soaking wet clothes and his own exhaustion. When he came level with the door, he glanced back at Karriana.

"We should check what's in there, just in case."

She looked fearful, but nodded. "Okay."

Wishing he'd armed himself with one of the many spars of wood that had drifted past them, Todd placed his hand on the door and pushed.

He knew the resistance he felt was only water, but it was unnerving to feel it all the same. As the door opened, he directed his torch beam through it, not only to illuminate the room beyond, but also to dazzle anyone who might be in there.

The light showed him shelves cluttered with model boats, lumps of coral, the spiny carapaces of crustaceans, and chunks of colored glass, their edges smoothed and rounded. Next to an ugly electric fire was a TV stand half-submerged in water, supporting a large-screen TV. On the green-painted wall, packed tightly together, were dozens of family photographs, and a glass-fronted display case containing the skull of a large fish.

Bobbing on the surface of the water was a mug, some waterlogged books and DVDs, and the loose pages of a newspaper, now resembling lumps of gray porridge. From the position of the TV, it was clear that any furniture in the room would be to Todd's right, and so he pushed the door wider and stepped through, shining his torch in that direction. What he saw gave him such a shock that he jerked backwards, almost dropping his phone into the water.

There were two people sitting on the sofa.

After the initial shock, he realized that the couple were dead. Shaking with reaction, he again illuminated them with his jittering torch beam, and saw that one of the dead was a slim woman of about forty, the other a teenage boy.

Todd's guess was that the woman had been strangled, judging by her face, which was bloated and dark, her eyes bulging from their sockets, her blackened tongue lolling from her mouth. The teenage boy (her son?), who was leaning forward with one listless hand trailing in the water, appeared to have been bludgeoned to death. His head and the left side of his face was a mess of congealing blood, and the top of his skull was horribly dented and misshapen.

Todd's torchlight played over them for a few seconds before he directed it away. Hurriedly he stepped back, dragging the door closed, then bent forward as a wave of nausea rushed through him.

"What is it? What's in there?" Karriana hissed, eyes wide and scared.

"You don't want to know," Todd said.

"I do. Tell me. Not knowing is worse than knowing."

He took a deep breath, then straightened up. "Two dead people. A woman and a boy."

"Haugen's wife and son?"

"I guess."

"Did he kill them?"

"Looks like it."

Karriana blinked rapidly and licked her lips. Finally, she said, "At least the house is likely to be empty."

Although Todd knew the dead couldn't hurt them, the proximity of the corpses made him more eager than ever to find the keys and get out. He waded along the hallway, giving the second door on his right no more than a cursory glance. The kitchen door at the end was closed, and as he put his hand on the handle, his heart quickened. He was aware that if there *was* someone in the kitchen, he or she had access to a variety of weapons: knives, bottles, even pots and pans. Pressing his ear to the door, all he heard was the tinnitus-like hissing of the rain outside. He glanced at Karriana.

"You ready?"

She nodded.

He sucked in a breath, then shoved the door open, brandishing his phone like a weapon, or a crucifix to ward off a vampire. Because of the water, the door opened more sluggishly than he would have liked, revealing the kitchen with agonizing slowness. The light slithered across a floor-to-ceiling food cupboard, a work surface, a cooker and a stainless-steel sink on the left side of the room. Beyond the sink was a window, which streamed with rain, and a closed door that presumably led into a backyard or garden.

Todd felt the muscles in his body bunching as the door opened wider. He knew if there *was* someone in the kitchen, it was likely they'd be behind the opening door on the right side of the room, from where they could launch a surprise attack. Slowly revealed on this side was a fridge, a long breakfast bar beneath a glass-fronted crockery cupboard, and three tall stools, all of which had toppled over and were bobbing gently on the ripples created by the displaced water.

The room, though, was empty of people.

Seeing this, Todd expelled a long, relieved breath and looked around, taking in further details. Along with the stools, a tea tray, a canvas shopping bag, and a plastic bin, plus all the rubbish that had spilled out of it – vegetable peelings, soggy food packaging, chicken bones and other kitchen waste – were undulating on the water's surface.

"Gross," Karriana said, wrinkling her nose.

Not as gross as the people in the front room, Todd thought, and shrugged. "Let's find those keys."

They moved into the room, Todd shining his torch around. "I was hoping there would be a row of hooks on the wall with keys hanging from them," Karriana said.

Todd grimaced. "That would have been too easy. Why don't you look in the cupboard there, and I'll check the drawers?"

She nodded, splashing across to the cupboard. When she tugged it open, more sodden foodstuffs floated out to blend with the rubbish from the bin. "Great," she said, as flour, pasta and rice drifted around her knees.

Todd rooted through the drawers, shining his torchlight into each and sifting through the contents with his fingers. In one drawer he found a packet of Ziploc freezer bags.

"These might come in useful for keeping our phones dry," he said, handing a bag to Karriana, "especially if the water gets deeper."

She took the bag and said, "But our phones are no good. There's no signal on the island."

"No, but if we get far enough away the signal might come back. And if it does, I want to get help for Robin sooner rather than later. If we wait 'til we get to the mainland it might be too late."

She looked dubious, but conceded, "You're right. We must...what's that English phrase? Grab whatever straws we can?"

"Close," he said, smiling, and went back to rooting through the drawers.

He was closing the eighth and final drawer, the cutlery inside it jangling, when Karriana gave a triumphant cry. Turning, he saw her upending a bulbous vase made of smoky blue glass. With a clatter, a set of keys slid out of the vase and into her hand.

"Is that them?"

"It is."

"Great. Let's go."

They splashed out of the kitchen and along the hallway, Todd's phone light jerking before them. Todd didn't realize how oppressive he had found the house until they were back in the open air, the rain beating down. As he turned off the torch and sealed his phone in one of the Ziploc bags before pocketing it, he looked up and down the street, and was relieved to see it was still deserted.

Making their way back to the main street, they found the water level there had risen by several inches; it was now just above Todd's knees. What this meant for Robin and Dev, in their cave in the forest, he dreaded to think. One thing was certain, though – staying on the island was not an option, because in a couple of days there would *be* no island. The only thing sticking up out of the sea would be the dormant volcano at its center.

Although the rising water level was a problem in itself, it was now bringing additional problems with it. The deeper and faster flowing the water became, the larger and more dangerous were the objects becoming caught up in it. Splashing along what had once been the pavement, Todd pointed at a branch some eight meters long that sailed past them at speed, its girth that of a man's torso.

"If we get in the way of something like that, it'll pulverize us."

Karriana nodded, and drew his attention to the toppled truck further up the road, which was also now beginning to creep in their direction. "The flow will soon be strong enough to start carrying along cars and vans. All the more reason to go across the fields."

They trudged on, Todd with his hood up to keep the bandage around his head as dry as possible, Karriana preferring to leave her hood down, despite the driving rain, so it wouldn't muffle her senses. Defying her bruised and swollen throat, she glanced around constantly as they walked, alert for any hint of danger. Some of the buildings on the main street were in a state of near-collapse now, and the two of them steered clear of the 'whirlpool' areas that seemed to gather around these sagging edifices. It was not so easy, though, to dodge the smaller chunks of wood and masonry that flowed either side of them, and occasionally ricocheted off their legs.

Grateful to make it out of town without sustaining anything more than a few bumps and bruises, they headed into open country as soon as they had left the last of the buildings behind. With no streetlamps to light their way, they used the torches on their phones to illuminate the path ahead.

Not that there was a path to follow. In low-lying areas the land was now little more than a shallow lake. It was unnerving, especially as beyond the island was nothing but the North Atlantic ocean. If it wasn't for the trees, which at least gave *some* definition to the landscape, Todd thought a sense of panic might have started to set in. As it was, the sooner they reached the harbor and boarded a boat, the better he would feel.

The journey, though, was exhausting and treacherous. Once they'd left town, the route to the sea became a wide and gushing channel, choked with debris, barely contained within banks and hedges and the occasional stretch of crumbling stone wall. At Karriana's recommendation, they walked not along this route, but struck out into the fields that flanked the road, where the water was at least flatter and calmer.

As they quickly discovered, though, the fields were not without their own dangers. Unlike the flooded crop fields and grazing land that Todd had waded through before reaching the Frifelts' deserted farm and appropriating the family truck, the land between the harbor and the town was untenanted, and therefore wilder.

Although the surface of the water *looked* flat and constant, the ground beneath their feet was anything but. One moment Todd and Karriana were wading through water that was knee-high, and the next the ground dropped away, and they found themselves up to their chests, or even shoulders. A couple of times the ground disappeared completely, and they had to swim along cautiously in their heavy, wet clothes, alert for hazards beneath the surface – bushes, tangles of undergrowth, small trees. The second time this happened, swimming side by side and gasping for breath, Karriana said, "I don't know how long I can keep going. The things in my pockets are weighing me down."

"What things?" Todd gasped.

"Food, drinks, medical supplies..."

"Give some of them to me. We'll share the burden."

Karriana did so, pulling Ziploc bags from her pockets and passing them to Todd. By the time the harbor came into view, they were both drenched to the skin, shivering with cold and exhausted to the point of collapse.

The only way they knew they had reached the harbor was because of the boats bobbing on the water. In fact, they were doing more than bobbing. Where the floodwaters met the sea, the water was turbulent, waves rearing up and crashing down, and the eight or ten boats they could see were riding the foamy swells like cars on a roller coaster.

Throughout their journey, Todd had been using the torch app on his phone to light their way. To keep the phone dry, he had kept it in the Ziploc bag. Now, standing in water up to his chest, feeling the tidal pull trying to drag him this way and that, he held up the bagged phone and scanned the area around them. In an attempt to pinpoint their exact location, he was searching for the cluster of dark buildings that he knew ringed the harbor. After ten seconds or so he managed to pick them out, or at least their roofs, which were jutting above the water's surface like squared-off rocks.

The buildings were twenty or thirty meters ahead of them, over to their left. Of the jetty, however, which should be even further to their left, there was no sign. Judging by the buildings, Todd estimated the water level here had risen by some six or eight meters. The boats were beyond the buildings, maybe a hundred meters away, although in the darkness and the driving rain it was hard to judge distances, especially with few landmarks to provide perspective.

Although their objective was in sight, Todd felt his spirits sinking. "How the hell are we going to get across to them?" he said, indicating the boats.

"Swim," said Karriana.

He eyed the churning water dubiously. "We'll drown."

"No, we won't. It looks worse than it is. Once we're out there it won't seem as bad."

Todd wasn't sure whether her confidence came from a lifetime by the sea, or whether she was just trying to convince him, and maybe herself too.

"Yeah, right."

"No, really. We can do it, Todd. We have no other choice."

He sighed, but he knew she was right. Soon this entire island would be part of the seabed, and their only lifeline was one of the flimsy-looking vessels soaring and plunging on the waves a hundred or so meters away.

"Okay," he said, "so once we're across to the boats, how do we get on board without killing ourselves?"

"We'll have to time it right. There are a few seconds of stillness between each wave. We'll have to go for it then."

It seemed the most basic of plans, and fraught with peril, but again, what choice did they have?

"Last question," he said. "Which is Haugen's boat?"

She shrugged. "I won't know until we get closer. I do know it was named after his son. Milo."

An image of the slumped body with the bashed-in head immediately flashed into Todd's mind. The memory tightened his throat, but a second later he was distracted by a spark of orange over to his right. He turned his head, and saw something enter the water with a tiny splash.

What was that? A fish? Were there sharks around here? He turned back to Karriana.

"Did you see that?"

"What?"

Before he could reply, a ball of fire streaked over their heads and splashed into the sea ten meters in front of them. Todd's first thought was that the volcano was erupting, and he twisted to look behind him. What he saw was not an erupting volcano, but it was something almost as bad.

"Shit," he said, switching off the torch through the Ziploc bag to make them less visible. "Look!"

Because of her neck, Karriana turned slowly. When she saw what Todd had seen, she let out a gasp.

A couple of hundred meters away, silhouetted against the rain-lashed sky, were seven figures. They were standing on the highest point of the banking beside the road that rose up from the harbor, but if it hadn't been for the burning torches that three of them were carrying – burning, Todd thought, with a fire that didn't quite seem natural – they might not have been visible at all.

Six of the figures were squat and hunched, standing in water that lapped at their knees. It was the seventh figure, though, the tallest, at the center of the group, that caused Todd's guts to clench in regret and dismay.

Yrsa.

His emotions must have been apparent on his face, because Karriana asked cautiously, "Are you okay?"

He glanced at her. "Not really."

"I'm sorry," she said, so softly that Todd barely heard her above the rain.

Staring at Yrsa, whose black hair thrashed around her bone-white face in the howling storm, Todd suddenly noticed something that sent a jolt of shock through him.

"Fucking hell!"

"What?"

"Look at Yrsa. Look at her feet."

Karriana frowned. Then her eyes widened. "Is that real?"

"I think so."

What they could both see, but didn't quite believe, was that Yrsa's feet, toes pointing downwards, were visible *above* the water. She was floating. Levitating. Which suggested that whatever force inhabited her had the ability not only to control her body as a driver might control a car, but to propel it through the air, like some…

…*like some fucking inflatable,* Todd thought.

It would have been ridiculous if it wasn't so obscene. And worse still was Todd's suspicion, the more he stared at Yrsa's distant figure, that the thing inside her was no longer propelling *her*, the Yrsa he had known and loved, but simply her corpse. The way her body hung in the air, the slackness of her features, suggested there was no spark of animation left in her anymore. Her body, it appeared, was now nothing but a vessel. Yrsa herself had been not only subsumed, but obliterated.

Movement among the jötnar to Yrsa's right diverted his attention. One of the creatures, holding a burning torch, was leaning towards its companion and appeared to be lighting something that the second creature was holding. Next moment, the second jötnar turned in their direction, a small flame dancing in front of it, and raised its stubby arms. Todd was puzzled, then the flame shot upwards into the sky, describing an arc through the rain that would bring it down close to their location. A thrill of horror ran through him as realization dawned. It was a flaming arrow! They were under attack!

Karriana tugged at his sleeve. She too had realized the danger.

"Swim, Todd!" she cried, and plunged into the water. Legs kicking, arms scissoring frantically, she made for the fishing boats.

Todd hesitated, at first reluctant to turn his back on the approaching arrow, before quickly realizing how futile that was. The arrow was coming so fast that even if it had been heading straight for him, it would have been too late to take evasive action. And so, as the arrow sliced into the sea some twenty meters to his left, he hurriedly zipped the bag containing his torch into the inside pocket of his coat and threw himself into the water.

Like Karriana, he plowed towards the boats, but for long, agonizing seconds, it seemed they were getting no closer. In fact, he wondered whether they were drifting out to sea at roughly the same speed that he and Karriana were swimming towards them. His layers of waterlogged clothing were now so heavy he felt like Jacob Marley encumbered by the chain he had forged in life. He was so close to exhaustion that simply giving up and allowing himself to sink like a stone was actually starting to seem like an appealing prospect.

Doggedly, though, he kept going, flinching as another burning arrow plunged into the sea some fifteen meters ahead of Karriana. Then, less than a minute later, another arrow landed so close to him that he imagined he felt the heat of it, even though he knew that was impossible.

Teeth chattering, muscles cramping with cold, the water seemed to thicken as his efforts became feebler. Another arrow came down somewhere to his left, this one little more than a flash of fire in his peripheral vision. All he could see were waves, surging into his face, stinging his eyes even though he had squeezed them into slits. He had lost all sense of how far away the boats were now; he no longer had the strength to lift his head to check.

A burst of sparks somewhere ahead of him. A firework exploding. His eyes flickered in that direction, and beyond the clash of waves, the flying foam, he saw a metal wall tilting from side to side, the last few sparks tumbling into the sea. He realized the wall was the side of a boat, surprisingly close, and that the sparks had come from another burning arrow that must have hit the boat and bounced off.

Then, above the rushing hiss of rain, which was pockmarking the cement-gray surface of the sea, came another, shriller sound. A human voice, calling his name!

Karriana! But where was she? He halted, treading water, lifting his head to orientate himself.

Another burning arrow flew overhead, and by its light he saw her. Her dripping, bedraggled form, mostly in silhouette, was standing on the pitching deck of a shabby fishing boat some twenty meters to his right. Her hands were gripping the rail, and her back was arched in a semi-crouch as she leaned forward, yelling his name.

Although it took a huge effort to do so, he raised a hand to acknowledge her. She pointed frantically to her right, and at first Todd thought she was gesturing at the name, white on black, on its peeling hull – *Milo*. But then he noticed the metal ladder attached to the side of the boat, which appeared and disappeared as the waves surged and fell.

With what felt like the last of his strength, Todd swam towards it. Another arrow, like a tiny comet, flew over his head and struck the hull of the boat a few meters to the right of the name *Milo*. This one too burst like a firework, before the sparks, one by one, fell into the water and were extinguished.

Encouraged by Karriana, he swam to within a few meters of the *Milo*, then trod water as he watched the boat rearing and plunging in front of him, creating a ripple effect of waves that threatened to push him back in the direction he'd come. How was he going to get close enough to grab the iron ladder? He'd have to do it when the boat tilted low in the water, then establish a firm enough grip not to get his arm wrenched from its socket when the next wave tilted the boat back the other way, yanking him upwards.

He was moving tentatively closer, stretching out his arm, when something long and winding and muscular came hurtling out of the rain-lashed sky. He jerked back so violently that he gulped a mouthful of seawater. Choking, his first thought was that an eel or a sea snake had leaped out of the water to attack him. Then, as his streaming eyes cleared, he felt something drape itself across the top of his arm – a tentacle? Alarmed, he looked down, and saw it was a thick rope. Realizing that Karriana must have flung it, he glanced up and saw her standing on the deck a few meters away.

"Grab it!" she yelled. "Reel yourself into the side."

Her face was white and shining with water, her hair plastered to her cheeks. Todd was about to grab the rope when he saw her eyes and mouth widen in horror. The next instant she threw herself to her right.

Her shoulder hit the rain-slick deck just as another flaming arrow passed no more than three meters above Todd's head. Almost before he could register its presence, it sliced through the space in which Karriana had been standing, and hit the deck of the *Milo* in a burst of fiery light. Ricocheting off the deck, it flew over the rail on the far side of the ship and landed in the sea, where it was immediately extinguished.

It was the closest shave yet, and it galvanized Todd into action. Grabbing the rope, he hauled himself up to the side of the boat, waited for the *Milo* to tilt obligingly towards him, then lunged for the ladder and pressed himself tight against it, clinging on for dear life as the vessel tilted back the other way.

How he scrambled up the ladder and over the side with the boat lurching like crazy he wasn't sure, but seconds later he was sprawled face down on the deck, almost hyperventilating as he tried to get air into his lungs, while simultaneously puking up the seawater he had swallowed. He could feel the deck rolling beneath him, could hear rain battering the drenched clothes clinging to his back.

Somewhere, blending with the rain, he heard what he guessed was Karriana rushing about, clangs and thumps as she made preparations to get the boat moving and away. Then he heard an engine roar into life, followed by what sounded like the rattling of a heavy-duty chain. When the boat began to pitch even more alarmingly, he realized he was hearing the sound of the anchor being reeled in.

The deck, already awash, soon began to take on more water as waves crashed over the rails, sluicing around his body and splashing his face. He pushed himself groggily upright, aware that the deck was vibrating beneath his hands and his padded knees. His head swam, and then suddenly Karriana was crouching beside him, draping an arm across his back.

"Are you all right, Todd?"

Her delicate face was drained of all color, her lips gray-blue, her fair hair flattened into a tight-fitting cap by the rain.

"What's happening?" he asked. "Are we moving?"

Her face broke into a grin so tired it looked in danger of crumbling. "Yes, we're moving! We're heading away from the island. We've done it!"

He felt hysterical laughter bubbling out of him. He lurched into a half-kneeling, half-sitting position, and wrapped his arms around her. For several seconds he and Karriana clung to each other, half laughing, half sobbing, neither able to believe they had got away.

Then there was a flash above them as if something had exploded, and they jerked apart like teenagers caught necking. Todd looked up to see a flaming arrow spinning away from what it had hit – the U-shaped radio aerial sprouting from the roof of the wheelhouse. For a second sparks fell with the rain, then winked out. Both of them looked towards shore.

"We should take shelter," Karriana said. "We'll be out of range soon."

Todd nodded, but remained where he was, too exhausted to move, as Karriana lurched towards the enclosed wheelhouse, arms raised for balance as the deck seesawed. Still staring across at the island, Todd found it reassuring to see it receding from them, the flaming torches of the jötnar dwindling.

He crawled to the side of the boat, where waves were still bursting against the hull in great clouds of spray. Eldfjallaeyja was now a dark hump against the night sky, slowly bleeding into the blackness. Coming here with Yrsa, he thought, was the worst decision of his life. Suddenly all the terror and trauma overwhelmed him, and tears, hot in contrast to the cold rain, began to pour down his face.

Although, like Yrsa, he had been manipulated, he felt ashamed of the lives that had been lost because of him. He thought of Robin and Dev, huddled in their cave, and took comfort from the hope that they were lives he might yet save. Pulling the Ziploc bag from his pocket, he tried switching the phone on through the plastic. Despite the tears rolling down his cheeks, he gave a bark of laughter when the screen lit up. Hunched over, he saw not only that he still had over thirty percent charge left, but also that the 'No Service' message had been replaced by a couple of bars of signal. He hesitated, then clicked on his 'Contacts' folder and scrolled down until he found 'Dad'. He considered calling him, but his mind was so scrambled with shock and fatigue he doubted he'd be able to make himself understood – not to mention heard above the storm. So he selected 'Message', and when the box and the winking cursor appeared, began to stab feverishly at the buttons:

> Dad, somthing terrible hs hapened on the island. Ive escaped on a boat but Robs still there with Dev, badly injured. Plese inform authorties &send help but be careful. Everyones gone mad, theres no law and order & whole place is flooded. Robs in a cave in a forest, unconcious, losing blood. Devs with him. Cant tell you much more. Get on to this strait away. Matter of life and death. No joking. Many have died. I love ou. Im sorry. Txx

He paused, then added:

> island near Iceland. Dont know name but itll be in Robs paperwork.

He pressed 'Send', hoping it would be enough. Anxiously he watched the buffer icon on his screen spinning for several seconds, and then he let out a half-sobbing cry of relief as it was replaced by the word 'Delivered'. Pocketing his phone, he decided to join Karriana in the wheelhouse. He grabbed the rail at the side of the boat with hands that felt like chunks of frozen meat and hauled himself to his feet.

As he straightened, Yrsa's dripping corpse rose up over the side of the boat, two meters in front of him.

Todd had never actually screamed before, but he did so now. It was shrill and full-blooded, and it felt like it was ripping its way out of his throat. He stumbled, and fell on his backside. Yrsa's corpse continued to rise like some deep-sea revenant, until she – it – was hovering in the air, above the rail at the side of the boat.

Up close, she was even more hideous than he could have imagined. She looked not only like a drowning victim, but one whose body had been horribly damaged on jagged rocks before being vomited onto the shore. Her clothes were hanging in tatters, and her gray-white limbs were twisted and broken, with splintered bones sticking out through the torn flesh in several places. There was no blood, because the relentless rain had washed it away, but in some ways that was worse, the inner flesh of her terrible wounds showing through pink and ragged. Her naked feet, pointing downwards, looked as though they had been mangled in a machine, and she was missing at least half her fingers.

Worst of all, though, was her face, which had sustained appalling injuries. Her forehead was gashed and partly crushed in; one of her eyes had become dislodged and was bulging like a gray egg from its socket; and her shattered lower jaw was hanging loose, stretching her mouth open in a terrible, black-tongued yawn. Todd couldn't help thinking of the many times he had kissed this woman, of the times he had slept with her, made love to her. His stomach convulsed and he puked onto the deck.

Although Yrsa's ravaged face was blank and dead, and although her broken limbs hung slackly, Todd knew that the thing inside her, the thing that was manipulating her like a puppet, meant him terrible harm. He scrabbled backwards as Yrsa's corpse drifted towards him like a grotesque kite, her black hair lashing like serpents, her ragged clothes flapping.

His only thought was to run for the wheelhouse and lock himself in with Karriana. Slamming his hands on the deck, he tried to push himself to his feet – but all at once he felt a weakness invading his body, and then a crushing, paralyzing tightness filling his limbs and chest.

What was happening? Was he having a heart attack, or a seizure? He felt his throat closing up, as if a hand were squeezing his windpipe. As black sparks danced in his vision, he suddenly realized the attack was coming from the thing, the entity. Its influence had entered his system like some airborne virus, and was now swarming through his body.

He desperately wanted to fight back, but could do nothing. His mind was like a trapped rat, scrabbling in panic. Yet, terrified though he was of dying, he was more terrified still of being used like Yrsa had been used. He felt himself sinking, blackness crawling across his vision, like grave dirt shoveled on top of him.

Then suddenly Karriana was beside him, brandishing something long and slim, a javelin perhaps. With a furious screech, she thrust the end of the javelin right into Yrsa's gaping, black-tongued mouth.

As though struck by a giant arrow, Yrsa's corpse flew backwards, shattered arms and legs flailing like the limbs of a broken doll. Karriana pressed home her attack, still screeching as she ran across the slippery deck. With Yrsa's corpse impaled on the end of the javelin – *boat hook*, Todd suddenly realized – Karriana resembled a fisherman spearing a particularly large fish. When Yrsa's corpse had been forced back over the side of the boat and was once more hanging over the sea, Karriana halted – then, with a last defiant yell, she thrust the boat hook savagely forward, so that the metal spike burst out through the back of Yrsa's neck. Then she immediately yanked it backwards, dislodging the corpse, which fell bonelessly into the sea.

Sprawled on the deck, Todd saw all of this peripherally. He saw Yrsa's corpse fall, but he didn't see it land, although in his mind he had a picture of it hitting the black, churning ocean, of the waves folding over it.

Gasping, his heart hammering with reaction, Todd saw Karriana stagger back from the rail. She dropped the boat hook, which clattered to the deck, and turned towards Todd, shock and trauma stark on her face. Feebly he raised a hand to let her know he was okay, but she stared at him without reaction. Then she stumbled past, heading back towards the wheelhouse.

Todd closed his eyes. He would join her in a minute. But for now it was almost peaceful lying here, the boat rocking like a cradle, the thrumming engine making the deck vibrate beneath him. The waves – calmer now, as the boat moved away from the island – were like a wordless lullaby as they slapped against the hull, and even the monotonous drumming of the rain was soothing, reminding him of camping trips as a boy.

Eventually he stirred, and sat up. His body felt pummeled, tenderized, and he tried to recall how many hours it had been since all hell had broken loose in the tunnels. Ten? Twelve? It seemed like an eternity.

Sensing movement, he looked towards the wheelhouse, and saw Karriana marching back across the deck towards him. She no longer looked shell-shocked. She was walking with confidence, striding in fact.

Perhaps fending off the entity had galvanized her. Wearily he raised a hand.

"Hey," he called. "I was just about to..."

But then he realized something was wrong. Karriana had an odd expression on her face, a kind of taut blankness, as if she was under...

"No," he groaned.

He knew immediately what had happened. It had jumped. The entity had jumped. At some point during Karriana's attack, it had passed from Yrsa's ravaged corpse to her. Perhaps that had been its intention all along – to vacate the damaged body, and relocate to a healthy one. And now Todd saw what Karriana was holding in her hand. It was a large knife for filleting fish, its blade thin, curved, and no doubt very sharp.

"Karriana!" he shouted, scrambling to his feet, adrenaline overriding his fatigue. "Don't let it control you! Fight it!"

It was an approach that often worked in movies, but this wasn't a movie, and Todd's words had no effect. Instead of stumbling to a halt, Karriana began to *run* towards him, raising the knife.

Todd backpedaled, raising a hand as Karriana closed the distance between them. She slashed out with the knife, and Todd felt a stinging pain as his palm was opened neatly from the base of his thumb to his little finger. Blood poured from the wound and was instantly diluted by rain, thin red streams running down his upraised hand and wrist.

"*No, Karriana!*" Todd screamed, but she kept coming, slashing out again, this time opening a long slit, at chest level, in his thick, protective coat.

The third time, when she slashed at his face, Todd threw himself backwards, though not quite quickly enough. He had a split-second impression of the long, thin blade arcing towards his eyes, and a stinging pain across his left cheekbone as he jerked back, and then, not for the first time, his feet skidded from under him and his back slammed against the deck with spine-jarring impact.

There was so much water on deck that he slid backwards as if on an ice-slide. Instinctively he threw his arms out to steady himself, and his right hand came down on a wooden pole that rolled away from him.

Realizing what it was, he glanced to his right and saw the boat hook lying six inches from his outstretched fingers. Aware that Karriana was looming over him, knife upraised, he lunged, grabbed the boat hook, then swung the long pole up and over in an arc.

It was an impulsive reaction, his intention being to knock Karriana off-balance. Instead of batting her aside, though, the curved hook on the side of the implement smashed into her temple with enough force to puncture her skull and embed itself in her brain. Instantly her left eye filled with blood, while the other rolled up into its socket. A shudder, like an almighty electric shock, passed through her, and she collapsed, the knife flying from her hand and spinning away as she hit the deck.

It happened so abruptly that for several seconds Todd could only lie on his back, staring at the space she had occupied a moment before. He wasn't even aware the boat hook had been wrenched from his hand when Karriana fell, until he eventually raised his head and saw the hook still embedded in her skull, the long pole jutting out obscenely.

"*No*," he whispered and crawled across to her, so shocked that all he could think was that if he pulled the hook from her head, maybe she'd be okay.

"Karriana," he whispered, "Karriana." She didn't respond. From the terrible wound in the side of her head, thin tendrils of rain-diluted blood writhed away in all directions. Todd looked at her open eyes and slack expression and realized it was too late. He laid the back of his uninjured hand on her cold, white cheek and whispered, "I'm sorry."

Taking hold of the boat hook, he pulled it out of her head and threw it over the side of the boat, watching it spin away and splash into the sea. Instantly more blood came gushing out of the hole in Karriana's skull, running into her eyes and ears and open mouth. Quickly, though, the rain did its job, diluting the blood and washing it away. Todd pulled Karriana towards him and laid her lolling head in his lap as he sat cross-legged on the deck, rocking gently to and fro.

For a while his mind went away, and when he came to, he realized the rain had stopped. He looked down at Karriana's body, at the awful hole in the side of her head, and knew that if they were found like this, people would think he had murdered her, and that might delay them going to the island and rescuing Robin.

Sliding out from under her deadweight, he stood up, then bent down with a groan and picked up her body. He staggered with it to the side of the boat, and heaved it up onto the rail. Without her life force, her face looked like a crude mask, made of putty.

"Sorry," he said again, and then he heaved her body over the rail.

He didn't watch it hit the sea. Instead, he turned away and trudged towards the wheelhouse. He wondered if he could steer the boat towards land, but when he entered the little shelter and saw the long seat, upholstered in some faux-leather material, running the length of the wall, he was suddenly overcome with a deep and overwhelming exhaustion.

Soaking wet, dripping, shivering, blood pouring from his slashed hand and seeping from the smaller cut on his cheek, he stumbled across to the long seat and lay down.

Darkness came for him immediately, and he slipped blissfully into it.

CHAPTER FIFTY

He emerged from his dreamless sleep with an overwhelming sense of regret. So overwhelming was it, and so akin to grief and terror, that he felt an instinctive urge to flail and fight against it.

"Hey, hey," a soothing voice said. "It's okay. You're okay. No need to panic."

It was a woman's voice, and he immediately recalled another occasion, waking up in a hospital bed, with a woman beside him.

"Yrsa?"

"No, my name is Frida. Are you Todd?"

"Yes," he whispered.

"You're in a helicopter, Todd. You're on your way to hospital. Your father got your message. We managed to find you."

Todd was soothed by her voice, and by the simple phrases it conveyed. He sensed that in time there would be more difficult things to talk about, and many questions to answer, but that could wait.

There was one thing he did need to know immediately, though.

"Did they find Robin?"

"Robin?" she said lightly.

"My brother. He was on the island."

"Ah." A hesitation. "I don't know anything about the island, I'm afraid."

Todd knew she was lying. With an effort he opened his eyes, and through his blurred vision he saw a young woman, pretty, her blonde hair interwoven into a thick braid on top of her head. He was lying on some sort of bunk and she was sitting beside him. She was smiling, but her face looked tense.

"What did they find on the island?" he asked.

Again that hesitation. "I told you, I don't know anything about the island."

His surroundings were gray. The chopping roar of the helicopter was loud but somehow soothing. Todd remembered what had happened on the boat. Yrsa, and then Karriana. Karriana had killed Yrsa, and then he had killed Karriana.

But Yrsa had already been dead when Karriana killed her. Yrsa had been dead, but the thing – the entity, the Old God – hadn't been. It had passed into Karriana. And when he had killed Karriana…

"Where is it now?" he said.

The woman, Frida, frowned. "Where is what, Todd?"

"Is it…" Todd began, but then he checked himself. "Sorry. I'm confused. I'm tired now." He closed his eyes.

"That's it," Frida said. "You sleep. We'll be at the hospital very soon."

Todd had said he was tired, but he was lying. He was wide awake, his mind whirring. What he had been going to ask Frida was: *Is it dead?*

Yrsa and Karriana had grown up on the island. The islanders too. So maybe whatever had been in those caves – that ancient, malevolent, powerful thing – had been imbuing them with its essence for years, saturating and poisoning them, as if with radiation, making them easier to manipulate when the time came.

But he, Rob, Dev, Big Andy, Sean and the rest, those who had only been on the island for a short time, they had resisted it, hadn't they? *They* hadn't succumbed. Okay, so there'd been Luke, mumbling in some ancient tongue, but he'd been injured, unconscious, vulnerable – and even then, the thing hadn't fully possessed him, had it?

I'll be okay, he told himself. *I am okay*. He had to believe that. He had to believe that the thing couldn't get a foothold in anyone it hadn't been 'preparing' for years. Had to believe too that it was not an old Norse god, as it claimed, but simply some unknown…*thing*. Some *entity*. Powerful, yes, but not *all*-powerful. It had simply soaked up the legends that the islanders had brought with them to their new home, generations before. And in turn, it had affected *them* with its poison; had laid dormant within them, until triggered by the events that Yrsa – poor, possessed Yrsa – had set in motion.

But now the thing had trapped itself. Confined itself to the island. Destroyed its habitat, its ecosystem.

He had to believe that. He *would* believe it.

I'll be okay, he told himself again. *I am okay*.

He *felt* okay. Physically and mentally shattered, but fundamentally okay.

I'm me, he told himself. *I'm definitely me*.

He made to reach into the pocket of his coat, to retrieve the Ziploc bag containing his phone, but realized he was no longer wearing his soaking wet clothes. Instead, he was wrapped in blankets, on top of which had been laid a thick foil emergency blanket, which crackled when he moved.

Raising his head a little, he said, "Excuse me."

Frida was beside him immediately. "What is it, Todd?"

"Where's my phone?"

He expected resistance. Expected her to say he didn't need it right now; that he shouldn't worry; that everything was under control. But instead she said, "Don't worry, it's right here." And she placed it in his hand, smiled, and moved away, giving him some space, some privacy.

Todd removed the phone from the Ziploc bag, and tapped the camera app, and when the photo screen came up, he flipped the screen to selfie mode.

He stared at his face for a long time. Stared into his own eyes.

He looked terrible. Washed out and shell-shocked. But nothing looked out at him from behind his eyes. There was no indication that he was carrying a passenger.

"I'm me," he whispered to his image on the screen, and saw his reflection moving its lips in time to his words. "I'm just me."

He looked at his own face for several more seconds, and then, letting his hand, with the phone still clutched in it, sink slowly to his side, he laid his head back and closed his eyes.

FLAME TREE PRESS
FICTION WITHOUT FRONTIERS
Award-Winning Authors & Original Voices

Flame Tree Press is the trade fiction imprint of Flame Tree Publishing, focusing on excellent writing in horror and the supernatural, crime and mystery, science fiction and fantasy. Our aim is to explore beyond the boundaries of the everyday, with tales from both award-winning authors and original voices.

•

Anthologies edited by Mark Morris:
After Sundown
Beyond the Veil
Close to Midnight
Darkness Beckons

You may also enjoy:
The Influence by Ramsey Campbell
The Wise Friend by Ramsey Campbell
Somebody's Voice by Ramsey Campbell
Fellstones by Ramsey Campbell
The Lonely Lands by Ramsey Campbell
The Haunting of Henderson Close by Catherine Cavendish
The Garden of Bewitchment by Catherine Cavendish
In Darkness, Shadows Breathe by Catherine Cavendish
Dark Observation by Catherine Cavendish
The After-Death of Caroline Rand by Catherine Cavendish
Dead Ends by Marc E. Fitch
The Toy Thief by D.W. Gillespie
One By One by D.W. Gillespie
Black Wings by Megan Hart
Silent Key by Laurel Hightower
Will Haunt You by Brian Kirk
We Are Monsters by Brian Kirk
Those Who Came Before by J.H. Moncrieff
Stoker's Wilde by Steven Hopstaken & Melissa Prusi
Stoker's Wilde West by Steven Hopstaken & Melissa Prusi
Land of the Dead by Steven Hopstaken & Melissa Prusi
Whisperwood by Alex Woodroe

•

Join our mailing list for free short stories, new release details, news about our authors and special promotions:

flametreepress.com